Praise for Keith Scribner's

OLD NEWGATE ROAD

"A bracing, knotty exploration of abuse and its impact across decades. . . . With grace and a fine eye for detail . . . [Scribner] writes beautifully." —*Kirkus Reviews*

"Highly emotional. . . . A complex and introspective account of one family's plight of abuse and heartbreak." —*New York Journal of Books*

"Affecting. . . . [A] dark rumination on domestic violence." —*Booklist*

"A portrait of an American family still threatened by the past as its members labor to construct a sustainable present." —*The Anniston Star*

"Events and emotions long buried are unearthed, a home and childhood filled with rage, fear, violence and trauma are explored. *Old Newgate [Road]* shows us that one can escape from a broken home, but the shackles of abuse remain tightly in place." —*Connecticut Magazine*

Keith Scribner

OLD NEWGATE ROAD

Keith Scribner grew up in Troy, New York, and then East Granby, Connecticut. His previous novels are *The Oregon Experiment*, *Miracle Girl*, and *The GoodLife*, a *New York Times* Notable Book of the Year. He currently teaches at Oregon State University in Corvallis, where he lives with his wife, the poet Jennifer Richter, and their children.

keithscribner.com

OLD NEWGATE ROAD

OLD NEWGATE ROAD

Keith Scribner

VINTAGE CONTEMPORARIES

VINTAGE BOOKS

A Division of Penguin Random House LLC

New York

FIRST VINTAGE CONTEMPORARIES EDITION, OCTOBER 2019

Copyright © 2019 by Keith Scribner

All rights reserved. Published in the United States by Vintage Books,
a division of Penguin Random House LLC, New York, and distributed in Canada
by Penguin Random House Canada Limited, Toronto. Originally published
in hardcover in the United States by Alfred A. Knopf,
a division of Penguin Random House LLC,
New York, in 2019.

Vintage is a registered trademark and Vintage Contemporaries
and colophon are trademarks of Penguin Random House LLC.

The Library of Congress has cataloged the Knopf edition as follows:
Names: Scribner, Keith, author.
Title: Old Newgate Road / by Keith Scribner.
Description: First edition. | New York : Alfred A. Knopf, 2019.
Identifiers: LCCN 2018009881
Classification: LCC PS3569.C735 (print) | LCC PS3569.C735 O43 2019
(ebook) | DDC 813/.54—dc23
LC record available at https://lccn.loc.gov/2018009881

Vintage Contemporaries Trade Paperback ISBN: 978-0-525-56346-4
eBook ISBN: 978-0-525-52180-8

www.vintagebooks.com

For Tracy Daugherty, for Marjorie Sandor,
and in memory of my mother, Ann Keithline Scribner, 1937–2016

OLD NEWGATE ROAD

1

HE LEAVES HOME BEFORE DAWN. THROUGH THE WINDOW OF THE train Mount Hood rises up, draped in moonlight and snow. Spectacular. Standing guard over the sleeping city.

Then again, he thinks, it could blow any day.

At the airport, security's a breeze, so on the other side he sips a coffee over yesterday's paper, picked from a heap by the lids and cream. As his plane ascends eastward a sunrise blooms in fast time, from night to morning in a minute. He sits back. Two blue eyes are watching him through the small space between the seats in front of him—the sleepy toddler he waved to before buckling in, traveling, he believes, on his grandmother's lap. He leans forward, pointing out the window, mouthing "Look!" and the little boy presses his nose to the glass—a Band-Aid strapping his chin—and gapes at the orange-yellow sky and the bright, beautiful dawn they're hurtling into.

After a moment Cole pulls back from his own window, slipping a three-ring binder from his briefcase, and studies the paperwork for a huge bid he'd hoped to make before this trip—a four-room addition and new second story on a 1920s bungalow, along with two porches and a new garage. But then a sheet of paper rolled into a tube pokes him in the knee—a crayon drawing of yellow and red scribbles, a fiery orb, and a silver X, their plane. He flips pages in his binder to an elevation drawing of the house and, using a drafting pen, adds a sun rising over the roof and draws the boy standing on the porch, a big smile, the Band-Aid. He snaps the paper free, folds it in thirds, and slips it through the space until it's tugged away.

When the plane levels out, he studies the excavation and electrical proposals and clowns with the kid every time he peers over the seat and drops out of sight giggling, but after a while his grandmother settles him down to sleep.

Once they've landed, Cole reaches for his carry-on. The boy and his grandmother are sitting tight until the plane empties out. Cole waves at him going past. "Bye-bye, sunshine. You're a good artist."

The boy grins hugely, then presses both palms to his mouth and throws kisses, like showering Cole with handfuls of confetti.

In Newark he changes to a small plane, and before long, off to the east, he glimpses Hartford's two big domes—one yellow, the other blue. The capitol and Colt Firearms. His great-grandfather painted the gold leaf on the capitol dome, or so the story goes. And his grandmother carefully inserted firing pins at Colt during the war.

The plane follows the Connecticut River north, and then circling Bradley they swoop in low over the tobacco fields he worked in Suffield and Windsor Locks. He's never thought of tobacco nets as anything but an agricultural fact of the place where he grew up, no different from a hoe, a tractor, a bag of lime. But now, after thirty years, seeing the nets from the air and then driving with the windows wide open past fields of Connecticut Shade, he imagines them as an art installation by Christo, acres of undulating white cheesecloth rolling in swaths over the terrain toward a dense line of elms and cottonwoods. There's the art—the regularity and surprising beauty of red cedar poles poking through the nets—and also the mathematical symmetry. The poles are thirty-three feet apart. The squares they form are called bents, which contain ten rows of twenty-seven plants that typically produce eighteen leaves each. The drying sheds differ in size, the biggest as long as a football field, and their vent design varies, but they all have the simple New England lines of a covered bridge.

He's here to buy a shed and oversee its dismantling: thirty thousand board feet of American chestnut, as prized as mahogany by woodworkers until the trees were wiped out by blight in the early decades of the twentieth century. He'll use the wood for a post-and-beam addition he's been planning to build onto his own house in Portland for years. He's always called it the family room, but at this point he should think up another name. Whatever chestnut's left over—and there'll be plenty—he'll dole out to paying customers.

East Granby. His hometown, so to speak. It's taken him nearly thirty years to come back—three decades and three thousand miles to feel he was ready to see it again. This is his busiest season with work, but he's carved out five days for the trip; he'll return to his real home with a piece of his past. Two flatbeds' worth. He worked summers on tobacco as a kid, and though he was big for his age the labor was still as hard as it was reputed to be. He complained along with everyone else but secretly enjoyed unfurling the nets, skidding along behind the Farmall in a setter, shimmying between rows on his butt for suckering on cold wet mornings late in the spring, the temperature rising so fast that by coffee break it was a hundred degrees under the nets. He loved the obsessive care shown to each valuable leaf, the rich smell of alluvial soil, the sticky juice on his fingers, arms, and hair.

He drives along winding roads north of town past stone walls parceling up the cow pastures and the brick saltbox where his music teacher lived. Sprawling fields once tented with nets are now squeezed between new housing developments, a commercial nursery, a gun club. When he reaches Alex Bearcroft's house, he immediately recognizes it and can almost come up with the name of the kid who used to live here, running all wobbly with his trombone case down the driveway when the school bus stopped for him.

Cole pulls in and parks beside a stack of chestnut timbers. The big carriage doors of the shop are open, and though he's never met Alex, or even seen a picture, he knows it must be her running chestnut through the planer. She's young, early thirties, and a woodworker of the first order. For five or six years they've had a good business relationship, mostly by email but also on the phone. When he needs something as simple as a handrail or as complex as the paneling and French doors for the entire first floor of that house in Grant Park, Alex never fails to deliver. She's got a great eye for grain—its pattern and flow always working with the architecture of her pieces, showing off the wood's character as much as her exquisitely crafted pilasters and corbels. She favors chestnut from tobacco sheds but also reclaims black walnut posts and beams from defunct mills, random maple flooring, and even teak one time from a lobster boat tossed onto the rocks in a nor'easter.

He sends her photographs of a house, they discuss style and woods, she emails sketches that he can show to the customer, and a few months later another of her dazzling creations arrives in a crate. Her work is often the centerpiece of his remodels.

Alex doesn't see him and he doesn't want to shout over the planer and startle her, so he stands by a stack of chestnut that she's already planed; the patina of tobacco has brought out the color, some boards a light honey brown, others deep chocolate. Chestnut's more rot-resistant than redwood, lighter than oak, and easier to work with. Before the blight it was used for everything—railroad ties and telegraph poles, houses and sheds and bridges, furniture and paneling, pianos and violins.

After a few minutes she glances over her shoulder and smiles at him, kills the machine, and takes off her earmuffs. And as she's stepping toward him he shivers despite the heat: with her dark loose curls, the soft round shape of her face and hips, her long straight nose, she resembles—no, she *looks* like his mother did back then.

He extends his hand to shake, but she opens her arms like they're old friends separated for years, and they embrace.

She pours coffee and stirs a heaping teaspoon of sugar into their mugs. He hasn't taken sugar in his coffee since high school and the taste brings him back to driving his grandmother's canary-yellow Cadillac on roads circling and crisscrossing this town, creeping by Liz's house, hoping for a glimpse of her, and also by his own, searching for an explanation in a cracked pane of glass or a broken shutter, searching for meaning in the damage, for understanding to rise from the destruction. But that house always kept a tight grip on its secrets, and when he rolled by was as silent and lifeless as the night they were taken away.

Alex slides a package of biscotti across the table saw. "You'll probably need to dunk it," she says, rapping one on the steel. "They've been sitting out awhile." Then, as if reading his mind, "So where's the house you grew up in?"

"Old Newgate Road. At the far end. Just the other side of the creek."

"There's two old colonials along that stretch, right?"

"The one closer to School Street."

"Center chimney?" she asks. "And the Palladian window?"

He nods.

"We'll go right by it on our way to the shed," she says.

He glances over at maple panels she's got clamped up on the bench.

"You must be excited to see it after so many years."

What can he say? He'd planned to wait a few days before driving by the house, but in fact he's ready. The sooner the better. "I am."

They're quiet for a moment until he says, "What's the maple for?"

She points with her coffee mug. "A Greek Revival in Rhinebeck. Newel posts and banisters, window and door trim, a mantel. I never made Ionic columns before. Or so many dentils. It's technical as hell but also, weirdly, makes me feel sort of Greek and precise. Kind of symmetrical." She squares her shoulders and chin. "I can't stop eating stuffed grape leaves from this old Greek place in Hartford. A week or so into the project I pulled the *Iliad* off the shelf, and last night *Oedipus the King*."

He dunks one of the stale biscotti. The anise and nutmeg and sugary coffee are like a treat from the Old Country. He eats a soggy second and then a third, sucking them down with the warm drink. "I built a Japanese teahouse for a client last month," he says, "and was craving sushi the whole time."

"Right?"

"And come to think of it"—he wipes his messy chin—"I do loads of work on Craftsman houses, and after a while I felt like I needed a fedora and a wool topcoat, and bought them, even though I only ever wear Gore-Tex and fleece. After a long day oiling dark paneling and chunky trim and hanging mica lanterns, I'll sip an old-fashioned and get reserved. '*Brooding*,' my wife would call it," and immediately he fears he's said too much.

She raises her mug. "To brooding in the aughts."

HE STARTS THE CAR TO GET THE AC GOING, AND A MINUTE LATER Alex emerges from the shop. She's put on deep-red lipstick and tied up her hair in a floral scarf. Her lipstick and smile and even the tilt of her head match his mother's in her soft-focus yearbook picture.

Wearing a polka-dotted vintage shirt, she slaps sawdust from her jeans and gets in. "Let's go see your shed."

As he drives, she turns the vent on the dashboard to blow on her, and he notices that the big wooden ring on her thumb looks like chestnut. She rolls up her sleeves.

"Sweet chisel," he says.

She stretches out her arm so he can get a better look. A bench chisel and a Japanese *dozuki* saw are tattooed up the inside of her forearm. He glances at the road, then back again when she holds up her other arm, where *Fig. 12* and *Fig. 7* have curving arrows pointing to details in a mortise and tenon and a row of dovetails.

"I love all that," he says. Even with the AC on high, he's starting to sweat.

"I'm getting a jack plane next." She runs a finger over the bare spot below her elbow. "Antoine wants me to get a tobacco shed on my back, but I think I might just keep it to my arms." She pushes up her sleeve to show him the auger on her bicep, then makes a muscle. "Wait," she says. "Isn't that the house back there?"

"Oh, yeah," he says. "Right," his foot easing off the gas pedal. As if he'd forgotten. Pulling to the side of the road, he looks over his shoulder and makes a U-turn.

"A few years ago," Alex says, "we bought a shed that was back there by the swamp."

"I remember that one," he says, barely accelerating. "Another one beside it burned down when I was a kid."

Viets's truck farm is long gone, their cucumber and tomato fields a tract of characterless houses. The acres of tobacco beyond are now a nursery's long straight rows of flowering dogwoods and birches. But the fields immediately behind his old house are still tobacco, the red cedar posts sticking up through the white nets all the way back to the swamp. He stops on the soft shoulder twenty feet shy of the driveway.

"I wish I'd known this was the house," she says. "One of East Granby's great old colonials." The grapevines have spread like jungle plants, swallowing the currant bushes and snaking up the long hanging branches of the weeping willow as if to pull the tree to its knees. The vines have climbed pear trees that haven't been pruned in years, suckers shooting skyward like antennae. He remembers when gypsy moths infested those trees. He and his little brother splashed gasoline on the gauzy silk cocoons—as big as paper lanterns—and set them on fire; when they fell to the ground, he and Ian hit them with another dose of gas, the mound of caterpillars squirming and crackling. Afterward, they spelled out their names in gasoline on the tractor road in huge letters and ignited them with a match. He'd imagined ten-foot flames—his name burning so bright it could be seen from outer space!—but the gas barely flickered.

Alex is talking about the entablature and dentils under the eaves ("dentils everywhere I look!"), but what he hears is his mother's voice expanding over the words: *the old colonial.* She was proud that her family, all on their own, were restoring this 1780 home—*the restoration,* she'd describe reverentially—adhering strictly to the period and filling it with antiques that registered their respect for the past. Instead of a rec room, they had a keeping room, a borning room, a buttery. No shag carpeting or Naugahyde La-Z-Boy, but wide floorboards and ladder-back chairs. Family trips were to Old Sturbridge Village and Williamsburg, where they dipped candles and made brooms and tin lanterns. Their father bought them knickers. Their mother, for special occasions, made succotash and cornmeal mush with molasses.

When he opens his door, the rental car chimes a warning.

Alex turns toward the house. "Why'd they sell it? Why'd you ever move?"

He looks at her over the car's roof. The house *wasn't* sold, as far as he knows. Just years of rentals arranged by his uncle Raymond. "Long story," he says, and considers one of his lines for stifling such inquiries: *The family split up early on* or the ironic *I come from a broken home* he deploys when people persist. The car's still ding-ding-dinging, and then his phone rings. His wife. "Sorry," he says, "I should take this. It's about my son." He bumps the door closed with his hip. "We're having an issue."

Alex gestures that she'll go on ahead, and he leans on the car as she walks up his old driveway.

"What did they decide?" he says into the phone.

"One more chance," Nikki tells him. "If he misses another day, or even part of a day, he's expelled."

"Christ." He's relieved, though at the same time knows that one last chance might not make much of an impression on Daniel. There are only two weeks of school left before summer break. But Cole will stand guard at the front door if that's what it takes.

"With the other thing, it looks like he'll be paying a fine. The judge'll let us know how much next week."

"So he'll have to get a summer job."

"Which won't be easy. There was an article in the paper. Even college kids can't find jobs. Never mind a fifteen-year-old."

"I'll hire him if there's nothing else. I've got a big job going once I get this bid in. But I really think it's better if he gets out of this mess on his own."

He hears Nikki exhale.

"I know," he says.

"I just wish you weren't away so you could help with this."

"I wish I were there too. But I'll call him. And I'll be back in five days."

"All of this is so you can watch some guys dismantle a barn?"

"You know they're called sheds."

"Oh, yes. The amazing Connecticut tobacco sheds where you had amazing sex when you were Daniel's age."

He laughs. "Are you really still jealous of my girlfriend when I was fifteen?" He knows it's more complicated than that, but Nikki lets it drop—kindly, he supposes. They're silent long enough that he remembers the metal Sucrets box Liz always kept loaded with pot, cash, ChapStick, gum, as if she was ready to escape at a moment's notice.

Finally Nikki says, "Do you think he's having sex?"

He *wishes* Daniel was, since none of the activities he and Nikki propose distract him from committing juvenile misdemeanors that have twice landed him in court. He looks at his watch. "I'll call him after chemistry." God, they know his whole schedule by heart.

"Okay, then," she says.

"Okay."

He starts toward the house. A bird shrieks. The three grand sugar maples still line the front yard. He used to climb these trees and can still identify the branches he scrambled up. He peers through the overgrown grapevines, but Alex is nowhere in sight. A battered Pontiac sits far up the driveway. The grass needs mowing. The place needs a coat of paint. Cole painted the entire house the summer he was thirteen, still too young to work tobacco. Is this the same paint he brushed on thirty-two years ago, blistering and peeling away from the clapboards in flaps the size of his hand?

On the driveway, gravel crunches beneath his feet. Then, drifting out an open window: piano music. It sounds like a recording until he hears a wrong note, a pause, the music resuming. His sister Kelly took lessons on his father's old upright. According to their mother he'd played brilliantly when they married and hoped to devote his life to it, but quit when he was in the army and never played again. His kids tried over and over to coax him back to the piano, and his refusal seemed to Cole, even when he was just a boy, like willful stinginess. His mother had also played when she was young, but a broken wrist that didn't heal right finished that for good.

The soulful, brooding piece comes to a final note, the resonance still hanging in the air until pounding chords begin a new movement, this one louder and more insistent. Farther up the driveway he glimpses around back and what he sees is impossible: his old bicycle, red and black frame, pitted chrome fenders. He'd built it from salvaged parts to ride the tobacco roads with his girlfriend. A plastic grocery bag hangs from the handlebar, bright and blazing in the hot afternoon sun, weighed down with what looks like a dozen eggs and a quart of milk.

He's baffled. He wants to show Alex the bike but can't see her anywhere. He looks toward the house. Bricks have come loose in the bulkhead that his father once spent a weekend rebuilding. He's watching himself like he's in a flickering Super 8 film, soundless and luridly colored, wrestle a ping-pong table down those steps into the cellar with his father, then level it up on the dirt floor. With each serve and stroke and slam, their feet burrowed deeper and deeper into the dirt until the table rose so high they had to rake the mounds back into the troughs. When his father took the lead, he started laughing uncontrollably; with each point he won, he burst out cackling, raising his hand and calling for time to catch his breath before the next serve, his eyes brimming with tears.

Cole continues toward the kitchen door, from the weedy patch where his mother tried to grow early-American herbs to the shaded spot where they'd planned to lay a flagstone patio for summer dinners but instead only ever heaped up lath ripped with the plaster from walls. He can see his sensitive, frightened little brother hunched over the wheelbarrow after school, even in the rain, hammering bent and broken eighteenth-century iron nails from the lath because they had to be saved, Ian *pounding lath*, as they called it, resigned to drudgery like one of Courbet's stone breakers.

Stepping up onto the back porch, he walks through an invisible spider's web, sticky as a gypsy-moth cocoon across his face, and he wipes at his cheeks and chin. The back door's wide open, and though the light inside is dim, he can make out their massive old kitchen table and somehow even the smells of their meals. And now he sees his mother standing at the stove in her beige skirt and white blouse and apron, her necklace of red beads the size of cherry tomatoes. When she cooked she used to speak to the food in French. Cole would slip into the kitchen unnoticed and listen to a pouty, round-lipped *"un petit peu plus d'ail,"* shaking garlic powder into hamburger; a sulky *"tu sens si bon,"* forming balls with the squishy meat; a playfully scolding *"non, non, arrête ça,"* slapping the balls into patties. Then she'd spot him—*"Ah, salut, mon chéri"*—and that would be the end of the French. "Set the table, please. Ketchup, pickles, ranch."

"Cole," he hears, seemingly from inside, and he stands paralyzed at the threshold, his chest thudding. But then he turns his head, and beyond the driveway, through the curtain of the weeping willow, he spots Alex back on the road beside the rental car, waving her arms at him. "Cole!" He steps down off the porch and strides away from the door, but stops at his old bike again, mystified how it's still here. And even more that someone's using it. The milk carton pokes out of the plastic bag, and he runs his finger along the cool sweat condensed on its side. His eyes follow the tobacco road until it disappears between the nets, and in a flash he remembers that night: standing on the pedals, pumping his legs and gazing up at the golden sky rimming the Metacomet Ridge, then spreading purple as a bruise except for a single star, which wasn't a star, but Venus.

He swerved around a puddle in the tractor road, sweat worming down the insides of his thighs, and Liz's thumbs tugged harder on the belt loops of his cutoffs. The bike wobbled—the front tire catching in a rut—and they nearly crashed, but she just laughed and kicked out her legs, which reminded him of the musical montage in *Butch Cassidy and the Sundance Kid*, and with Liz's hands on his hips he began singing that song—" 'Raindrops keep falling on my head—' "

"Ha!" Liz said. "Do you remember when you didn't get it?"

"You've been reminding me for a year and a half."

"Such an innocent boy," she teased, goosing him. "It's so obvious Butch isn't really riding Etta on the bike. He's riding *her*."

"I know. I know. But they're *on the bike*. I was still in eighth-grade English. Metaphors confused me. You were in ninth grade reading *Hamlet*."

"Etta scurries up to a hayloft," Liz said, "bats her eyelashes, fixes her hair. They're *balling*!"

"I know, I know!" He laughed, steering around the back of the shed. "Now it's my favorite metaphor ever."

After ditching his bike in tall weeds, he pried open the vent and they slipped inside, pinched off their sneakers, and walked barefoot through the cool dirt, as fine and rich as cocoa powder. The narrow vents reached to the rafters, evening light casting long angled stripes across the ground. As they ambled the length of the shed, Liz's joints loosened, her hips swayed; she swung the sneakers hooked in her fingertips, tossing her straight pale hair from side to side. His voice mellowed, dampened by the tobacco curing over their heads, as thick as a jungle. She leaned back against a wide chestnut post, pulled him to her, and kissed him deeply, then spread out their small blanket and lay back, a band of light crossing her bare thighs, and another her flushed face. She plucked a joint from her Sucrets box and struck a match. The light darkened, then slowly re-emerged bright yellow-blue with the rising moon. A gentle buzz rose through them. "The present is actually eight milliseconds in the past," she said, "because that's how long it takes your brain to deal with it all. You're looking at my face like it's *right now*, but you're really seeing it in the past. Through time." Her hand curled and twisted like the smoke in the heavy air.

"Especially if you're stoned," he said.

She formed pea-sized spit bubbles on the end of her tongue and flicked them out floating above them. School was beginning in a few weeks, he'd be a sophomore and she a junior, but next weekend they had a plan: she'd told her parents she was going with a friend to her family's cabin on the reservoir; he told his he'd be camping with Paul. "If the sky's clear," he said, "let's sleep under the stars."

"And pie for breakfast," she said, her voice dreamy, unfocused. They were stoned and kissing and warm, the sweet sharp tobacco smell all around them. "Hostess cherry pie."

She'd brushed some hanging leaves as they walked through the shed, and her forehead and hair were sticky and fragrant with tobacco juice. He loved her with the reverence you're supposed to feel for God. Their love was a release for them both, from the fighting in his home and, in hers, from her parents, big drinkers both, and her brother Kirk, who she shut up tight about when Cole touched the bruises on her arms and legs and begged her to confide. "I can handle it!" she'd snap. "He doesn't fuck me if that's what you're worried about." But he'd been watching Kirk, making a plan.

Wriggling out of their cutoffs, staring into each other's eyes, they escaped into ecstasy.

THEY HEARD SIRENS WHEN THEY GOT TO THE BLACKTOP, COLE BIKing her home, and he thought, *What if?* He'd kept himself awake many nights imagining every detail, waiting for what hadn't come. But what if it was happening now?

Spinning down the hill past the cemetery and Old Newgate Tavern, they came to the center of town. Liz's house was just beyond the town hall and elementary school. Her father had an insurance business and their place was a modest estate by local standards—brick and handsome with ivory trim, black shutters, and a circular drive, the detached garage converted to his office, perfect lawn and orderly flower beds, English ivy clinging to the chimney.

He coasted around back, both of them relieved that her brother's Chevelle wasn't there. In the darkness they kissed goodnight, deep-throated and sloppy, and as she ran across the lawn to the kitchen door—passing through the dingy splotch of carriage light pulsing with mosquitoes and moths—he felt the familiar empty tug that he might never see her again.

He rode past the Cumberland Farms—gearheads smoking cigarettes by the phone booth, a pregnant woman with a gallon of milk getting into her station wagon. He pedaled by Hair It Is! in an old house on the corner, looped behind the Congregational church, and then was back on a tractor road that took him through fields where he'd just done a fifth priming. This was his second summer working tobacco—he'd turned fifteen in April. Since Cole was big for his age, the straw bosses called on him for the heavy lifting and expected him to move faster down the rows than the other kids. It was the same with the restoration, his father having him rip out plaster and haul sheetrock. And in gym class, too, the teacher choosing him to demonstrate wrestling moves and recruiting him for the football team two years early. Even to himself he seemed to become a teenager overnight. In seventh grade he grew a foot, his arms and thighs and calves thickening. He'd been a child and then suddenly wasn't. He'd felt powerful in the football gear, invincible, but he played on his heels, he was told, lacked the killer instinct he needed to learn how to hit. And at the moment of impact he always balked. By ninth grade the coach had lost interest—calling him a gun-shy bird dog—and no one cared when he quit the team.

He biked the dirt road between two walls of nets, smelling leaves ready to be picked, thinking of Liz's hair tonight, but then he caught a trace of smoke: above the treetops, the sky was glowing. He stood up on the pedals. The fire was behind the Viets farm, where two sheds sat close to the swamp, and he steered in that direction, pedaling faster, his heart picking up speed. Another fire. Insane! He got close enough to see sparks rising on the heat, then ditched his bike, ducked under the tobacco nets, and hurried between rows of plants to the far end, where he spread the net open to peek out. Beyond Viets's fields of tomatoes and zucchini, the shed itself—loaded with leaves worth a hundred thousand dollars or more, partly cured, maybe already sold—was a dense inferno. Torched.

Swirling red and blue lights reflected off the smoke. Radios squawked, water surged and splashed, the trucks rumbled and the fire roared. They had given up on the burning shed and were now dousing the one beside it—water pouring off its roof—to keep it from catching.

It was late and he knew he should get home, but the fire captivated him. He and Liz had a nest in that shed last fall. He'd discovered a platform high up off the ground—no telling what it was built for—and Liz brought an old quilt from home, and they climbed up those massive chestnut timbers and made love and talked. Sometimes a bird got trapped inside or they watched a feral cat stalking invisible prey, and she played Pink Floyd on the portable cassette player, and as he watched the fire now he could hear, *I'll see you on the dark side of the moon* . . . It was a great spot until Marianne Viets saw them going in one day after school, and she started spying, and then the place was no longer theirs.

Cole wanted to get closer but knew he shouldn't be seen. It was the fifth shed to burn since early spring. At the second fire, back in June, when Cole walked right up to watch, the police came at him, asking questions, writing down his name and address, itching with suspicion.

They also questioned kids at school and pulled two kids right out of Liz's algebra class. Because Boulger Tobacco was multinational, people said the FBI was involved. There were rumors of undercover agents posing as teacher's aides and cafeteria workers. Rumors that the arson was related to the bomb scares that had already emptied out the high school twice that spring.

With an explosive crack the roof finally caved in, the fire flared, and sparks plumed into the sky. Within the flames he could now see the dark skeleton of timbers. The police had his name and address but never contacted him, though since the third shed—out on Spoonville Road—he'd known who was setting the fires.

LATER THAT SAME NIGHT HIS MOTHER SCREAMED OUT HIS NAME and he sprinted from bed, and as he pivoted toward the door, the throw rug slipped and his feet skidded out from under him, and not until his cheek hit the corner of the dresser—pain expanding in his head like a whiff of ammonia—did he know he was really awake.

He shot into the hall as a boom from their bedroom shook the house along with a startled cry. Even with the lights blazing and his covers kicked off, he'd fallen asleep. *Damnit!* For a week this fight had been building, starting with a highboy his father had bought that she said they couldn't afford, then taking its usual course—*the oil bill, the kids' braces, marriage has to be a partnership!* Her protests were met with gruff muteness. Last night at dinner she was crying while Cole and his brother and sister pushed mashed potato around their plates, so silent as to become invisible until finally his father punched the table and their dishes jumped. Figuring this would be the night, Cole fought off sleep and kept alert as her grievances pierced the walls, never knowing what was happening during the silences. He'd never in his life heard his father raise his voice.

Cole burst through their door as her bedside lamp hit the floor, light slashing sideways and too white across the room: his father's arm cocked, his mother's leg hanging off the bed. "Dad!" he shouted as Ian tore in behind him. "Stop!" And for a long moment they were all frozen. In the sudden quiet he heard her whimpers spill out, muffled through her hands, and Ian stifling the gasps that would explode into sobs, his own heart thumping in his ears as a horror-movie shadow of his father, fist still raised, blotted across the ceiling and down the far wall. When his arm dropped, he turned into the light glaring up from the floor, one side of his face twitching with anger, the other as black as a cave, and moved toward his sons, who stepped aside. Avoiding their eyes, he walked between them and out the door.

Cole picked up the lamp and set it back on the nightstand, righting the shade and switching the bulb to low. He touched his mother's shoulder, her skin bare and hot, the nightgown strap moist with sweat, and she sobbed violently into her palms. Rage rose up in his throat—an acid burn—and he swallowed hard against it while clutching his mother's wrist and pulling it gently from her face. Her left eye and cheek were already swelling red, and when she turned into the light he saw a heavy drop of blood clinging to her nose. He lightly touched her forehead before leading Ian to his room and telling him, "Try to sleep." Halfway down the stairs he heard the TV, so he went the long way around to the bathroom, shook two aspirin from a bottle, and filled a bag of ice in the kitchen.

Upstairs, his mother hadn't moved, still cradling her face in her hands, her back rising and falling as she wept. He passed her tissues and waited as she wiped away the blood, blew her nose, and gave them back in a wad. She accepted a cup of water, swallowed the aspirin, then pressed the ice bag to her cheek. Kissing the top of her head, Cole took in a low-tide smell of hairspray and snot and something from under her scalp, chemical and singed.

"I'm sorry," she said.

"I'll get Ian from camp tomorrow," he told her, knowing she'd have to call in sick for the rest of the week, staying indoors until makeup could hide the bruises.

"This is the last time." She spoke the words precisely, angrily, defiantly, as if doing so would make them come true. "Lord help us."

He sat beside her on the edge of the mattress, resting his hand on her back, until finally she dropped to the pillow. He draped the sheet over her and kissed her again, the ice bag sitting on her cheek. He pulled the door closed until the latch clicked.

At the top of the stairs he heard machine-gun fire, explosions, a scream. From Ian's door, listening to him cry, he stared across the landing at the blanket chest with the Canton ginger jar set on top like an urn, focusing on the hairline cracks in the porcelain's depiction of a coastal village. The elements of Canton, his father had taught them, were rain clouds, water, birds, and trees, a scholar in the teahouse, a bridge that no one is crossing. There'd been a lid, shattered now into a dozen pieces, swept into an envelope and stowed inside the jar. That fight had been a year ago, or was it two? By the time Cole ran from bed, his father had hit her here (was she stumbling toward his room?) and she'd fallen into the chest, knocking over the Canton jar.

Not until Cole was laid out flat in his bed, his sheets clammy from the feverish humidity and sweat—it was over for now, but he left his fan off so he could hear anything even in his sleep—not until he'd turned out his light and punched up his pillow did he erupt into sobs.

By one o'clock and then one thirty, he had nothing left. Released and spent, he blew his nose and thought how good sleep would feel. At eight a.m. he'd be picking leaves under the tobacco nets. His father would be gone when he woke up. At dawn Cole would hear the car start, then the rest of the family would straggle downstairs, cringing at their mother's bruises but saying nothing as they entered the week-long period of afterward: silent, wounded, sometimes tender with one another, sometimes trading deadly stares of blame for a fit over staying out late on Friday or asking for new cleats. For setting them off.

Cole would get his sister to drive Ian to camp, then he'd tell the straw boss he had to quit an hour early, and he'd bike out to the brook and ride Ian home on the handlebars.

His father would be home as usual for dinner. His mother would bang pots, muttering, weeping, but she'd serve them a meal just the same; she'd keep the family running despite it all. They'd go through the motions of eating, of making believe that everything was normal. Which it was . . . all of this . . . normal.

Then his breath caught: his father's footsteps dragging up the stairs. But he didn't stop at their room. He turned down the hall—*a scholar in the teahouse, a bridge that no one is crossing*—and passed Ian's door and Kelly's. Cole pulled the sheet up over himself. His latch clicked, the door opened, and he pretended to be asleep. His father came toward him. He stepped between the twin beds, the spare now heaped with sleeping bags and a backpack, a mess kit and hatchet, and just stood there looking at the pile, picking up a packet of freeze-dried food, unsure about whether to clear off the bed, shoulders slumped and head dropped, defeated. Cole couldn't let him go back to their room, and almost offered to move the gear, but the beatings were a secret even among themselves, and to acknowledge that his father was sleeping in his room would've been too close to admitting that this had happened, that it happened over and over.

He tossed the foil package back onto the bed and turned for the door. As he moved down the hall Cole clenched his teeth, his stomach churned. *Don't go in the bedroom!* Then he heard his father descending the stairs, and he could breathe.

After five minutes, or ten, Cole silently padded to his brother's room. He touched the sleeping boy between the shoulder blades and went back into the hall, pausing at his sister's door. In the past, she'd come running with him—since they were little children, as far back as he could remember, when Ian was an infant and could sleep through it all; and then, in later years, the three of them racing in pajamas to their parents' bedroom in the dead of night, like children escaping a fire, just moments ago asleep and suddenly watching their house burn. *Daddy, stop!* Kelly would shout, but then one night she stayed in her room, and afterward her light, as it was now, would be shining from under her door.

When he got back in bed it was just after two. His alarm was set for six o'clock.

After running through a checklist in his mind—his mother with plenty of ice and quiet in their room, Ian asleep, his father on the couch—he finally let himself relax, a visceral release. The fight had played out. Unless she went downstairs. Cole suspected one reason his father sometimes came into his room afterward to sleep—it wasn't just for the bed, the couch was large and comfortable—was so she wouldn't follow him. So he could sleep. So it would be over.

But he should've thought to move the camping gear. How could he be so stupid? Next weekend, with Liz, would be their first time spending a whole night together, the two bags zipped to each other, drifting off entangled, still inside her, waking, stirring, and making love again, which was what he called it even though she got a charge out of saying *balling, screwing, doing it*—as tough and unsentimental as she'd been from their first encounter. He'd seen her—a small town, you saw everyone—and he'd always been drawn to her taut body and blasé expression, giving nothing away. And she was known for being the girl who got shot.

In the winter, kids skated behind the elementary school on the duck pond—a dredged swamp, actually, so full of mosquitoes the rest of the year that even the ducks stayed away. Cole was sitting on a bench lacing his skates with two boys when Liz glided off the ice and stomped up through the packed snow to the bench where she'd left her coat. She was alone, and that confident loner quality—she seemed self-contained—was something else he'd found alluring. Like her, the other boys were a grade ahead of him, but they sometimes treated him as an equal, so when they started taunting her—"Did you see *The Dick Van DYKE! Show* last night?" one of them said— Cole knew how to play his hand and muttered, "Lesbo." She stopped in front of him and waited until he looked up at her, face-to-face for the first time. When their eyes locked, she kicked him in the shin, the teeth at the front of her skate blade stabbing through his jeans and driving right to the bone.

A year and a half later he could still hear the thud, still feel the pain barreling up his leg, the numbness in his groin slowly spreading to nausea. God, it hurt. But he smiled, remembering it, and remembering tonight, making love twice in the shed, the drooping corners of her stoned blue eyes, her bony naked shoulders. He could see her sharp pretty nose scrunching up when she comes, and his cock stirred, and her scent rose off his body—the intoxicating smell of red currants beginning to ferment.

HE WOKE WITH A START, THE HOUSE QUIET, CRICKETS CHIRRING. He was desperate for sleep to carry him off, but his mind raced. If he hauled himself out of bed, he could put on the record to help him drift away: *I'll see you on the dark side of the moon . . .* If only he could let go of the hyped-up watchfulness. From a week of his mother's shrill complaints and his father's threatening stares and futile violence—slamming a door, hurling a coffee mug at the side of the concrete cistern—Cole was always on guard for the moment he had to run to them and hold back his father's fists. From a week of that to one of tense, funereal placidity. He'd considered calling the cops and had even floated the idea with his mother—never more than a hint because that would violate the code, the secret—and she responded with equal indirection: *Private matters staying within a family, that's the real bond . . . My clients get involved in this sort of messiness . . . I could tell you stories, social services whisking the baby right out of the high chair . . .*

He could've killed his father. Who'd blame him with her bloody face as his defense? Knifed him in the kidneys in the middle of a fight, hiked up Metacomet Ridge to the cliffs that overlook Old Newgate Prison and shoved him off, kicked out the jack when he was changing the oil.

His heart was pounding so he finally got up and put on the record, side B. His turntable was old—Liz's cast-off—and sometimes the needle picked up at the end of the album, sometimes not, but it was 2:45, too late to care if it spun around in the dead zone for a couple hours.

He fell heavily back into bed—God, he could hardly breathe in this swampy air—and the music transported him to that loft in the shed with Liz, their nest now collapsed, still smoldering, incinerating all traces of them before the exhausted gaze of firemen and cops. And along with Liz's scent there was the smell of smoke and tobacco juice from skulking under the nets for a view of the fire, a combination that reminded him of smoke pouring from the censer as the priest walked up the aisle swinging it over his head, clanking the chain against the brass, and Father Mally acting holy and solemn, when he actually must be feeling how cool it was to walk through a crowded church whipping around a huge incense burner pouring off sweet clove smoke like a Rastafarian. And when Liz came to church with them she got a kick out of tossing her coat over their laps then easing her hand across his thigh and getting him hard so when he went to the altar for communion he had to bunch up his hands in his pockets. And if they made love before church—up against the washer while she was helping him iron a shirt, maple syrup sweetening the corners of her mouth—they melted into each other in the varnished pew, calling out with the chorus of parishioners how culpable they were for their sins, their thoughts, and their words, what they'd done and failed to do. *Lord, I am not worthy!*

In the shed, her body striped with long bands of light, he'd inspected—surreptitious, clinical, instinctual—for bruises across her back and thighs. And now he was drifting up to their nest on the platform, embers hot enough to melt nails, the staring faces of firemen and cops in the hot yellow light, mesmerized by the flames. Dreaming that he and Liz were embraced on the platform in a cloud of curing leaves, and then there were noises—shrieks and a boom like one of the huge shed doors blowing closed—and she said, *It's just one of the barn cats and her kittens.* But he heard a rhythmic crackle and smelled smoke and within seconds the tobacco and the timbers and the roof were in flames; clutching each other, she gasped for air. *Help me, Cole!*

He kicked off the sheet. He *had* to sleep. Or he could call in sick and go back to bed after Ian went to camp, then bring his mother cold drinks and more ice, sit on the edge of her bed with his hand over hers while she wept. He could clean the house. Make dinner. He touched his face. Below his left eye, his cheek was throbbing.

The rhythmic crackle was the needle spinning around and around at the end of the record. He got up and as soon as he lifted the arm, there was a tense quiet. No crickets. His ears rang, and the pressure pulled at his eardrums and temples and the skin up the back of his skull. More than silence: absence. The dead hollow of the night pulling him with a distant resolute force out into the hall.

Why was his parents' door ajar? He peered into their room—

too dark to see if his mother's body, or his father's, lay beneath the twisted sheets.

He was so thirsty now he could hardly breathe, but it was something else, ghostly and certain, drawing him downstairs past the wing chair and pie cupboard through the keeping room to the kitchen for a drink of water, and then he heard a familiar animal noise, like the scratching and hissing that rose up from under the porch when a family of possums had burrowed down there last winter. Lots of holes and cracks in this house where wild things could sneak in, so he moved back through the keeping room and grabbed the fireplace poker as he stepped across the hearth, peering behind the dining table, gripping the poker in front of him like a sword, defensively, knowing he could never club a possum, and slowly his eyes focused in the eerie darkness, and he saw him: deep in the dark corner, sitting on the floor, his arms locked around his knees, his head on his chest.

And the sound was coming from him—not crying or weeping, but *sniveling*. Cole stared at him in the feeble light that seemed to have traveled to this spot from another galaxy, another time. He stared because he knew—though he shouldn't, no one should—what he was going to find next.

Under the window, moonlight glared off a bare leg. He bent low to see beneath the table: her bunched-up nightgown, the underside of her wrist. A grunt slipped out of him as he rushed to kneel close to her; she was slumped against the upright piano, bruises around her throat and mouth, deep scratches down her neck. He shook her— she was warm but her head dropped forward. "Mom!" he shouted. He put his face to her mouth—no breath—and his ear to her chest. He jumped back, jumped to his feet. His father still curled in a ball.

"Jesus Christ!" Cole yelled, and he raised the poker over his head.

2

"NOBODY ANSWERED WHEN I KNOCKED," ALEX SAYS OVER THE hood of the rental car, "but I heard somebody playing the piano."

The seats and steering wheel have gotten hot in the sun. "It looks just the same," Cole says. "A little too much the same. Ha!" He forces a laugh. He glances at the house as he swings a U-turn. He's not deluded about the lasting trauma of this place or the emotional and even metaphorical significance of making this trip thirty years later. He knew that coming back might rattle the healthy distance he's cultivated. But seeing the house so much the same, then his bike standing by the back door . . . he wasn't prepared to dive in so deep so fast.

But this trip's about looking forward: a shed, seventy-five feet long with thirty thousand board feet of old-growth chestnut that he'll mill into neat fat stacks of lumber at his shop in Portland. And Alex, who he's known from afar for years yet met only today—many shared divulgences, even a few flops, failures in engineering or aesthetics, disagreements over money, all infused with an expectant new friendship. Hell, even this car smells new—he looks down at the odometer—only 623 miles old. He stops at the corner, then hits the gas hard. "I love that ring," he says to Alex. "Is it chestnut?"

"Yeah, I turned it on the lathe and then Antoine did that minuscule carving." She raises her thumb so he can get a better look. "It's a traditional Slovak pattern."

"Cool," he says. "Really beautiful."

"Antoine looked like he was doing scrimshaw or something, all hunched over a bright light and a magnifying glass in a clamp. It looked like the Renaissance." She spins the ring and admires it in the sunshine pouring through the windshield.

They drive five more miles east of town. Just beyond a defunct little schoolhouse—shuttered since before he was born—Alex directs him left, and as he turns under the canopy of two enormous black walnut trees he expects to see the fields he worked, tobacco nets filling the low stretch of land that bottoms out at the river, but there's only a new sign, meant to look historic: Connecticut Shade Estates. They pass houses in varying stages of completion. Some are finished, already lived in. A woman in flip-flops pushes a power mower across her lawn, though the houses on either side are foreclosures, back on the market. And the next three are roofed but lacking windows and doors, flaps of Tyvek dangling from the sheathing in the stagnant air.

He hits a speed bump a little too hard and the car bucks. There are no trucks or materials on site, no evidence of ongoing work, not even a dumpster. Just rutted and mounded-up dirt—the best and richest alluvial soil on earth for growing cigar wrappers, which now looked dried out and crusted over, like the site of a bomb blast next to hyper-green sod yards.

Alex points left again and he turns. Ahead, in a cul-de-sac shaded by a weeping willow, he sees the shed he's been studying in photos all spring. He'd convinced himself that he remembered it from childhood, but now he's less sure. And he can see the developer's vision of this shed—evoking, at a distance from his ten or fifteen new homes, the history of this land, which Cole guesses is mostly too close to the flood plain to build on.

The crew has already stripped the shingles off the roof and peeled back half the skip board, exposing the rafters. Cole parks behind a flatbed, older than he is, with "KLK Crane" painted on the door of the cab. And the crane, a grimy yellow Cat, sits close by in the shade, its operator beating the long arm of an oversized crescent wrench with a hammer trying to loosen a bolt. A man up in the rafters raises a gloved hand in a wave, and Alex waves back.

"Antoine?" Cole asks her.

She nods.

He tightens a cable around the first rafter and shouts "Ready!" down to the crane operator, who keeps pounding on the wrench—arrhythmic, frustrated—sucking on the stub of a smoldering cigar. When Antoine shouts "Ready!" again, he sounds pissed off. "Now!"

After three or four more clanks on the wrench, the guy flings the hammer into the weeds, climbs into his seat, and fires up the diesel engine. Black soot coughs from the exhaust, the pulleys engage, the cable snaps taut and jerks the rafter from the shed. Jarred off-balance, Antoine grabs hold of a timber and shakes his fist, but his angry shouts are drowned out by the motor as the huge timber swings high and light as a bird before dropping smoothly to the ground. The crane operator, who Cole can already see is an asshole, hops down from his seat and unhooks the cable.

Cole leaves Alex at the car and walks through the tall grass and weeds and kneels down beside the timber—six-by-eight, twenty feet long. He flicks open his buck knife and carves a slice off the edge—tight-grain chestnut, hard as oak, with the patina and sweet smell of curing tobacco. He holds the shaving to his nose, flooded now with memories of these sheds, of carrying in leaf bins to the women chatting with each other in Spanish, who'd then sew the leaves to the sticks of lath and hand them up to the men who moved as nimbly as acrobats through the beams to hang them.

And in the corner of his eye: a dark swoop. He twists his neck and jumps back as a second rafter barrels at him like a missile and strikes the ground so close he feels the thud in his spine. He spins around as the crane operator trots up. "What the fuck's wrong with you!" Cole spits.

The bastard bends over the hook and releases the cable.

"You could've killed me!"

He yanks the cable free, then straightens up and twists his head toward Cole. "If I wanted to hit you, I would've." He's chewing on the cigar stub, stuck in the corner of his mouth, and through the horseshoe mustache, greasy cap, and thirty years of hard living, Cole identifies him instantly.

"You gonna use that knife or just dangle it?"

Cole looks down at the hand gripping the buck knife pointed for attack, and for a blurry moment it seems to belong to someone else. He slowly turns the blade until it glints.

"I wouldn't hit you, Cole." He laughs. "You're practically blood. I can work this crane the way some people aim a gun."

Cole takes his time folding up the knife. The cigar smoke, which he usually finds pleasing, turns his stomach. That face, lined and grizzled, stained by the years—if you could scrape away the gnarled outer layer, he'd look exactly as he did back then.

"You look like you seen a ghost, Cole."

"Ready!" Antoine shouts from the rafters, but neither man looks up at him.

"Welcome home." He smacks twice on the cigar and picks it from his mouth. Exhaling a big cloud of blue smoke, he jams the stub back beneath the heavy mustache. "Careful on the jobsite now." He turns, and Cole watches him lumber back to the crane, a hitch in one knee, arms hanging long at his sides, leather gloves burnished at the palms from the crane's knobs and levers.

Cole holds the slice of wood to his nose, watching Antoine hook the cables around the next rafter. As it sails skyward, the diesel roaring, he walks back to Alex at the car. "Do you know him?" he asks.

"Kirk?" She raises her eyes. "Oh, yeah."

"He still trouble?"

She nods. "Our regular guy threw out his back."

Sweat creeps down his skin beneath his shirt. The air is so dense with humidity it's hard to get a breath. How did he ever live here?

"Are you okay?" Alex asks.

He feels a little dizzy, both hunger and the hot sun beating on him. "Yeah," he says, his eyes on Kirk grinding gears, the burnt-clutch smell toxic. How easy it would have been to stick that knife between Kirk's ribs. How easy to ignite the rage he thought he'd put forever to rest.

DRIVING OVER HATCHET HILL, THE BACK ROUTE INTO TOWN, THEY pass the trailhead where he and Liz planned to hike and camp that summer.

"The shed's really a prize," Alex says. "We considered keeping it ourselves, but we're pretty overstocked, and I'm guessing things'll be slow for quite a while. If not for the housing crash, I don't think it would've been for sale."

With the bust, she explains, the developer who sold him the shed is strapped for cash, and Cole's ten K will float him for another month.

"And when do you and Antoine leave on your cruise?" he asks.

"Five days. As soon as your trailers are loaded. That's why we had to use Kirk. Tight timeline."

They drive by the house of a childhood friend whose family had snowmobiles; straddling the machines, he and Paul would choke down Yukon Jack and then blast up the ridge, smoke a bowl at the top of the quarry, and race along the edge. A miracle he wasn't killed. "The Danube, right?"

"Steaming the river to the Old Country. Vienna, Bratislava, Budapest."

He glances up the hill at the high school as they go by, then at the old pizza-and-grinder shop once they come into town. Two gas stations still face each other across the main intersection, one of them heavily shaded by an enormous elm in the cemetery. The *Ulmus americana* blight wasn't as devastating as the one that wiped out the American chestnut, but it cheers him to see this majestic tree thriving. Old Newgate Tavern's still here, and the Cumberland Farms.

"Antoine hopes that just being in those places where his ancestors lived—touching the stone walls in the churches, eating cabbage and lamb, lots of paprika and coriander . . ." She looks out her window at a little strip mall—just three shops—sitting where the skating pond used to be. "He hopes he'll find a connection there."

Liz's old brick house hasn't changed on the outside, but it's no longer a home. A lawyer, therapist, and accountant have wooden signs on the lawn. Her father's detached office belongs to a realtor. It's still the stateliest property in town.

He sometimes can't remember the order of things, but he believes his last time here—a year after his mother's funeral, maybe two?— he'd taken the turn into their driveway too wide and he felt the ground go soft under the right front tire of his grandmother's Coupe de Ville. The house would have looked as it does now except that the blinds would be drawn, and when Mrs. Schaler opened the front door, a cigarette in her hand, he would demand to see Liz. "You!" her mother says, eyes full of venom, so he pushes past her up the stairs, then searches room by room until he finds his girlfriend's denim jacket hung over a bedpost, a *Dark Side of the Moon* prism on the wall, brown clogs under the desk. But no Liz. He knows she's home from boarding school for spring break. She can't be far.

He lies down on her bed to wait, his face buried in her pillow, and when they come for him—a cop's tight grip around his upper arm—Cole pleads: "It's not true what I said. None of it happened like that." Harsh sunlight burns the edges of the shades like an atomic flash. Four of them squared off in the smoky living room on a Saturday afternoon—Cole, Liz's parents, and the cop, who's the only one of them who isn't drunk. He rips free of the cop's grip—"I just want to *talk* to her!"—and his arm gets wrenched up his back, his face pressed into the dining table.

LIKE AN ARC ON A WHITE SEA HE SOON SPOTS THE ROOF OF THEIR old house above the tobacco nets on their way back to Alex's shop. As they get closer, a shadow moves across a window—or is it a reflection on the glass, a trick of the sunlight flickering through the maples?

"Watch out!" Alex screams, and he slams on the brakes—a raccoon is lurching across the road. They rock to a halt and the animal stops too, on the yellow line, turning toward the car. "Why's it out in the daytime?" she says. "Rabies?"

The raccoon rises up on its haunches and reaches its tiny hand toward the car—its markings and dark coat out of place in the bright sun—and just as it loses interest and turns away, a pickup comes barreling around the curve. It swerves but the rear tire strikes the animal with a quick and awful crunch. The truck slows as the raccoon drags itself with its forelegs to the edge of the road, but then speeds away.

"No," Alex laments. "Oh, no." Cole swings the car onto the shoulder and jumps out. The raccoon is clawing at the base of a maple tree on their old front yard, trying to pull itself up. It rolls onto its side, strains to right itself, and rolls back again, all the while scratching at the bark.

Alex has tears in her eyes. "Shit. What do we do?"

Cole searches the ditch for a rock, and the biggest he can find is no larger than a baseball. He approaches the animal tentatively. He can smell it now—wild and dirty, the smell of fear that predators detect or maybe of rabies ravaging its body under the thick pelt. "You might not want to watch this," he calls.

Alex lowers her head, a hand hovering over her mouth, but keeps looking at him.

And when he raises the rock, the raccoon's black eyes, squinting against the sun, grow wider in Cole's shadow. It tumbles again onto its side, exposing a row of swollen nipples. She focuses on him, seeming to know what's coming, and he smacks the top of her head with the rock. She falls back, the soft belly fur turned skyward. She's only stunned—not dead—and after a moment her eyes flicker open. He gently presses her snout back with the sole of his shoe and slips the knife from his belt.

As the blood drains out, coloring the fur, the slight resistance he felt beneath his foot surrenders. He can see now that her belly was split open, and he smells the guts still warm with blood.

There's no blood on his hands or his clothes. He wipes his knife blade in the grass but doesn't fold it, just lets it hang to his side as Alex crosses the road toward him.

"Can you get rabies from blood?" she asks.

And strangely her question sparks a long-forgotten afternoon carefully drawing pictures, copied from the encyclopedia, with colored pencils. "No," he says. "But I bet it's not rabies. I gave an oral report once."

"What?"

"In fourth grade. Rabies can bring raccoons out in the daytime, but usually it's nursing mothers who need more food."

Alex nods. She can't take her eyes off the dead animal.

"Rabies and babies," he says. "I hope her pack's old enough to fend for themselves." He remembers his mother helping him with the drawings on the floor in front of the keeping-room fireplace, how expertly she shaded the fur with the side of the pencil lead. "A gaze," he corrects himself, "not a pack. A gaze of raccoons."

He looks at the house, then down at the carcass. He's gone from feeling like a mercy-killing Good Samaritan to a hit man with a body on his hands. He wishes he knew the renters, but hasn't been in touch with any for eight or ten years. "I'll have to bury it," he tells her, looking out over the fields across the road; there's plenty of loose soil back by the tree line, so digging would be easy. "I'm going to rinse my knife off, then I'll knock on the door and see if I can borrow a shovel."

"*I'll* go ask about a shovel," she says. "You go clean up."

Cutting along the currant bushes and under the pear trees, he can see at the back of the yard the mossy concrete cistern that's probably a hundred years old. When Cole was a kid, it's where they got water for their rabbits and chickens.

He bends down and twists the spigot, which doesn't budge, and he fears a frost has done it in, but then it snaps open and a rush of rusty water splashes onto the grass. Alex is at the back door, still thrown open as it was earlier, and he can hear her calling "Hello?" over the piano music, the same tumbling, off-balance piece they heard an hour or so ago. After a moment the water runs clear and he washes the knife and then his hands, one in the other. Alex calls again into the house. He closes the tap and wipes his hands and the knife on his pants, which makes him think of his son. Cole's jeans from the knees down were Daniel's towel, from the time he could stand until he was eight or nine—his hands sticky with ice cream, slimy with pumpkin guts, numb and gritty from saltwater and sand. As he straightens up and flips the knife closed, he looks back at the house, where Alex is gone from the door, but the piano's still going. He passes by the grapevines and ducks beneath the branches of an apple tree, feeling apples squishing under his shoes through the thatch of grass and weeds.

At the back porch he's about to knock on the open door, but the sight of their kitchen is so astonishing that he steps inside. Almost nothing's different after all these years—the long heavy table where they ate, the straight line of Formica counter and pressboard cabinets, now painted a fiery yellow that someone hoped would brighten, the same brick-patterned linoleum rolled out over most of America in the seventies, scuffed through in spots to the asbestos backing.

Then he's tracing his fingertips along the dent in the paneled wall, remembering how that particular fight began: she wanted him to go to a cocktail party at the Dovers' and he refused. Simple as that. From there it built for days, the kids quiet and cooperative but glaring at each other as if to say, *Stop it! Don't! Don't set them off!* Then at dinner—they were going to Ian's Little League trophy night and, as always, were running late—everybody was seated except for Kelly, who his mother had asked to get a serving spoon for the salmon wiggle. "It's not here," Kelly groaned, digging through the cluttered drawer. "Lord help us!" their mother responded. "Now we'll *really* be late," and she pushed back from the table declaring, "I could've found it *ten times* myself by now," her heels pounding across the floor as his father's whole body jerks, as if jolted by electricity, and he flings the stack of paper plates on top of the casserole, stands up, punches the plates down into the bowl, punches again, hot food spewing like lava, then lifts the big bowl and hurls it the length of the table at their mother. She jumps aside and it smashes against the wall. Ian is screaming now, holding up his bare arms helplessly, and before Cole understands what's happening his father is wiping the scalding food from Ian's skin with a potholder. When Cole begins cleaning up, he finds the deep curved dent that the bowl's rim made in the paneling, realizing that Ian's scalding skin is the only thing that prevented, on this particular evening, a beating.

The music picks up momentum, a violent pounding on the keys, and Cole looks into the keeping room—the big slab of a hearth and the huge fireplace now stripped of its iron. He steps through the doorway, the wide floorboards giving beneath his feet. Alex is turned away from him, standing beside the piano, right where his mother died. Her body blocks all but the curve of the pianist's back. But by now, he knows.

Alex's head sways gently. The room is mostly empty, with only a broken chair and some junk along one wall. The music picks up speed and charges to the end. "Wow," she nearly shouts.

Cole stands motionless as the final chord settles like dust. "Hello, Dad."

The two of them turn from the piano.

"This is your *dad*?" Alex says. "Did you know he was here?"

Cole shakes his head.

She's looking back and forth between them, pure delight on her face. "How could I have missed it? Oh, my God. The resemblance is so obvious."

With difficulty his father pushes to his feet and straightens up, like someone collapsing in reverse. Stiff hips, the forward pull of a low-slung paunch, shoulders pinched back to compensate for a stoop. When he shuffles clear of the bench, leaning on a palm on the edge of the piano, fingers curled into a loose fist, he says, "Son. What a surprise. Welcome home to you both."

"What're you doing here?" Cole's sharp tone ruffles Alex, but his father is enlarged by it.

He takes a deep breath, seeming inexplicably serene, and says, "Renters moved out a while back, and after your uncle Raymond passed, there was nobody to find new tenants. My gig was up in Baltimore"—he glances at Alex—"and it's no fun living in my car. Did you know Raymond passed?"

"But what are you going to *do* here?"

He gives the question more thought than it probably deserves. Cole doesn't even know what he's asking, his head swimming in confusion. What the hell? As dismissive as he is of his father's conversion to the Bridgeport Correctional Center's religion of positivity, he's spent the last decades nurturing much the same thing in himself—a calm and centered peace that seeing his father here is instantly shattering.

"Live," his father says. "I guess I plan to *live* here."

The irony fucking kills Cole, and he's about to say so, but Alex extends her hand over the piano bench. "I'm Alex Bearcroft. It's a pleasure, Mr. Callahan. You play beautifully."

His father takes her hand in both of his and holds it like a baby bird. "Tell me about you. How have you been?"

"I live just over on Suffield Road. Your son and I have known each other for years."

"But you've never come to the house before?"

"I didn't even know this *was* the house."

He releases her hand, suddenly. "Yes," he says, his eyes flashing on Cole. "This was the house." He drops the cover on the piano keys, and then his spirits rebound. "Let me give you the grand tour." It's his mother's phrase, one that his father never would've used back then.

Alex nods, smiles, and then glances at Cole, puzzled, as if her loyalties are shifting. "I'd like that, Mr. Callahan," and she lets him take her elbow.

"But please call me Phil."

"Certainly."

"Good, then." And he leads her into the parlor.

Despite his unrestrained laughter when creaming Cole at ping-pong, his father was usually reserved, even sullen. In the few times Cole has seen him since prison, he's proselytized gratitude and looking toward the future. He's spent these years working at halfway houses for parolees, and like the army culture that always seemed second-nature to him, he obviously felt comfortable inhabiting that world. Cole's mother used to say that as a Catholic, no matter where you went around the globe, you could walk into a church for Sunday mass and be at home. For Phil, six months in DC and two years in St. Louis, with a constant stream of ex-cons to soak up his advice, then on to Little Rock and San Diego, sleeping in a bunk or his car, made him feel more at home, more settled and content, than he ever seemed when Cole was a boy. He'd hated running Marks & Tilly, a home store in Avon that his mother-in-law owned; he didn't have the personality for it. He might even have hated restoring the house. As a kid Cole suspected that his father's responsibilities provided nothing more than a reason for him to get out of bed in the morning, and that the life he perceived as oppressive helped explain—and Cole also believed this was normal for every husband, every man—his occasional brutality.

As in *erupting on occasions*: Mother's Day one year. Easter. The day of her father's funeral. Never every week or even every month.

This was probably why his mother truly believed *This will be the last time* every time she said it. Nevertheless, in between, the sword was always dangling over their heads. Some years ago, when Nikki pointed out that Cole's depression and impatience kicked in on weekends—as his father's violence often had—he hated recognizing his father in himself.

He hears the two of them clomping upstairs and walks back through the kitchen, which still smells like a bin of potatoes going soft in the pantry, so he peers in there—but no potatoes. He remembers how the eyes grew as long as tentacles. Looking around, he can't tell whether Phil has been here for a week or a year. The fridge is mostly empty—leftovers, mustard, horseradish—and the light has burned out. Dirty dishes are jumbled in the sink. Half a loaf of bread on the counter. In the keeping room, other than the piano, there's a rolled-up carpet, a broken chair, tangled telephone wire spilling out of a box, a keyboard, and floppy disks. He picks a fork up off a beanbag chair—dried food in its tines—and drops it in a paper bag of trash. The place, as his mother would say, *looks like who did it and ran.*

Uncle Raymond always had trouble with tenants because the house was always sort of unlivable and naturally still is. Rooms were left with bare studs after they ripped out the plaster for insulation. Windowpanes rattle in the wind, most of the upstairs still without heat. Plumbing runs to a room that's the upstairs bath in name only—no tub or sink or toilet. Drains are stuffed with rags. Wires hang from ceilings and walls where there were, or will be, but are not presently, fixtures. Somehow, though, Raymond coaxed enough people into the house over the years that he got the taxes paid. The house apparently still belongs to Phil. And Cole catches himself before feeling too critical: in his own house in Portland, wires have been curling out of a hole in the sheetrock beside the French doors where he's been intending to put a sconce for years.

Despite its condition, this *is* a beautiful house. And not merely what realtors would call *good bones*. Exquisite colonial paneling and mantels, floorboards twelve inches wide, high ceilings, five fire-places, massive stone hearths and steps, gorgeous doors with their original iron hardware. The perfect house for someone with loads of money to spend.

He sits down on the porch steps and calls Nikki. It rings once, then she answers with "How'd you know?"

"What?"

"Expelled. Our son no longer has a school."

"Permanently?"

"Forever."

"Christ."

"Halfway through honors algebra he quietly got up, left his notes and textbook on the desk, and walked out. The school called the police and they picked him up at the skate park."

"Where's he now?"

"In his room."

"Doing what?"

"I have no idea."

"Shouldn't you be talking to him?"

"How would you handle it, Cole? Have a man-talk about the importance of high school? We've been working that angle for a year."

"How are his spirits?"

"Never been better. As soon as I got him home, he put on his pajamas and robe and comes into the kitchen and opens the cup-board. I'm like, 'So what's your next move?' and he says, 'Making some toast,' and I say, 'Your next move *in life*,' and he says, 'Toast might be my favorite food.'"

"Jesus."

"He loves that robe."

It had been Cole's robe, which Nikki bought him a few years ago for Christmas. The following winter, when Daniel had a bad flu, he took the robe off the bathroom hook and lay wrapped up in it on the couch in a cold sweat for a week. When he recovered, there was no discussion whatsoever—Daniel kept the robe through the spring when Cole and Nikki began couples counseling, kept it through the summer when Nikki went on yoga retreats in Baja and Vancouver Island, and kept it for good when she moved into her own apartment over a chocolate shop with a second bedroom for him, every other week. Nikki's own shop is only a few blocks from the apartment, a tiny, trendy boutique where she designs and sews and sells dresses, skirts, and tops.

From the backyard Cole looks down the driveway and across the road to where two nursery workers maneuver the blades of a tree cutter around what looks to be a two- or three-year-old dogwood, then lift the tree and root ball into the air.

"We'll have to work out a plan," he says. "I'll call Daniel later." Through the upstairs window, in what had been his parents' bedroom, he sees Phil's hand sweep to his side, and Alex nodding, as he explains something about the raised hearth or the hiding place under the closet floorboards, big enough for three people to curl up inside.

"Are you there?" Nikki's saying.

Sunlight spots the old glass, texturing both their faces. Does Phil notice that Alex resembles *her*? "I'll call him in a while."

In the toolshed Cole finds a shovel—certain it's the same one they had when he was a kid—and out front he scrapes the dead raccoon onto the rusty blade and, propping it out to his side, walks past rows of red maple and black-walnut saplings to the thick weeds at the edge of the swamp, the air even heavier there, seething with humidity and the click of insects. He was right, the digging isn't difficult, but after the animal's buried and he's refilling the hole, a splinter from the brittle old shovel handle stabs into his palm. It's broken off under the skin and he can't pull it out with his fingernails, so he gnaws at it, biting into his palm as he looks back over the young trees at the house.

THAT NIGHT, THE FIRST COPS TO ARRIVE SMELLED LIKE SMOKE from the burning shed. His mother, still uncovered, lay propped up against the piano. His father was on the floor, moaning, his face turned to the wall. The cops kept the children at the far end of the room, jotted notes, their gazes roaming but always coming back to the dead woman on the floor: attractive, even beautiful, though it was difficult to tell with the welt on the side of her face and the bruises around her mouth and throat; she had brown hair and was overweight, her summer nightgown stretched tight. Cole's arm was slung over his brother's back as he silently sobbed; Kelly kneeled behind them, steadily petting Ian's hair.

The cops had called for paramedics, though it was obviously too late, and for state cops, who'd carry out the investigation; he'd also heard one say into his radio "someone for the kids." They glanced at Cole, noting his black eye, how it strangely matched his mother's. His pulse was pounding in his ears, throbbing from his heart down to his hands. The cops looked at his mother again, whispering between themselves, and he considered their gaze an outright violation.

Although the three of them were comforting one another, Cole felt like it was already starting to happen—in the stiffness of Kelly's hand, the purse of his own lips, Ian's elbows and arms cradling his guts as if trying to keep them from spilling out onto the floor. They all had known he might kill her, yet they allowed it, and because each was blaming the others, they were—even tangled together in a twisted mess at the end of the room—already ripping apart.

COMING UP THE DRIVEWAY HE HEARS THE PIANO AGAIN—HIS father playing the same dark and moody piece. There's an unnerving absence or emptiness underneath the melody, as if half the notes are missing. He stows the shovel, and walking toward the kitchen door he sees Alex slip the plastic grocery bag off the handlebars. They meet in the kitchen, where she's wiping condensation from the milk carton. He rinses his hands—there's no soap—and she reaches toward him with the towel. Spreading his palm open in the light from the window, he examines the splinter, nearly an inch long, in a sheath of blood. Alex puts the milk in the fridge and removes the eggs from the carton one by one, placing them in the twelve empty cups in the door. He'd never seen her until a few hours ago, yet here they are in his boyhood kitchen, putting away groceries, tidying up.

"What a great house," she says.

"How did it look up there?"

"The paneling over the fireplace in his bedroom's chestnut."

"Ha. Now I know why I always liked that paneling." He hangs the mildewed towel in a hoop of pitted chrome.

"Why'd it take you thirty years to come back?"

"That," he says, smiling, "is a longer story than we have time for right now."

She looks at her watch—"Oh, rats"—and taps it with the empty egg carton. "I'm meeting a client in twenty minutes."

"I'll drive you home," he says, feeling suddenly like she's his little sister; he felt it earlier too, at the shed: when Antoine got angry, though rightly so and at *Kirk*, a protective impulse gripped Cole. Until he knows and trusts them, he tends to eye warily the husbands and boyfriends of women he cares about.

"It's really great to meet you for real." She wipes crumbs off the counter and, after wringing out the sponge, holds her fingers below her nose, inhaling cautiously, then rubs her hands together under the faucet. He looks down at his shirt, which he's sweat through digging the grave. She sniffs her hands again, eyes the towel, then wipes them on her pants. His heritage: mildewed and musty, hard to discern what's half-demolished and what's half-restored. And all of it gouged with resentment. For the last few weeks he'd imagined arriving fresh and crisp and striking—flying in from a hip West Coast city, a man Alex has developed such an easy friendship with on the phone. He and his company, Greenworks, have been featured in *Fine Homebuilding* and *Architectural Review*, and received awards from *Sustainable Living* for his commitment to low-impact building and design. He wanted to present himself as who he's become, not who he used to be.

His father pounds on the piano keys. Cole will come back tomorrow and clean the sinks and toilet. He'll look for a vacuum or at least sweep the place out. He'll see if there's a working mower. He pulls some ancient food wrapped in tin foil from the fridge and packs it into the garbage pail, then carries it out to the can in the backyard. He started this short trip with a light heart and sense of adventure. He didn't *need* to come at all—he supposes Nikki's right about that. But he thought it would be inspiring to see the wood standing as it has been for eighty-five years, not as another stack of lumber delivered to his Portland shop, and to see how well his old house and the town itself match his memories. He wanted to prove to himself that he *could* come back, that Nikki's wrong about the danger of this trip stirring up the long-settled muck inside him. He's forty-five years old, for God's sake; it's about time. But then he laughs out loud: he wasn't here for half a day before he was killing a raccoon right out front. *That can't be a good sign!* he wants to tell Nikki. He shoves the garbage in the can, comes back inside, swings the kitchen door shut, and locks it.

Alex takes a few dishes from the drainer and stows them in the cupboard overhead. Cole pushes in the chairs, then puts a couple spoons and forks away automatically, knowing which drawer to reach for. They sidestep and slip past each other easily—that intuitive domestic dance—and with a feeling he can only compare to the dry, brittle chafe of the shovel handle on his skin, he suddenly misses his wife.

3

JUNE 10TH, HIS MOTHER'S BIRTHDAY, HER THIRTY-NINTH. DINNER at the Magic Pan in West Hartford. From the table Cole watches his father drape his arm over Ian's shoulders, the two of them leaning on a brass rail as the chef, wearing a tall paper hat, dips the bottom of the pans in batter and sets them bottom-side-up on the carousel for their slow turn around the ring of blue flames.

They come back to the table grinning. "Twelve pans," Ian says, "Fifty-two seconds for one revolution. Dad timed it."

"That's an actual gargoyle hanging above the kitchen door," Kelly says, smoothing her hands over the white tablecloth. On the wall behind her there's a photo of a kissing couple on a wet Paris street, and beside that a painting of water lilies.

"Beef Crepe Bourguignon," their mother murmurs. "Crepe Chicken Divan. *Je ne peux pas me décider.*"

"Ian, look at the desserts," Kelly says. "Chantilly Crepe."

Everything about the restaurant amazes Cole. He'd like to bring Liz here on a real date, romantic and classy. Their fancy family nights out are most often to the Jack August in the airport Ramada Inn, where the dining room has plush carpet and low lighting; they go on Wednesdays for popcorn shrimp and the salad bar. It's delicious and all you can eat, and while their parents are having coffee the kids play pinball in the hotel game room by the pool.

They also go to the Chart House and Four Chimneys once in a

while with his grandmother Tilly—Easter dinner or her birthday—
but those places feel mired in a crusty 1950s. Oil paintings of clipper
ships and fox hunters in heavy gold frames, a dish of green peas or
steamed cauliflower going cold beside his plate.

The waiter sets down a carafe of white wine and pours a glass
each for his parents, then asks about the young lady. "Oh, no," Kelly
says, blushing.

Cole wonders if the waiter is putting on the accent, but then his
mother asks, "*Vous êtes français?*"

"*Non, non,*" he says. "*Je suis de Montréal.*"

"*J'adore cette ville. Ça fait longtemps que je n'y suis pas allée. Avant
les enfants. Avant le mariage.*"

Their conversation continues, and Kelly's cheeks never pale as
she gazes at the waiter, who isn't much older than she is; Cole's father
sips his wine; Ian looks back and forth between the crepe carousel
and his mother; and they all watch her intensely. She sits back in her
chair, her wineglass loose in her fingers, her French speeding up. She
makes a comment about Montreal, the waiter nods, and they both
laugh, the rest of the family just looking and listening—not understanding, but watching her lips move into shapes they've never seen,
hearing the music of the words lift and carry her far away. Not only
her mouth moves differently but also her wrists and elbows, her chin
juts when she makes certain sounds, her laughter turns gravelly—
transforming before their eyes into another woman entirely, the
woman she might have been.

4

KIRK ISN'T MANNING THE CRANE THE NEXT MORNING. IT'S A KID about Daniel's age. The day is already heating up, the sun high above the cottonwoods along the river. They got all the rafters to the ground yesterday afternoon, and the kid is hoisting them onto the first of two flatbeds that will carry them cross-country to Cole's shop.

He catches sight of Antoine inside the shed and he goes in, sipping a coffee he brought from the hotel buffet. Antoine has two other guys up in the timbers, drilling out pegs. "Work across the top," he calls up to them, "then we'll bring in the crane."

"How's it going?" Cole says.

"Real good. Lots of wood in this one."

"I owe that to you and Alex."

"It's all her. She finds them. I just tear them down."

"And sometimes you put them back together." He knows Antoine's just being humble. This time it's salvage, but often he's marking every stick and reassembling the sheds better than ever on another site, building stone foundations, and converting them into studios and homes. Like Alex, he's a master.

"This one would make a great house," Antoine says. "I'd build a second story at that end"—he points into the sun—"and a loft over here above the living room." He describes windows and exposed beams, flooring and a dry-stack fireplace in such loving detail that a scene emerges complete with children's laughter and a sleeping dog on the Persian carpet.

"I can practically smell the bacon," Cole says, then taps his chest with a fist. Heartburn. "Or maybe that's thanks to the hotel breakfast buffet."

"Knock that purlin off first!" Antoine shouts up to his guys.

"Too bad you can't put this one back together."

"No matter. The spirit of the chestnut will keep on living in your family room. That wood's as alive as you and me."

Cole's surprised by Antoine's moonbeamy sentiments, even though he pretty much agrees. "Well, thank you," he says finally, and reaches out his hand.

Antoine hollers instructions to his guys again. The confidence of youth, Cole thinks. And he was probably wrong to be suspicious of him. He seems gentle and good-hearted, a wonderful husband to Alex. Kirk could stir up anger in anyone.

Back outside, the kid has shut off the diesel and is cinching down straps over the timbers on the flatbed. "Where's Kirk?" Cole asks.

The kid pumps the arm on a ratchet strap. "Running late."

"So you work for him?" Cole notices he's wearing Kirk's gloves, smooth and shiny at the palms.

"I help him out."

"Good summer job?"

"I just help out. Summer I'm working tobacco."

"Kids are still doing that?"

"Not really."

"I worked tobacco back in the day."

"Yeah, I know."

Cole stares at the boy.

"My father told me."

He's got deep brown eyes, pouty girlish lips, a sharp chin. Cole's legs go watery: he looks like Liz.

"Little Kirk Schaler," he says, extending a gloved hand.

ROLLING PAST FORECLOSED HOUSES IN THEIR SUSPENDED HALF-built state, he flips the vents so the AC blows straight on him. He presses his palm into the steering wheel—the swollen red spot sore from the splinter—and then presses even harder so the pain flows to his molars and the base of his spine. It turns out that Little Kirk is exactly Daniel's age. He seems decent enough. Is it remotely possible that Kirk could raise a good kid?

He checks his phone, but there's no message from Nikki. She's putting on coffee now, or maybe stepping out of the shower. Almost from the moment her eyes open in the morning she sings—Rickie Lee Jones, Nina Simone, Bonnie Raitt. Her memory for lyrics is astounding. For twenty years Cole woke most mornings to Nikki brushing her hair at her bureau and quietly singing marmalade rhymes—"flying too high with some guy in the sky"—never a trace of performance or self-consciousness. She drifts into melodies as easily as Cole drifts into daydreams, in his case often dark recollections. Sometimes, for no reason he can identify, his blood starts racing, like the pain from his palm now, shooting up his arm and pooling in the back of his mouth. Sometimes it's fear that Daniel might be in trouble. Or disgust at himself for losing Nikki, or a nagging suspicion of looming secrets.

Secrets. He spoke of that night to almost no one for ten years, as if he'd just jumped town and what happened here, his entire childhood, didn't stow away with him. The beatings were always a secret, until his father killed her, and then the truth spread like fire. But when Cole left for the West Coast, he snapped the latches closed and left all the secrets behind, like the footlocker full of clothes and trophies and souvenirs he'd stored in Tilly's attic. A decade later, that night had almost become a secret to himself. By now, honestly, he mixes up his memories of that night with Nikki's retelling. She's the one who sensed when the time felt right to tell their friends, good friends who she thought should know. She'd decided it was important for Cole to have it out in the open.

But even if she's right—that it's good for him to "let in some light"—the story she told makes him uncomfortable. She made him out to be a hero, beating his father off of her, trying to protect his mother, trying to stop it, when he knows it wasn't like that at all. He listens, accepts the sympathy and hand wringing and pats on the back, endures the long silence, then slaps the table and jumps up: "Okay. Who wants marionberry pie?"

He never resented Nikki for talking about that night, but when she left and he started meeting new people—women, to be precise—he didn't know how to tell the story himself, and it could be one of the reasons why nothing clicked with any of them.

The truth is he has plenty of options. Within weeks of Nikki moving out (two weeks seems to be the official mourning period for a marriage pronounced dead) he was getting calls from friends, mostly female friends, who knew a "wonderful" or "brilliant" or "drop-dead-gorgeous" woman. A landscape architect, a potter, an ER doctor, a lawyer, a yoga-slash-Pilates instructor. There were Stumptown Coffee dates and drinkable chocolate at Cacao. Dinners in the Pearl, shows at the Schnitz. Afternoon rendezvous at Powell's Books and bike rides through Forest Park. Winery loops down the valley. After the strained and angry final months with Nikki it was all light and fun, even thrilling. But the time would come in their shared divulgences when the lovely woman sitting across the table from him, open and generous, wineglass at her lips, would ask about his childhood, and they would've already become too intimate for his usual sidesteps, but he wouldn't know how to *tell* the story, he didn't *know* the story, and she'd lower her glass and sit back in her chair, sensing his dishonesty.

It's early morning in Portland. He conjures Nikki in her sunny kitchen, singing "The Last Chance Texaco." She's sprinkling cinnamon over oatmeal, slicing on strawberries, and tossing in a handful of caramelized walnuts. Daniel's standing at the toaster reading texts, wearing the robe.

HIS FOOT LAYS OFF THE ACCELERATOR AS HE APPROACHES THE house, surprised again that it looks so much the same, so perfectly preserved in his memory. He hadn't intended to drive down Old Newgate Road, or at least not to stop, but then he glimpses Phil sitting on the front steps, his arms crossed over his knees, his head resting on his arms, and his pulse flutters. Only once has he seen his father sitting like this—when he found him that night. He hits the brakes and swings into the driveway.

Phil lifts his head.

"I was just passing by," Cole offers.

"Great day for a drive," he says hopefully, his eyes yellow and distant.

"I came over Holcomb Road."

His father looks at him vacantly.

"Not the new cutoff but the old Holcomb Road." Far back in the tobacco fields a few workers are rolling up a net to open a bent. They might be suckering already. "Anyway"—Cole's beginning to sweat, standing there in the sun—"aren't you hot sitting out here?"

"I was cold. I left my groceries on the bike, but they're gone."

"Alex took them in."

His gaze is totally blank.

"Yesterday. The woman I came by with."

"Lovely lady," he says. "I think I met her once a long time ago." He drops his head back down on his arms.

"Did you have breakfast? Let's go inside." He steps by him and thumbs the latch, but the door's locked.

"That's the snag right there," his father says.

"Is the kitchen door open?"

He doesn't respond, so Cole goes around the house checking all the doors—all locked.

"Do you have the keys?" he asks once he loops back around.

"Stuck out here since suppertime yesterday," his father says.

"All night?"

"The car's locked too."

From behind the shed he grabs a mossy cinder block and sets it below the keeping-room window. He steps up, pries out the screen, and climbs inside, as his father could've easily done. Replacing the screen, he hears water running, and follows the sound to the kitchen: the sink is overflowing. He sloshes across the floor through water up to his ankles and twists the knobs shut. First he thinks: a lot of water. But next: there should be more. He stands still and listens—a loud and steady trickle from below. Although plenty of water has run out into the keeping room, the kitchen floor slopes down toward the sink and most of it flowed under the cabinets. He rushes to the cellar, where it's showering down between the joists and cascading from around the holes cut for plumbing. The dirt floor's puddled and muddy but absorbing it all pretty fast. He'll get some air moving down here and it'll dry out in no time.

But then he sees some soaked cardboard boxes beyond the oil tank. Through the soft mud, water raining down on him, he carries the boxes straight outside through the bulkhead. His father glances at him as he sets them down in the sun and rips them open. Miraculously, the cardboard has shed a lot of the water. Inside the first box there's a loose stack of damp photos—Ian's third-grade class picture right on top, the kids lined up in three rows, his brother in the front on his knees with crooked teeth and a zippered shirt, bangs in his eyes. Miss Patterson, who was Cole's third-grade teacher too, looks a bit bonier than he remembers her. He shuffles through the pictures. There's his father stirring flaming logs in the keeping-room fireplace with the brass-handled poker, his face turned to the camera—someone has called to him just before snapping the shutter. And there's his mother lighting a new tapered candle, probably at Christmas or Easter, with dangly earrings and a beaming white smile. *Young.* Which is always his first thought when he sees a picture of her. She should grow older with him, old enough to be his mother.

He spreads out the photos in the sun, then digs down through a few paperback books, a stapler, a coffee mug stuffed with pencils and pens, and at the bottom of the carton finds the rosewood tea caddy she kept on her desk, the lid inlaid with ivory, the handles brass. He sets the box on the brick walk, where it looks like a foot-long casket. His grandmother insisted he be a pallbearer. Tilly had a vision for the funeral involving a particular card stock for the programs, a harpist in a black satin dress, and Kelly and Ian arranged like Caroline Kennedy and John Jr. She orchestrated the funeral from a hospital bed; the same eye that had distinguished Marks & Tilly Ltd. would bring dignity to her daughter's funeral, despite the shame.

He goes down through the bulkhead and up to the top of the cellar stairs, where he slips out of his muddy shoes before stepping through the house and opening the door for his father, who pushes by him, straight for the piano, and begins playing the familiar piece. In the kitchen Cole removes the stopper and stares at the hunk of iron sitting there in the sink. These are the nails, the thousands of nails pounded from the lath by Ian and left in the cellar in a cardboard box, where for thirty years they've rusted into a block the size of a small, impenetrable safe.

"What were you trying to accomplish here?" he calls, but gets no reply. Did Phil think that water dissolves rust? Or is he just not thinking straight at all?

He opens the window and cabinet doors and drops the towel on the floor. Most of the water has already drained through to the cellar, but his socks are wet and he takes them off and carries them along with his muddy shoes out to the steps and sets them in the sun. As he listens he realizes his father keeps hitting the wrong notes at the same places.

"Do you want some eggs?" Cole asks from behind him.

Still playing, he nods. Cole rummages kitchen cupboards and drawers until he finds what he needs. The milk and eggs are where Alex left them in the fridge, otherwise empty except for the sketchy-looking stuff he saw yesterday.

Cole scrambles the eggs with milk and shakes in some salt. There's no toaster, but after sniffing the tub of margarine he spreads some on the bread. While the eggs are cooking, the music stops and his father appears in his armchair at the head of the kitchen table. Cole serves them each a plate and takes his old spot, but then Phil gets up and disappears into the back room for a minute and returns with a small canning jar. He unscrews the metal ring, pops off the seal, and heats a paring knife under hot water at the sink before slicing the disc of paraffin on top. He slides the jar to Cole, who picks it up and looks at the oval label decorated with berries and his mother's handwriting: *The Callahans, Red Currant, 1978*—a year before she died. Before he killed her. They spoon jelly onto their bread and eat.

"Why didn't you come in through a window?" He can see that his father is getting back to himself with the food. "Didn't you know the sink was running?"

He doesn't answer.

"What if I hadn't come along?"

"I would've snapped out of it. I always do."

He's gaining strength by the minute. He was famished, is all. Who knows how long it's been since he ate? The delicate taste of the currant jelly brings him back to this table, this kitchen. His father reaches out and clasps his hand over Cole's beside his plate. "Good to see you, son."

Cole nods.

Phil takes a bite of bread and chews slowly. "That's the last jar of the currant." He stares off through the window. "We should let her know."

5

HER FINAL SUMMER SHE DOESN'T MAKE JELLY. THAT JUNE, EARLY on a Saturday morning, it's barely light outside, too early for anyone in the house to be awake, yet Cole is sitting on the stairs listening to his parents in the living room. His arms are wrapped around his legs, his bare feet cold. There's the roasted-chestnut smell of instant coffee.

"Can you at least say you'd *like* to spend a week with me in France?" she asks. He's been listening for a while; she's the calmest he's ever heard her in a dispute, and his father the most forthcoming, as if the day's too young to work anything up.

He clears his throat. "Not really."

She soldiers on, even-toned. "But this is deeply important to me."

He's silent.

"So that's it!" Her voice sharpens. "It's not about the money at all." She emits a clipped cry. "Good God! How long have you so *loathed* spending time with your wife?"

Cole wishes she hadn't asked him that. In the long pause he tries to picture them: his father staring at the floor, lips pursed as if he's cycling through memories, arms crossed high across his chest and resting on the rise of his paunch like a pregnant woman might rest a coffee mug there; his mother hanging on the edge, impatient with his silence, with waiting to hear how completely he'll shatter her delusion.

When Cole was very young—four, five, six—and he woke in the night and went to his mother's bedside, he'd never have to wake her. "What is it, *mon petit*?" she'd whisper. Her radar for activity in the house, or disturbance in her child, is the same instinct that woke Cole up this morning, and now he's wondering if his father slept on the couch last night.

Finally he says, "Since Bermuda."

"Lord help us!" she cries. That's where they spent their honeymoon. For a time he hears her weeping, and waits for the scrape and gasp of sudden movement, but in the end she just blows her nose. "And it's because you've always cared so little for me that it was so easy to smack me while I was pregnant with Cole?"

"You said we'd have a reasonable discussion."

"Are you denying it?"

"Pregnant and *smoking*. And so pleased with yourself in front of your girlfriends, telling that same idiotic story." This was fifteen years ago, but his disgust surges as if it were yesterday.

"So you twisted my arm until my wrist snapped."

"And you still wouldn't shut up."

"Talk about dumbfounded. They knew at the ER that I was telling lies."

Cole backs slowly up the stairs to avoid a squeak, and sits on the edge of his bed. Just after five thirty. If this was a weekday, he could escape to school in a couple hours, but it's a Saturday in June. Two weeks until summer break and his tobacco job.

Through the window screen birds chirp, squawk, warble—a frenzy of feeding, fighting, sex. Jays swoop down on the currants and tear off clusters of bright red berries, already overripe. They're early this year. Everything is. When he filled out the employment papers at Taybro they told him the tobacco starts were two weeks ahead. "That warm stretch before Easter," the farm boss said. "The whole season's jumped the gun."

The numbness that often seizes him takes hold and he drops back in bed, curls his knees to his chest and, as if he's been drugged, falls immediately, deeply asleep.

Until.

A scream.

She's screaming his name and he's running out to the hall, then flinging open his parents' door. Their tangled bed is unmade and empty, the curtains and windows open to the sun. He's flying down the stairs when she shouts "We're waiting, Cole!" and he stops, standing on the step where he was just sitting and listening. "You can't sleep all day!"

He leans into the handrail. His head drops. He can see his own heart thumping beneath the tight skin of his bare chest.

He starts across the keeping room, his hands still shaking, and spots her through the open door outside on the driveway, her back turned, the soles of his bare feet cool on the hearthstone and then blistering on the hot granite steps, the bright sun blinding him, voices twittering. He squints through yellow and black sunspots floating in his vision like a scene in a psychedelic movie: standing around their battered, wine-colored Malibu, all four doors flung open, are five round and full-bodied high-school girls, two of them holding newborn babies on their chests, standing ragtag by the car—tall and short, black, brown, and white, hair feathered, permed, or ironed straight. He knows who they are, though he has no idea why they're here.

His mother turns. "And ladies," she says, "I present my son." Then finally looking at Cole, she dials up her shock at the sight of him shirtless and in gym shorts, and she says, "Good gravy, make yourself decent!" at which the girls laugh.

"Your momma told us you're only fifteen," one of them says, stepping forward. Her face is as round as a paper plate, all dark lips and eyes, heat rouging her cheeks and forehead. Her small hands grip the bottom of her equally round belly like she might otherwise teeter backward.

"He looks older than that," another girl says, "with those shoulders." They all giggle again.

"How old are *you*?" Cole asks the girl in front of him.

"Seventeen."

They break out laughing. "She lies," one says.

The girl cracks a smile—her puffy lips parting to reveal an adorable overbite—and he knows she can't be much older than he is.

"She's perfect for you," another says.

"That's enough," his mother cuts in, shooing him into the house. "Cole, you go make yourself presentable. Ladies," she says, curling her index finger, "follow me."

At the upstairs window, pulling on cutoffs, he watches the girls totter around the long row of grapevines to the six currant bushes planted in a lopsided circle. The two with the babies sit in the shade of a pear tree, unbutton their tops, and slip them underneath to nurse. Another picks a few currants and pops them in her mouth, and when her face puckers, the others laugh. His mother comes across the grass with mixing bowls and the blue-speckled turkey-roasting pan. She's been working with the unwed mothers at St. Mary's in Hartford for a few years, and regularly brings home their stories but never before the actual unwed mothers.

With their bundles and babies the girls look out of place in the yard—like pictures on the news of boat people arriving in foreign lands and plopping down on any patch of ground to feed their children. He puts on a T-shirt that smells of smoke; last night was the bonfire at the high school. A year from now—*next* year's bonfire— he will no longer live in this house, and he'll drive Uncle Andrew's car over from Bloomfield after dark. He'll park and trudge down the hill as a bottle rocket stashed in the burning tower of scrap lumber and logs ignites and shoots across the grass. He'll keep his head low, hoping to spot Rochelle or Paul. Liz will already be away at boarding school in Florida. In a letter she'll have told him she's staying in Boca for the summer, serving cocktails and club sandwiches at a golf course. He'll sit down at the back of the crowd, huddled in shadows. When the fire lights one side of his face, a girl from freshman English will recognize him, her eyes shooting wide with the red and yellow flames. She'll poke her friends' shoulders, urgently whispering. An M-80 will blow—sparks bursting and a leg of the fire collapsing—and the boom will hit him in the chest, indistinguishable from the wallop of shame that will keep him away from his hometown for thirty years.

But for now he has brushed his teeth and he's back outside with the girls, who've plopped down cross-legged at the bushes, tugging off handfuls of currants and dropping them in bowls wedged between their bellies and knees. They're picking at least a week late so some of the berries burst at a touch and red juice trickles down their bare arms.

"Here, Cole," his mother instructs, and he kneels beside the girl who said she was seventeen and begins pulling berries from the branches and adding them to the bowl on her lap. She's from New Bedford, she tells him. All the girls are from somewhere else. Girls from here are sent to Philly or Providence or Boston, which Cole already knows. Hartford's the pits, she tells him, and in New Bedford they know how to party, so when she gets back home she's going with Celia and Mary Beth out to the island first thing. Does he have a car? she wants to know, and he doesn't remind her he's fifteen, just shakes his head. She says he should call her anyway, and she wipes the juice from her hands in the grass, digs a scrap of paper and a pencil from her bag, and writes down a phone number. "Ask for Monica," she tells him, "and be quick about it—I only got seven weeks left."

When the bowls fill with berries he dumps them into the turkey pan and stockpots, then returns them to the girls dripping with juice to be filled again. He wonders if his mother hopes this will be a cautionary tale for him, that he'll imagine Liz pregnant and think twice.

But if so, her tableau has the opposite effect: he thinks they're gorgeous. He's always been drawn to pregnant women, but that's just it—they're *women*, adults. These are girls his age, bursting with sensuality. Carnality is removed. Horny doesn't enter the picture. Fifteen years old and he just wants to gaze at them, be near them, discover whether they smell sweeter than the girls at school. He wants to bring them lemonade, pour cool water over their feet. Years later, when Nikki's pregnant with Daniel, he'll love how maternity imbues her—her belly and face, her glowing skin and swollen lips. That's also when he'll begin to feel less sexually inclined toward her. Not, he'll explain, because he finds her less desirable, but because the nature of his passion for her has shifted. He'll want to care for her—God, he'll want to *worship* her. Sex will feel too rough, too reckless. She'll never believe his explanation, though. Or if she does, she won't accept it.

"Cole could have been an altar boy," he hears his mother tell the two girls burping babies. (He's never *considered* being an altar boy.) "Father Mally asked him specifically. But we decided that with the restoration taking so much out of our weekends, it wouldn't be possible." The girls turn their faces toward the house—plywood nailed over a rear window, the heap of lath in the backyard waiting to be pounded and beside it the massive dump pile. "Before we go back to St. Mary's I'll give you the grand tour." And *he* remains her theme for the rest of the afternoon: Cole is in honors English; he learned to shear sheep with eighteenth-century clippers and weave on an antique loom at Old Sturbridge Village; he builds bicycles from spare parts; he's studying French. She emphasizes the importance of paying close attention to every detail while restoring a house. Paints from a colonial palette. Drapes and furnishings strictly period. A passion, yes, but a responsibility as well—safeguarding the house, the antiques, for those yet to come as they've been kept over two hundred years for us.

And slowly he gets it. She hasn't set this up as a cautionary tale for him: she's giving the girls a glimpse of a respectable life. And a worthy boy. Only a few hours ago her husband, unapologetic for beating her while she was pregnant, confessed that he can't stand spending time with her, yet she's proudly dangling this life as a model for the unwed mothers. He suspects it wasn't a bicycle crash, as they've always been told, that left her with the gimpy wrist, but his father's violence. *He's* why she doesn't play the piano anymore. On TV the abusive husband is always a mean drunk, though his father barely drinks; it's undiluted rage. On TV the violent husband begs his good wife for forgiveness, charms her, swearing it'll never happen again. But in their family his mother makes the declarations about never again and spends her considerable charm talking circles around the aftermath of a beating, sealing it up, providing the excuses her husband doesn't care enough to make for himself.

COLE CARRIES ALL THE RED CURRANTS INTO THE LAUNDRY ROOM, out of the sun, while his mother guides the girls around the house before loading them in the roasting car for the ride back to Hartford. Ian, hunched over the wheelbarrow in the hottest part of the day, is pounding lath and doesn't look up as Cole passes by. His father has returned from a few hours at the store—he's left it in the weekend manager's hands—and changed out of his blazer and tie into his work clothes. He intercepts Cole in the kitchen. "We're going to rip out the buttery today, so get yourself ready."

A few minutes later, from the doorway, Cole watches his father widen his stance and swing the sledgehammer full-force over his shoulder, burying the rusty head in the plaster. He swings again, punching a fist-size hole in the wall and shooting out white dust that cloaks the hair on his sweaty arms. Animal hair used to be mixed into wet plaster, and Cole can see long black strands, encased for two centuries, dangling from the ragged hole. His father moves aside and Cole hooks the crowbar behind the wall and yanks on the splintered lath, popping out chunks of plaster that bust apart at his feet. Stepping onto the rubble, he tears in again, and as a cloud of dust billows off the floor his father pounds the sledge hard enough to shake the house.

They get to work, finding a rhythm with his father bashing holes between the studs and Cole prying and jerking out the lath. Years later Cole will come to know this is a stupid way to rip out plaster. A Sawzall or even better a Skilsaw with a junk blade would do the job much cleaner, and he'll wonder if his father asked for any advice before they started. They're in over their heads, his parents. With everything. Always struggling just to get a breath.

A minute later the small room's thick with dust, and he breathes heavily through his nose. His father's hair is powdered white and sweat streaks the dust down his cheeks and nose. Cole's lips are chalky and every few minutes he sticks his head out the window for a deep breath before hawking up a ball of white spit. And again he hooks the crowbar, yanks, and explodes the plaster. When his father sets the sledgehammer down, Cole grabs it and starts swinging. He beats and smashes and pulverizes the wall—in the thrill of demolition—and when he stops to catch his breath, his mother's standing in the doorway, hands on her hips. "You should be wearing masks."

His father swats the plaster with the crowbar.

"Suit yourself," she says, "but *he's* going to wear one," and wordlessly Cole slips past her and searches the toolshed until he finds a couple dirty masks hanging from a nail.

"Asinine," she's saying when he gets back to the buttery. "Common sense." And rage twitches his father's face and wrings his spine. Cole holds on to one mask and hangs the other on the doorknob but she grabs it, twirling it by the elastic on her finger. "You too," she says.

His father eyes the mask Cole is fingering and says, "Put that on." Then, hefting the sledgehammer, he squares his feet and, with his backswing, breaks a glass sconce off the wall. Cole's glance darts from the shards on the floor to his father's face and to the doorway: his mother has vanished.

Once they've stripped the studs, they shovel the plaster into garbage cans and toss the lath out the window. Room by room, the walls are coming down so they can add insulation. They drag the cans out to the edge of the road, then sweep and mop, coughing and spitting. The *restoration* has been going on for years: it's not a process working toward completion, it's a state. Ripped-open walls and torn-up floors, exposed wiring, a toilet drain covered up with a wastebasket, split clapboards that let mosquitoes into his bedroom in the summer and snow on windy winter nights—this is who they are.

DINNER BEGINS WITH THE METAL-ON-METAL SCRAPE OF THE SPATula gouging a cookie sheet as she serves fish sticks and tater tots, and the family eats in tense silence broken by his mother whimpering between bites, blowing her nose. A fat housefly circles his parents, scrabbles along the ceiling, and then lands on the green ribbon of fly tape hanging from the light fixture over the table.

"Maybe I should insulate the spare bedroom tomorrow," Cole says. "Get it ready for drywall."

The fly struggles against the sticky goo—the buzzing slowly muffled, then silenced.

LIZ'S SKIN IS SALTY WITH SWEAT. HE KISSES THE SMALL ROUND scar on the right side of her neck and the larger tattered one on the left. The bullet grazed her voice box and she talked like a Munchkin for a year. It was her father's revolver, the trigger pulled by Kirk's friend Matt Gosling, who snuck into her parents' bedroom and was pawing through her father's sock drawer looking for money when he found the gun. It was an accident. Liz was roller-skating in the driveway. The bullet shot through the bedroom window and straight through her neck. She stuck an index finger in each of the holes and Kirk, who was fifteen and didn't yet have his license, grabbed the keys off the hook on the fridge and drove her to the hospital in Hartford. Cole met her two years later and she talked about the shooting like a minor incident she barely remembered.

As the sun sets, the band of light travels up their bodies. This shed has been used to store equipment all winter, and early in the season it's still full of tractors and setters, stacks of flats, and an old school bus painted like all the tobacco buses, the color of coffee with cream. They've made their lair in a heap of nets that smell of dirt and winter and Connecticut Shade.

"What's wrong?" she says.

His body goes stiff. He never wants to tell her, but she always knows. He clears his throat—the plaster dust now settled deep in his chest.

"Are they duking it out?" she asks.

"Waiting for the inevitable."

She rises up on an elbow. Her face pinches. "It's *not* inevitable. You could stop it."

He sighs. "I try to keep the peace."

"You work so hard to harmonize, but it's never enough. It doesn't work. And anyway, do you ever tell your mother to just stop talking? I've heard her nagging. For a Catholic Family Services counselor with a *master's in social work*"—she mocks his mother putting on airs—"you'd think she might see a pattern. It always ends the same."

"What can I—"

"Tell her to shut up, and tell *him* that if he hits her again you'll beat the piss out of him." She sits up and punches his chest. "You have no idea of your own strength. Anyone can see you could take him. It's just your image of him as your father that's stopping you. You're not seeing this objectively." On her knees she fishes around for her underpants, then stands up and slips them over her narrow hips.

As he pulls on his T-shirt, he imagines beating the piss out of him and saving his mother. He'd pull him off of her and punch him flat on the jaw before he knew what was happening. *Think fast!* was how Cole's wrestling matches with him always began since when he was little. His father might start in tickling him on the couch and then Cole—thinking fast—would jab a finger into his ribs, and pretty soon they would've rolled onto the floor, going at it. As a kid, his father would toy with him for a while before pinning both of his ankles to the floor with one hand and tickling him madly with the other, until Cole begged for mercy. But more recently his father has struggled to get on top and pin his shoulders with his knees and declare victory. They haven't wrestled now in a year, he realizes. The last time—yes, it was a summer ago and they both worked up a tremendous sweat and Cole was pushing on his shoulder, trying to force him onto his back, but his father whipped his leg around and knocked him off-balance, drilling a knee into his back, and as he came in close to flip him over for the pin, Cole twisted and his elbow caught his father in the side of the head, breaking his glasses and driving the nose piece deep into his skin. His father groaned, holding his face, and for a week or more he wore the glasses taped together at the bridge, a Band-Aid running down one side of his nose. He looked like he'd been in a fight, or like an old man who'd had a growth removed, and no one said a word about it.

"RABBITS," HIS FATHER SAYS, FROM THE HEAD OF THE TABLE, thumbing through a catalog. "New Zealand Whites. Apparently they pretty much take care of business. Do everything but butcher themselves."

Cole imagines them hopping in the grass, their soft fur and whiskers. "Butchering seems like the hard part."

"Nope. A knife, a club, and a meat hook. That's all it takes."

He backs out of the kitchen. In the living room, Ian looks up at him and then returns to watching TV. In front of the fireplace his mother stands at the ironing board, spraying starch and pounding his father's shirts with the iron. Starsky and Hutch are making a deal with a pimp to nail a lowlife who has shot a fellow officer. Music from Kelly's stereo rattles down the stairs.

He brushes his teeth before kissing his mother goodnight, never sure how much of Liz's scent lingers on him. She's moved to the couch, reading a paperback, *The Women's Room*. His father's shirts hang stiff from the wrought-iron candelabra standing in the corner. "'Night, bro," he says, slapping his brother's knee, but Ian doesn't take his eyes off the commercial: he hovers close to their mother at these tense times, head down yet watchful.

At the top of the stairs, light's showing around his parents' door; his father has come up to bed. A soft rap swings it partway open. "Goodnight, Dad," he says.

"One male and three females," he says. He's got *The Rabbit Breeder's Guide* propped up on his belly. "The docile ones you sell for pets. The mean ones you eat."

He knocks on Kelly's door. "What?" she calls over the music, and he pushes it open.

"Dad's in bed," he tells her. "You should turn your stereo down."

She's standing in her closet doorway, pressing out on the jamb with both hands as if trying to widen the door or, by the looks of her muscles, taut as cables, trying to bust the house apart. Isometrics— pushing one palm into the other until her face turns red, linking her fingers and pulling apart like busting out of shackles, pressing her arms and legs and the side of her head into walls. Sweat drips down her collarbone and chest, darkening her tank top. "If you knock her up," she says, "it'll ruin your lives."

She doesn't like that Liz is in her same grade—both of them sophomores—as if he's stalking her territory. They were even made lab partners last winter, dissecting a fetal pig together. Cole smelled formaldehyde in Liz's hair one afternoon, and later that same night he smelled it coming off his sister's skin, here on her braided carpet, as she performed the leg lifts prescribed by the *Royal Canadian Air*

Force Exercise Plans for Physical Fitness, her personal bible. In the lab she and Liz swabbed the tips of their ring fingers with rubbing alcohol, then jabbed each other with razor-sharp skewers, and squeezed blood onto a test strip.

"Don't lose sleep over it," Cole says. Not long after he and Liz started going out, her menstrual cramps became severe and her cycle irregular, and the doctor put her on the pill. A month later Cole, who'd been drawing a timeline for world history of major events from Stonehenge to the launch of Skylab, plunged into her bareback on a hot afternoon under the nets and said, "This is the most spectacular event since the Chinese invention of gunpowder in one thousand BC."

"It's your future," Kelly says. "Not mine."

And Kelly's future is determined: her walls covered with posters of F-16s screeching across a blue sky, pilots geared up and walking badass from their jets, the Thunderbirds mid-twirl. And another, with photos of Venice and Switzerland, urging her to *Discover the World as a Woman in the Air Force.*

"Can you hold my ankles?" she says.

He gets down on his knees while she does sit-ups. "Do you know he wants to get rabbits now?"

"Ian'll like that," she says. "I wish we'd get a dog."

"The rabbits aren't for pets."

"Ugh." She fires off the sit-ups like a marine. "Barbaric."

She turned mostly vegetarian the first time they butchered chickens, and only ate meat that had no obvious connections to an animal. Pepperoni on pizza. Bacon bits on salad. Slim Jims. Getting the chickens had been her idea, inspired by a Sturbridge Village trip. Their father got on board immediately and together they designed the coop, selected the breed, and made several trips to the Agway in Southwick for supplies. Kelly imagined plump, demure birds quietly clucking around the yard, pecking at bugs and roosting serenely in the coop, laying rich, delicious eggs. She made outstanding omelets.

But she was put off by the smell of twenty-five chickens right away, and when they slaughtered the roosters she bailed on the project completely. Their father took over with zeal, ordering another twenty-five day-olds and giving away eggs to everyone they knew.

"Okay," she says, lying back on the carpet, and he releases her ankles.

"You should turn your stereo down," he says. "I think he's trying to sleep."

She flexes her biceps in the mirror.

"You're an Amazon," Cole says.

"Getting there."

LIZ IS PREGNANT, STRADDLING HIM IN A SHED LOADED WITH DRY-ing leaves, the heaters hushing with soft blue flame . . . then a shout and he shoots up in bed . . . a muffled cry, and now he's tearing across his room, still half in the dream, and bursting out the door, and this has always been his biggest fear: he doesn't wake up in time, doesn't hear the scream through the pillow smothering her. He slams open their door—he's on top of her and turning now toward Cole, his face red. "No!" his mother calls out from deep in the pillows. "Dad, stop!" Cole shouts as he leaps onto the bed and grabs his ankle, twisting and yanking him off of her. Ian comes running into the room, then Kelly rushes up the stairs wrapped only in a towel, her hair hanging wet. His parents, naked in the hot night, quickly cover up with the sheet but not before they see his father's erection, his mother blushing in the lamplight, smiling and stifling a laugh. "Okay, kids," she says. "Back to bed."

6

WITH HIS PHONE PRESSED TO HIS EAR, COLE PULLS RIPE BERRIES from a bush and tips them into his mouth.

"I was sitting in American history," Daniel's saying, "learning how American democracy and capitalism have made the world just so amazing and free and full of opportunity, and out the window there's a homeless couple pushing a shopping cart with a little girl in it, collecting cans from garbage bins. And I don't mean 'out the window' like some synecdoche for 'in the city' or 'in the nation,' I mean I'm looking out the literal window of my high school at these *Americans* with their *American child* picking through garbage for the Rock Star empties my classmates tossed out before first period. I couldn't stay in that room another second."

"But Daniel, you're smart enough to know you can't change the world without an education."

"Last time I looked up 'education' in the dictionary I didn't see 'lies,' 'hypocrisy,' and 'propaganda.'"

Cole swirls sour berry juice around in his mouth, then swallows. "What do you propose?" he finally asks. "You have to go to school. You're fifteen. It's a law."

Daniel sighs. "Yeah, laws. Right."

They get nowhere and agree to talk later. The joke among their Portland friends is that—liberal parents all—they'd end up with kids rebelling into rabid conservatives, but Daniel has out-lefted the lefties. And to call it rebellion doesn't do him justice either. He's smart as hell, and his politics are more complicated than some knee-jerk reaction to his parents driving a Prius and favoring good wine, bike lanes, and Obama.

Cole calls the school's principal to see what can be done to allow him to finish ninth grade.

"He can't come back this spring," she tells him, "but he'll pass. He had A's in all his classes, so even with F's on his final papers and exams, he'll be fine."

"What about next year?"

"He can apply in August to have his expulsion lifted. You could also think about alternatives. He's very gifted, Mr. Callahan. Some of his teachers feel he's not sufficiently challenged here."

The next call is to Cole's foreman, Ben Salverson. They have two jobs going—a wraparound porch with new entryways in Laurelhurst and a complete gutting and renovation on a Craftsman in Sellwood. Ben's working through a punch list on the job they finished last week when he answers the phone. "I pulled two guys off the demolition to bang it out here. We'll be done by lunch."

Cole, who'd pushed the crew hard before this trip, is relieved by the news.

"Got a problem in Sellwood, though. Asbestos behind the drop ceiling in the kitchen."

"No, no," Cole says. "We checked that."

"It was hiding behind the abandoned ductwork."

"Damn. So now you've got them working upstairs?"

"Back to front."

"All right. I'll set up the abatement, but we'll lose at least a few days. If the guys are spinning their wheels, send them to the shop to make room for the chestnut. Looking at all those gorgeous timbers this morning, I realize we're going to need racks on the whole south wall."

"So it's good?"

"It's such beautiful wood, Ben. And there'll be lots left over after the addition on my house." The family room.

"There was a message about the Richmond bid," Ben says. "Sounds like they're getting antsy."

"Yeah, I've gotta get to that. It's been a hell of a trip so far. Hard to believe it's only been two days."

"Ghosts popping up everywhere?"

Just then, inside, his father hits one of the wrong notes. "Every time I turn around."

"Well, figure that bid pronto or else we'll lose the job."

"Will do, Ben. You keep the guys busy."

Cole slips the phone in his back pocket and picks berries until his palms are full, then he goes inside and spills them into a cereal bowl. He carries it into the keeping room, and his father stops playing and peers into the bowl as if looking down a well. "Oh," he says. He drops a few berries in his mouth and sucks on them while returning to the keyboard.

Cole steps back and listens for a few minutes, then goes in the kitchen and fills a glass with water. The music's mournful, in part because of a hollowness; it's like the notes are calling out into darkness, but no reply comes back. Listening, drinking the cool well water, he walks into the parlor. The moldings are ornate, and he runs a finger over the wood overlay on the mantel that his mother cut from half-inch stock with a coping saw. His father had stripped a dozen layers of paint off the mantel, and when he got down to bare wood they could see the ghostly imprint of a frieze torn off who knows how long ago; so they traced the outline and remade it perfectly. Inspecting the interlocking circles now, he sees how skillfully it's done. Through the years it's been easy for Cole to fault his parents, critical of their bad judgment and incompetence. He doesn't need a shrink to tell him that his entire career is—at least partly—an attempt to correct his parents' restoration mistakes. But it's more than that. They taught him to appreciate craftsmanship and artistry, and a beautiful piece of wood. Being here reminds him how much he still loves the New England colonial aesthetic, closer than people might think to the Craftsman houses he works on in Portland. Despite everything they did wrong, he respects what his parents were trying to create here, and he understands the hard work of living in a jobsite. The constant battle with frozen pipes and their own learning curve, with their Sisyphean progress and dwindling bank account. The long cold trudge to the bathroom in the middle of a winter night. Once a roof leak's repaired, the medieval furnace conks out. Never a weekend or an evening when the list of what must get done could be ignored.

Although in truth there was the occasional Saturday or Sunday at Sturbridge Village, buying a paper sack of penny candy from the store on the common, touring the Fitch House, then walking past the tinsmith and the waterwheel beside the gristmill to give sheep shearing a try. He remembers feasting on pounded cheese with gourd soup and Tunbridge cakes at the tavern while his parents drank hard cider from pewter mugs. Then they all got on a stagecoach so big it was pulled by a team of dray horses over the covered bridge and past the clanking and smoky blacksmith. As soon as his mother heard a Quebecois family on the coach behind them, she turned and spoke to them in French, her face flushed from the alcohol and the thrill of loosening her tongue in the language she loved. When they stopped in front of the meeting house, his father jumped down to the ground first and reached out his hand for his wife, caught her in his arms when she stumbled, and they started across the common after Cole's mother bid her new friends adieu, walking hand-in-hand for several steps until they broke apart. Other than the night when he pulled his father off of her because he thought he was stopping a beating, it was the only time he ever witnessed any intimacy between them.

What does it mean that his own failure at intimacy is what drove Nikki away? It wasn't like that at the start. They began as friends, part of a little clique in college, and when the two of them started meeting separately for dinner or a movie they'd laugh into the night. The first time they slept together it really was just to sleep: two in the morning and pouring down rain, and they'd been bingeing Louis Malle movies at his place. After he suggested that she spend the night on his couch instead of going home, she floated her contacts in tea-cups while he brushed his teeth, then rinsed the brush under a long blast of hot water and held it out for her. Nikki was poised to put his toothbrush in her mouth but stopped, and they stared at each other, and he parted his lips, mirroring her, and they fell into an explosion of passion that had been building for a year. They kept their romance a secret from their pals for a while, and when they finally went public some of them felt betrayed; their group wasn't as tight anymore, and before long it dispersed.

Even now Cole remembers that time with Nikki as a love that all others could be measured by, the kind celebrated in poetry and mov-ies and dreams, so ecstatic that since things started falling apart he's wondered whether he was romanticizing their early years, romanti-cizing his own past.

Their love for Daniel, though, never wavered. Despite the dif-ficult delivery and the hard toll it took on Nikki, their baby was born wise, a step ahead. He aced his Apgar tests. Nikki spent a few days in the ICU because of the hemorrhaging, so Cole held their baby beside her and combed the thick red hair he'd grown in utero. His eyes appeared focused and penetrating, watchful. He *envied* his baby, his past only a few hours old, a clean slate.

He realizes the music has stopped, and when he peeks into the keeping room his father isn't there. He goes to the piano and sits on the warm bench, looking out the window across the backyard, where Phil's pulling up nettles half his height from around the chicken coop. The sheet music's flopped open in the scroll-top rack, and Cole flips the pages to see the cover: Brahms's Symphony no. 2 arranged for four hands. Which explains the emptiness he's been hearing in the music. It's a composition for two players. And when he turns to the first page he again recalls the image that he's flashed on thousands of times: his parents holding hands on the Old Sturbridge commons, her good hand in his, her lame one hanging at her side—because on that sheet, in his mother's handwriting, is her name for one player and her husband's for the other.

LATE IN THE AFTERNOON, AFTER MAKING SOME DISTRACTED BUT still decent progress on the Richmond project and a few phone calls in search of educational options for Daniel, he finds the kitchen tap running and, on the table, the old turkey roaster overflowing with currants. When he turns off the water, he can hear his father rummaging around in the laundry room, where he's down on his knees and trying to stand with his arms around two flats of Ball jars, still in their tattered and dusty cardboard cases. The blue-speckled waterbath canner's teetering on top, and Cole swoops down to catch it. "Let me help you with that."

Phil loses his balance and stumbles into the washing machine, the canner slips and clanks to the floor. "Don't treat me like a pissant!" he snaps. "Now pick up that kettle and put it back on top!"

OUT IN THE YARD, COLE STARES AT HIS BROTHER'S FACE IN A PHOTO, then sets it aside and rummages through the box. It's full of stuff from his mother's desk. A pack rat, she crammed drawers, bookcases, shoeboxes, whatever, full of virtually anything: a receipt for stockings, a blouse, and a girdle from G. Fox & Co., for lipstick and a purse from Marks & Tilly; Cole's fifth-grade report card and his permission slip for a field trip to Hartford; birthday and Christmas cards, canceled checks. Who is the woman who emerges from these archives? What could it mean that she saved a slip from Valley Dry Cleaners ("1 dress, 1 slacks") in 1974?

Like whoever years ago packed this stuff into boxes—Uncle Raymond or her brother Andrew, most likely—he feels the need to save it, too. Maybe he can't expect meaning in each scrap of paper, but the mere accumulation—the records of a short life's transactions—must add up to something.

He needs new boxes, then he'll move it all to the attic where it'll stay dry. Before long, a time will come when he and his brother and sister will converge here, do the culling, and sell the house.

His father has been banging pots on the stove for the last half hour, and now a waft of stewing currants settles around Cole, conjuring images of his mother in a steamy kitchen, a cotton sleeveless dress, her face red, a bead of sweat dripping from the tip of her nose.

He spreads everything out in the sun, then carries the tea caddy into the kitchen and sets it on the table. "How's the jelly coming?"

His father doesn't respond.

"Hey," Cole says. "I'm driving over to the liquor store to get some boxes. You need anything?" He'll take some of the photos and maybe even the tea caddy home with him to Portland.

"I need boxes too. Eight or ten." Phil's staring into the rising steam. "I'm ordering some day-olds. They can live in boxes till I get the coop cleaned out. Fifty rings a bell. Fifty's what we got when you were kids."

"You're talking about buying chickens? Is now the time to buy chickens?"

"It's a great time. Warm and getting warmer. With chicks, the cold can be a battle. Do you remember how much Kelly wanted chickens?"

"I didn't really mean the time of year. I meant . . . this time in your life."

His father stares at him for a long moment and then at his wrist, where a watch would be if he had one. Finally he looks back at Cole, rheumy-eyed, and says, "At eight weeks you can kill the roosters."

. . .

WITH A DULL PARING KNIFE COLE HACKS AT A ROASTED CHICKEN.
He's done some shopping at the new supermarket on the edge of
town. Cracking a leg from the carcass, he remembers how Daniel
has repeatedly told him to quit saying *supermarket* (*grocery store,* his
bemused son instructs, or just *store*). He also shouldn't say *knapsack*
or *high-test gas* or *Wash'n Dri* ("Jesus, Dad, they're *wipes*") or refer to
his iPod as a Walkman. But all these old words feel revived in this
house.

From the foot of the stairs he calls his father down for dinner,
then puts the food and dishes out on the table. He's stocked the
fridge. The cellar and the cabinet under the counter have pretty
well dried out. He plans to repack his mother's old papers, give his
father a good meal, and then leave him to his jelly making, his fifty
day-olds, and the rooster slaughter in eight weeks. He's got Daniel's
troubles to tend to, not to mention his eight employees who depend
on him to keep the jobs running. In a few more hours he could finish
the Richmond bid and get that off to the client. He doesn't even want
to think about his father's finances or long-range plans or the house
or his broken-down car . . . Suddenly he laughs out loud, shaking his
head: those are the same damn things he listened to his parents fight
about year after year. He'll get his father settled this evening, go back
to his airport hotel, and stop in just once more at the end of the week
before returning home.

Phil drags out the chair at the head of the table.

"You want a drink?" Cole asks. "I got you seltzer, grape juice, OJ."
When he finally looks up he sees that his father has put on long flannel pajamas over his clothes.

"What?" he responds, noticing the look. "I go to bed early. It's
what I got used to inside."

Cole sits down and fills their plates with steamed green beans,
brown rice, and chicken.

His father hunches over his plate. "Pass the ketchup," he says, and
Cole gets back up and swings open the fridge—still dark in there, he

meant to buy a bulb—and grabs it from the door. His father squeezes ketchup over everything, scrapes a few forkfuls into his mouth, and while he chews his back straightens as if he's rising out of the chair, his face softening, his eyes going limp. "This is a *meal*," he says, "tasty as any I ever had," coming out of the gloomy confusion that dogged him all afternoon and recovering the easy charm he displayed with Alex, like a man in a seersucker suit with a highball in each hand. But then Cole smells something sharp and weirdly intimate: his father is *pissing*. Cole jumps from his chair. Piss soaks through his father's khakis, through his flannel pajamas, and drips off the edge of his seat.

"Who the hell are you?" Eyes burning, Phil shoves his plate away, knocking over the seltzer, chugging fizz across the table before Cole snatches up the bottle. "What are you doing in my house?" He pushes away from the table and Cole takes a step back, flashing on the bowl of salmon wiggle his father tossed from this same spot, the explosion of hot food and glass against the wall, his mother's screams, Ian's cries and burning arms, food splattered on his Little League uniform.

Phil trudges into the keeping room, leaving a puddle in the seat and a trail of urine dripping down one leg of his soaked clothes.

Cole's heart is racing, then his phone rings: Nikki. Catching his breath, he says, "Hi."

"What's wrong?"

"Nothing." The opening chords rise from the keeping room.

"Airport piano bar?"

"Something like that."

"So glad you're enjoying your holiday while our son's getting arrested."

"Oh, shit."

"You said it. Shit, shit, friggin' shit."

"Is he in jail?"

"He's out now."

"What, on bail?"

"Tony called in a favor and got the charges dropped."

"Thank God. What did he do?"

"Breaking and entering, destruction of property, vandalism. He'll have to pay Safeway some money, or else."

"He broke into a Safeway?"

"No, just into their dumpster."

"Oh," Cole says. "He's told me about those. He's right, too. They're shameful."

"Turns out you can do a thousand dollars of damage to one of them with a hacksaw and a small gang of homeless people and freegans."

"The freegans again."

"You know, we've been blaming them for a year, but Daniel's the only one who got arrested. The one with the hacksaw. The rest of them were just standing around. You can watch it all on YouTube. It's pretty obvious he's the ringleader."

He listens to the somber chords preceding the run of trills that by now he's memorized. When Nikki was first pregnant, they both sensed the baby was a girl, which was a relief to Cole since he wasn't sure he'd know how to raise a boy. A few days after the ultrasound he was driving the pickup home from the shop and passed a park where a Little League game was being played. He looped around and sat up in the small bleacher with the fathers and studied them for how to act, but could think only about his own father, which was maybe what he'd feared.

Daniel's ideas of fairness were strong. In pre-K he pointed out to the teacher that she was favoring boys when they lined up to go outside. He returned kindnesses religiously. After one boy's birthday party, Daniel told him to take off his shirt, then—a four-year-old son of a seamstress—peeled off his own, got down on his knees in the driveway, and taught him how to fold.

When he was five, walking down a sidewalk in Portland, they

passed a panhandler they'd seen for years, and Daniel asked, "What's his sign say?"

"He wants us to give him money," Cole explained.

"What for?"

"Food."

They walked a few more steps before Daniel stopped, yanking on his father's hand, confused and angry, and said, "Why *wouldn't* we?"

Cole had felt it at his birth, but looking at his incensed boy on the sidewalk that day, he *knew* Daniel's spirit and intelligence and heart were limitless. That he could do what any father dreams his child would: reach further than his parents, live a richer, more meaningful life.

"Hello? Cole?" Nikki says, exasperated.

His father has arrived at the dreamy middle of the piece. Cole half-listens, knowing where the mistakes will come, anticipating them like a skip in a favorite record. "I'll call him," Cole says. "And I'll try for a flight back tonight. Maybe there's a red-eye."

Phil's piss has run the length of the kitchen floor and pooled in a depression in front of the sink. Cole straddles the puddle and finds a rancid sponge in the cabinet, and putting all squeamishness aside he sops up the urine, rinsing the sponge repeatedly in the sink before bending over to wipe up some more. This takes long enough that by now his father has finished the piece and started in again from the top. Cole wipes down the chair, thinking of Daniel's pee-soaked diapers, of having to chase him down in the summer to get them off—he never wanted to stop running—and when he released the Velcro tabs, the diaper would drop to the floor heavy as a melon, and he'd dash away, naked and ecstatic to be free of the hindrance.

He sponges up dribbles on the wide floorboards that lead like a trail of breadcrumbs to the piano. He'll have to make arrangements for his father—he needs real care—but he can do that by phone. He'll have to pay for it, and he'll also have to get in touch with Kelly and Ian.

He stands beside him for a minute, waiting for a transition between movements before interrupting. "You should hop in the shower and get a change of clothes."

Phil turns to him, smiling serenely, then nodding in time to the music. "It's fine. It's fine." He chuckles. "Change in the shower and hop into clothes." He plays on.

"Really, Dad," Cole says, and reaches out to touch his forearm.

He reels back as if stuck with a knife. "What in the goddamn hell!" His lips trembling, teeth bared.

"You need to clean up."

He looks around the room as if trying to place where he is— fireplace, windows, piano, his own wet pants, and finally the sponge in Cole's hand. "It was an accident," he says flatly.

The words hang between them, piano strings still quivering. Their eyes meet in the piercing stares of animals. "*What* was an accident?"

His father's head drops. He looks at his lap. "Just . . . just . . ." He slides off the far end of the bench and stands as if ready to fight, but quickly his fists fall to his sides. "Just let me wash up, will you?" Stiff-legged, he walks into the bathroom and cranks the shower on. "It's fine," Cole hears over the water.

FROM THE BACK PORCH HE CALLS THE AIRLINE. THERE'S NOTHING tonight, but he books a flight for six a.m. Alex and Antoine can sign off on the shipment for him.

He calls Daniel, who instead of "Hello" says, "A thousand bucks is such bullshit, Dad. I cut through an eighty-nine-cent bolt."

"We'll deal with the money part," Cole says. "The main thing for you is not getting arrested again."

"Trumped-up BS, and they knew it. They couldn't hold me for two hours."

"The only reason they let you go is because Tony boxes with some cop."

Daniel bristles—he can feel it right through the phone. "This is much bigger than some old boys' network. It's about feeding people in a state with the disgraceful standing of number one in childhood hunger. And these goddamn *'fully-enclosed waste removal systems'* are criminal! Safeway sends enough food to the dump to feed every hungry person in Oregon. The solution's pretty fucking simple." And Cole lets him vent, listening to the rant he's heard before. Crates of wilted lettuce, bushels of bruised tomatoes and peaches, heaps of pasta, damaged boxes of Bisquick and brownie mix sent down the dark conveyer belt through the hanging rubber flaps and into a compactor as big as a truck, fully enclosed, impenetrable from the outside. "They don't even look like dumpsters. They look like space pods."

How could he and Nikki have raised a boy so principled? Cole thinks of himself at that age—the summer of his mother's death. Sex with Liz, and getting high with her—those were *his* passions. He supposes he believed in the careful and accurate restoration of old colonials. He disapproved of vandalism and littering and would call people out when he witnessed it. He understood the value of hard work. But he felt he'd missed the moment—his whole generation had arrived late. The sixties were already over, the seventies had turned sour, and the groundwork for Reagan's eighties was solidly in place. It was far too late to save the world.

But Daniel feels the urgency of *his* time. America's been at war for half his life. Climate change has become undeniable yet is all the more fiercely denied. World economies implode weekly. "Our neighbors are starving," he says, "while we're enjoying French cheese from Whole Foods."

As Daniel continues on the phone about the other people in among his freegans, Cole walks out to the chicken coop at the back of the yard, some of the wire fence pulled down by weeds but for the most part intact. He has to yank on the door of the coop until it finally flies open. Inside, a motorcycle. No front tire, no seat, surrounded by cardboard boxes of greasy parts, all of it coated with years of dust. A tenant's project, long ago abandoned. And then from the back corner, dark except for bright stripes of sunlight shining between the siding, he hears squeaking, like chicks, but when he squats down to look, he sees a nest of baby raccoons, three of them piled up like kittens, their long snouts pointy as a rat's, black masks, their eyes chips of light.

He leaves the coop's door ajar and back in the kitchen pours a dish of milk and fills another with stale saltines and the remnants from a bag of peanuts in the shell.

"I'm sorry, Dad, but if anything we've got to step up the action."

Cole slides the dishes under the motorcycle.

"Anyway, I should go. I've got a meeting."

"With the freegans?" He wanders over and kneels beside the contents of his mother's desk, sifting the papers and photos, now crinkled but dry, in his fingers.

"For work."

"You got a job?"

"The People's Farm."

"Can you save enough on that job to pay Safeway?"

"Dad, it's a co-op. And I donate my share back for the food boxes. As you know. I'm not giving Safeway a penny."

"You don't have a choice, Daniel. That was a condition of them not pressing charges." He begins stacking his mother's things in the fresh cartons.

"I'd sooner give money to the Klan."

"I don't think the Klan and Safeway are in the same category."

"Ah, *that's* where you're mistaken, my friend."

So now they're on to this. "Okay," Cole says. They're getting nowhere. "I'll see you tomorrow and we'll make a plan." He lowers the phone and watches Daniel's picture on the screen until it fades. After loading the boxes, he carries them inside to the kitchen table. The shower's still running. He pulls the drawers open but can't find any tape. He just wants to get back to the hotel. He has to be up before dawn. He has to get his father a phone. He has to make sure his car's running. From Portland he can make arrangements to have an aide come in and assess his needs. He'll email Kelly and Ian. He'll get everything rolling.

Wondering why the shower's still on, he goes to the bathroom and sees a trail of water and footprints across the floor. The shower curtain's pushed open. Christ. He twists off the tap and starts through the door into the parlor but stops short. The wing chair's still here, pushed up against the wall. He hadn't noticed it earlier. The upholstery looks like a dog bed. It's a repro, made by his father's friend Tom Mace, who charged them, according to his mother, an *astronomical* price. Something was always off about the chair. It looked right, with elegant colonial lines, but was never comfortable, and if you shifted to find the fit, it was hard not to slide off the seat. But his father made a point of sitting in it to read. And then there was the night that Cole got out of the shower and half dried off and came through the parlor to go upstairs but stopped in his tracks: his parents seemed to be kissing, something he'd never seen them do. His father was sitting in the chair, a book open in his lap, his mother leaning down to him, her palms flat on his chest, his hand reaching up to her. But he wasn't holding her face, as it first appeared. He was gripping her throat.

"Hey!" Cole shouted, and his father's hand sprung open.

She stumbled backward, choking. "You could've killed me," she croaked, in a voice not even recognizable as hers. Hoarse and rasping. Possessed. And over the following days the voice he knew began to re-emerge, slowly, cautiously. She made their dinner and sat at the table, but she didn't eat. She drank tea, asking Ian about Little League, Cole and his sister about their classes, a blood spot in one eye, purple dots dusting her cheekbones and brow.

The water trail leads up the stairs, where he can hear a TV playing. "Dad," he calls, but there's no reply. The steps squeak as he ascends, the crack down the length of each board widening under his weight, opening enough to let through the smell of the dirt cellar, earthy and dank as a grave.

Evening light washes through the Palladian windows on the second floor, the shadows of balusters like bars on the white plaster wall. The blanket chest and Canton jar are gone, replaced by a low black-and-blond IKEA-looking cabinet with a glass door, weirdly out of place on the rough wide floorboards beneath the decorative colonial window moldings. The trail of water continues into his parents' old room, and he pushes open the door. The bed's positioned where it always was, on the far wall, and there's a TV on a nightstand, an old set with rabbit ears, and behind it lies his father, still dressed in his pajamas over his clothes, soaking wet, fast asleep. His white whiskers look sharp as quills. Dirty dishes, a sandwich crust, and a mossy brown apple core litter the other side of the bed. The TV screen is mostly fuzz—a Red Sox game, the desultory observations of commentators. Cole touches the antenna and the screen goes white, the voices staticky, and he switches the set off.

He opens Ian's door. The small room has been turned over to storage, packed so full with furniture and boxes, rolled carpets flopped over a cot, a stack of games—Yahtzee, Operation, Chutes and Ladders—that he can't see the fireplace, or the closet with its secret compartment under the attic stairs, where Ian sometimes slept. He wouldn't recognize the room at all.

The carpet his mother braided is still in the center of Kelly's room. Her canopy bed, too—stripped of its canopy. It has been rearranged, the desk and all her decorations are gone, but it still feels like a dusty gray preservation. He runs his finger around the rings pressed into the closet doorjambs where her pull-up bar was.

At his own room he pauses with his thumb on the latch, and after taking a deep breath and blowing it out he bursts through the door to find his room even more impossibly the same. The twin beds are right where they were. The curtains are yellowed and dusty, but he instantly recognizes the Williamsburg fabric—a bare-chested Indian leading a colonist through a lush forest populated with peacocks, dogs, and lions; the years have made the print look more cartoonish. What's most different is that the walls, which they'd gutted to the studs for insulation, have been sheetrocked and painted, making it feel like his room's been transported to a museum and reassembled.

He sits on his bed, rests his head on the pillow, and closes his eyes. Beneath the dust is the familiar damp-wood smell of his childhood. Promptly, he falls into a fitful sleep and then wakes abruptly, running into the hallway before he stops in the moonlight shining through the windows, his heart pounding. His father is shouting out gibberish in his sleep.

Downstairs, he finds his phone. It's almost midnight. He tries to remember . . . Yes, when he closed his eyes it was still light. The thud in his chest begins to let up. He takes the grape juice from the fridge, can't find a clean glass, and sits at the kitchen table, swigging from the bottle. In front of him, the rosewood tea caddy. He lifts the lid and pulls out a square of card stock, ink-stamped with a newborn's foot—*Kelly Marie Callahan, November 4, 1962*—and then their marriage certificate, yellowed and ancient-looking. And darker still, as if it's been stained with tea, a newspaper clipping he carefully unfolds: an ad for the grand opening of Marks & Tilly Ltd's second store in Avon, the store his father would manage. They always called it *his store, Phil's store,* but everyone knew it was Tilly's.

Tilly's father, Mark O'Brien, had owned Mark's Five-and-Dime, and when he got sick, Tilly took it over just as rural Simsbury was becoming a Hartford suburb. Within a few years of his death, Tilly had transformed the store—which had never made even enough money for him to move his family out of the dark apartment at the rear of the shop—into Marks & Tilly Ltd., a small but fancy department store catering to Simsbury's new residents flocking to big new homes and restored old colonials, founding members of the country club, insurance-company executives, and bigwigs from Pratt and Whitney, Taybro, and Boulger Tobacco. She carried expensive women's clothes, luxurious sheets and towels, and there was a nook of English teas and biscuits in tins. As a boy, Cole was only allowed in the store with clean clothes and hair neatly combed.

When Phil got out of the army, Tilly opened the second store, in Avon, and hired him to run it. Year after year, as the Simsbury store flourished, *his* store struggled to break even. Everyone knew this because Tilly talked about it incessantly. Or did she? Suddenly he wasn't sure. But it was known, a fact that hovered around them always, suffusing the very air they breathed.

In a small blue envelope Cole finds a plastic hospital anklet typed with his name, his mother's, and his birth weight. A lock of hair is tied up in a flattened blue ribbon. He thumbs through his mother's high-school diploma, report cards, snapshots of her as a girl, her grandfather Mark in front of his five-and-dime. He pulls out a postcard—a photograph of the Queen Mother with adolescent Margaret and Elizabeth, taken in 1941 in a Windsor Castle garden. They're posed, straining to seem at ease: Margaret fiddles her fingers, Elizabeth pets a small dog, broodingly, and the Queen Mother has perched her hands on the handle of a parasol, its tip planted in the grass. Lording it over the girls. She looks exactly like Tilly, and the card is from Tilly to his mother, dated June 1964: *Fashions changing for the worse. I'll stick with tried and true for my customers, thank you. England bleak. Get that baby weight off. Your self-respect never amounted to a hill of beans (as you know) and a layer of fat doesn't help. A cigarette takes the appetite away. Men get their shots in—Lord knows your father was difficult—but they're only stronger in the arms, not in the backbone. Stiff upper lip. With affection, Tilly.*

Cole was two months old then; Kelly less than two years. His father, still in the army, was making the trip home from Fort Devens every few weeks. What makes Cole feel sick now isn't so much what Tilly wrote—he'd heard many versions of this straight from her own mouth—but that his mother had kept the card, and kept it in her box of sentiments and memories. Why hadn't she torn it up and burned the shreds?

He pulls out a photo of him and Liz sitting side by side on the back porch steps. She's wearing her blue rain slicker, a little small on her, gripping the cuffs to tug down the sleeves, her arms wrapped around her knees. Cole's looking at the camera and smiling while Liz stares off, far away. He remembers that his mother came outside to get a shot of the copper weathervane his parents had bought that morning at an auction. The weathervane never made it to the roof, and the picture of it isn't here with the others. It was that last summer, in August. Squinting, he thinks he can see that his fingers are stained from tobacco picking. His head's cocked toward Liz, but she's leaning away from him. He wonders why this is the photo of them that his mother chose to keep in the tea caddy, both of them wet from the rain, scraggly, coming down from a joint they'd smoked earlier. Liz looks tough. He imagines she's still the same girl she was then, except she's sitting in a high-rise making deals for coffee beans or Brazilian hardwood or whatever it is she imports. But of course she isn't the same. *People grow up. People move on.* It's Nikki's voice he's hearing now. He *thought* he'd moved on, but he's beginning to feel like he only moved away.

He looks at another picture: Phil holding a rooster in front of the henhouse. They'd just built it from rough-cut Southern pine and it looks new, surprisingly, as Oregon homesteads out on the high desert are surprisingly new in old photos. His father has long, thick sideburns, and his black plastic glasses are held together across the bridge with tape. The Band-Aid runs along his nose. Although he isn't smiling, he looks as proud as he would in a 4-H portrait, presenting the rooster he fattened up and will butcher in a few weeks.

And then he sees a flash of Daniel in the face of his father as a younger man—a skeletal resemblance, the curve of the cheekbones, the insistent jaw—and he's suddenly afraid for his son. Christ, he was arrested, he went to jail! How can Cole protect him if he continues to seek out trouble? The most basic and essential duty of a father is to keep his children safe; that's what you sign on for. They had to get him away from his crowd of freegans—ha!—away from his strident, if honorable, principles. Getting him out of Portland for a while might be the only solution.

Until he's slipping the photos back in the envelope he doesn't realize his hands are shaking. He's looking forward to driving back to the hotel and having a stiff drink at the bar off the lobby. He'll check on his father and go.

Upstairs, he pushes open his parents' bedroom door. The bed's empty, and he jerks his head around like he's being stalked: in the dark room his father's standing in the moonlight at the window.

"One of the females was pregnant when we got them," he says.

"You just need to sleep now. Why don't you get back in bed."

"We thought she might be sick, but it was babies. Seven of them. Minus the one that died."

"The rabbits," Cole says, "the New Zealand Whites," squeezing his father's elbow and nudging him toward the bed.

But Phil cups his hands around the sides of his eyes and presses his face to the glass. "Did you bring the garbage cans in?"

"They're not out, Dad."

"On Tuesdays." His father turns from the glass, his face so vacant it could belong to anyone. It could be Cole himself.

When he's finally got Phil in bed, he closes the door and leans on the railing in the hallway, the mullions in the Palladian window etching moon shadows over his body. He texts Nikki—she's not going to like it—and then Daniel.

Then he shuts off his phone but doesn't go downstairs. He doesn't drive through the night with the windows open wide to the airport hotel. He steps quietly down the hall to his room.

7

IT'S A FRIDAY AND SCHOOL WILL BE OVER IN A WEEK, BUT IT FEELS like summer already after a spring so long and warm, and this morning, eleven a.m., they're all outside in T-shirts and shorts because of another bomb scare.

Cole's friend Roxanne says, "The Red Army, the SLA, the Communists. It could be anybody."

"It could also be a senior," Cole says. "Any kid in school."

"Don't be so naive," she tells him. "Our little town in the New England countryside isn't immune from the threats of the world. In fact we're the target. This enemy strikes at the heart."

Cole thinks her politics are shaped by some combination of English class, where she's reading *Beowulf*, and gym, where they're on week three of dodge ball. Behind her he sees seven or eight boys have lifted up Miss Huebler's Datsun and are carrying it over the flowers ringing the circle and will set the car down on the grass beneath the flagpole, which was exactly what they did at the bomb scare last week. "I think," he says, "the enemy is within."

"What about the tobacco sheds?" she says. "You think that's just a kid from school too?" Two have burnt down in the last two months. "It's ugly corporate tactics. Tobacco's on the way out in Connecticut and these guys are desperate. Torch the competition. No different from Rockefeller and the Standard Oil Trust." He happens to know she wrote a paper on that subject for American history.

"When corporations aren't busting up unions, they're busting up each other."

Kids are spilling out of the smoking pavilion, lounging with cigarettes in the grass while a senior girl sits on a picnic table playing a guitar. Another two strum and sing "Southern Man" in the shade up on Bonfire Hill. Others play catch or tennis or, on the far side of the baseball field, chuck clumps of dirt attached to long weeds over the barbed-wire fence at the bull who's grazing just beyond their range. They all call him Buford, though nobody knows his real name or whether he even has one; in the school's mythology he's a menace and a constant threat but also an ever-watchful protector.

At the center of the soccer field, Liz catches a Frisbee on the run. She flings it back where it came from—two masses of kids, three Frisbees slicing the air—and then ambles toward Cole and Roxanne. "Too hot," she says, plopping down between them. She kisses Cole and he tastes her sweat mixed with peppermint Lip Smacker; he smells green grass and body heat. She gazes back at the Frisbee players, or beyond, to Buford; the bullet scars on her neck have reddened, as they always do when she's hot.

"Roxanne thinks our town's the front line of a ruthless corporate war," Cole says.

Liz's shoulders stiffen and the damp spot on the back of her T-shirt sticks to her skin.

"What do you think about it?" Roxanne asks. "You know, the bombs, the arson."

"Oh," she says as the first of the police cars pulls away from the school. "I don't really think about it at all."

And then the fire alarm blares two short bursts. School's back open, in time for fifth period. French I.

IAN NEEDS HELP DESIGNING AN ECOLOGICAL CITY FOR CIVICS class, so that afternoon Cole cuts Palmolive and Herbal Essence bottles into tiny solar panels and Kelly glues cotton balls on the tops of factories, Ian's answer to noise pollution. Smoke and factory waste travel in bendy straws to treatment plants that transform it into fuel for the monorail. "Fresh drinking water from the mountains," Ian tells them. "Laid-off people pick up litter. The recycling plant's attached to the school, so kids collect newspaper and bottles and bring them in on the bus."

Cole straightens a wall on the monorail station.

"How about a slingshot at the airport," Kelly suggests, "so jets don't burn so much fuel taking off?"

Ian's eyes widen. "Or a catapult."

And then they hear the Impala in the driveway. It's their father, but at the wrong time for him to be coming home. They rise from the floor and move toward the window cautiously. Cole pushes a curtain aside, kitchen shears in his hand.

Pressure-treated lumber is roped to the roof, and the trunk's half open, tied down against a heavy load, sinking the back of the car like a boat taking on water. When Cole steps outside, his father calls, "Come look!"

Three liquor boxes sit across the backseat. Cole opens the door, bends down inside, and pulls up the flaps on the closest one. Two pink eyes swimming in a puff of white fur peer up at him anxiously.

His father's in high spirits. "Get over here!" he shouts toward the house, flipping open the tops of the other boxes. Ian and Kelly crawl into the car, kneeling backwards on the front seat—their four heads now in a tight huddle. "New Zealand Whites," their father says. "Two females. One male." He reaches into a box and scratches the scruff of a neck. "Sweet little things."

"Time crunch," he announces, looking at his watch, and they start unloading. "But as a reward"—from under a bag of rabbit pellets in the trunk he fishes out a skillet and waves it like a flag—"we're making crepes for dinner!" And when they don't react, "It's a *crepe* pan!"

Ian grins. "A real one?"

"Made in France."

"Whip cream?" Ian asks. "Chocolate chips?"

"I got it all. But first, work clothes. Everybody."

Cole changes quickly and comes down to the kitchen to call Liz and tell her he can't meet her at the shed before the dance.

"Bogus," she says.

"Sorry. But after, for sure."

"Yeah."

"And I've been thinking," he says. "We should go camping, just us."

"Tonight?"

"Later this summer. We'll plan it."

"We could hitchhike to Maine," she says, "and live in your pup tent next to a lake. There's land up there that people have never even been on. In the winter you break into a summer house and live beside the fire and drink their booze and ball in every room."

It's still afternoon, but he can hear the raspiness that's come and gone since the bullet grazed her voice box, the raspiness that means her parents are sloshed.

"Let's just leave tonight after the dance," she says.

For the next two hours the four of them work together. His father paces out the size of the hutch, and Cole slams down eighteen inches with the posthole digger. Falsetto harmonies of Earth, Wind & Fire glide from Kelly's window, where she's propped her speakers on the sill. Together, she and Ian heft a bag of cement mix and dump it into the wheelbarrow, then she trickles water on the dusty mound while he mixes it with a hoe. Their father cuts 4x4s to height and chooses long pieces of lath from the pile and sets them to the side. When the holes are ready, Cole drops in a post and holds it plumb with the level, Ian shovels in cement, and their father nails on lath for stays. Kelly assembles the cages using hog-ring pliers to crimp the galvanized wire together. And they all keep stopping to pet the rabbits, huddled in the liquor boxes a few feet away on the grass.

Their father holds one in his arms, scratching it under the chin. "What do you want to name them?"

"Breakfast, Lunch, and Dinner," Ian quips.

They're all a little stunned, silenced, looking at him cautiously as he hoses out the wheelbarrow tipped on its side, the hard spray of water ringing on the steel. Then Ian looks up with a grin.

"Exactly," their father says, tucking the rabbit under one arm and slapping Ian on the shoulder. "And I think . . . I don't know much about these animals"—he kneads the rabbit's belly with his fingers—"but we might have hors d'oeuvres too. This one could be pregnant."

In the kitchen, Kelly cracks eggs in a mixing bowl, the bass from her stereo thumping through the ceiling. "Two cups of milk," she tells Ian, bending to the counter to read the recipe that came with the pan. Cole melts half a stick of butter over a low flame. Their father squirts dish soap on a sponge.

"This is the only time we'll ever wash it," he's saying. "You just wipe it out with a paper towel. It has to season. If you wash it, you ruin it."

Kelly sets Ian to mixing the eggs with a fork, then empties the rest of the carton into the egg holders in the door of the fridge. She rests her chin on Cole's shoulder. "Don't let it boil," she says, as he stirs the butter with a spoon, then she bonks him on the head with the empty egg carton, singing along with the song playing from her room.

The batter now ready, their dad drops a hunk of butter into the hot pan, and once it's sizzling he pours in a ladle's worth, and Cole wishes his mother were here, speaking French to the crepe as the edges, swimming in butter, begin to brown. In fact, where is she? She should be home by now. His father bangs the pan on the burner, jiggles it until the crepe slips loose, lifts it off the flame with a two-handed grip, flicks his wrists, and launches the crepe into lazy flight above their heads—a slow-motion flip—then catches it, cooked side up, as they all four cheer.

. . .

AFTER THE DANCE THE HEAT IN THE SHED PRESSES CLOSE, DENSE
with humidity and dust. "We'll go for the summer," she murmurs,
her breath heavy on his face. "We can decide in September if we ever
want to come home."

"But I'm working tobacco as soon as school's out. I can't just leave
like that." He kisses the hard ridge of her collarbone. "Let's go camping for a weekend. It'll be amazing."

A spit bubble floats from the tip of her tongue, then another, hovering in front of their faces.

Decades later, early on a Saturday morning in their kitchen in
Portland, Nikki will touch his shoulder and suggest they take their
coffee back to bed, but he'll say, "I'm already into this coat," wearing nitrile gloves and holding up the rag and the cup of tung oil.
She'll cinch her robe tighter, clutch her mug to her chest, and say, as
she turns from the room, "I'm going dancing with my book group
tonight," and Cole will know he's hurt her again, but he'll keep rubbing oil into the chestnut trim he's just installed around the big bay
window, and he'll get the idea to go to the club later and surprise her,
imagining he'd dance into her circle of friends where she'd open her
arms to him. Peeling off the tight blue gloves to refill his coffee, he'll
remember that night with Liz in the shed, their legs still entangled,
her voice distant: "Maybe I'll just hitchhike to Maine by myself."

WHEN KIRK'S CAR ISN'T PARKED IN THE DRIVEWAY, RELIEF LIGHTS
Liz's face, and she kisses Cole quick and runs for the house.

He pedals through the center of town, past the old cemetery and
the library, headlights coming at him in the distance. The car slows
and stops a hundred yards down the road, sitting there for a minute
as Cole gets closer, but then it jumps left, accelerating onto a trac-

tor road, and from the silhouette and parking lights and the throaty rumble of the 350, Cole recognizes it as Kirk's Chevelle.

By the time he gets there, he can see only two faint red lights through the turned-up dust. He stops and leans on his handlebars, watching, and then steers his bike onto the dirt road.

He stays near the edge, the tree line shading him from the bright moon. The road bends to the right, drops into a mud puddle, and then cuts like a long corridor between the tobacco nets on either side. He's never worked these fields—they're Boulger—but he's been back in here snowmobiling, exploring, smoking cigarettes or weed. Straight ahead, he sees Kirk's car lights go out.

He stashes his bike in the woods and slips through the nets. The plants are six inches or better, ready to string up any day. It's ten bents or more to the far end and he walks between rows, Kirk's voice becoming distinct as he gets closer. It occurs to him that he might find Kirk having sex with somebody, though he's never heard of any girlfriend. But he could be pressuring some girl, forcing himself on her, and Cole's heart races: he'd bust out from the nets and fling open the car door and pull Kirk off, throw him to the ground and stomp his balls, saving the girl, then spin the Chevelle's tires and throw mud on his body lying there in the dirt.

Squatting down, he parts the net. Kirk's leaning against the car and passing a joint to Matt Gosling. He watches for a few minutes, hoping one of them will drop his pants and bend over the hood. But when they finish the joint, Kirk opens the trunk and the two of them stand there staring into it.

Just as Kirk reaches in, a police siren pierces the quiet. Kirk slams the trunk shut and jumps behind the wheel, and without flipping on the headlights they shoot down the tractor road. Another siren starts blaring and Cole feels guilty and suspicious hiding inside the nets at the scene of . . . Was it a crime? What were they doing? Their car long gone, he decides the only thing to do is sprint back down the ten bents, get his bike, and stay hidden in the woods. But by the time he gets there—dusty and out of breath with dirt in his sneakers—the sirens are fading north of town. And riding back toward the street, the dust from the Chevelle still hanging in the air, he wonders if he actually saw what he thought he did back there: Kirk lifting a gas can halfway out of his trunk before dropping it back in and speeding away.

HE WAKES UP, SUNLIGHT SUFFUSING HIS EYELIDS—OR HE'S *ALMOST* awake, because he doesn't know where he is. Or when. Dust tickles his nose. He sneezes and sits up, looking around his boyhood room.

At the kitchen table his father's eating a piece of bread heaped with currant jelly, leaning on his elbows over a newspaper. "The Patriots won," he says.

Cole glances down at the table. It's a November paper, three years old. "Good season?" he asks.

His father snaps the page over. "I wouldn't know." He suddenly seems miffed. "It's a violent game."

Cole turns on his phone: voice mails, texts, and missed calls from Nikki and Daniel that all came in last night. It's now only four a.m. in Portland, so he's got time.

"Hey, listen," he says. "I'm thinking I'll hang around a little longer. No rush getting back home."

His father is silent, staring at his half-eaten slice of bread and jelly, then finally scrapes back his chair and rises, spreading his arms wide, and reaches around Cole, hugs him hard, and slaps him twice between the shoulder blades. "That would be fine, son," his father's breath on his ear. "Superlative."

BY EIGHT O'CLOCK HE'S WATCHING KIRK HOIST A MASSIVE CHEST-nut beam and swing it onto Cole's stack. One of the flatbeds is already half-loaded. Christ, it's a lot of wood. He grins. Double what he imagined. Over the crane's diesel he hears the blat-blat of a two-stroke engine: Little Kirk's darting toward him on a dirt bike. When Cole waves him over, he skids to a stop in the gravel and kills the engine. His helmet looks too small, capping him like an old leather football helmet, but it's silver and scratched up with a gold star on the side like maybe he swiped it from a pinheaded human cannonball in the circus.

"Hey, I wanted to ask you something," Cole says.

He pulls off the helmet and sticks it over the throttle.

"My son's coming out for a while. I was hoping to get him working tobacco."

After a pause Little Kirk says, "And?"

"I thought you might tell me who I could speak with to find him a job."

He gazes off at the crane, chewing his lip with a petulance so similar to his father's that Cole feels it might as well be 1979, not 2009. "How old is he?"

"Fifteen."

"He ever work tobacco before?" He's milking the opportunity: an adult asking him for a favor.

"We don't grow tobacco in Oregon."

"Right." He nods, as if considering. "Does he know how to bust his ass and not complain?"

"He does."

"And what it's like being the new guy?"

"He will."

Little Kirk takes a step toward his dad, then turns back. "I work for Boulger, out in Suffield. Ask for Jim Stanton."

HE'S DRIVEN LESS THAN A MILE DOWN THE ROAD AND JUST TUNED in NPR when his phone rings. It's Nikki, up before six. Unheard of. He stops on the shoulder.

"Have you lost your mind?" she says.

"We've got to get him out of Portland. At least for a while. What if Tony can't get him off the next time? God, Nikki. What if he ends up in juvie?"

"So your solution is to have him run away. That sounds familiar. How did that work out for you?"

He ignores the swipe. "It's not running away. It's temporarily getting him out of an environment that invariably leads him to doing stupid shit."

"Why's it going to be any different there?"

"Because there's no fucking freegans or foragers or squatters for miles."

"So you think you'll rent an apartment? Do they even *have* apartments in that backwater? Where the two of you can spend your days discussing responsible adult choices?"

"I'm arranging a job for him . . ." He pauses. "Working tobacco."

"This is weird, Cole. You want him to do all the same crappy stuff you did?"

He might as well just spring it: "And we can live in my old house. My father's back here. His health isn't great and he could use a hand."

The line is silent for so long he wonders if she's hung up. But finally she says, "You want to move our son to Bumfuck, Connecticut, force him into a job that you've said is the most miserable thing you've done in your life, and live in a house that destroyed any chance you had at a normal childhood, *and* be nursemaid to the man who strangled your mother?"

"I think it could be good for him."

"The answer's no."

"Daniel's with me for the next two weeks, as per agreement. And we're taking a trip to Connecticut. Your lawyer will tell you there's nothing you can do about it." Tony is her lawyer.

. . .

A TOBACCO SHED TOWERS OVER ONE END OF THE GRAVEL LOT with a huge Montecristo medallion on its side. He parks in front of the office—a tidy wood house with a big front porch and gable dormers, part colonial farmhouse, part southern plantation. Back toward the fields a few Hispanic men are unloading flats from a tobacco bus; they're still using retired school buses painted light brown. A white man wearing khaki pants and a dress shirt speaks briefly to one of them, pointing at the greenhouse with the hand holding his cigar, then sticks the stogie in his mouth and walks briskly off.

Inside, Cole asks to see Jim Stanton and is told he's in the field, but at that moment the door in back opens and the receptionist looks up. "One minute," she says and follows the man he just saw into a rear office. He comes right out to the small front room and shakes Cole's hand suspiciously.

"Kirk Schaler told me I could speak with you about getting my son on tobacco."

"Junior or senior?"

"Little Kirk."

The man warms at this. "He's a good kid. Good worker." He folds his arms across his chest. Although he's left his cigar behind, he smells sweetly of the smoke—the whole office does. "Your son a friend of LK's?"

"No. But I know the family from way back."

"Why isn't your son here in person?"

"Well, he's in Portland." Then he adds, "Oregon. But he'll get here tomorrow."

"He's away at school or something? How old is he?"

"Fifteen. He *lives* in Portland. We both do. But we're here taking care of my father. And I worked tobacco as a kid, for Taybro. Loved every minute of it."

Jim smiles. "Now I *know* you're lying."

"Well, it's true. Maybe I felt miserable now and then, but it was all part of the experience."

"Times have changed. It's really not a local kids' summer job any-more. It's all migrants now. Little Kirk's the exception. Special dis-pensation, you could say."

"Can't you just give him a shot? Meet Daniel and try him out for a week? Look, I'm a contractor myself. I know the value of a good man with a little training."

"I got eighty-four Mexicans who know tobacco backwards and forwards. I don't need to train some fifteen-year-old from who the hell knows where." He sticks out his hand to shake goodbye.

8

"SHE WANTED TO GO TO GRAD SCHOOL IN PARIS AND GOT ACCEPTED. French literature and film at the Sorbonne."

"So why didn't she?" Alex says.

He's told them everything, and the unloading has left him spent. They'd heard much of the story already—town folklore—but they hadn't known it was Cole's family, hadn't known which house. They stopped short of saying "the Old Newgate Strangler," but he could tell they knew more than they let on.

"My father had his ROTC commitment, and I *think*—I don't know, I might've heard this in a fight or from my grandmother—he was all panicked to get married before the army, so they had a wedding while they were still in college and nine months later my sister Kelly was born."

Antoine leans into a mound of dough with a rolling pin. "So she never went to the Sorbonne?"

"She used to say she'd planned to stay in France, to live in Paris and direct movies, and when I was a kid that always seemed like a perfectly reasonable alternate life for her. But as I got older I realized, who the hell moves to Paris and turns into Truffaut? She'd talk about these films she loved—*Hiroshima Mon Amour, Elevator to the Gallows, The 400 Blows*—and I'd imagine growing up in Paris, my mother a famous director"—he shakes his head, sips his wine—"like with a megaphone and riding boots and a beret. It was a compelling but absurdly romantic story about who we might've been. I never questioned it until I was"—he forces a laugh—"way too old."

Alex smiles. "She had a notion of escaping, don't you think?"

"Just like you and your brother and sister," Antoine says.

"Escape her marriage before it began." Cole shakes his head. "Like she knew how that romance would end."

Why does he feel so comfortable talking to these two? Across their kitchen's chestnut island, Alex skewers chunks of marinating chicken alternated with yellow and orange peppers, zucchini, red onion. Antoine cuts neat squares of rolled-out dough and folds the peaches and berry and sugar filling into elegant puffs, shaping them like acorn finials. Flour dusts his dark forearms. He's deeply tan from working outside, and Alex, who works in the shop, is milky white. Side by side, it's striking. They're the same height, but in his thick arms and shoulders and weathered face he carries his Hungarian stock, generations of craftsmen, in every muscular move. She's wonderfully plump, the figure of a pastry chef rather than a woodworker, skin as soft and white as dough, and today she's in a vintage dress, a paisley scarf in her hair, dark red lipstick, and an apron printed with ladybugs that his mother might have worn.

"Sometimes she'd stand in front of two long bookshelves in the parlor lined with the Livres de Poche she'd studied." The books are gone, he realizes, and he hopes they found a good home. "She never even plucked one off the shelf. Just stood and stared like she was at a museum looking at relics from another era. You'd think she might've resented her kids, but . . ." He shakes his head. "Not a word of regret. I guess it's doubtful she was destined to be a star of the French New Wave, though even my father admitted that not going to the Sorbonne had been a sacrifice. But she'd interrupt him and insist, 'No, no, not at all. There's nothing I wanted more than a family.'"

When Cole has been lucky enough to meet someone he can open up to so freely, it's usually been while traveling. And he *is* traveling now. Traveling back.

It was like this with Nikki at first. Easy to talk to, eager to divulge, to allow himself to be vulnerable. When did they start sniping? If falling in love involves a series of ever more intimate divulgences, do you plumb the depths at some point and bottom out, leaving you no place else to go?

"She sounds like an amazing woman," Alex says, spearing a wedge of onion.

"It's tragic," Antoine says. He reaches around his wife's back for a carton of eggs, then cracks one open in a blue ceramic dish. She sprinkles crushed herbs over the skewers. The whisk rings in the bowl. The colorful platter of meat and vegetables is more than they could ever eat. Antoine brushes egg on the pastries. It's a domestic scene as beautiful and tranquil and timeless as a Vermeer. He hasn't cooked much since Nikki moved out. He's become a solo binge watcher, with dirty dishes and takeout boxes piling up in the kitchen; he forgets to open windows and the house gets stuffy. He misses their domestic life. He misses her.

From his breast pocket Cole slips out a photo he found in the tea caddy, probably taken at a wedding. She's in front of a church wearing a dark A-line dress with white polka dots and a sun hat in the same fabric.

Alex's eyes go wide. "She's beautiful!"

Antoine studies the picture. "She looks like you, Alex," he says.

She glances at the photo again. "Thanks for the compliment, and I'd kill for the outfit, but . . ." She shakes her head. "Your mother would've made amazing French films." She pops the cork on another bottle of wine. "She would've rocked a beret."

He puts the picture back in his pocket as Alex reaches over the counter to refill his glass. He's been in Connecticut three days, but it feels like weeks. He's exhausted. Maybe it's the shifting time zones. He drank the first glasses of wine too fast, and telling anyone new about it always drains him, which is partly why Nikki told it for him. He stares into the wine, as red as blood.

"When I was a kid I had very involved fantasies of getting myself set up in Paris—a job and a great apartment—and then I'd bring her over. I'd introduce her around at my favorite cafés and *boulangeries,* and show her out-of-the-way museums I'd discovered. Take her to mass at Notre-Dame. Bring special cheeses and pastries back to the apartment, and we'd drink heavenly red wine at a tiny table over-looking the Seine. I knew she'd never get divorced, but while she was with me at least she'd be safe. I imagined that with me she'd be as happy as when she spoke French with strangers." He smiles, shakes his head. "Sort of embarrassing, really."

Once they've moved outside Alex spins the skewers on the hot grill. They sizzle and the charcoal flares.

"She wanted all of us to take a trip like yours," Cole says. "'We'll do Ireland right,' she'd say. 'We can find our ancestors' graves, eat shepherd's pie in their villages—hardly changed in generations—and meet cousins we never heard of, who'll embrace us like fam-ily. Because that's their way. *Our* way. The kind of people we come from.'"

Antoine's sitting on the railing of the deck, sipping his wine. "I try not to romanticize it," he says, "but I'm sure I'll feel a connection. The stories passed down from the time I was a baby, they're so real inside me. Like I've lived there already—another time, another life."

"Be careful," Cole says. "You might meet some ghosts."

Antoine rubs his chin, his rough hands chafing against stiff whis-kers. "I guess that's what I'm hoping for." Then he slips inside and Cole can hear the oven door opening and closing.

"She wanted each of us to change the world," Cole says, "but none of us has."

"It's the small acts," Alex says.

"Small wasn't what she had in mind. I fear we'd be a disappoint-ment."

"I don't believe it. And you can't speak for your siblings."

"You're right. I barely know them. It's pretty disgraceful."

One by one she picks the skewers from the grill and sets them on the platter propped against her hip. "And by the way," she says, "this isn't just to make you feel good, but you're an incredibly gifted architect and builder, certainly the most talented I've ever worked with. I show off your stuff on the website all the time. And if you believe that the spaces we inhabit change us, as I do, then you're creating an environment where people are more inclined toward beauty and insight."

"Thanks," he says. "That's nice of you to say." They're quiet as she fills the platter with skewers, and then Cole says, lowering his voice, "Antoine has pretty high expectations for this trip. Do you worry he's setting himself up for disappointment?"

"We *should* have high expectations. For everything. What's the alternative?"

Cole admires them both and wishes they weren't leaving so soon. Since his mother died, it's felt like people are always leaving.

"And you've got super expectations for the work you buy from me," she adds. "Remember that corner cupboard you got all pissy about because the angle of *your* walls was so fucked up?"

"You sent some nice trim to cover the gaps. *My* gaps." He lifts his glass to her.

She steps toward the kitchen door, then stops. "I can't save him from feeling let down," she says, "but I can be by his side to share in the disappointment."

He wonders about Nikki's disappointments, and whether he's shared in them.

"You haven't mentioned your wife." It's like Alex is reading his mind.

"Things aren't going so well."

"I gathered." She's holding the platter on her forearms, like a load of firewood, making no moves for the house.

"I think I've tried to shield her from my letdowns and worries. You know, from my dark underside." He laughs, but Alex doesn't. He notices that since all the skewering she's put the chestnut ring back on her thumb. "I didn't think I should drag her down into those dank places with me. I'm not sure that's the reason, but now after twenty years it seems like there's just too much festering for us to ever air it out."

BACK AT THE HOUSE, HIS FATHER ASLEEP, COLE FULL FROM HIS meal with Alex and Antoine, he lies naked on top of the sheets in his old bed in the dark.

His mother wanted grandchildren to sleep over in the homestead, to be surrounded by laughter and singing on Christmas morning in a meticulously restored old colonial. She wanted them all to be happy and successful and Catholic and nearby.

9

AS THEY CROSS THE TOWN LINE THE SUN DROPS BELOW THE NETS, a fiery sky above the acres of cloth. This afternoon, before returning the rental car, he jumped his father's Bonneville, filled the tank, and added two quarts of oil; except for a clackety-clack in the engine, it runs okay. The alignment's out of whack, though, the car leaning toward the yellow line, so he steers against it to keep them from veering into the oncoming lane.

"A, it's smoking, which if you haven't heard . . ." Daniel shakes his head. "B, they're cigars, which maybe at one time were partaken of by GIs and cabbies and plumbers, but now are nothing but a phallic symbol of wealth and class and I don't know—like guys at a bachelor party getting lap dances and pretending they're Wall Street tycoons. Oh, and that old president sticking his Cuban in the intern. So yeah, I have a slight problem jumping on board with the whole tobacco-industrial complex."

He hasn't seen Daniel in nearly two weeks, and to suddenly see him here, so strangely out of context, is disorienting. It had occurred to Cole that his arrival might be grounding, might bring along familiar and welcome elements of his life, but instead it's like those dreams where he goes to a new client's house to discuss a sunroom or whatever, and the door is answered by his mother, the age she was then, an ice bag over one eye. He has a nagging feeling that Nikki's right, that Daniel doesn't belong here.

"Dude," Daniel says, "are you messing with me? This is where you grew up?" The car creeps up the gravel drive. "This is the sticks! Somehow, I thought . . . I don't know *what* I thought, but not this. And pre-internet. What did you *do* all day?"

In the driveway, Cole turns off the ignition but the car diesels and he floors the gas pedal to flood it silent. "There's still no internet."

Daniel stares at his phone, then out at the tobacco nets, and at the house with its peeling paint. "So this is my Peace Corps experience."

"DAD?" COLE CALLS FROM THE KEEPING ROOM, BUT THERE'S NO reply.

Daniel drops his duffel. "This place is hammered."

"Just needs some furniture and a good cleaning."

"I've been in crash houses that look homier than this."

"Jesus, Daniel. You don't belong in those places."

"They have actual couches, for example." He nudges the broken chair with his foot like nudging an animal to test if it's alive.

"Dad?" Cole shouts again, walking to the front stairs.

"Hey," Daniel says from the front window, "check this out."

When Cole joins him he points up the road. A hundred yards away Phil's wobbling toward them on Cole's old bike, an enormous plastic bag weighing down one side of his handlebars; each time it swings the bike lurches to the side, nearly crashing him into the ditch. "That looks like a cartoon."

"In fact that's your grandfather."

Daniel laughs. "Far out."

They go to the door. Coming up the driveway expends Phil's last ounce of energy, so Cole jumps down the steps and grabs the handlebars just as he's about to keel over, sweating and panting. Stretching the seams of the plastic bag is a huge watermelon and a gallon of ice cream, chocolate, melting through the rim of the cardboard lid.

He dismounts as Cole steadies the bike. "This must be the lad."

Daniel steps down onto the grass and stands straight, arms at his sides. "Yes, sir," he says, and for a moment Cole suspects he's up to no good, some irony that'll slowly sour.

"Are you hungry?" Phil asks.

"I had something at the airport," Daniel tells him.

"They used to serve nice meals on a plane."

"Back in the day."

"I haven't flown in forty years." He looks up at the sky, and then Daniel does too.

"That's a long time." Daniel's voice is tender.

Phil nods. He holds out his arms and Daniel hugs him. "I got you some ice cream."

Cole carries the bag into the kitchen and slices watermelon on the counter.

"Used to be," Phil says, "you waited till August for watermelon. We always got ours at the Liss farm. Corn and tomatoes too. Tomatoes that actually tasted like a tomato. Now you buy watermelon trucked in from anywhere. Where's it say?"

Cole rolls the melon over and spots a sticker. "Texas."

"Who the hell knows?"

"I'm a locavore as much as possible myself," Daniel says. "There's the spoilage of trucking, never mind the carbon footprint."

Cole sets a couple plates heaped with melon wedges on the table and Phil stares at Daniel, nodding slowly. "Like I say."

Cole sits, and they eat. It's sweet and delicious, the long ride north notwithstanding. Pink juice runs down their arms. His father and his son sit side by side, elbows on the table, and there's no missing the resemblance in the slope of their shoulders as they lean forward to have a bite.

"What else did they grow on the Liss farm?" Daniel asks.

"Zucchini and squash," Phil says. "You gotta be careful picking those. Mr. Liss would get peeved if we scratched the skins on the leaves."

Daniel spits a seed. "Did *you* work on the farm?"

"Not really peeved, I guess. He was a kind man, but even back then it was hard to scratch out a living as a farmer. I worked on his farm before I got old enough to work tobacco."

Cole sees his mother in Daniel's eyes, and strong as ever, even as his face is becoming the face of a man, Nikki's nose and lips and chin.

"And pickles," Phil says.

Daniel laughs. "How do you grow a pickle?"

"They were cukes for pickling. 'Load them bushels of pickles on the truck,' he'd say, and the next morning he'd drive them into the market in Hartford and be back by eight when I showed up to work. Not an easy life at all for him."

"I know a guy," Daniel says, "he pickles everything instead of composting it. Watermelon rind"—he holds one up—"the entirety of a pumpkin. Lemons, pears, okra. Eggs, of course. Brussels sprouts make amazing pickles. They're called frog balls."

"That's a new one," Phil says, and they both laugh.

The conversation sounds so natural that Cole thinks back to last night—how easy it was talking with Alex and Antoine. How good it was. And those endless nights talking with Nikki, laughing and holding hands on the couch. Why did they stop?

"Ice cream," Phil says, their bellies bloated with watermelon. "Who'd like a big dish?"

THOUGH THE AC WINDOW UNITS ARE CHUGGING, THE FARMHOUSE is hotter than last time, the reek of cigars staler, danker. They sit waiting silently for Jim Stanton in the cramped front room's only two chairs, Daniel texting and Cole flipping pages in *Cigar Aficionado*.

Finally Daniel slips the phone into his front pocket and slumps to his feet, antsy. "Want some water?" he asks. Through a glass door leading to a small conference room they can see a bubbler.

Cole shakes his head and glances at his watch.

On the other side of the glass Daniel sips from a Poland Spring paper cup, studying a blown-up historic photo of tobacco pickers under the nets. A side door opens and bright light sweeps into the room, and through the glass Cole sees his son look up at a woman in oversized bubble sunglasses and a wide-brimmed hat. Over the noise of the air conditioner he can't hear them, but they're speaking to each other: Daniel looks surprised, he's nodding, and the woman steps closer to him, then reaches out, heavy gold bangles slipping from her wrist to her elbow. Suntanned arms, blond hair cut smartly at her shoulders. She touches his chin with her fingertips, gently turning his head to profile. Her face is mostly hidden by her hair and the big blue brim of the hat but, strangely, Cole recognizes her hand, her long, hyperextending fingers thicker than they used to be. His son seems uncomfortable, his eyes flitting through the glass, and then he points and she turns: her sharp chin and painted lips, her small nose barely poking out from under the enormous sunglasses. In one motion she draws off the hat and slides the glasses on top of her head. Their eyes meet, but still it takes her a moment. Cole stands up, straightening his shirt, and her face flashes with recognition. She comes through the door, and he thinks how tall she appears in high heels and poofed-up hair.

"You look just the same," she says, reaching toward him with a straight stiff arm.

Cole clasps her hand, then tugs her closer and they embrace, and except for a few spots the fit is familiar, a sort of muscle memory, and he says, "You're just the same too," and their first words strike him as lies until her sharp hipbone cuts into him, and through the lingering smell of cigars, her cinnamon-and-pepper scent, the essence of Liz, long ago vanished from his memory, is as present as his own breath.

He hadn't realized his eyes were closed until he opens them to see his son, and he waves Daniel over as he and Liz release each other. "This is a very old friend of mine. An old flame."

"Duh," Daniel says flatly. "Get a room."

Cole's face warms. "And this is my boy, Daniel."

"You're a dead ringer for your father at fifteen. Even the shaggy hair." While she's focused on him, Cole steals a closer look at her. Her narrow shoulders are fitted with a cream-colored linen top and a scarf that drapes across her chest. Her clothes appear expensive, as if they're *meant* to. Except for a few lines around her mouth and the corners of her eyes, she really doesn't seem that much different to him.

When the silence grows awkward, he says, "What the heck are you doing here? I thought you lived in Brazil."

She laughs. "Brazil? Where did you hear that?"

"I have no idea." He actually knows *exactly* where: an email from Sherry Devereux, who'd found him through his company website a few years back. They'd exchanged updates on their lives, and she'd been full of gossip about their old classmates; when he declined to meet her in Seattle while she was there on a business trip, the emails stopped.

"I've lived for twenty years in Miami, but my husband's Brazilian." She lowers her head and he notices a bump in her nose that he doesn't remember, and also that her nose is a little crooked. He remembers a straight and petite nose, sharp as a blade. "What are *you* doing here?"

"We're trying to get Daniel a summer job."

"In the office?"

"In the field. Or the sheds."

"Oh, that's all changed since we were kids. It's only migrants now. The same folks come back year after year."

"We ran into your nephew—"

"But wait. Are you *living* here?"

"Portland, Oregon," he says, then tells her about the shed he's buying and crossing paths with Kirk. "But what are *you* doing here?" he asks, pointing at the floor. "At this farm?"

"I'm a buyer. If it's a good year, we take all their leaves."

"A Connecticut Shade buyer?"

"And broadleaf."

"I heard you were an exporter. Or an importer."

"The leaves ship to rollers in the DR and product comes back in through Miami."

"Amazing," he says. "Here I am scavenging an old shed for chestnut, and you've got a big career in cigars."

"Where are you staying?"

He forces a laugh. "At my old house. Sleeping in my old room."

"But . . ." She tips her head to the side. "Has it just been empty?"

"Actually, my"—the words catch in his throat before he finally ejects them—"my father's there."

Not quite a gasp, but a quick sip of air, and then her face goes red, her eyes darting to Daniel and back to Cole, and in the moment it takes his heart to thump three times, each more powerful than the last, she's regained her composure. "Wow," is all she says.

"It was a surprise to me too."

"So he's out?"

"For sixteen years now."

"And he's been living here the whole time?"

"Just the last few months. From what I can tell."

"He hasn't told you?"

"I'm not sure he totally knows. His mind . . . it's not too sharp." He turns to Daniel again; they haven't had time to discuss this yet. "He seems to not want to remember anything."

She gives him a long, hard stare.

Jim Stanton pops out of his office and stops short—apparently not expecting that Cole and Daniel were still waiting.

"You hooking this young man up with a job?" Liz asks him.

"As I told them, we've got what we need for the summer."

"Jimbo," Liz says, looking at her fingernails, "don't be a douchebag."

Five minutes later, Daniel's signing a W-4.

10

COLE DOES WHAT HE KNOWS HE NEEDS TO DO, FINALLY. CHRISTMAS was when he'd last heard from his brother and sister. Every year he sends a card and a few lines come back by email: frustrations with the school board in Toyohashi, where Ian teaches English; a clipped description from Kelly of breaking the sound barrier over the Mojave Desert or screeching low over jungles in the tropics, often ending with the wish she could say more but "most all I do is classified." He believes she flew missions for a time, then became a flight instructor. She might still be, though a while back she mentioned hitting the age limit for flying.

In the parlor he switches on a lamp, sits in the old wing chair, and stares at his laptop screen, hands hovering over the keys, and finally he just starts typing. "I hope all's well. I happen to be back in East Granby. The town looks just the same. I'm surprised by the connection I feel to the place. At every turn—a deep familiarity. There's a particular smell of humidity sitting heavy in the nettles beyond our backyard that transported me in a snap to searching for the boomerang. Remember that, Ian? The damn boomerang that never came back? Tobacco nets bright in the early morning, the Metacomet Ridge at sunset—it's beautiful, and it's stirring up our childhood. I wish we all saw each other more often. And the house—it looks the same too, and the main issue I'm writing about is Dad—"

"Dad," he hears behind him. "Yo, *Dad!*"

He jerks his head around.

"Phil's outside."

Cole goes to the front window, cups his hands to the glass, and peers out into the twilight, where his father's tromping down the road. "Crap," he says, and charges through the door. He gets halfway to him before calling out.

Phil looks over his shoulder, then jumps the ditch and runs through the high weeds into the tobacco field.

"C'mon," Cole hollers, "come back," breaking into a jog, and just as he catches up, his father trips and falls.

"Damn you!" he shouts. "Back off!"

Cole drops to a knee beside him and takes hold of his arm. "Dad—"

"Quit harassing me." He yanks his arm free. "You're *harassing* me!"

"Let's get you into the house."

"What the hell are you doing here?"

"Dad—"

"Why are you calling me that?"

"It's okay. It's me, your son."

At that he quits fighting and goes completely limp. "Ian," he says. "You were always a pipsqueak"—he chuckles—"but very steady. A solid kid. Never any trouble. You made those damn labels for everything I owned."

Cole remembers: the alphabet on the dial, Ian feeding in the plastic strip and squeezing out the letters, embossed and precise as Braille.

"You stuck my name on saws and crowbars, on my briefcase and razor, even the car door."

Pulling him to his feet he says, "I'm your other son. I'm Cole."

With a sideways glance and a smirk—as if he knew all along—he says, "Yes, yes. You were always *her* boy."

. . .

DANIEL'S IN THE KITCHEN WHEN HE GETS HIS FATHER INSIDE. HE'S wearing nothing but a pair of nylon gym shorts and holding a glass of ice water to his cheek. "Doesn't it ever cool off here at night?" he asks.

"If you can't stand the heat," Phil says, "get out of the kitchen." His face goes blank. "No, that's not what I mean. . . . Heat of the moment. Dead heat." He wanders into the keeping room, shaking his head.

"Why don't you wash up for bed, Dad," Cole says. "We should all hit the hay."

"I'll tell you something about freedom and free will and the great journey we call life et cetera. That when you reach a certain age you decide for yourself when it's time to brush your goddamn teeth." He takes a few more steps, then stops. "'Humidity'! That's what I was looking for." He smiles at Daniel, wide and warm. "The one that goes 'It's the humidity.'"

After a moment they hear his father's surge of piss in the toilet bowl. Daniel clinks ice around his glass and presses it to his bare chest. "Why are we here, Dad?"

Cole swings the back door shut, the old iron latch clanking like in a dungeon. "He needs help. What would happen to him if I just left?"

"I'm not staying here indefinitely. I'm really not."

"Don't worry. This is very temporary," Cole says. "I've just got to get him eating right. Get him a phone. He doesn't even have a doctor. I'm waiting to hear back from the senior center about activities. I'm hoping there might be a van that could take him grocery shopping."

"You can't fix it this way, you know."

"I'm just trying to—"

"You think that hunkering down and just sort of being together, quiet and with good intentions, solves problems. But only action solves problems. Bold, decisive action."

"So that's what this is about? Why we should all be vandalizing dumpsters? You're going to land in juvie, Daniel, if you don't come up with a thousand bucks for Safeway. It's hard to see how that's a model for how I should be caring for my father."

"I'm talking about fixing our family. Do you remember you, me, and Mom sitting in a triangle and holding hands and meditating together? God, what was I—like *eight*? And you wanted us to align our breathing, which was going to bring us all into harmony. And making us go to that cabin on the Olympic Peninsula. Cold and raining every time. And I'm sorry to break the news, but I don't like hot tubs. They sap you of energy instead of cranking you up. The opiate of the privileged class. And Mom never liked them either."

Blood rushes to his face. "Yes she does."

"They make her feel bloated. Actually, I think she said *stewed*."

Cole takes a step away from his son. He can hear the bathroom sink running and hopes his father's cleaning himself up.

"You're a great guy, Dad. I really mean that. You just can't always be in the hugging-it-out mode. I'm sorry if this sounds harsh, but it doesn't take Dr. Phil, no pun intended, to recognize that you ran as far from your disastrous childhood as you could get without falling in the ocean, and now you've run back here to avoid Portland."

"I came here to buy thirty thousand board feet of chestnut."

"But you *should* be back living your actual life and doing whatever it takes to convince your wife that Tony's an asshole and that your marriage . . ." Daniel's eyes fill with tears and he chokes on his words. "You can't just let it implode."

"Oh, son," Cole says, opening his arms and stepping toward him.

"No!" He wipes his nose with the back of his hand. "I don't want a fucking hug. I want . . . I want . . ." Tears are streaming down his face. "I want everyone around me to quit deluding themselves. I want everyone to grab the world by the collar, stare it down, and shake some sense into it. Jesus, he strangled your *mother*. Instead of trying to save him, you should be saving your own family."

Cole opens his mouth, but nothing comes out.

Daniel wipes his cheek. "There's not even a friggin' toaster in this house."

HE SPENDS OVER AN HOUR SETTLING HIS FATHER DOWN. HE STIRS honey into warm milk, turns on the bedside TV, and gets him talking about his boyhood in Suffield.

"Henry Harrison came up from the South like so many during the war because the GIs wanted cigars and there were labor shortages with everybody fighting overseas. He was from Georgia, a black man, and he lived in the barracks by where the tracks cross Konkapot Creek. So one day I happened to be kicking by the fields during coffee break and Henry Harrison started telling me about *his* boy, who was about my age—and what grade was I in? What comics did I read? Anyway, he sets his coffee on the tractor's footrest, opens his lunch pail, unwraps some wax paper, and hands me a hunk of cornbread. 'Go on,' he says, 'take it,' and I'll tell you now it was the richest, most delicious thing I've ever tasted. My eyes went wide and then all soft, like I was drunk on the bread, and he must've seen that because he laughed out loud and gave me a second piece, which I devoured and then licked my fingers and palms and even the crumbs that had fallen on my shirt. I knew right then that anything I ate in the rest of my life would be a disappointment." He takes the last swallow of milk and hands Cole the mug. "And I wasn't wrong."

He's cleaned up the cuts on his father's feet and the scrape on his palm. No luck getting him out of the pajamas, stuck with nettles and dirty at the knees. He switches off the lamp and turns the TV volume down, his father looking staticky in the fuzzy light. "Did the man ever give you cornbread again?"

"After coffee break he took off on the tractor—he was plowing ahead of the setter—and he was standing up, preparing to swing around the pole at the end of a bent, looking back over his shoulder, and when he saw me he gave a little wave, and I'd like to believe he was thinking of his son at that moment—his hand still raised to me as he drove the tractor under the net wire. It sliced his head clean off."

PAST MIDNIGHT HIS FATHER'S ASLEEP AND DANIEL'S MOVING around overhead in the attic. In bed, he opens his laptop and returns to the email, but he freezes up. No hurry, he decides, since he's not even sure where he can find wi-fi in town. In Japan it's already tomorrow, and his sister—well, he really has no idea—she could be streaking over Afghanistan, miles above the surface of the earth, where time zones don't seem to matter. It's a weekday. Ian's probably standing in front of forty-five uniformed high-schoolers. Eight years ago—when he last saw his brother and Michiko and his nephews—Cole made the trip to Toyohashi. Ian was late meeting him at the station, and once they got to their small house Cole felt he was imposing and immediately regretted coming, but a few days later he wasn't so sure. It might have been that he simply felt large and obtrusive because the rooms and doorways and tables and chairs were so small. Michiko waited on him attentively, completely, but that, too, made him uncomfortable. Showing Cole the city and its historic parks and temples Ian sometimes seemed indifferent, but when he took him into a *robatayaki* he was suddenly overeager, showing off his Japanese, calling the owner to their table, patting backs, spending money, becoming the little brother seeking approval for his success, for a life well lived. Despite being an inch taller, Ian was bald on the top and chubby up front. Even his teeth had changed—gray and crooked, obscured by a push-broom mustache hanging over his mouth. On nights when he got to drinking Suntory whiskey, which was most nights, he'd start in on the school administration—restrictive and authoritarian— treating teachers like minions, and then that the whole culture was no different and he always felt scrutinized, trapped like a zoo animal.

Michiko could be a relief, he said, but she had plenty of tricks for keeping the upper hand. And the whole kid thing had been a disappointment; he thought they'd be more like friends to him, that he'd be able to reason with them, but instead—just so they'd brush their teeth, sit still on the train, or practice the piano—he had to spank them. By the time he got to the last bit he'd be so loaded that he didn't know what he was saying, and one night he hit such a dark drunk he looped back to the beginning: I hate that school, I really hate teaching, I hate this whole fucking country and everyone is conspiring against me. And then, on Cole's last night in Japan, as if it was all the same thread: "You were just as bad as her, you know. The two of you saying 'It's the last time. Never again. Everything'll be okay.' But you knew it was a lie, didn't you?"

Cole gripped the edge of the table, still as stone.

"HEY," NIKKI SAYS.

"Can you talk?" he asks.

"Yeah," and then after a pause, "I'm home."

"Home?"

"At my apartment."

"Oh." It's cooled off a little, and he pulls the sheet up to his chest. "How's Daniel?"

In their last call—and after a long talk with her son—she resigned herself to his working tobacco, even admitting that it might do him some good. "He's rummaging through the attic. He should get to sleep, though. He starts his job in the morning, early."

"Make sure he's got sunscreen. And plenty of water."

"He's all set. He even made his own lunch."

"And you?" she asks. "Long days watching the barn come down?"

"Actually, my father's taking a lot of my time."

"I heard you reconnected with an old friend."

He smiles, and somehow through the phone she knows.

"Feeling randy?" she says.

"She's married." They both know what he means: Nikki's married too.

She takes a deep breath.

"Is it true you don't like our hot tub?" The long pause that follows is familiar and therefore perversely comforting: at least they still have this dynamic between them.

"I liked it," she finally says, "because it relaxed you. I was hoping it would help."

"But wasn't it pretty sensual, too?"

"Sensuality-wise, I needed a little more than taking a bath together. I can wait a while. I waited for years. But we're not young anymore, Cole."

"I just felt—"

"Stop!" She hates his victimized tone as much as he does. "Do you really want to claim you're a little hurt to hear I was faking it with our hot tub when you couldn't even fake it with me in bed? Jesus. I gotta go." She waits for him to say "Goodnight," then says "Bye."

He switches off the lamp. Moonlight angles sharply through the front windows. It's quiet overhead. He hopes Daniel has gone to sleep.

IT STARTED A FEW DAYS AFTER THE ULTRASOUND, WHEN THEY learned their child was a boy and he stopped off in the afternoon at that Little League game. At bat, a small boy in a baggy uniform swung at two wild pitches but then made contact and ran like hell. The ball rolled only halfway to third base—a perfect bunt, if he'd been bunting—and when he was called safe he couldn't restrain a beaming grin, accepted pats on the back from his coach, and then gazed into the stands to find his father as the first baseman punched his fist into his glove, spitting and kicking up dirt. When all eyes were on the next batter, the first baseman—twice the size of the kid on the bag—elbowed him hard in the ribs, doubling him over. Cole shot to his feet shouting "Hey!" instantly so enraged that he could hear his blood pounding. A grandstand full of fathers—and not a single one of them noticed!

He left before the game was over and, at home, stood at the fridge staring at the ultrasound photo that Nikki had stuck on the door with a magnet. What if it had been *his* boy taking that elbow? How easily could he have controlled his rage? He opened the fridge and grabbed a beer. He drank several more through the evening, and later in bed Nikki held the ultrasound in her fingers—the baby cradled inside her, his giant head, a raised arm, a tiny fist—and cooed, "Hello, Daniel." Then she set the picture on her nightstand and turned to him so full of love and passion and straight-up horniness that any man would catch on fire, but Cole couldn't do it, couldn't let loose. That was the first time.

Nikki was understanding. "A baby coming," she said. "It's a lot to take in." But she had no idea, neither of them did, that it was the beginning of the end of what for six years had been a crackling sex life.

The end came fifteen years later. On that Saturday morning when he didn't accept her invitation to come back to bed with his coffee, he cleaned up the tung oil and worked on a bid for dormers in a bungalow, or maybe it was a wraparound porch on a foursquare. When he made Daniel breakfast around noon, he realized Nikki had gone out, and he didn't see her until dinnertime, when she came home with shopping bags from two other dressmakers like her with shops on Alberta. Then, around nine o'clock, Daniel texted that he was going with friends to a late movie, and Cole shaved and put on his dancing shoes to surprise Nikki at the Iguana.

Inside, over the tops of a hundred heads, he spotted two women from her book group, martini glasses in hand, talking at the bar. The music was loud, the bass thumping his spine, so he was dancing already as he shouldered through the rowdy crowd and the dizzying fumes of bourbon and beer, perfumes, orange slices and bitters. He scanned the dance floor and saw her bopping under the lights in a blue and green dress he'd never seen, and he was seized by desire as her beauty rushed through him, swift and sparkling. She was a slinky, sexy dancer. He pushed by a few more bodies, ready to spring onto the parquet. Though he was still fighting through the crowd, her eyes seemed to lock onto him, her playful appraising gaze, her knowing grin, her inside-joke wink—*Don't sit under the apple tree with anyone else but me*—and he fell in love all over again. She reached out a hand, and it was taken. She twirled once, then twice, fell into Tony's arms, and popped back out for another spin. Cole stopped dead. She hadn't seen him, and neither, apparently had anyone from the book group. He turned away, dropping his face into his collar like a spy, and at home he scrubbed the stamp off the back of his hand at the kitchen sink. Then he vomited and smoked a joint and watched half a season of *Six Feet Under*. At one point Daniel was in the kitchen eating a bowl of cereal. When Nikki came in he pretended to be asleep on the couch, the only light in the living room coming from the TV. Though she didn't try to wake him, she did spread a blanket over his body. Like a shroud.

He never told her what he'd seen at the Iguana. He didn't think she'd forgive him for not blowing up.

11

HE OVERSLEEPS—DIDN'T HEAR THE DAMN ALARM!—AND THEN races into Kelly's room, but Daniel isn't in her bed. Smelling warm butter, he goes downstairs.

"*Beurre*," his father is telling his son at the stove. "The best *beurre* in the world is French."

"I take Spanish," Daniel says. "Now step back." He wields the pan like a sword and flips a crepe in the air. It's the same pan from back then, with that simple turning at the end of the wooden handle. "Dad, you're up," he says looking over. "I searched this place top to bottom for a toaster. *Nada*. But I found a reasonable substitute."

"Lower that flame," Phil instructs him. "And more butter in the pan."

"Crepes are the rich man's toast. Congratulations, Dad. You've reformed me. A couple days in New England have turned me bourgeois."

They spread jam and sprinkle sugar, the three of them eating faster than Daniel can cook. "*Mangez voilà magnifique qu'est-ce que c'est*," Phil says. Gibberish. He's off somewhere, his face blank, but blissful too, chewing, swallowing, holding out his empty plate for more. Daniel gulps a tall glass of milk, snatches his lunch from the fridge, and they all three load into the car.

Cole fights the steering the whole way, and at Boulger he points out Little Kirk, parking his motorbike by a shed. Daniel walks across the dirt and shakes his hand, and the two of them, along with a couple dozen Hispanic men and boys, board the dusty bus, and the two fathers sit in the car watching it pull away. "You can't say we didn't do something right," Phil says finally, smacking Cole on the knee.

THE END OF THE JOB HAS COME ON FASTER THAN HE EXPECTED. He'd planned to stay less than a week, and it's been ten days, but it's Alex and Antoine who are suddenly leaving. He's taking Daniel over to their house this evening—excited to show off his son—for a final quick goodbye.

For now they're standing in the hot sun outside the bank in the center of East Granby. Cole's check has already been deposited in their account, the documents are notarized, he's signed the bill of lading, and the cargo's insured. The two flatbeds loaded with his chestnut are lined up the length of the cemetery, idling.

Cole leans back against the hood of Phil's Bonneville. "Where's your first stop?"

"Bratislava," Antoine says.

"At a hotel," Alex adds, "that actually has the same name as Antoine's great grandfather."

"Maybe just a coincidence," Antoine says.

"Maybe not." Alex reaches out her arms. "Well," she says. "It's been really wonderful, Cole. And I've got—"

"Wait, I'll see you tonight. With Daniel."

"Didn't I text you? We're driving down to Brooklyn to spend the night with Antoine's brother. We got a security warning from the airline saying to get to JFK extra early, so this way we won't have to leave at two a.m."

"Oh, shoot. So this is really it."

"Until next time."

He's terrible at goodbyes. He can remember fearing even before his mother died that there wouldn't be a next time.

Antoine hugs him, his arms like rocks. And then Alex, soft and strong. "I've got something for you," she says, and pulls the ring off of her thumb and slips it on his finger. "And one more." From her pocket she produces a smaller chestnut ring. "Antoine made this one last night. That design comes from traditional Hungarian embroidery."

"It's beautiful. You're so kind."

"It's for your wife," she says, sliding it onto his pinkie. "For Nikki."

He admires the two rings, side by side on his fingers, and his eyes fill with tears. "Thank you."

Antoine opens the pickup door, and Alex hugs Cole again.

"Bon voyage," he says.

They climb inside and she starts the engine. Cole's last sight of her is through the windshield, her hair tied up in a scarf. She clunks it into reverse, looking out the rear window over her shoulder. She waves at him, rolling backward, and then stops, trying to work the old transmission into gear, and in that halted moment with the sun igniting her hair and glinting off her cheeks, she looks more like his mother than ever.

WITHIN A COUPLE MINUTES THE TRUCKS PULL AWAY WITH HIS chestnut, shooting long black clouds of smoke drifting over the cemetery. He's got time to spare before his lunch date with Liz, and should go back to the house and wire in the new ceiling light he bought for the kitchen, but instead decides to take a drive. He heads south and turns up the long entrance to East Granby High School, which has a new façade and new bleachers; the pasture where Buford used to graze is now a subdivision with small houses, thrown together in the eighties by the look of the siding and wrought iron.

Then he takes the twenty-minute drive to Bloomfield, where he and his brother and sister moved in with their uncle Andrew and Sandy after their mother died. Bloomfield High has put in a new track, and there's a Warhawk banner fading in the sun, but otherwise he guesses it looks about the same. He went here for two years but hardly has a memory of it. Nearly straight A's, piling on extra classes—all a blur, as if one night he crept downstairs to find his mother slumped against the piano and the next moment he was in Seattle at UDub.

Across the street from his uncle Andrew and Sandy's house he parks in the shade. It's been painted a blue that's probably too bright, but it still looks cozy with its steep roof, gingerbread details in the fascia, and deep turnings in the front porch columns. The street's less run-down than it used to be. The houses are close together, separated only by the driveways. Down the side of theirs, the cedar fence is gone. And the hot tub, too. The garage isn't in the spot he remembers.

A woman with a trowel appears on the opposite side. Could she be Sandy? She must be. There's no reason she and Andrew wouldn't still live here. Her hair's shorter, her hips wider. He watches her set down a flat of pansies and kneel beside it. Then a little girl comes running around from the back. "Mommy. Where are you?"

What could he have been thinking? Sandy was twelve years older than he was, and this woman's in her thirties. With a five-year-old daughter. He's off by twenty-five years.

He was a college junior when Andrew wrote to say Tilly had died, and that was the last Cole ever heard from him. The letter also said she had set up a trust to continue paying Cole's tuition, and that Andrew would cover his airfare to the funeral. It took him a week to write back—*really busy time . . . midterms . . . advanced calculus,* some of it nearly true. She died four years and two months after his mother, and leaving Bloomfield now, driving along a golf course to Simsbury and Tilly's old house, he knows that, even taking self-preservation into account, not coming back for her funeral was unambiguously wrong.

The grand and stately house looks just the same—red brick with black shutters and ivory trim—and he can easily imagine Tilly still sitting at the head of the kitchen table. Then he notices, in the side yard, an elderly woman half-hidden by the mulberry bush sitting at an easel, painting. On a garden table beside her, brushes fan out in smudged jars among squished metal tubes and what look like small apothecary bottles. Though her hair is white, it's permed in the style his mother's used to be.

Another woman, younger but with long silver hair, comes out from the breezeway, carrying a tray with a teapot. She pushes aside the rags on the table, sets down a teacup, pours it full, and makes space for the pot. She stands behind the painter—maybe her mother—resting one hand on her shoulder, pointing out details on the canvas with the other, and chatting, although at this distance Cole can't hear a thing.

HIS MOTHER'S BURIED IN TARIFFVILLE, THE NEXT TOWN OVER. THE fifteen-minute drive takes him past some beautiful old colonials, through fertile countryside, and across a silver steel bridge right into the restaurant's parking lot. He gets out and leans a foot on the guardrail, white water surging through the gorge below, and decides to visit the grave another day.

When Liz pulls up in her Mercedes, he says, "I'd have bet this whole town would've slid over the cliffs by now."

"It's not Nantucket, but no, they've had a little renaissance." Her Mercedes chirps and they kiss on the cheek. Again she's in a killer outfit—a fuchsia blouse with a white silk scarf, a bright yellow skirt, open-toed pumps. Her purse looks like Park Avenue—stiff, shiny leather with gold clasps and a wooden hoop handle. It's impossible to connect the dots to her frayed cutoffs and tube tops, the girl with stringy blond hair sitting cross-legged in the dirt rolling a perfect joint.

"How long has this place been open?" Even when he was a boy these carpet and textile mills along the river had long been shuttered. All he remembers here was an army-surplus store, a single-bay garage that sold retreads, and a dreary market with a butcher in back where his mother bought their meat for the week on Sundays after church. Local kids wore secondhand clothes that didn't fit, exposing their bony wrists and bare ankles, and they stared at you with a squint, like the next blow could come from any direction or like they were fixing to pull a rock from their pocket and hurl it at your skull the moment you turned away.

"I don't know," she says cheerfully. "Things change."

The organic restaurant, a former mill, is beautiful inside, and the air-conditioning feels good. Massive posts and beams rise up from wide plank floors to a clerestory. On their table, white linen and three purple tulips. A live recording of Miles Davis playing an upbeat "Springsville." He sees he's underdressed. Clean jeans and a collared shirt will get you anywhere in Portland, but now he suddenly feels like some contractor out with a client.

She orders a glass of Sancerre and then he does the same, and when the waiter brings them Cole raises his in a toast. "To meeting again," and they clink.

"I've had some good news," she says, "so lunch is on me. Driving over here I got a call from my lawyer and found out I just bought a flower farm." She grins with unrestrained delight and Cole catches a flash of the girl he knew.

"Where?"

"And ferns. Flowers and ferns. North of Miami."

He's not sure what to say. "I like flowers."

"Everybody does, and that's the idea. I'll always keep a toe in shade tobacco. Ten or fifteen years from now, though . . ." She shakes her head. "It's already a labor of love, but tobacco in Connecticut is history."

"So flowers are the future?"

She takes a sip, widening her eyes. "And ferns."

He laughs, mostly because she's so giddy.

"The farm's gorgeous, all the colors and fragrances, and it's huge—fourteen employees. But what clinched it for me is they do lots of growing under nets. I bought it on an impulse, though I figure that boom times or bust, in sickness and celebration, people want flowers."

"So does this mean you're leaving town now?"

"We don't take possession until October. My husband'll spend time there this summer while I'm here, and by fall . . ." She shrugs. "You know, it's an investment. If it doesn't work out, we'll sell it. But until then"—she rotates the small vase, scrutinizing the tulips—"we've got heaps of flowers in our lives."

Their meals come, along with more wine, and as they eat he tries to steer the conversation to when they were kids, but she keeps looping back to her Christmas plans with Manuel's big family in Brazil and the Portuguese lessons she's going to resume for the third or fourth time.

Once they've finished Cole goes to the restroom, and when he returns, Liz is talking with two women and a man who are standing by their table. "Cole," she says, "you must remember . . ." followed by their names, jarring loose washed-out images as misplaced as Daniel and Phil together in his old house, Kirk and his son manning the crane, or Liz's face across the table—older but truly the same—pasted into a glossy ad for Chanel. Everything's at once familiar and strange, as in a dream where you walk into your office and it turns out to be your childhood bedroom, and then a masquerade party where you're the only one without a costume.

And yes, he remembers the three of them. The man a year ahead of him in school, married now to the woman who'd been in Cole's class, while the other one's rolling "How's the West Coast?" off her tongue like they'd all met for drinks a month or two ago. And Cole's saying, "Beautiful coastline. Microbrews. Rains a lot," and Liz mentions a recent trip to San Francisco. Okay, just three people who used to be classmates—they look just like them and act like them, and he remembers that one of these girls, whose name he couldn't have summoned in a million years, had bad allergies and scrunched up her nose to keep from sneezing and always breathed through her mouth. And now she's married to this boy, and they're all grown up and wearing dressy business clothes, all grown up, whereas Cole's dressed essentially as he was when they last saw one another, aged fifteen.

HE POURS THE BOYS TWO TALL LEMONADES AND DROPS A HANDFUL of ice in each glass. It's good to see Daniel with dirt covering his arms, and his jeans and T-shirt, too. The rich smell of under the nets so familiar to Cole.

"How was Phil this morning?" he asks Daniel.

"He did fine," his father says as he comes in the kitchen. "Bigger question is how was day one as a tobacco picker?"

"We ain't pickin' yet, Mr. Callahan," Little Kirk says.

"It's good," Daniel answers. "Real work. I just wish we were growing carrots and broccoli."

"But you like it?" Cole asks.

"I like working in the soil. The heat. The intensity of it. And I'm using my Spanish, which is cool. It's a privilege to be working with such folks—"

"Like that one babe," Little Kirk blurts.

"And it's very labor intensive—"

"Fuckin' A it is." LK drains his glass.

"—so it provides a lot of jobs."

"Now, when I first worked tobacco," Phil says, "there were some serious initiations for the new guy. I had my pants tore right off me."

"I'm keeping an eye out," LK says. "Nobody'll mess with my boy."

"I met Connie Stevens back then," Phil notes. "She looked right at me and said, 'Nice to see you.' And I saw Karl Malden in the Windsor Family Restaurant. Karl Malden, eating a plate of eggs. Imagine."

Cole heard this story many times as a kid, but he wants to keep Phil reminiscing. "Was that when they were filming the movie?"

"*Parrish*, starring Troy Donahue. I never saw him. *Thought* I did, several times, but it was always somebody else."

"I love that movie," Little Kirk says. "I've seen it a hundred times. And you know the speech about tobacco leaves being like a baby—"

"'You gotta keep it warm, sheltered,'" Phil puts on the voice, "'water, hoe, sucker. It never leaves you alone. Like a baby.'"

LK lights up with a wide grin. "Exactly! Our farm boss gives the same speech. Right from the movie."

"Well, it's accurate. There's not a thing in that movie about tobacco farming they got wrong."

His father's making perfect sense, his mind clear, and Cole wonders if the episodes of the last week might have been aberrations. There's a bang on the door and Cole opens it to a UPS delivery woman. "Phil Callahan," she says, setting two big boxes down on the step, "Live Chickens" stamped on the cardboard. They can hear the frantic chirps. She holds out her electronic clipboard for Cole to sign.

He's about to say this must be a mistake—as if just saying it would change his father's mind and make her take them away—but instead he simply signs. Half the people on their street in Portland have a few exotic chickens, but he's got a bad feeling about what's in this box. "How many?" he asks his father, looking down at the boxes once the woman leaves.

"Thirty-five."

"That's awesome," Little Kirk says. "Your coop looks like a classic."

When they built it, Cole remembers, his father was working from a few Polaroids of a board-and-batten henhouse in Sturbridge Village and drawings in a coffee-table book of colonial outbuildings. They'd paid extra to get rough pine instead of smooth.

Phil tears open the top of a carton and the chirping goes wild like . . . well, like hungry chicks. "About half hatched," he says.

"Do you have any feed?" Cole asks.

His father's silent for a moment, like he's thinking, but then his face slackens.

"I *had* some," he says, turning to Cole. "Did you throw it out with the garbage?"

Cole shakes his head.

"Everything's been disappearing since you showed up."

Christ. How can any of this work out? Daniel has asked the only sensible question in days: *What the hell are we doing here?*

"We got feed," Little Kirk says. "Don't take much for the day-olds. They'll peck at some food scraps for now."

"Ha!" Phil points at Daniel, seeming right back on track. "No scraps with my grandson in the house. What's it you call that?"

" 'Scrappetizing,' " Daniel says.

"His own coinage." Phil nods proudly.

"Huh?" LK looks blank.

"Tell him." Phil chuckles. "He's committed. Got suspended from school for it."

"All I was doing was eating off the trays on the conveyor belt before they went into the dish room."

"He started a movement."

"I got some other kids doing it too. You don't need to buy food in this country. Half a sandwich, a cup of pudding, a carton of milk barely touched, most of an apple."

"Got him kicked right out of school."

"Only for two days," Cole adds.

Little Kirk's face twists up. " 'Scrappetizing'?"

Phil pats his grandson's arm. "Tell him about eating from dumpsters."

"That's just wrong." LK turns up his nose. "I won't even eat left-overs."

EACH OF THE BOYS CARRIES A BOX, AND THE MEN FOLLOW THEM across the backyard to the old henhouse in the weeds, then Cole suddenly remembers. "Hold up, guys. We got squatters in there."

They open the door and see the eyes reflecting the sunlight. On the other side of the motorcycle, the three raccoons are curled around one another in their nest.

"Their momma must be dead," says Little Kirk. "They'll make quick work of thirty-five chicks." The dish Cole put out for them has been flipped over and swatted into the opposite corner. The three Callahans all stare blankly at one another, and after a moment LK asks, "You got another carton?"

Cole jogs back to the house, and when he returns Little Kirk lifts the raccoons into the box along with much of their nesting while Cole drags the one-wheeled bike out of the coop.

"Will they make it?" Daniel asks.

"Say what?"

"Don't they need food?"

LK stares at Daniel, seemingly fascinated. "They can fend for theirselves by this age." He closes the cardboard flaps and bungees the box to the back of his motorbike. "I'll let them go by that shed closer to town." He claps Daniel on the shoulder. "They'll live a nice life there. And now we still gotta patch those holes," he adds, pointing at the sunlight shining through two spots. "Keep the chicks in and the critters out." Then he starts giving them all orders, setting them to work. For twenty years Cole has supervised every detail of extensive, complex building projects, and here Little Kirk Schaler is telling him how to nail a piece of wood over a hole. And it's a relief, really, to have the kid take charge.

When the holes are sealed, the boys straighten up the chicken wire, pounding the highway stakes solidly into the ground. Cole and Phil work on the henhouse door, so warped by time that it won't swing freely or latch.

His father had gotten angry back when they were building the henhouse: his mother thought the chickens—and the Chinese geese, the mallards, the rabbits, the goat—were *fool's errands* that took him away from restoring the house, and the night before, he and Kelly and Ian had listened to them arguing—or listened to their mother's side—late into the night. But when it was finally quiet he fell asleep, and his father woke him up early the next morning. Cole endeavored to keep the project going smoothly, without complaining about hunger as they worked through lunch, measuring precisely and cutting fast even though he was tired from staying awake and vigilant so late. But things didn't go well. They were short a sheet of plywood and had no idea how to cut a birdsmouth or set rafters. By dinnertime, with only the framing done, his father said, "If we fly through the siding we'll be done except for the roof." Cole set to cutting, exhausted by now and knowing they'd be working until dark, and he promptly cut through the cord of the circular saw—always an awful sound, like a snake choking on its own tail.

"Damnit!" his father shouted, then chucked the saw as far as he could, the severed cord dangling, and marched into the house. Cole stayed out there sawing the bats and boards by hand until his mother called him in to eat. He picked up the circular saw, nosed into the dirt, and collected the rest of the tools. No one spoke over the meal except his mother: "Everything always takes longer than anybody thinks."

That night Cole was so exhausted it was almost a relief that it came so fast. When he stepped out of the shower his father was leaning into the sink with the Waterpik stuck in his mouth, and his mother stormed into the bathroom shouting at him—"Chicken coops! When there's no money to install *heat* upstairs!"—and he turned the Waterpik on her, the pulsing spray needling her cheeks and eyes and inside her mouth, and she held up her hands—"Stop it! Phil! Listen to me!"—and then with one swift backhand he sent her slamming into the wall beside the toilet and pounded out the door. Wrapped in a towel, Cole kneeled at his mother's side, blood running from her nose. She was howling. The toilet paper, ripped off the wall, unrolled across the floor, the Waterpik tip spasming where it dangled off the counter from its slim coiled hose.

Once the henhouse is patched together, LK stays for dinner, and while the boys are doing the dishes, Cole takes a shower. Afterward, standing at the upstairs window, he watches Little Kirk take off on his motorbike, kicking up a tail of dust down the tractor road. At the back of the field along the tree line, he stops. One by one, he lifts the baby raccoons from the box, snaps their necks over his knee, and flings them into the woods.

IT'S NOT TOO LATE ON THE WEST COAST, SO HE MAKES A FEW BUSI-ness calls he should have made days ago. "We're losing money on this one, boss," Ben Salverson says.

"Isn't the abatement done?"

"Yep. But behind the asbestos there's dry rot. Every layer we peel away on this job leads to something else."

"Well, okay. So get the jacks over there and let the customer know we're adding a week. Can you pull Travis and Dylan off of shingling?"

"Travis sprained his ankle yesterday, really bad."

"Damn. On the job?"

"Yep. Just stepped wrong off a ladder. He's out for a few days at least, and then I'll get him making window trim in the shop. That job's hit some snags too."

"Handle it best you can—"

"Fact is we could use you here *now*. I couldn't pull the permit for the bay window on Thirty-Third."

"Why not?"

"Setback issue. The neighbor produced a survey from nineteen-ten or something. They still want it, but you've got to do a redesign."

"Well, I can do that from here. And I'll finish that bid tonight."

He can sense disappointment in Ben's silence. Or worry. "I thought they called you."

"Who?"

"They gave the job to somebody else."

"No. The Richmond job? Damnit. That was supposed to carry us through September."

"I know, boss. I looked at the numbers this morning. At best, this summer's a wash."

LIZ DIDN'T TELL HIM ANYTHING ABOUT HER HOUSE, AND HE WAS surprised by the address—way out on Airport Road. He guessed it was in a new development, but at the mailbox he turns into a long, pristine gravel driveway that winds up through nursery fields with rows of holly and dogwoods; on a rise in the distance a tobacco shed is set against the Metacomet Ridge, and as he gets closer, the sunlight reflects off its hefty steel overhangs suspended from cables, its expansive windows and polished doors. Ha, meeting her in a *shed*!

After that night—*the* night—Liz's parents forbade her from seeing him, and since he'd moved to Bloomfield and neither of them had a license, they'd hitchhike to each other, or get a ride from a friend. Her parents caught her twice when she couldn't get home until long after midnight. The third time, they sent her off—gone in what seemed like a matter of days—to a boarding school in Florida. For the first months they wrote each other long letters full of promises, but then hers stopped. He never knew why, but he was crushed.

He parks beside her Mercedes and shuts off the engine. She told him to enter on the left side, which makes him wonder about this particular arrangement. An exterior flight of stairs—slabs of chestnut—lead up to her second-floor entrance and a west-facing deck. Bossa nova's pouring through the screen door, and she's standing at the kitchen counter chopping at a butcher block.

"Knock knock," he says, and she turns, a chef's knife raised.

"*Olá,* Cole! *Bem-vindo.*" She wears a starched apron covering her skirt that swishes around her hips like silk. They kiss on both cheeks and he hands her a bottle of Oregon pinot noir that he finally found at a shop in Avon.

"Magnificent," he says. The chestnut timbers are exposed and finished with oil, in an expanse that's sparse and clean with evening air passing through the big windows. He bends down to smell the huge bouquet on the dining table as Liz explains that she owns the whole place but rents out the main house and keeps this apartment for her Connecticut trips. She'd like to move here permanently someday, though her husband isn't as interested.

"The place you come from will always have that pull," she says. "I feel that homing instinct most powerfully when I'm blue. Or even when I get a bad cold—I just want to come to Connecticut and curl up for a nap. With Manuel it's Brazil. Somehow we've decided that Miami, right in the middle, is the sweet spot."

She makes a production of the cocktail, rattling the shaker over her shoulder to the music, then pouring their drinks in martini glasses—citrus and cucumber and gin.

They clink glasses. "To coming home," he says.

He offers to help but she waves him away, so he sits on a stool at a soapstone counter and takes it all in. A dozen pendants, two chandeliers—twenty-five K, give or take, for the lighting alone, and worth every penny. It's a comfortable, elegant, and very functional kitchen that Liz moves around in like a pro. She forms ground pork meatballs in her palms and rolls them into a pan of hot oil. He can see the scarring on her fingers where they meet her nails, painted the color of midnight, and before long their talk turns to Kirk.

"For years I refused to see him at all," she says, "and even now I don't see him very often. I'm in and out of town in the summer, then sometimes we come at Christmas for a little snow, but that's about it."

"What's it like, though? I mean, what do you say to him? How can you stand to look at him after what he did to you?"

She laughs. "I guess I don't look at him much. His teeth are a mess, he doesn't shave. He's let himself go, don't you think?"

"But why . . . why would you even want a *relationship* with him?"

"Brother *is* a relationship. It doesn't matter if I want it or not." She wipes her hands on her apron and sips her drink, wincing approvingly at the sting of the gin. "My parents died within a year of each other, my mother just this past Easter after endless doctor consults, bedside sitting, crying one minute and arguing with nurses the next, funeral, burial, lawyer meeting, and house cleaning. Kirk was good with that stuff. Respectful. It brought out his best. It's really only since my mother died—just a few months now—that I decided to let it all go and reconcile with him."

"But after what he did—"

"You don't have a clue about what he did to me."

He feels like he does, like he witnessed it through her bedroom window or through her own eyes.

"I know you don't because I never told a soul."

"So what, exactly, did he do?"

She tips back a long swallow. "Cole, dear, here you find yourself all these years later trying to figure out how to cope with your own murdering father. This whole conversation's about *you*, not me. I'm over it. I barely remember what he did."

"Before your mother died you remembered it, but now you don't? I'll bet you think of it every day."

"But that's *you* again." She sips calmly, reasonably. "You're a middle-aged man. How can you let yourself be consumed by something that happened when you were just a kid? A horrible thing, okay, but you've got your own kid to deal with now. Focus on him. The past only has the meaning we give it in the present. I've simply chosen to not allow what Kirk did a lifetime ago to matter to me. Since it never affected you back then, it certainly shouldn't now."

"It did, though. I wanted to protect you."

"That was *your* deal. Some male thing."

He takes a swig, but most of it sloshes onto his shirt. "If it's so trivial, why not tell me?"

She eyes him, squinting coolly—not an expression she made back then. "Okay," she says, "if it means so much to you. He'd get a little drunk and a little high and he'd grab my wrist and twist it up behind my back, yank down my jeans, and then . . . is it called *dry humping*? I don't even know the name of it, so it couldn't have been too traumatic."

He knows she registers the blood in his face, his shaking hands.

"He'd flail at me like that for a while, twisting my arm the whole time, and when he pushed me away I'd gouge at his face with my nails but usually ended up hurting myself more, and he'd tell me he knew what a slut I was with you so I had no right to judge *him*. I'd spit that he'd burn in hell, and a couple times he said, like some creepy Eddie Haskell, that it's not a sin if he doesn't penetrate or ejaculate. And voilà, fifteen years later he's part of a trial against that priest—"

"Father Mally?"

"Exactly."

"Holy shit."

"The lawsuit gets momentum and pretty soon Kirk joins as a plaintiff and gives a deposition. Mally did the same thing to him, even used the same penetration-ejaculation line. But the men who brought the suit were altar boys a few years after Kirk, so by that time I guess Jesus had changed the policy and anything was game. The full monty. The lawyers dropped Kirk from the suit because they thought his case weakened the others."

"I'm surprised he didn't change his story."

"He did. Or tried to. But then they thought he *really* undermined the credibility of the, you know, *penetration plaintiffs*."

"Well, it's to his credit that he at least tried to do the right thing."

"Actually, he did it for the money."

"Why didn't you ever tell your parents what he was doing to you? Or tell me?"

"He said he'd beat you to a pulp every single day, and if that didn't work he'd burn down your house. And I knew he would."

"So you knew he was burning the sheds all along?"

She nods. "He learned that tactic from Mally too. He'd get altar boys into confession and then threaten to reveal their secrets. 'Things could become much worse for you,' he'd say."

"You know, I can't feel sorry for Kirk, even hearing all that. It doesn't change what he did to you. It's no excuse."

"No, he really is a bastard." She smiles. "But he's *my* bastard. And he seems to be doing okay as a father. I'm only now getting to know Little Kirk—" she stops herself, pursing her lips. "I guess the truth of it is I want a relationship with my nephew. Manuel and I tried a little late, and with my parents gone, my brother and LK are the only family I've got left. And to me he seems like a decent kid."

"I hope so. He's Daniel's only friend here." Turning his thoughts to Daniel begins to calm him down.

"What does he say about him?"

"I guess . . ." He pauses. "Not much. I mean, they're pretty different, but I think they get along fine. I'm glad Daniel's got a job. Thanks again for that, by the way."

"Little Kirk told me that Daniel feels like a cousin to him," she says. "He doesn't have any real cousins or siblings. He can be sweet about that sort of thing. I'm sure for years all he heard from his father about me was venom, but when I started making trips back, he warmed to me immediately. Long before I reconciled with Kirk, for my birthday and Valentine's Day, he'd send me Hallmark cards. 'For My Special Aunt.' He's very loyal. To his father, too. Lots of people in town think my brother's an asshole, but his son has only the most glowing words for him." She studies a cookbook, measuring cream and quarter teaspoons of spices from Ziploc bags. "What about your brother and sister?"

He explains what they do for a living and implies he's in closer touch than he is. He describes his two nephews as if he has a sense of who they are, though he probably knows more about Little Kirk. He hasn't gotten the image of LK snapping the raccoons' necks out of his head, but he's convinced himself that it's just the unsentimental, practical side of country living. No different from wringing a chicken's neck. And if those raccoons had lived, they'd be stalking Phil's new chicks night after night. He tells himself that Little Kirk was just doing what needed to be done.

AT THE END OF LIZ'S DRIVEWAY HE TURNS LEFT INSTEAD OF RIGHT and drives north with the windows of his father's car open wide. It's a clear night, the black sky splattered with stars, moonlight glowing in the tobacco nets. The car rumbles louder when he speeds up on the country roads, shuddering in the curves as he tightens his grip on the wheel, fighting the skewed alignment. He thought he'd loop back on Alex and Antoine's road, but instead keeps going and before long crosses the Massachusetts border. There was a roller rink around here where he and Liz would sometimes skate. Even then the place was a time warp, the relic of a family resort built in the 1930s on a lake with an Indian name. Canoeing, archery, ballroom dancing. The roller rink, in a massive wood-sided building, was probably all that survived of the resort itself when he and Liz used to skate in circles, holding hands, and in the dark corners tongue M&Ms back and forth into each other's mouths. As the night went on blisters formed on their feet—an exquisite sting streaming up their legs.

He turns around in the muddy lot of a dairy farm, his headlights sweeping over a field of chest-high cornstalks engulfing a long-abandoned gas station. He and Liz would whip each other in the tight curves; she was light as a bird and fearless. They'd extend their arms and she'd lean out hard away from him, and he felt powerful sending her soaring. He tries another dark road, and another, weaving all over for miles without ever finding the roller rink, so he veers back south toward East Granby.

At an intersection, he recognizes a small brick house and follows the route up the Metacomet Ridge toward the Connecticut border and the northern tip of Old Newgate Road, which he can take all the way home. The car bucks a couple times going uphill, the road getting even darker in the trees, and he tunes in the same scratchy rock 'n' roll station from Hartford he listened to as a kid. God, they're playing the same music, and when Pink Floyd's *Dark Side of the Moon* comes on, he thinks of Liz blowing those spit bubbles off the tip of her tongue. By now she's finished cleaning up her first-class kitchen, maybe listening to a contemporary Brazilian band and changing into an elegant nightgown, while he's rattling in his father's old Pontiac beater down a pitch-black road blasting music from ninth grade.

Just ahead he sees a yellowish glow hovering in the darkness. He backs his foot off the accelerator and rounds a bend where the road drops so suddenly that his stomach rises. It's Old Newgate Prison.

In the gravel lot he lets the engine idle until the song ends, then cuts it off and gets out to have a look. The night air's cooler up here on the ridge, and the heat from Liz's cocktails is fading. He was in middle school when the state took this place over—a historic landmark. They've built it up a little since then—a new ticket kiosk he doesn't remember, handicap ramps, heavy iron chain strung between low columns of granite. Other than the high stone wall with the old brick guard tower perched on top there's not much more to see from the outside, and it really hasn't changed much since he came here on rowdy school buses with his classmates, winding the eight or ten miles past their house at the other end of Old Newgate Road.

He gets back in the car and twists the key. The engine turns over, fires for a second, then quits. He keeps on cranking. Shit. After a minute he tries a few more times and pretty quickly can hear that the battery's charge is dropping. "Fuck," he says aloud, and senses that he's starting to blame Phil for this new annoyance. He finds the AAA card in his wallet and calls it in, and then texts Daniel to tell him he'll be late.

He gets back out, and swinging the door shut sounds even creakier and tinnier than it did before. The car sits at a careless angle in the middle of the lot, like it was dropped there from a crane. He punches the hood.

A text from Daniel dings in: "How do I get to work tomorrow?"

He replies: "Little Kirk??"

Then his phone rings: AAA, telling him it'll be an hour.

So he takes a deep breath and slips the phone in his pocket, his eyes traveling up the 250-year-old prison wall. This place was chartered as a copper mine around 1700, but by 1760 the copper ore—poor quality anyway—was running thin, so the Connecticut Colony sealed the shaft openings with iron grates and turned the mine into a prison. The inmates were of every stripe—murderers, thieves, counterfeiters and, during the Revolution, Tories; in fact, in a glass case of yellowed documents a letter ordering the incarceration of a band of Loyalists was signed "I am, &c, George Washington."

When he was very young, Cole would climb forty feet down an old wooden ladder into cold, damp caverns where water dripped from the rock, rotting the wooden bunks. The rusty remains of iron manacles hung from bolts driven into the stone. At times there were a hundred prisoners here, and Cole was riveted by the stories of their deathly hardships and harrowing escapes. One man sliced open his wrist and pressed filthy sludge off the floor into the wound, hoping that he could slip a gangrenous hand through the metal cuff.

"You were just sent down into those old dungeons to crawl around?" Nikki used to ask. "I'm incredulous."

"There was a guide, but I think he was too old to get down the ladder. He mostly just did a head count to make sure everybody got out."

A few years later the state backhoed a new entrance to the shafts and put in stairs, a handrail, and better lighting. Some of the terror was lost, but in the darkest, deepest shafts, he'd told Nikki, he could still hear moans and cries.

She was particularly fascinated by the human-sized gerbil wheel. In the morning the prisoners were brought up from the caverns to work, and one task involved a gristmill; with no river there to power it, they traded their manacles for neck irons and climbed paddles to turn the wheel.

"It's all I can think about on the StairMaster," Nikki said. But he wonders now if his prison stories rattled some lockbox hidden inside her ribcage. When they met, she guarded herself with swagger and irony and forceful opinions. And one night he was telling her how for punishment the convicts were double- or triple-shackled, and in the severest cases left manacled in the mines for weeks, and that the guards dumped their daily pickled pork on the floor of the black-smith shop, and they had to scoop it up and boil it in the same vats of water they used to cool the iron they'd forged. And then, in turn, she began a story about her own hometown, but her voice suddenly cracked, her eyes filled with tears, and she unloaded: her mother was a drunk, long divorced, a serial restaurant owner, failure after failure, and that ever since Nikki was a little girl her mother would come home plastered after midnight and shake her awake, demanding a back rub until she passed out. Year after year. Sometimes it seemed like the only childhood memory she had: working her small hands into her mother's broad back until, stinking of booze, she started snoring. As her older brothers got into high school they became big partiers too, and their small house was rowdy until two or three in the morning most nights of the week. She never had a sanctuary. Later, she even moved in with her boyfriend's family for a while, embracing his parents as her own. The first time Cole told her he'd fallen in love with her, she said, "I love you so much. I've never felt safe like I do with you." Whether he knew it or not, Cole had been looking for someone to save, and Nikki, despite her swagger, was looking for someone to save her.

He leans back against the cool granite at the base of the prison wall, spinning the chestnut ring around his finger. Then he decides to chance it, and calls Nikki.

After four rings she picks up. "Hey."

"You'll never guess where I am."

"In a hayloft with your old girlfriend?"

"Not quite. I'm—"

"Singing all the old songs from *Hee Haw*?"

"Old Newgate Prison."

"Oh, shit. Daniel?"

"Jesus, Nikki, *no*. The colonial prison. The old copper mine."

"Thank God. How *is* Daniel?"

"He's good. Really good, I think. He likes the job and he's finally got a normal friend. Just a regular high-school kid who cares about girls and cars and money in his pocket."

"That's a relief," she says.

"I'm urging him to go to this Fourth of July barbecue at Little Kirk's house—"

"That's his actual *name*?"

"Well, his father's Kirk."

"Banjos, man. I hear banjos."

"Look, Nikki, this isn't the backwoods. It's been really cool to meet Alex and get to know her and her husband. Their lives are so rich. And their marriage. I loved how—what is it?—they take care of each other but can also stand back. Admire what the other person's doing or saying. To let them figure stuff out. And Liz, too. You should see her house. With *her* marriage it seems like—"

"Holy shit. So you *are* sowing your oats."

"I'm not, in fact."

"You must get a little rise out of—"

"Nikki, please. Cut it! I'm trying to say I appreciate how patient you were with me, and I'm sorry that for all those years I couldn't work out what was wrong with me and I couldn't . . ." He looks up at the stars.

"Fuck me proper?"

"So you're not going to let me say this."

"Hasn't the chance for saying things expired? Like when you agreed I should move out."

"Or maybe a little before that," he says, "like when you started sleeping with Tony."

"I was begging you to tell me not to. Tell me to stop looking for my own place. Begging you to take some fucking *control* of the situation. I mean, it's amazing, Cole. You run a million-dollar business with eight employees you boss kindly but very firmly. You fire guys for shoddy work or having a beer at lunch. I've heard you bring subcontractors and suppliers to their knees when they dick you around. Your authority and competence and skill make Greenworks a success that anyone would envy. And you constructed a life you thought would immunize you and me and Daniel from any trace of your fucked-up childhood, but the problem is that you can't be immune and all buttoned up and also be intimate with your wife. Never mind the sex. How do you think you can be in a relationship if you're afraid of passion and intensity? Afraid of becoming your goddamn father? There's a difference between letting go of control and losing control. Not to put too fine a point on it, but letting go's mandatory for having an orgasm. For good sex, period. That's why it's called reckless abandon."

"When did you figure all of this out?"

"I've been in therapy."

He's embarrassed by what she's divulging. "With who?"

"You don't know her."

"Oh." He's still embarrassed. "Anyway, we *were* intimate, and we didn't just *stop* making love."

"You were a wonderful husband, Cole. I always felt loved and cared for. But then you got spooked by conflict and stopped... I don't know how to say it. You stopped melting into me. Always stayed a little on guard, like you didn't dare let yourself go. It's why I hated our hot tub. You could release yourself to a vat of chlorinated water, but not to me. Not to my body. I was jealous of it. How do you think I felt when you'd come back from a massage and say what an amazing relief it was to have somebody else's hands all over you for an hour? Yes, we did have sex sometimes. But the fact that you could swing it once a month just made me feel worse. It would be one thing if you'd got your balls shot off in a war or something. But knowing it was only the fraught complexities of desire that kept you from me... well, I've told you before, it hurt my feelings."

"Really fun catching up."

"That's a deflection."

"That's your therapist talking."

"Another deflection."

"I don't see the benefit of a lecture about my inadequacies while Tony has his gloriously unfraught prick inside you."

"Nice one." He thinks she might hang up, but then she says, "So why did you call?"

"Because I'm at Old Newgate Prison. I thought we might, you know, *intimately connect* over the long-ago suffering of convicts. Like we used to."

"Oh, nostalgia."

"I didn't realize the prisoners made nails," he says. "On a sign-board here by the entrance it lists all the different jobs."

"Probably the same nails you had to hammer out of the old lath."

"Prison nails. Ha! Forced labor at both ends. But that was *Ian's* job."

A fat possum, with little ones clutching onto its fur, lumbers along the top of the prison wall, disappearing into the guard tower.

"Isn't it late there?" Nikki says.

"Almost midnight."

"And you're out being a tourist?"

"The car broke down."

"Oh, no. Are you okay?"

The possum squeezes out through the hole in the bricks. She's left her litter behind in the nest and trudges back along the wall into the darkness. "It's so quiet here," he says. "Really peaceful."

For a long while they listen to each other breathing, and he wants to say how much he used to love listening to the rhythm of her breath beside him in bed. How much he misses it. And her voice, too. Nothing gratified him like hearing his wife singing in the next room on a sunny Sunday.

But through the thick black woods that swallow the road, flashing yellow lights grow brighter and brighter with the deepening howl of an engine. "Goodnight, Nikki," he says, "sleep tight. Here comes my tow."

"YOU ARE *DÉLICIEUX*," PHIL SAYS, SPEARING THE LAST BITE OF crepe with his fork. It's only seven o'clock, but the kitchen didn't cool off overnight and the morning's already heating up. They're all three bare-chested, wearing nothing but gym shorts—Phil sitting at the head of the table, Daniel tipping crepe batter in the pan, and Cole texting Ben about joist fasteners for the Laurelhurst job.

"That thing is *art*," Daniel says.

Cole looks up from his phone. "What thing?"

He flips the crepe and catches it in the pan. "That work of art at your elbow."

It hasn't moved from the counter for these weeks. The forged-iron nails had filled a liquor box flush to the top; they'd corroded impermeably together over the years, so when Phil tore the cardboard away, what remained was a near-perfect cube of countless small square-shank nails—some still oil-black against the red and orange and powdery-brown flames of rust.

"Put that on a pedestal made from your chestnut," Daniel says, "and watch it change lives." He slides a crepe onto a plate.

When Cole studies it now, he can't think of anything but wretched men in leg irons hammering the heads flat, the same nails holding fast the lath in this house for two centuries until he and his father ripped out the plaster, and Ian pounding enough of them into a wheelbarrow to fill at least this one box, where for twenty-five years they hardened into this hundred-pound barbed-iron block. He supposes Daniel is right. The block is brutally beautiful, so perfectly formed, each twisted and curved nail showing the hammerings of the convict who shaped it.

He sprinkles cinnamon sugar on the crepe, rolls it up, and eats half in one bite. "Amazing," he says, and Daniel winks at him. And then they hear the motorbike. Through the window, Cole sees LK shoot out between the nets on the tractor road and drop the kickstand at the back of the yard. He lets himself inside the chicken wire and opens the henhouse door. A couple chicks venture cautiously into the light, but then he upends a plastic bag: food scraps hit the dirt and squawking baby birds stampede through the door, flapping their wings, pecking and tackling one another.

Daniel rushes upstairs for his work clothes. "Great day for a drive," Phil calls.

"Little Kirk's taking him in this morning." He hasn't yet told his father about the car, and to avoid doing so now he steps out the back door and meets LK where he's closing the chicken-wire gate.

"What's their calcium source?" he asks.

"Oyster shell," Cole says. "Plus what's mixed in the grain."

LK rubs his chin, purses his lips. "That oughta do 'er."

Daniel runs out from the house and LK squeezes off the old helmet and tosses it to him.

"No, no," Daniel says. "You wear it."

"My bike, my rules," LK tells him. "If my brain hits the dirt, no big loss, relatively speaking. But you're a smart dude. Now put your nut in that shell."

Daniel hesitates, then slips the helmet on and straddles the seat behind him. Cole holds out his fist, and Daniel bumps him. He's excited to be on the bike but plays it cool, so Cole does too. *Normal kid,* he'd tell Nikki, *normal stuff.*

"You make it all the way to Boulger on tobacco roads?" Cole asks.

"Technically, occifer, there might be a couple miles of pavement." LK fires it up. "Don't worry. I take good care of my friends." Pulling Daniel's arms around his torso, he says, "Hold on tight. None of this macho shit." Two quick revs, then he clunks it into gear and spins up a tail of loose dirt, taking off toward the nets.

LK's assurances aside, Nikki would kill him if she knew he was letting Daniel tool around on a motorcycle.

He can still hear the whine of the motor in the distance when he steps up on the back porch, where his father, fists on hips, is blocking the doorway. "Where the hell's my car?"

"It's in town at the—"

"You sold it!"

"Ha. That's a good one. Not exactly a high-value—"

"Go buy it back!"

Touching his father's shoulder to get by him, he says, "Look, last night—"

"Hands off my person!"

He has such violence in his eyes that Cole steps away. "It broke down last night. I had it towed to the Texaco."

"Bullshit!"

"I'll call them at eight and you can listen in."

"You! You're cheating me. You're saying . . . twisted words!"

"I'd like another crepe," Cole says. "Want one?"

Phil shakes his head emphatically, like a child. He's confused, and

Cole finally admits to himself that his mind's definitely on the fritz—
something not explained away by an empty belly, a sweltering afternoon, or a sleepless night. It's not going to be a matter of just stocking
the kitchen, replacing washers in the sinks and shower, paying a lawn
service in advance through the summer and fall. His father needs
blood tests, a brain scan. He probably needs regular care. Dripping
faucets and a houseful of burned-out bulbs are not the issue here.

"Well, I'm going to cook myself another." He doesn't reach forward but inclines his head toward the doorway, and Phil steps out
of his path. He turns on the flame and knifes butter in the pan and
scrapes the last of the batter from the mixing bowl. As the edges
sizzle, he loosens them with the spatula and the crepe seems to hover
on the heat rising off the steel. He considers flipping it in the air but
instead turns it over with the spatula, then slides it onto his plate and
sets it behind him on the table. The last time he made a crepe was at
this stove, passing the plate to Ian, who promptly zigzagged it with
Hershey's syrup, then to Kelly for a blast of whipped cream. "*Ooh
la la!*" or "*Formidable!*" their mother would exclaim as they set the
plate in front of her.

He runs water into the bowl and turns to the table to chow down,
but his father, sitting in his mother's place, is eating the crepe. Cole
laughs. "How is it?"

Phil stops chewing, his face drops, and he places the last bite
down on the rim of the plate. His eyes dart around the kitchen—a
drowning man searching for a buoy. But then he reaches for his own
chair, empty beside him at the head of the table, and grabs hold of
the arm. "Great day for a drive," he announces again.

"It's gonna be a warm one," Cole says. "Let's give the chicks some
cold water this afternoon." He squirts dish soap in the rag, scrubs
the sticky plates and forks. "We used to like maple syrup on crepes,
remember?" he says, and when he reaches for the pan, he's startled
by his father standing there at his shoulder.

"Not in the water!" he commands. "Just wipe it out with a paper towel. René himself instructed me on that." Phil holds the black pan in front of his face like a mirror, staring into it, and his voice softens. "I had to go all the way to Glastonbury for that pan. René's French Kitchen. He had a nice store. Quality stuff for customers who were serious about good cooking. Like a highly specialized restaurant supply. None of the pretentiousness of Marks & Tilly, those foofy aprons and pillow shams and potpourri. God, the reek of it still sours my mood."

And just like that, his father's perfectly lucid.

"Maple syrup and banana is how you liked them," Phil says. And he's right. "Ian loved the chocolate syrup," he remembers. "Kelly was cinnamon sugar with whatever berries we might've had. I went for the red currant jelly." He laughs. "Truth be told, I liked that jelly on anything."

Phil wipes out the pan and sets it on the stove. "Thanks for doing the washing up. Always good to have a clean kitchen." He clasps Cole on the shoulder. "Hard to think clearly with dirty dishes piled up."

As Cole is getting dressed, Phil digs into the piano piece, notes rattling through the house, spilling out open windows and through cracks under the doors. He grabs his laptop and shoulder bag. Even if a clean kitchen has wiped the clutter from his father's mind, Cole has to figure out what needs to be done for him.

In the keeping room he pantomimes that he's going out for a while, then mounts his old bicycle and coasts down to the road, and even once he's long out of earshot, the music's haunting melody is still playing in his head.

Phil's car is tucked in where the tow truck left it last night, next to a green Charger with a bashed-in front end. The mechanic looks up from under the hood of a Toyota when he steps into the bay. "I'm Cole Callahan. I called earlier about the Bonneville."

With thick red hair and a goatee, he's about Cole's age, a navy tattoo on his forearm and a pack of cigarettes in his breast pocket. If he grew up in East Granby, Cole would've known him, a couple grades up or down. "Haven't looked at it yet."

"I figured," Cole says, "but I was passing by. Just wanted to put a name with a face. I appreciate you fitting it in." He likes the sweet oil-and-grease-and-Gojo smell of a garage, and also likes to look someone in the eye when work and trust are involved.

"Shouldn't be later than noon." The man twists off a distributor cap. "I wrote down your number."

"Thanks. And hey, is there a place in town that has wi-fi? You know, that I could use."

He snaps a spark-plug socket onto his ratchet. "I'd have to say no to that one."

"The grinder shop, maybe?"

"They barely got a working toilet."

Cole laughs. "All right," he says, backing out into the sun. "I'll check with you later. Thanks again."

As he turns, the mechanic calls to him. "Try the library. They've got computers and all that."

Cole walks the bike over to the compressor and blasts some air in the tires, then pedals along the stone wall past grave markers, the names of the dead worn illegible from the centuries.

The colonial brick library was the town's original school. He swings into the lot and finds that it's closed three days a week— yesterday, today, and tomorrow—and keeps rolling, standing on the pedals to get up the rise, and his sweat comes on hard.

Approaching the house, he cocks his head and listens for the piano. Nothing. Inside, he moves quietly through the rooms until he finds his father asleep in the wing chair. He fills a glass of water at the kitchen sink and drinks it down. *Nikki,* he thinks. She could search for a few things, so he calls her and she picks right up.

"I guess you got rescued okay by the big white truck."

"Nice guy," Cole says. "He was dispatched from Hartford, which is why it took so long."

"Triple A," she says, nothing more—a friendly volley in their long-running disagreement over the value of their membership fee. Cole has always argued it's a waste of money, that if they break down driving together he'll take care of it, and if she breaks down alone she only needs to call him, and that furthermore, AAA's a conservative organization that lobbies Congress for more roads, cheap gas, and weakened regulation of the auto industry. But Nikki says Cole needs to stop acting like he's solely responsible for fixing every situation, and that she feels safer with the card in her wallet, so every year he writes another check.

"You're right," he says, and she knows what he means.

"Everything good with Daniel?"

"Great." He thinks about the motorbike this morning. "I want to ask you a favor, though."

"Yeah?"

"Can you Google how you can tell if you have Alzheimer's?"

"So you're finally past the denial stage."

"Hilarious. Not me. It's my father."

"Seriously? Oh, no."

"Yeah. He's really in and out of it."

"Just a second. I'm right here at my desk." Her keyboard starts clicking. "Okay," she says. "Top ten signs." As she reads them aloud, Cole mentally checks the boxes.

"Well, this sort of sucks," he says. "I think he got a perfect score."

"Really?"

"Yeah, if 'cow juice' for 'milk' counts as 'problems with words.' "

"At least partial credit. And bonus points for charm."

"Damn," he says. "Well, can you look up some other stuff for me?" And when he hangs up he has phone numbers for a geriatrician and a neurologist in Hartford and an 800 number for the VA. Once he gets the car back, he'll go online himself.

He tiptoes into the parlor—the wing chair's empty. "Dad?" he calls up from the bottom of the stairs, and there's no reply. Then, from the keeping room, he looks out the window and spots his father doubled over beside the chicken coop. He doesn't panic but hustles out the kitchen door and across the yard to where Phil's hunched down, sitting on a cinder block by the henhouse door.

Cole opens the chicken wire. "You okay?"

"These runts need looking after." In one hand he's got a chick tucked against his chest and in the other he's cupping a handful of grain. He nods toward the corner of the pen. "Scoop up that one over there."

Cole sneaks behind the bird and snatches it—smaller than the others, with scraggly feathers and a scabbed-over bald spot on its head that he strokes with his finger.

"That's where the rest of them are pecking her," Phil says, without taking his eyes off the bird cradled to his chest—a tenderness Cole doesn't recall ever seeing in him before. Either he developed this gentle and nurturing impulse in the years since they were a family or Cole has forgotten—the moments all chewed up and spit out by memories of violence.

Violence is always annihilating, not only when it's inflicted with malice. When Nikki went into labor, neither of them expected soft music and pastels and a bundle of joy magically appearing in their arms, but they also didn't imagine that childbirth would nearly kill her. She had a dreamy pregnancy at the start. No morning sickness, lots of energy. She loved her lush body. Their pleasure was intensified in everything they shared—from chocolate to pesto to the long massages he gave her at night. Her hair smelled like she'd been baking ginger-molasses cookies.

Then, in month seven, her blood pressure shot up—preeclampsia—and she had to go on drugs and take to bed. Except for doctor visits she almost never left the house, but somehow she still came down with the flu. By the time her water broke she was completely sapped. She labored for eighteen hours, her blood pressure off the chart. She was in agony. Beside her, squeezing her hand, he'd never felt more helpless. And then as Daniel started descending, a wave of relief. But the delivery stalled out and Nikki was screaming for help, screaming as the doctor calmly worked scissors along Daniel's crowning skull and cut her open. But Daniel stayed put, his mother now screaming even harder, and they were trapped in this state—Nikki in excruciating pain, their baby half born, masked and unalarmed strangers draped in blue paper gowns surrounding them—until Daniel shot out like a rocket.

Nurses took their baby away for a time, and Cole pressed his cheek to Nikki's and her breathing quieted. Although he was relieved it was over, his gut clenched with his failure to protect her from this suffering. Soon Daniel was laid on her chest, amazingly in tiptop shape. Cole was crying, a gushing release, and then, without warning, a nurse snatched their baby back: Nikki was hemorrhaging. They tried to pull Cole away from her, but he refused. When an aide, his arms like a bouncer's, grabbed his shoulders, Cole threw an elbow. Blood poured from her, glugged as if from an upturned jug. They stuck an oxygen mask over her face. Needles, IVs. Monitors wheeled to her bedside, more people draped in blue. With metal trays of clanking tools they worked like butchers, maddeningly calm, to stop the bleeding. Heaps of gauze, pillows of it soaked with her blood, piling up on the floor. He had no way of knowing if they'd stopped the bleeding, except that eventually the doctors and nurses in their bloody gowns took a step back from Nikki and her eyes were still open and her chest rose and fell. Or *mostly* stopped it. She bled for three more days, but she was stabilized. She wasn't going to die.

In a couple weeks she was up and around. In a couple months her doctor told her she had the strength of any woman two months postpartum. They'd saved her uterus, which was good news, because she and Cole had planned to have two children or even three.

His father finds another runt cowering in the henhouse and carries it against his chest to the watering fount. He scatters the other birds and holds this one to the trough while it drinks, then reaches into his pocket and comes out with a handful of grain spilling between his fingers.

The violence that Nikki suffered annihilated everything except his desire to save her, and that was how he lost her.

12

THE SIGN FOR HOLCOMB ESTATES NO LONGER STANDS AT THE
entrance on Route 20, and so many trees have matured since this
cow pasture sprouted thirty or forty houses that he drives right past
and has to turn around at the high school and come back. "Unbe-
lievable," he says to Daniel. "This was the new fancy neighborhood
when I was a kid." Scraggly lawns, torn screens, peeling paint, and
on one house a window shutter dangling from a single screw. Denise
Cowl and C. J. Gibson lived here, brand-new Pontiacs in the two-car
garages, Winnebagos in the driveway. Split-levels and colonials, finished basements with wet bars. Some had above-ground pools, and
Denise's parents had a Jacuzzi on the patio. Between the huge leafed-
out trees and the overall shabbiness, the neighborhood he envied no
longer exists.

He turns in and pulls up behind a few cars parked in the cul-
de-sac, and with a six-pack under his arm he and his son walk up
the driveway. Kirk's at the grill wearing a yellow polo shirt and an
American-flag apron. "Happy Fourth!" he calls as they come across
the yard. He's got a cigar stub stuck in the corner of his mouth.

"Danny boy!" comes from the circle of lawn chairs.

"Hey, Jim," Daniel says to his boss at Boulger.

Kirk rings his spatula on the grill. "What are we drinking?"

Cole pulls a beer from the six and sets the rest on the picnic table.

"I'll have water," Daniel says.

"The water boy," Jim Stanton says, mocking and endearing at once. "From the tap, am I right? Don't offer this kid a *bottle* of water unless you want a lecture about who the hell knows."

Kirk grabs a bottle by the neck. "Water's for fish. But tequila!" He splashes some into the plastic cups everybody's holding out and pours new ones for Cole and Daniel.

"He's fifteen, Kirk."

"When I was fifteen me and Jim put down a pint of Yukon Jack before the party even started. Isn't that right?"

"Yes sir," Jim says, raising his cup.

Daniel's hands remain in his pockets. "Is LK inside?"

"Follow the music," Kirk says, emptying Daniel's red plastic cup into Cole's. "You'll find him."

As Cole watches his son go into the house, Liz comes out carrying a tray of guacamole and blue chips. It hadn't occurred to him that she'd be here. She moves the tray to her hip, kisses his cheeks, and dips a chip in the guacamole; he thinks she's going to feed it to him, but she pops it in her own mouth.

Cole introduces himself around and sits down in a lawn chair with a beer. Before long they're all very loose. Though Kirk's sipping Dr Pepper from a can, he's the sort of reformed drinker who enjoys getting everyone else drunk. Cole's faking it with Jim's wife, who says she remembers him from middle school and goes on and on about some birthday party at the shore; he has no memory of the day, or of her at all. But then she says, "We climbed on top of the picnic-table pavilion and jumped off into mounds of sand," and now he recalls the asphalt shingles scorching his feet, and instantly the whole afternoon, her included, comes back to him.

"That huge lifeguard," Cole says, "he came after us when we wouldn't get down off the roof."

"Yes! We ran into the bathrooms to hide."

He can almost smell the damp concrete, the Coppertone and piss. "Kerry Jacobson's birthday," he says. A name, a girl, totally vanished from his mind until this moment. "She loved Juicy Fruit gum."

She nods. "Kerry could be a real bitch about the Juicy Fruit."

"She was a brand loyalist," he says. "In high school didn't she always wear a T-shirt with 'Marlboro' across her chest?"

"She was so proud of that shirt, she wore it constantly. And her left boob was bigger than her right, so we called her Marl-*burro*."

Cole laughs. "I wonder where she is now," he says, not really wondering. What he's thinking is how astounding it is that a chance meeting and random conversation can resurrect someone after such a long time.

"She lives in Enfield," Jim's wife says. "She's a CPA. It's sort of sad, actually. Her husband died of a heart attack, and a year later she got diagnosed with breast cancer."

"That's awful. How is she?"

"She's great. She had some work done after the mastectomy. Way beyond fixing the off-kilter thing. Her boobs look amazing."

"Whose boobs?" Jim shouts from behind the barbecue.

"Kerry Jacobson."

"Oh, yeah," he says and kisses his fingertips Italian-style. "Grade-A choice."

"You're single, aren't you, Cole?" Jim's wife asks.

"Separated."

She winks at him, sisterly. "You should call her up."

Daniel always accuses his parents of living in a bubble, a liberal Portland exclusion zone where they pretend the forces of racism, sexism, and economic injustice barely exist anymore, not since the bad old days. Cole's not sure how his son would react to this conversation, but he'd at least accuse him of failing to speak up because he fears conflict. Which he does. He's been sneaking glances at Liz, who's listening to every word but revealing nothing. He's about to change the subject when Kirk does it for him.

"I heard your dad ordered up some day-olds," he says.

Cole smiles and nods, indicating his dismay.

"What's he gonna do when *you* fly the coop? That's a lot of work, all those chicks."

"Good question. Maybe I'll come back to help him butcher the roosters, but I'm not even sure he can remember to feed them, so I may have to . . ." He sips his beer. "I really don't know," he says, and he doesn't.

"LK and I could help butcher."

"Thanks, man. That's a nice offer."

"He can pay us in fryers."

"Sure," Cole says.

"Has the old man ever butchered on that scale?"

"When I was a kid we got fifty white rocks. In no time the roosters were waking us all up before dawn, and eventually the whole family was so damn sleep-deprived I think we would've machine-gunned them all if we had the hardware. So we start in on a Saturday morning, and of course Ian and I want to see a chicken running around with its head cut off, so my father agrees to give us a chance. He's got a plan—probably he read it somewhere—and he makes a little noose out of string and holds up the first rooster so Ian can slip the noose over its neck. Then my father pins the chicken down on a tree stump and Ian starts pulling on the string to stretch out its neck. 'Okay, go!' my father says, the chicken fighting to get loose, and I swing the ax. But it's so dull it barely crimps the feathers, and this chicken who's getting bludgeoned in the general vicinity of his throat looks up at me with one eye like '*You gotta be fucking kidding me.*' And my father shouts, 'Again! Swing harder!' and I do, but the ax just crushes the neck, doesn't *chop*, and the poor thing's making these terrible squawks and moans. By this time Ian's crying, so he lets go of the string and my father grabs it so now he's got one hand holding the bird down and the other yanking on the neck—" and suddenly Cole realizes how uncomfortable everyone is: Jim Stanton's looking at his hands, his wife has shrunk back into her lawn chair, Kirk's swishing Dr Pepper around his mouth and eyeing Liz, who has one hand at her throat. He's told this story before but never to an audience familiar with his family saga, and looking at their faces he knows what every one of them is thinking, and he makes them even more uneasy by stopping so abruptly, then saying flatly, "I chopped once more and the head popped off and my father let it go, but it didn't run around like in the cartoons, just clawed and flapped furiously, spinning in circles in the dirt until it died." Finally he stands up. "I'll go see if Daniel and LK want some food."

Liz walks with him to the house, pulling open the screen door with one hand, a plate of pie in the other. He follows her through the kitchen—surely an early-seventies original, with almond-colored cabinets and gold-speckled Formica. He can hear the music pounding from upstairs, LK's laugh, "Bite me, bitch!"

"I want to show you something," she says through a mouthful of pie, and leads him down the steep basement stairs, the temperature dropping with each step.

"God, why don't they have the party down here?" he says. The basement's paneled in knotty pine, the bar built from packing crates with "This Side Up" stamped in red, upside-down. The clock behind the bar has crooked arms and numbers running counterclockwise. There are tiny statues of drunks in top hats leaning on light posts and St. Bernards with casks strapped to their chests.

Liz reaches around behind the bar, clinks some bottles, and all she comes up with is crème de menthe. "Kirk was a lot more fun before he quit drinking." She leaves the bottle and takes him around the pool table, pointing at the far wall, which is covered with old framed photographs. "Here's what I want to show you."

The first he notices is Liz's freshman-year school picture, and he recognizes the calico shirt, the leather choker with the wooden bead. And the smile, wide and aggressive, her eyeteeth prominent. Most of the photos are of Kirk—toddler, Little League, altar boy, honeymooner—but there are others of Liz, too: school pictures from earlier grades, on a cruise ship, standing at a table where someone's carving a ham. He's scanning for one of himself but instead sees her wearing a bikini next to Kirk, in cutoffs, bare-chested, his arm draped over her shoulders, and Cole's face twists up with revulsion. "How can you even *look* at that?"

"Cole! Settle down."

"I just . . . I wish I'd punched his face in thirty years ago."

She sets her paper plate on a cider barrel and clutches his hands to her chest.

"Same goes for my father. But he's an old man who's losing his marbles. Too late now to pop his jaw."

"I heard you popped him pretty hard."

"That was only reactive, spur-of-the-moment. What I wish is that I'd looked him in the face, thought about it for a second, and then watched my fist hit him over and over."

"And you'd feel better now if you'd done that?" She squeezes his hands tighter.

"I'd feel I'd *done* something. I should've protected you."

"So now we're talking about Kirk again. You seem to mix them up. FYI, Kirk didn't murder your mother."

"It's not a joke, Liz. For Christ's sake, he stole your childhood."

"Ha!" She laughs. "A little dramatic, isn't it? I told you the other night I barely remember what he did. The truth is, I barely remember my childhood at all."

"I doubt it."

"Who the fuck are *you* to tell *me* what I remember?"

"You don't *want* to remember, because your parents were drunks and your brother was an abusive asshole and it's easier to block it all out."

"Those are *your* memories of my childhood. I remember Easters with my cousins in Middletown. A cruise in the Caribbean. I remember being in love with a boy named Cole." She snorts. "And how my parents hated him after he turned my brother in. And truly, not a whole lot more."

"How about the spit bubbles?"

"The what?"

"You launched them from the tip of your tongue."

She shakes her head with exaggerated patience. "Doesn't sound like my style."

"You're kidding."

"No, Cole. I don't remember spitting."

"What about our plan to go camping?"

"I've never camped. I like room service and hotel robes—the plusher, the better."

"How about the creepy security guard who caught us smoking pot, and I was totally clueless to what was really going on?"

She smiles, shaking her head slow and wide.

"Look, I didn't get it about that guard until much later—I don't know, years—and I still feel terrible about being so blind. It always seemed you held it against me and that's why you stayed in Florida that summer."

"Cole, you gotta stop! This is intense. You're lugging around shit so old it's petrified. Big heavy sacks of shit stones. Protection, retribution . . . they're the big deals in *your* life. You can't unload them into mine." She kisses the back of his hand. "I stayed in Florida that summer because I met a guy, a college guy with an apartment, so I got a job waitressing at a country club. My parents were relieved not to . . . well, *parent* me. I'm not saying you shouldn't have done what you did, but they spiraled down after Kirk was arrested. Now they're gone, I have a wonderful marriage to a man I love, a fulfilling career, a good-enough relationship with my brother, and a decent kid who calls me Aunt Liz." She gives his hands a final squeeze, then lets go to signal the end of the conversation.

"But you *must* remember hiding with me at night under the

bushes outside your house, too scared to go inside. You were so afraid of Kirk you'd bite your cuticles until they were bleeding, and you—"

"Yes!" she shouts, then slaps him hard across the face. "So what? So I fucking remember! Does that make you feel better? What good does that do me? I'm not naive about what he did. I'm just sick of hating him." She raises her arm for another slap and he flinches, then she turns away and pounds up the basement stairs.

Shit! He didn't mean to upset her, he just wanted . . . what, exactly? He wanted to know that trudging through this muck he wasn't alone.

He rubs his stinging cheek. When was the last time someone slapped him? He considers this while his eyes drift over the photographed moments Kirk is using to create a life that could belong to any other boy—a skinny kid holding up a fish, or getting his first communion, his first car. He struggles to think of somebody else, but then decides the only other person to ever slap his face was his mother.

Outside the day has faded to a soft twilight. A few stars are out. Liz is coming out the kitchen door, and they keep their distance while walking back to the others. Two more couples have arrived, hefty and loud in pressed linen shirts and bright plaids, gold necklaces and watches and perfumes he can smell over the burgers getting cold beside the grill.

"Everybody," Kirk bellows over the ruckus, "this is Cole. Cole, this is everybody."

Liz sits, as she had before, on the very edge of a bench at the picnic table. She doesn't look up at him as he takes a fresh beer from the cooler and slumps into a lawn chair.

"Maxine," one of the newcomers tells him. Her bracelets jangle as they shake hands, and she takes the chair next to him. "Jim tells me you have a teenager. How old is he?"

"Fifteen."

"They grow up so fast," she says, as if she's known Daniel since he was a baby. "One day they're burping up milk and the next they're belching from beer. My boys are seventeen and twenty. Blink of an eye, I tell ya."

Liz takes a slow sip of her drink, adds more gin, then reaches into her purse for a long gold case, pops the clasp, and pulls out a cigar. She clips and trims it over the grass, flips open a fancy lighter, and patiently toasts the end.

Maxine's telling him about July Fourth on Cape Cod when she was a kid. "Fireworks over the sea," she says. "Nothing compares."

Liz finally lights up and puffs, her cheeks drawn in, the cigar at the very center of her mouth. She looks straight at him and doesn't appear angry, certainly not apologetic. And then her face is enshrouded in a dense cloud of smoke.

FROM THE FOOT OF THE STAIRS HE FUTILELY CALLS TO DANIEL over the music. He's about to shout louder but stops himself; his heart still jolts when he hears anyone shouting, flinging him right back to his mother's screams. When Daniel was three he'd wail out his complaints in a pitch identical to Cole's mother's. One time, after Daniel had been whining for an hour about watching another video, Cole left the house to go for a drive, just to distance himself from the sound. Not in a fury or frenzy, but calmly, therapeutically, he took a deep breath of cool air, put the car in reverse, and backed out of the driveway right into a UPS truck. The excitement of the crash brought an end to Daniel's tantrum; he was instantly fascinated, intent on inspecting all the damage. "That's an expensive way to quiet down a kid," Nikki said. "Hey, whatever works."

When he pushes open the bedroom door, it's so dark inside that it takes a moment for his eyes to adjust. Instead of the six or eight kids he expected, there's only Daniel in a recliner working a Game Boy and Little Kirk on his bed playing Nintendo on the TV. Music's blaring and the room reeks of hamburger and onion. The walls are mostly bare except for three centerfolds—a woman on her knees, another in nothing but cowboy boots propped up on a split-rail fence, a third splayed out on a Harley. Daniel swings to his feet and gives his father a quick *Let's go* nod. Then the music cuts off and LK jumps up, too. "You're not leaving already?"

"Yeah," Cole says. "You know, my father."

"Daniel could stay. My dad could drive him home later."

Cole is pleased that he can read the vibe from his son so clearly. "It really helps Phil to settle in if we're both there in the house."

They say their goodbyes in the yard, where Jim calls Daniel a pussy for leaving so early. Cole wants to give Liz a hug, but she doesn't get up from the bench so he bends down into her smoke and kisses her on the cheek. The cigar smells wonderful—pepper and eucalyptus—but up close her face is ashen. "Listen," he whispers, "I'm sorry I upset you."

"Oh, little secrets," Kirk blurts. "Some flames never burn out."

"Shut up, Kirk," Cole says. "You sound like a ten-year-old."

Everybody goes silent. Jim puts down his drink and stands up.

Holding the cigar to her lips, Liz says flatly, "He was just telling me what a fine nephew I have."

After a beat Jim picks up his cup. "Well, I can drink to that. Cheers!" And they all toast LK.

Cole extends a hand to Kirk and they shake, then he and Daniel walk to the car.

Driving back through town he asks, "Good time?"

"Whatever," Daniel says. "It is what it is."

"I thought he'd have more . . . you know, friends." Cole stumbles on the last word because he's not sure Daniel has many friends himself. He's got dozens of people he's close to, but they're more like *associates*. They're contacts, comrades.

"He's always talking about all his buddies," Daniel says, "but his father said the Fourth is just the inner circle. I guess you made the cut." They wait at the one red light in town, the blinker clicking.

He turns left and Daniel gets a text. Accelerating, he can hear how smooth the car's running since the mechanic put in a new fuel filter. The gas tank was corroding inside and out so he had that replaced, too. It feels good knowing there's a spotless zinc-plated tank underneath them, sloshing with super-clean gasoline. The alignment will come next.

Daniel replies to the text and then says, "LK's all right. He knows how to work hard. Hard as anyone. But some of the shit he says, the music he likes, the pictures on his wall, his attitudes . . . I'm not like personally offended, but . . . he's just sort of retrograde."

HIS BODY TEMPERATURE RISES IN BED, WHICH HAS BEEN HAPPEN-ing more and more in the last few years. He sometimes falls asleep and then wakes up in a sweat, his heart racing. The fan blowing on him isn't nearly enough. He bought Daniel his own fan and hopes he's not too hot to sleep. Working under the tobacco nets exhausted is hell.

Daniel didn't say anything else about the party before he went to bed. He's never known much of Cole's past—no family, no old friends, no childhood haunts—and this sudden immersion has to be strange for him. How can he reconcile all he's known until now of his father with this house and Phil, with Liz and Little Kirk? "Retrograde"—ha! His son's rock-solid, and the rush of respect Cole feels for him now makes him suddenly ache for his wife.

He checks his phone for texts, then powers it off. It's nine o'clock in Portland, and his mind keeps veering, as it does most nights when he gets into bed, back to Nikki. Tony fancies himself an aficionado of the latest restaurants, and he imagines they're now finishing a meal and he's bellowing to the owner about the dessert wine, the sort of bluster Cole especially abhors. And then they'll go back to Tony's house, which Cole essentially built, up the staircase made of chestnut that came from a shed in this very town, their hands on the newel post turned by Alex, to the bedroom and its wall of windows he installed with Ben in a soaking February rain.

He cuts himself off. Fuck, he'd love to forget all that shit someday. To never think of it again. Is it possible Liz has truly forgotten so much of their time together? Reels of the summer his mother died play endlessly, unstoppably through his mind: the taste of weed on her fingers after Liz rolled a joint; the sense of escape with her, how together they were flung to another galaxy and when kissing goodbye were dropped with a smack back into their lives; the strange lengthening of time with her, how an afternoon could fill days. And out of nowhere he remembers the currants his father picked last week, gets out of bed and goes downstairs into the back room, flicks on the light and sees the blue-and-white-speckled turkey roaster sitting there on the old broken freezer. He tips back the lid and the sweet, sharp smell makes him shudder like a swig of Robitussin. The mold has grown up so fuzzy it looks like a dead rabbit face-down in the fermented berry slop. He covers it up and can only think, *Nice day for a drive.*

A SUDDEN POUNDING SHAKES THE HOUSE TO ITS BONES, AND Cole's on his feet before he's awake. It's barely daylight and *boom, boom, boom.* He yanks on his shorts and rushes downstairs, where his father winds up and sinks a sledgehammer into the keeping-room wall.

"Stop!" Cole shouts.

Phil turns and stares into his face. "Progress," he says. "No time like the present. If you're not moving forward, you're falling behind." Then he slings the sledgehammer to his shoulder to swing again.

Cole raises his hands and rushes up. "No! We did this room already. It's done." His father's still wound up, so Cole closes his fingers over the hammerhead until he drops it to his side. "This is drywall," he explains, pulling away a broken piece to expose the insulation below. "We did this room years ago."

Phil steps back, scowling. "Not true."

"We did it together. We hung the sheetrock during an ice storm, and the power went out as we—"

"Don't lie to me! I told you not to lie to me."

"Look." Cole tears away the loose chunks and holds them in a stack.

"Tenants must've done this room," Phil says. "And how the hell do we know they did it right? You'll get a fire chute if you don't staple the insulation to the face of the stud. The *face* of the stud. A lot of people have no idea."

"I'll tell you what. I'll cut a big hole back to the studs so we can check. But for now, let's have some breakfast."

Phil goes off to the bathroom, and Cole hides the sledgehammer behind the pantry door.

Daniel's sitting there at the kitchen table eating a crepe with a tall glass of milk. "Dad," he says, "your shorts are on backwards."

Cole looks down at himself and laughs.

"I hope you're not turning into Phil." He takes a bite. "That'd be my cue to get on a plane."

He slaps drywall dust from his hands. "Pretty sure *my* noggin's still screwed on right."

"This house does strange things to people," Daniel says. "I haven't drunk so much milk since I was a little kid. And people start saying things like 'noggin.' It's the regression house."

A WEEK LATER COLE'S OUT FEEDING THE CHICKS AT SEVEN THIRTY on Saturday morning when LK comes shooting down the tractor road on his motorcycle with a milk crate of tools bungeed on back.

Phil's been good most mornings. He was eating an egg he'd boiled himself when Cole came down at seven, and then he went straight upstairs to get to work. Now, even out at the coop, Cole can hear him pounding away. "Is that our boy doing demo already?" Little Kirk asks.

"No sign of *him* yet."

LK glances at his wrist even though he's not wearing a watch. "Bullshit," he says. "It's time to get busy." Then he marches to the house with the squared shoulders and purpose of an admiral.

Cole fills the water founts and then takes a few minutes to look through a stack of invoices that came from Ben Salverson in yesterday's mail. By the time he's strapped on Phil's old tool belt, the boys are in the little upstairs room with his father, plaster dust thick in the air, Daniel pulling the disposable mask away from his mouth to sip coffee, LK shoveling debris into a garbage can. Thirty years ago the room was plumbed for a bathroom, but never got beyond water supply and waste pipes. There's still tearing out to do, so Cole makes long vertical cuts through the wall with a Skilsaw, Phil hands Daniel a crowbar and uses the claws of a hammer himself, and the two of them start popping lath away from the studs. What would Ian think to see these old lath nails going in the trash? Or does he think about any of this at all?

When the can's half full, LK tests the weight and after a couple more shovelfuls squats down to grab hold of it.

"Let Daniel help you with that," Cole tells him.

"Now that's just pussy shit," he says, rising up to heft the barrel onto his back. "It's a one-man carry." He humps it to the door and turns downstairs.

Phil yanks his mask away and spits out the window. "Your boy's a good worker," he tells Cole. "Focused and strong."

"That's the Schaler boy." He clasps his son's shoulder. "Daniel's right here."

Phil's eyes dart around the room suspiciously, as if he's searching for whoever might have left. "Back to it!" he barks. "We don't have all day."

They work a solid morning. When they break for lunch, Cole straddles the windowsill, one leg in and one hanging out, and Phil plants himself on LK's upturned milk crate, both eating sandwiches from paper towels. Cole believes his father needs to talk about what happened, that to allow him to slip into the fog that's waiting for him and eventually die without ever confronting his deeds face-to-face with at least one of his children would condemn him to a Hieronymus Bosch triptych.

The boys have finished their lunch outside in the shade. Little Kirk tosses a football from one hand to the other, grips the threads and cocks his arm as if to pass, then spins it to the other hand. Daniel twirls a Frisbee on the tip of his finger. Each has so little competence or interest in the other's instrument, it's as if they've come from different planets.

Cole and his father are tired and dirty, looking at the morning's progress and contemplating all that's left to do. There's satisfaction in demolition, but until construction begins you're aware that the difficult labor has only taken you backwards, that everything's less livable than when you started.

"So what's it like being back in the house?" Cole asks.

"I just want to get 'er done. Get this place right. You know, for . . . I suppose for posterity."

He lets his father believe in this pipe dream, though they don't have a prayer of ever finishing the house. His hope is to get the upstairs bathroom in, insulate and sheetrock the rooms with bare walls, and swap out a few light fixtures. He can cover that on his credit card along with the tools he bought last week. He'll get a short-term loan against the sale of the house and hire roofers; he fears the old oil burner might not pass inspection, so he'll have that replaced, too. He plans to contact realtors toward the end of the summer, hoping the house sells in the fall.

Though he's been in touch with the VA, he's frustrated as hell not to have gotten any real answers yet. The appointment with the neurologist is still a month out. He's been to the town hall and paid the real-estate taxes. More on the credit card. Incredibly, his father owns the house outright; Raymond paid it off years ago and kept up on the taxes until he died.

Meanwhile, he's been reading about competency paperwork and he spoke to a lawyer last week. Everything will be easier if he can move ahead on Phil's behalf.

And that's been the shape of his days. He makes Daniel breakfast and drops him at Boulger, then comes back and works with his father on the house. He makes dinner and Daniel devours enormous amounts of food, dusty from the fields, his hands black from tobacco resin. The smell of him—tobacco and dirt and sweat—in this kitchen, with Phil at the head of the table, can make Cole forget he has any life beyond this house. He can almost imagine that Kelly might walk in the door at any moment, that if he looks back over his shoulder he'll see his mother at the stove.

13

"I COULD'VE DONE IT *TEN TIMES* MYSELF BY NOW!" SHE'S STILL IN church clothes, covered by her apron, pointing a mixing spoon at Cole, who hasn't started vacuuming yet. Kelly's cleaning the bathroom, Ian helping their father pick up tools in the keeping room. It's Tilly's sixtieth birthday party, July 19th, and nothing is ready, nothing is right.

"How could we have come to this? Is it so much to ask for? First I can't have raised paneling, then you can't even get it done by Mother's birthday. What did I say in June? In *March,* for God's sake? I remember exactly when it was, because the kids were on spring break and we were making the big push to finish the insulation upstairs and Tom Mace came over on the Sunday before the kids went back to school and we were all insulating and I told him *raised paneling,* installed, sanded, and painted—*all finished*—by July nineteenth. We agreed. We were *in agreement.* I had your word. And the raised paneling goes out the window because Tom Mace wants to try something different. Does Tom Mace even know how to make raised panels, I'd like to know. I can't help noticing he's got raised paneling in *his* house. And now for Mother's birthday party, for which I've been promising the room would be done, a little chance to show off all we've accomplished, we've got a construction zone. Might as well hold the party in a shed. Mother's sixtieth birthday. In a half-built warehouse. Good Lord, Phil. The day that I have as much say around here as Tom Mace will be a glorious day indeed. I mean, a year or two living in chaos is one thing, but when it becomes an eternity, when it's all we know as a family, when it takes over our marriage . . ."

Cole pulls the Electrolux through the keeping room, past his father on his knees, rolling up insulation. Ian sweeps sawdust, bent nails, and puffs of pink fiberglass into a dustpan, then sprinkles it on top of the already heaping garbage can.

"Done by Mother's birthday. You and Tom Mace looked me in the eye and promised."

Through the parlor he drags the vacuum behind him, and hears one last word before switching the machine on again: "Ludicrous!" He climbs the stairs and works down from the top, the suction hushing, grit ringing through the metal wand, and is it the clack of the door latch at the bottom of the stairs that makes him turn, or a glimpse of her shadow, or the smell of her blood? One foot on the bottom step, hands cupped at her chin, she bursts out sobbing and blood leaks down her wrist and onto her blouse. He sets the vac on the landing and, still gripping the wand, opens his arms as she staggers up into them, her back heaving and hot. They sit down on a step and she leans into his chest, his bare arms sticky on her bare shoulders, and when his father comes through the doorway at the bottom of the stairs, Cole's arms flinch, tightening his hold on his mother. His father looks very small down there, reaching up toward them with a sandwich baggie of ice, three cubes. *He doesn't even know where she keeps the fucking ice bag.* His mother lifts her head and sees him, then buries her face back in her hands, wailing over the howl of the vacuum, and his father hasn't taken another step toward them, still just reaching, both of his parents waiting for him to call the next shot. And Cole stretches his arm down while his father climbs two steps up, then two more, and gives him the plastic bag of ice, their hands brushing. His father's eyes are downcast, or not even. Looking neither at Cole nor at anything else, his eyes blinking, his face twitching. His emotions are firing but he has no idea what they are, cannot discern between rage and remorse, sympathy or contempt, a short circuit visible in his nonexpression. Years later, it will be this face he sees when Phil—a decade after killing her—tells him, "She'd nag and nag until I finally hit her, so at the end I was always the bad guy." He'll remember his father at the bottom of the stairs appearing tiny, foreshortened, and there will come the nights when he can't stop seeing that image, sleepless in bed, his arms wrapped around Nikki's back, his leg against her thigh as she breathes heavily in deep sleep. And then he'll realize that this was his role in the family, to comfort his mother afterward, not to protect her before. To harmonize through jokes and upbeat filibuster and misdirection, to tamp down escalation: *Don't set them off!* He'll use these same techniques when Daniel is a toddler—"Guess what kind of bird I saw?" "Look at that school bus!"—and like Daniel they are children. Children with children. Cole's role is to keep the peace, but when he fails he doesn't protect her, merely waits to comfort her in the aftermath.

Her blood drips on the stairs. He gives her the ice and she holds it to her mouth. With a glance he dismisses his father. He rocks her, he murmurs.

THEY ARRIVE IN TILLY'S CADILLAC, UNCLE ANDREW BEHIND THE wheel. He gets out, tall and lanky, and stretches his back before swinging the door shut. He's a runner, a high-school math teacher and track coach on his second marriage. He has traveled the country running marathons, and in Boston and New York he places high in his age group; in smaller marathons he sometimes wins; he founded the Bloomfield Runners Club and for years has trained his students on weekends and summer break; he is a disappointment to his mother. Between her third and fourth Scotch, Tilly will ring the ice in her glass like a service bell, at which Uncle Andrew fetches the bottle, and she'll mutter "No ambition" as he pours. Somehow he's immune. In fact he dotes on her—cleaning her gutters, washing windows, chauffeuring, refilling her drink so attentively he sometimes has to carry her to the car.

Around the long hood of the Coupe de Ville, he opens Tilly's door. "Happy day!" he calls to Cole and his mother, who are spreading a floral linen tablecloth from Marks & Tilly over the picnic table. His mother has moved the party outside where they won't have to eat *in the midst of dust and drop cloths and debris,* but the main reason is so she can wear the big round sunglasses that are hiding much of her face.

Kelly comes out from the kitchen and weaves between the dump pile and the heap of lath waiting to be pounded. On the table in the shade of the pear tree, she sets down a tray with the ice bucket, three short glasses, a bowl of potato chips, and a bottle of Cutty Sark.

Tilly has made no move from the car, though Sandy has emerged from the backseat and is stepping carefully across the grass in platform sandals—four or five inches of cork sole strapped to her feet. She's tiny, no taller than a middle schooler, and she wears them to shrink the gap between her and Andrew. To meet her in running shoes—she, too, is a fiery distance runner, one of Andrew's former students—is to encounter a person so significantly shorter that Cole has to remind himself this isn't Sandy's little sister. Liz is small. Sandy is miniature. She's twenty-seven. Her college graduation coincided with Uncle Andrew's divorce, and only later will Cole learn how her high-school graduation and the team's trip to the New York City Marathon coincided with rancorous flash points in Andrew's first marriage.

The car horn blows, and through the windshield Cole sees Tilly reaching across the wide front seat to the wheel. "Go," his mother says.

He makes a beeline for the car before she blows the horn again—it's exactly what gets under his father's skin. "Howdy, Cole," Sandy says as they pass each other by the currant bushes. In a few months she'll start trying to mother him, but for now she's his young new aunt in heavy turquoise-and-silver jewelry and a thick brown pony-tail that hangs to her waist.

Uncle Andrew steps aside, a grandiose footman, and Cole bends down to kiss his grandmother on the cheek. "Happy birthday, Tilly. You look lovely." Beneath the brim of her sun hat, he can see she's had her hair done, as she does every week, in the style of Pat Nixon, the same watery-lemonade color. She's wearing pearls and a very smart pink and black dress that must have come back with her from London. "All set to party?" Cole says.

She checks her lipstick in the visor mirror. "Where is everyone?"

"Getting ready." Not precisely true. He looks out into the yard and sees that his mother's no longer there. She's gone inside to round up the rest of the family. His sister comes back out first and bends down into the car. "Happy birthday, Tilly," she says, kissing her cheek. "That's a lovely hat."

"Thank you, dear. What's that you're wearing?"

"They're shorts."

"*I'll* say." She squeezes Kelly's knee. "You're a leggy thing, aren't you?"

Kelly steps back, relieved to see Ian at her shoulder.

"Happy birthday, Tilly," he says. "You look lovely."

She pinches his cheek. "What grade are you in now?"

"Going on sixth."

"And still the baby fat."

At the picnic table, Sandy's pouring a drink.

"And where's the master of the house?" Tilly asks.

"Shaving," Ian says.

"At this hour?"

Ian stammers, fearing he's said something wrong.

"Grandpapa always shaved and put on a clean white shirt before he even took his morning tea."

"My dad drinks coffee," Ian says.

"Give Tilly your arm." She grabs hold of him and steps from the car, adjusting her white straw hat with its clump of cloth flowers on the wide brim. In a motley procession, Tilly and Ian out front, Cole and Kelly trailing off to the sides, Uncle Andrew bringing up the rear as he stretches his shoulders and wrists, they're all looking off at different angles and don't even seem to be moving in the same direction.

Sandy sits in the grass under the pear tree, stirring Scotch and ice cubes in a glass with her finger. Uncle Andrew pours a stiff one for Tilly. And with her first sip, her eyes brighten. She pats her purse, but her son jumps in and withdraws a slim cigarette from an enamel case and holds a flame before her. She takes two quick drags and a gulp of Scotch, then says, "There's a story, you know, about Grandpapa and the neighbors' lavender house." Cole, Kelly, and Ian all exchange glances, holding back smirks. "This is in Windsor Locks, mind you, the house directly across the street. The Flanagans. Mr. Flanagan was some sort of . . . oh, I don't know, a warehouse foreman or a trucking dispatcher. Heavy black shoes and white socks and lunch pail, though he did wear a collar. Well. Grandpapa comes home from the bank and sees Mr. Flanagan painting his house, which is all well and good, but the new color is lavender. Good Lord, he couldn't even eat his dinner. He closed all the curtains but still couldn't read the evening paper. He didn't sleep a wink. He'd roll over in his grave if he knew I was even revealing to his scions that we *ever* lived across the street from a house painted lavender."

"What did he do?" Andrew asks, although he could tell this story himself.

Tilly releases smoke from deep in her lungs. "We moved. What else could we do?" She waits for their reactions. "Grandpapa was a learned man. Such a shame you children didn't have more time under his tutelage. He lived in his mind. Literature, mathematics, accounts. He simply lacked the constitution to confront a burly laborer about delicate matters of class. A truly refined man."

Cole's mother comes around the dump pile, carrying a tray. His sister jumps up as if to lend a hand, when surely she plans to escape into the house. But his mother intercepts her and passes her the tray, so she returns to the picnic table with deviled eggs, a brick of Cracker Barrel cheese, a bowl of melba toast. "Grandpapa of course never had a radio in his car. Couldn't bear the racket. He appreciated what peacefulness can bring to the mind."

Cole's watching Sandy, sitting cross-legged with a magazine open on the grass in front of her, flipping pages. She makes no effort to conceal that she's not listening. She smiles over something she's just read and then snaps the page over, her necklace and bracelets clacking. *Andrew doesn't beat her.* Even as Cole thinks it he knows it's a strange thought, but not too long ago he assumed that all men eventually beat their wives. He'd also believed that the first beating he remembered was the first ever. There was that morning on the school bus when Vanessa Jones looked frightened and exhausted, and he did some nonsense math to figure out that given her age and her siblings and how long her parents had probably been married, yes, last night was the first time it happened in her house. Back then, horrified by what he would inevitably become, Cole had decided to never get married.

"He could not *fathom* sports," Tilly says. "Couldn't even begin to understand the basic rules. *I* knew more about baseball than he."

Sandy is too at ease to be a beaten woman.

Kelly successfully escapes on her next try and Uncle Andrew and Cole's mother have wandered across the yard, where he's inspecting the young ears on their cornstalks while they talk. Even from this distance he can see Andrew's face is grave; like peeking around a curtain, he looks for what she's hiding behind her sunglasses. She's telling him it's happened again, Cole supposes. She's telling him that her husband won't talk with her, just flies off the handle, too stressed out, all of them, this whole house, this whole life, it's too much. Cole can see Andrew's body slump helplessly. Does she say "hit me," "beat me," "knocked me around," "got a little rough"? After one beating she told Cole, "It happens in the best of marriages. Grandpapa could be a pill." And it was a few years before he realized she meant that Grandpapa beat Tilly. *A pill.*

She blows her nose, reaches under her glasses with a tissue to wipe her eyes, which Tilly notices and then figures out what's going on, but she doesn't miss a beat, still telling the story to Ian, Sandy, and Cole. "Simsbury was more suitable, truly. When the realtor told us that a neighborhood ordinance prohibited hanging laundry on a clothesline, Grandpapa signed the documents in an instant."

Andrew pulls his ankle up to his butt to stretch his quad, holding on to an old clothesline post that just yesterday Cole nailed a square of plywood to, mounted with a sharp stainless-steel hook. The first litter of rabbits, from the female who arrived pregnant, will be big enough to slaughter by the end of the summer. A week ago, Cole's father took him and Ian to the breeder's so they could all learn how to do it. They watched him demonstrate, quick and effortless; then they bungled through a few attempts themselves. You club the rabbits at the back of the neck, then impale a rear leg on the hook between the two bones just above the ankle, tug down on their ears, and slit their throats. If you do it well, the fur doesn't get bloody, and with a few slices around the feet and rump you can peel the coat off like a tight shirt. The breeder sold them a knife, a hook, and the rabbits they'd slaughtered, and Ian cried all the way home. Now Andrew leans into the pole to stretch his calves, the square of plywood still unbloodied, like gallows built from fresh lumber in Westerns, then he hangs his arm over his sister's shoulder and walks her toward them.

"Happy birthday," Cole's mother says.

Tilly feigns surprise. "Oh, *there* you are." She presents her cheek to be kissed.

"Ian, dear," their mother says, "get Tilly a lawn chair. Sitting on a wooden bench"—she shakes her head—"on your *birthday*."

Cole slides in behind the commotion to refill Tilly's glass—"A gentleman," she intones without turning to see him, then cocks her head at Andrew, who fusses over her with more ice. One cube? two? "No!" she snaps, slapping his hand—so nobody sees Cole pour a tall plastic cup half-full of Scotch before topping it off with lemonade. Ian drags up a chair. Cole tips a splash from the bottle into Sandy's glass; she stirs and sucks her finger. He sits near her in the grass and sips his own drink, the taste of Lemon Pledge and *cleaning for company*: behind schedule, no hot water, burned meat, yells crescendo-ing, a backhand, a trickle of blood, then putting on a good face for the guests. He puts the cup to his lips and swallows it all down, then he goes up to his room, takes a couple bong hits, and comes back outside to the picnic table wearing sunglasses himself. His mother and Andrew are laughing at Tilly's story about Atlantic City, and by the butchering post his father's pouring briquettes into the barbecue. On the breeze Cole smells charcoal dust and old meat and grease. He smells the henhouse, the ammonia sting of rabbit piss, his father's scalp. And his father is streaming more and more lighter fluid on the volcano of briquettes, squirting practically the whole can, so once he strikes the match the charcoal, the grill, and even the cook himself will vaporize. *Poof!* Greasy black smoke slithers skyward in twitchy flames.

His father then starts toward them, calling up his military stride, which he does less and less. He's become more of a stare-at-his-feet sort of walker, a reluctant, I'd-rather-not-be-joining-you shambler. "Happy birthday," he says. "Good of you to come." What does that fucking mean? It's *her* party.

"Indeed," she replies.

"The strangest thing," Cole's mother says. "Who walks into the Avon store but Ella Grasso."

Tilly registers surprise, but quickly catches herself. "And?"

"Madame Governor herself. Shopping in *your store*."

Everyone can see she's pleased. "Why do you imply she wouldn't? Please don't insult everything I've built."

"What did she buy?" Andrew asks.

"The whole place. A dozen of everything," Cole's father says. "She spent twenty thousand dollars in five minutes." He turns and goes back to the house.

No one says anything for a moment until finally Ian speaks up. "Really?"

"No, dear. Your father sold her a potholder. Gift-wrapped."

As the sun drops lower it feels hotter and they heft the picnic table to follow the shade, closer now to the chicken house, so once they're eating the rice, salad, grilled chicken, and rabbit the smell of the coop and hutch are strong, and in fact the rabbit meat *does* taste like a hutch, like the smell of their fur and fear. He washes the food down with another Pledge cocktail, aware that he's shitfaced, but with sunglasses hiding his eyes, it's easy to act normal. He doesn't speak. He just goes through the motions. He and his mother both— behind their sunglasses—acting natural. Stiff upper lip.

TWO MONTHS FROM NOW UNCLE ANDREW WILL MOVE TO A BIGGER house and make a good home for all of them. He'll sell his Corolla with the dented hood and the "Get High: Go Running" bumper sticker to buy a used Chevy Nova that fits five. Sandy will make family dinners and go to parent-teacher conferences. Everyone at their new school in Bloomfield will know that the math teacher's their uncle. They'll know about "the tragedy." Cole will blush with shame whenever anyone whispers anything in his presence.

Uncle Andrew will turn forty-five that fall, entering a new age bracket, and he'll train more rigorously to rank even higher now that he's younger than his competition. He'll be happy to include anyone who wants to hop on a bike and join him on his long runs in the evening or to races around New England on weekends; if not, he goes it alone. Cole eavesdrops on tense discussions between him and Sandy, hears her call him selfish. "But I could potentially *win* my bracket in Philadelphia" is, to Andrew, irrefutable and unarguable.

Consequently, Sandy will handle most of the parenting, or in the case of Kelly more like big-sistering. She takes her to a Rickie Lee Jones concert, which is so far off the mark that the next day Kelly calls several military academies around the country to request applications. And by January she's enrolled in the North Carolina Air and Sea Institute, a boarding school that Tilly pays for. She'll also pay college tuition for all three of them. The night before they pack Kelly off, Sandy bakes a cake. She's sitting cross-legged in the middle of their kitchen floor stirring batter in the big pottery bowl, keeping the bowl to one side of her lap because Ian's lying on the floor with his head propped up on her hip. She dips her fingertip into the batter and gives him a taste.

Uncle Andrew is out on his last long run before next week's marathon. Cole graphs parabolas on x- and y-axes at the kitchen table. And Kelly is doing pushups, clapping her hands midair and then catching herself before she hits the floor. She'll act grateful for the send-off meal, although she'll refuse her slice of cake. It's the first time Cole hears the term "body mass index."

He and Ian feel the hole left by her absence, and feel themselves falling into it. They're simply more *alone* with Kelly gone—from five to three to two. Cole writes her letters, and makes sure all three of them talk on the phone every few weeks, but he still comes to resent her for abandoning them. Ian's reaction is difficult to pin down: over the next year he trades off between sullenness, anger, and withdrawal. "Maybe he'd like the Boy Scouts," Cole suggests to Sandy, but her approach is to snuggle with him on the couch and lie with him in bed until he falls asleep. At times Cole thinks their relationship has become too secretive and cuddly and nonverbal. They're both five feet tall, both lean and hazel-eyed. They curl up together on the couch watching the sitcoms that Ian likes; she makes them herbal tea at commercials; he reaches for the afghan and pulls it up to their chins. All this time Uncle Andrew is grading homework and tests, reading about wind sprints and fartleks, or making plans on the phone with his star runners.

"Do you think you could get Ian running?" Cole urges him. "In a few years," Andrew says, and instead takes the boys to watch track meets and hockey games, and one night to see Kenny Loggins at the Hartford Civic Center. Andrew talks through much of the concert, bragging that there are no obstructed views in the arena because the roof doesn't require any posts to support it, as if he'd designed it himself. All the way home their car slips and slides in a blizzard, and a few hours after the concert, in the middle of the night when no one is present to witness it, the Civic Center roof collapses under the weight of snow.

When he hears Ian crying in his room at night, Cole lets himself in and sits on the edge of the bed as his brother rolls away from him. "It's all going to be okay," he says, and hears the same voice he used to soothe him after their parents fought. Ian recognizes this voice, too—even the words are the same—and Cole can feel his brother's bitter anger through the blankets. He's desperate to help Ian, and asks Sandy if he shouldn't start seeing a counselor again. She makes the arrangements, but Ian refuses, arms crossed, lips pursed, shaking his head.

Since he's taking extra courses, Cole studies long hours every night. There are a few kids at school who he sits with at lunch, but he knows they're dying to talk about the one thing Cole avoids, so he always cuts it off. There are also kids who approach him with sympathy, even charity, and he recoils from them even more quickly. He assumes it's much the same at school for Ian.

That summer, he works tobacco for a different company in different fields. Nobody here knows anything about him. The easy-flowing Spanish and musical Jamaican French sound like escape, like he's already far away. He tells everyone his name is Pedro.

Ian is in bed every night by nine thirty. Half an hour later, Sandy goes out back to the hot tub, an evening ritual she and Andrew used to share. One time when they have friends over for dinner Sandy blurts, a little drunk, "But now the hot tub makes his knees swell, so I soak alone and he gets into bed and puts bags of frozen peas on his joints. Can't have anything swelling up in bed, can we, Andrew?"

She's curvy. She looks sexy in her sweater-dresses. Her thighs are muscular from running and her hips are round. She hangs her robe on a peg and jiggles across the deck. From his darkened bedroom, his curtains barely parted, he watches her settle down into the tub. She soaks for a while, rises up to the edge with the steam pouring off her body, sinks back in the water, then out again into the open air. Turned straight toward his window, she's slow and patient, and so is he, silently climaxing. His own nightly ritual.

When Cole is in college, he'll learn from Ian that Sandy's pregnant. A baby boy. Ian doesn't take the intrusion well, and in phone calls and letters he says she's become distant. "Everything she's got goes to the baby. We don't talk like we used to. We don't go to movies or out to eat. She barely cooks anymore. I eat cereal and Ragú and tuna fish. It's like we're all in our own little orbits now."

"What about Andrew?"

"Since his surgery, he cycles. Everything's all about cycling."

"Another surgery?"

"Last spring. Jesus, Cole, you don't know anything. He blew out his knee."

In one such call Cole makes a proposal: "How about this summer you come to Seattle? You've been talking about learning Japanese, and there's a program here at UDub. One of my roommates is moving out for the summer. You'd have to get a job to pay expenses, but I'll write Tilly to ask if she'll cover the tuition."

"Yes. Holy shit, yes!" He feels his brother beaming through three thousand miles of copper wire.

But before that, before Cole leaves his aunt and uncle's house in

Bloomfield, when he's devoting all he's got to finishing his spring courses in good standing so he can go off to the University of Washington a year early at seventeen and a half, he slips into his bedroom one night without flipping on the light and walks to the parted curtain at the window, but Sandy doesn't come out to the tub. Although he's often felt shame over his voyeurism, this time he feels stood up. He'd heard her go out the back door, the wind chimes on the steps, so he waits. But finally he goes downstairs, stopping and listening in the kitchen, tiptoeing into the mud room, then sees her out the back-door window, sitting on the steps leading down to the deck, face in her hands, back heaving. He yanks open the door and rushes to her side, and she turns to him, startled, as he grabs her arms and examines her in a panic: her face, her wrists, her throat. Until he's sure she's okay, he doesn't even realize what he's doing. And simultaneously, as she understands too, her face collapses. She starts crying again, her arms going limp, and now he's holding her. "It's going to be all right," he murmurs. He rocks her, and after a time her jerky breathing settles down. They sit in silence, a warm breeze tinkling the chimes, and he thinks how much this feels like holding Liz.

The next day, after acing an AP history exam, Cole slams his locker, springs down the school steps, and cuts along the soccer fields to go home. He waves to his uncle across the track, but Andrew doesn't notice him because he's stretching in the grass with Ruthie Jacks, a senior hurdler and sprinter. He slows his pace, watching his uncle jump up and then reach out a hand to pull Ruthie to her feet. They walk side by side toward the gym, their heads inclined toward each other. He bumps her with his hip and she slaps his shoulder, both of them laughing, and now Cole gets it.

That night Andrew's out at a runners club meeting in preparation for their trip to the Marine Corps marathon. Cole sits on the edge of Ian's bed. "Last night was even worse," his brother says. He's been having nightmares. "I'm pounding lath in the backyard and when I lift off a piece I see Mom's dead under the pile, but I can't stop myself in time and I swing the hammer and hit her cheek . . ." He breaks off in tears. "I'm afraid to go to sleep."

"I miss her too," Cole says, then squeezes his shoulder. "You know we'll be in really close touch after I go to Seattle, right? You'll come visit me. You're always going to be my little brother."

After he's spent another half an hour on math, Sandy slaps off the TV. She passes through the kitchen and he looks up from his graph paper and compass, and they share a glance, both of them thinking Andrew should be home by now. Then she changes into her robe and goes out the back door.

After last night, and knowing what he knows, he doesn't go upstairs to his window. He's pissed off at his uncle, worried about Sandy, and scared by what this might mean for his brother.

He stacks his books, and when he reaches past the fridge to turn off the light he can hear her whimpering on the steps again. He listens for a minute before opening the door. She stiffens, then turns, anger set hard in her face until she sees it's him and not her husband. Eyes softening, she says, "I'm sorry. I didn't think you'd hear me."

He sits beside her, taking her into his arms, and she seems to break into pieces, shaking in a fit of sobbing, and he remembers holding his mother that night before filling the ice bag, before the bruise blew up on her cheek. If he'd called the police then, or if he'd gone downstairs and dragged his father off the couch and beaten him half to death right then and there, she'd still be alive.

A car comes down the road and she lifts away from him slowly, as if they're fused with tears and phlegm and body heat. Andrew's headlights swing into the driveway.

In bed he's slow to fall asleep, and soon after, awakened by a cry, he hurtles down the stairs. Andrew's shadowed back looms over Sandy, huddled in her robe on the ottoman, her face in her hands. His arm is raised. Cole yanks his wrist—"Off of her!"—and twists him around, punching him right on the mouth—"I'll fucking kill you!"—punching over and over as glass shatters and somebody shouts "Stop!" They're pleading, piling on him, and pulling at his arms as he holds Andrew down by the collar, and then he realizes that it's Sandy and Ian who are trying to restrain him.

In smoldering light, Andrew, on the ottoman, holds a bag of frozen peas to his face. Ian, in his pajamas, weeps silently into Sandy's chest. She strokes his hair. She's staring at Cole as if from miles away. "He would never," she says, shaking her head, baffled. Not bruised, not whimpering. "Never." Cole makes a fist and examines the blood on his knuckles, either Andrew's or his own. A lamp has crashed over and paper-thin shards of broken bulb litter the floor.

BUT THAT'S STILL TWO YEARS AWAY, AND FOR NOW SANDY IS HIS cool aunt sitting in the grass and leaning against the trunk of the pear tree, stirring Scotch and rocks with her finger. "Grandpapa," she whispers to Cole. "More time under his tutelage." She smirks. What Cole remembers of Grandpapa is his breakfast beer in a tall glass, the silver monogram flaking off, draped with a Kleenex to keep out the fruit flies and set on the counter overnight because his stomach couldn't handle carbonation. Feeble from diseased intestines, no longer strong enough to beat his wife, and so effete he had to move to another town to escape that lavender house. He loved *Moby-Dick*, the *Odyssey*, and *For Whom the Bell Tolls*. He loved to smoke Chesterfields and watch *Carol Burnett*. Cole is unable to sculpt these aspects into a coherent vision of an actual man.

The plates are piled with rabbit bones and chicken skin and gnawed corncobs. He drains his drink. He'll head upstairs in a minute for another bong hit. His mother's carrying a cake. There'll be singing and flames.

14

THE SEARCH FOR OSAMA BIN LADEN CONTINUES. AS THEY WAIT AT
the bank, Cole's reading an article in *Time* that quotes anonymous
sources as saying they're certain he's in a particular cave among a
vast complex of caves that have been inhabited and fortified for a
thousand years, but when the Rangers swooped in, they found only
small boys with goats. There's an accompanying photograph of Sad-
dam Hussein after he was pulled from his spider hole, disoriented
and weary, his hand at his throat as if he knew what was coming next.

Finally they're invited to the desk. "This sounds like a big project," says the young manager with gelled hair, whose tag reads simply
"Levi." "And just about all sweat equity."

"I'm a contractor," Cole tells him. "And I've got a couple strong
boys to help. I'll bid out the roof and the furnace, but we can handle
the rest."

"It's still a sizable loan," Levi says to Phil. It's his house, so it's his
loan.

"And an impressive property," Cole says. "Money well spent."

"As for repayment, I don't see any income other than—"

"That'll come out of the sale."

"But in this market—"

"I can cover the payments till then. Do you need me to cosign?
I'm more than happy to." Even as he says this he knows the cash he

laid out for the shed has left the business short, and that their personal finances are currently being examined by a divorce mediator.

Levi flips the pages, staring at the figures.

"It's a beautiful old colonial," Cole says. "When we're done, someone'll snatch it up in an instant. This is what I do for a living."

"Where's your business located?"

"Gotcha!" Phil has been silent, but now jumps forward in his chair and plants an elbow on the edge of Levi's desk. "'*Business*' is right. What's all this snatching and selling?" He reeks. Even with the long days of demolition he hasn't been showering. Plaster dust is caked in the furrows at the back of his neck.

"We talked it through, Dad. Once the house is in sellable condition we'll get a good price."

"And where does your big-business scheming leave me? Have you thought about that?"

"I told you, we'll find a place for you that's more manageable."

"What the hell kind of place?" As his voice sharpens, so does the sour smell in his clothes.

"One that makes more sense for you."

"A facility!" He's nearly shouting, and Levi looks over their shoulders, scanning the bank, uncomfortable. "An institution!"

"No, Dad. Just a—"

"I've *done* institutions and I ain't going back. I'll live in my car again before I do that. You can nag and push and taunt. *Beg* me to do it. Ganging up with her to humiliate me with that store in a shit location. Burger King grease wafting in. Doomed for failure—just what she intended." He pounds the desk with his fist. "And now you and sonny boy here"—he stabs a finger at Levi—"think you can run me out of my own house and lock me up and steal everything I've ever worked for, the only thing I've got. There's *gallons* of sweat equity in that house already. I was sweating over that house when you were still pissing in your bed, so don't start in with 'This is what I do for a living.' *She* wanted this house. She and her mother. The queen of fucking England—"

"Mr. Callahan," Levi says, flustered. "Please." He stands up and motions for them to shove off, his hands shaking. "Keep your voice down."

"Exactly," Phil says. "She could never just shut the hell up."

Cole maneuvers him out of the bank and into the car. Hot air blows in the windows as he drives. Both sweating, they doubtless look crazed in the heat. "Everything was A-OK till you and your boy showed up. I was making progress on the house, working through the rooms. Didn't you see I painted the two front bedrooms? I don't know what the hell the renters were doing in there, and I don't want to know. Mouse shit everywhere. Nests in a bureau and the kitchen cabinets. But I made the rooms look nice. Just in time for you to prance in and try to take over. Well, nobody's stealing my house out from under me, you got that? I don't see jackshit of you for ten years and suddenly you fly across the country to steal my house. And what about your own house? And your *wife*? Where the hell's she in all of this? Huh? She's eating her meals at another man's table, isn't she? Somebody else is ringing her register. I know what's going on. I hear your whispering and phone calls. And the boy's, too. You're just standing by while some other guy punches his time card in your clock. Let me tell you, boy, among the men I spent some time with there's only one way to deal with a snake in your grass, and running across the country to rob an old man ain't it. Where I come from they got names for men like you, and these are not respectful names. You're weak! An oversized weakling who whines just as bad as she did. 'Wah, wah, wah. My momma's an angel and my daddy's a brute.' What does your boy think of *you*? 'My daddy's a chump and momma's a whore—'"

Cole punches the steering wheel and pounds the brakes. The tires screech. "Shut your fucking mouth!" he screams, staring his father down.

Phil's sagging eyes startle wide, but as the smell of smoking rubber drifts into the car a smile creeps onto his lips. He squints at Cole's tight fist, raised to strike. "You want to hit me, don't you? One quick jab to the mouth." He forces a laugh. "Ha! Anything to shut me up, right?"

Having half-lunged toward him, Cole slowly uncoils and lets his fists go slack. He grips the wheel and drops his foot off the brake, but the car doesn't move. He hits the gas and they lurch forward, then stop. He reaches down to the floor to pull up the brake pedal and jiggles the hand brake until they finally start rolling again.

"What's worse," Phil says, "wanting to punch an old man or not having the balls to do it?"

Cole thinks *blind with rage* as he tries to focus on the road ahead, sweat running in his eyes, his heart and breath in a lathering gallop, his false calm utterly unconvincing. He's squeezing the wheel to keep his hands from shaking, and as they rise up and crest a hill he brakes and the car shudders all the way to the stop sign at the bottom. He's broken something in the pedal or the lines—he has no idea what. His father gasps, and when Cole glances over he's staring straight ahead down Old Newgate Road toward their house, where smoke's pouring into the sky. Phil must've left the stove on, messed with some wiring, tried to repair the furnace. Is Daniel at work?—he looks at his watch—yes, thank God, he's definitely not home.

He hits the gas and the tires spin out in gravel. Beyond the sheds and stand of willows there's a wall of smoke. He speeds around the curve, an impossible gray expanse, from the road right back to the tree line. Flames shimmer as they get closer, the house completely obscured. But he does see a fire truck on the tractor road, and a tobacco bus and a Taybro pickup. He floors the last stretch but then hits the brakes, the car bucking and grinding as they pass through thick smoke drifting over the road. A police car looms in their driveway, and irrationally Cole's seized by panic, his heart misfiring as he suddenly fears for Daniel's safety—irrational because the house itself isn't on fire and there's a line of men spaced fifty feet apart edging the tobacco field at the back of their yard, where all twenty acres are burning.

He pulls in behind the cruiser and the cop flips on his blue lights, spinning in their eyes and reflecting off the towering smoke, then he climbs out and waves them off. Cole sticks his head out the window: "We live here." The cop gazes at the house for a moment—a poor appraisal, judging by the curl of his lip—and then walks over, eyeballing the car and ticking off offenses, legal and otherwise. The fire hums like a crowd mumbling and muttering, urgent with the occasional snap and crack. "Your name, sir?"

"Cole Callahan."

He leans down to peer across to the passenger seat. "And you, sir?"

Phil stares straight ahead. Silent.

"Sir?"

"He's Philip Callahan," Cole tells him. "The homeowner."

The cop is nodding, first just his head but then somehow with his full torso. "Callahan," he says. "I see."

The wind shifts and they're all breathing smoke from wet tobacco, like burning soggy compost. "Is it wire worm?" Cole asks.

The cop puts a handkerchief to his mouth. "Blue mold," he says. "You can back onto the shoulder and let me out." He leans down once more and looks at Phil. "You have a good day, Mr. Callahan," but Phil keeps staring out the windshield.

"Asshole," he says when the cop's taken only a few steps away.

"Quiet," Cole hisses.

When they get out of the car, they stand at the head of the driveway surrounded on two sides by flames. From this spot in Cole's boyhood backyard, it looks like the whole earth is on fire, quickly closing in.

. . .

THE SECOND PRIMING IS DONE IN MOST OF THE FIELDS, AND THEIR shed—the one they've been coming to for much of the summer—is half loaded. The leaves hanging high above them, picked today or yesterday, release a clove-and-maple-syrup scent that drifts down onto them in the darkness. Liz is deeply asleep, drooling on his bare chest. And soon he falls asleep too, and he dreams what becomes his recurring dream: with Liz in a shed, flames blaze up the walls all around them, and he pulls her to her feet, grabbing up their clothes in his arms; at full sprint he drives his shoulder into a vent and they squeeze out between the boards into fiercely bright sunlight, naked and clutching at each other, cringing in the face of the flames, and though they're now safe on the tobacco road, barefoot in the soft dirt, Cole somehow knows this is the end.

Years later, when he's studying art history in college, images from Renaissance paintings of the expulsion from the Garden of Eden—cringing, naked, culpable, and no longer innocent—will follow him into sleep, so the dream, like memories, will develop over time.

Drool trickles down his ribs, waking him from his nightmare, and soon they're on his bike in the moonlight, Liz's thumbs hooked in the belt loops of his cutoffs, passing the cemetery and the bank. On the short road to Liz's house they hear the first siren. He rides across the side yard and they jump off behind the lilac bush in the dark, crouching down on the ground as Kirk's Chevelle barrels into the driveway. He's killed the headlights before the car even stops. A fire truck rumbles by, then another, followed by a police car speeding around the corner. In the sky now, over the trees, firelight begins to glow.

They back deeper into the bushes. Kirk shuts off the engine but doesn't get out of the car, just sits there behind the wheel. He lights a cigarette and takes a few long drags, then turns the radio on. Through his open windows they hear a commercial for McDonald's and a request for "Free Ride" going out to Gina from East Hartford.

Kirk smokes the cigarette down to the filter and lights another off the ember.

"What the fuck's he doing?" Cole whispers. Liz doesn't respond, but he takes her sticky hand in his. In the dim light, the blood dripping from her fingertips is black.

"I'm gonna sneak in the back door," she says, biting and tearing at her cuticles, and before he can kiss her goodnight she's crawling under the bushes toward the back of the house. He doesn't hear the latch, but he waits a minute and sees her bedroom light come on.

He sucks her blood off his skin, and watches Kirk smoke through three songs, and when the commercials start up again he clicks off the radio, gets out of the car, and walks back to the trunk. He looks over his shoulders, scans the house windows, and seems to gaze directly at Cole in the darkness. Then he opens the trunk, grabs two gas cans in one hand—empty, Cole can tell from how he swings them—and closes the trunk with a gentle click before hustling to the gardening shed behind the house.

ON THE BUS, THE PUERTO RICANS ARE FURIOUSLY DISCUSSING "*EL fuego*" and "*el incendio provocado*." From the local kids, more talk of conspiracy: it's a rival tobacco company, likely Diamond & Wentworth; it's cigarette companies trying to beat back cigars; or it's pot growers who want to knock out Connecticut Shade so when pot is legalized—any day now, they all insist—the land will be available. Cole spends his day under the nets out on Kennedy Road doing a third priming, carefully cradling each leaf like a baby under one arm, snapping it from the stalk with his thumb and index finger, and laying it gently in the plastic bin. Every six leaves he whistles to a kid on a bicycle pulley, who pedals the rope around a wheel, drags the bin down the long row, and loads it onto the bus. Like this, he and fifteen others work the bents through the long, hot afternoon.

At dinner he eats with his blackened hands, still sticky and sweet-smelling, picking up fish sticks less tenderly than he picked tobacco leaves and dabbing them in tartar sauce. The phone rings and Kelly jumps up to answer, stretching the cord into the keeping room and talking fast and muted to one of her friends. "Not during dinner!" their mother shouts.

"Just a sec."

"Another couple weeks," their father says, "those rabbits will be ready to butcher." Ian freezes, a fish stick in front of his open mouth. He sets it down on his plate.

Cole nods, nothing more.

"Airfare goes down in the fall," their mother says. "People say fall's as lovely as spring. The parks. The evening strolls."

Kelly giggles from the keeping room.

"I don't think I want to butcher them," Ian says.

"Nonsense," their father says. "Life is for new experiences."

"Like Paris," their mother says.

"In colonial times," their father explains, "everybody knew how to butcher."

"The museums aren't so crowded off-season. Can you imagine a private audience with the *Mona Lisa*? An intimate mass at Notre-Dame?"

"Back then you'd know how to stuff your own mattress."

"Kelly!" their mother shouts. "I said *now*!"

"*Okay!*" she snaps, and talks lower and faster.

"Kelly!" their father barks, and she comes.

"Jeez," she says, "it was important," and sits back down at the table.

"Hotel prices drop, of course, and even restaurants have special—"

"I told you it's too expensive!" He speaks sharply, glaring at his plate. "Enough!"

"We can afford chicken coops and tea caddies and bed warmers and ladder-back chairs. We can afford what *you* want but not what

I want. Who'd ever believe that with five fireplaces we could have too many andirons? But somehow you've bought enough to supply Sturbridge—"

There's a knock at the front door, the one they never use. It doesn't even open, so their father goes out the kitchen and around the side of the house. Cole stands up to follow him.

"Sit," their mother says. "It's probably Jehovah's Witnesses. Who bothers people during dinner? Can't we even once have an uninterrupted family meal?" Her lips are trembling, her face showing the heat. "Can't we live like normal people?"

"Looks like the sheds are definitely arson," Cole says. "That's what the straw boss said this afternoon. Piles of old clothes soaked with gas."

"Asinine," she says, staring at lettuce leaves on her fork before pushing them into her mouth and chewing hard.

"I'll bet it's some burnout potheads," Kelly says, glancing at Cole like maybe she thinks it's him.

Their father's voice and another man's rumble from the front room. Kelly stays at the table—"Suddenly interruptions are okay?"— and the rest of them go see the two men carrying a piece of furniture wrapped in a pad through the funeral door.

"Driving out," the man's saying, "I thought to myself, *How could anyone live way out here? What if you needed a hospital? Who picks up your garbage?*" Cole recognizes him as the owner of an antique shop in Hartford, a stout Italian with slicked-back hair and an Old World accent. He's stopped there with his father: "Lots of junk, but occasionally a find," he'd remark, turning over a flip glass and checking the bottom for wear.

"But now I see—" the man begins as they set the piece down, but then their mother tears off the furniture pad to reveal a highboy, exclaiming, "What in the name of Jesus!" and the antique dealer looks around the half-sheetrocked room, at severed wires and open radiator pipes, a missing closet door, rolls of insulation, piles of tools, furniture pushed away from one wall. "Now I realize that you don't actually live here."

THAT NIGHT, HE LIES IN BED WITH THE ICE BAG ON HIS CHEST, HIS fan off. His sweat soaks into the sheets. His mother's voice pierces the walls and rushes through cracks beneath the doors: "I'm taking charge of the money." And after a pause: "It's going back. You call him tomorrow and tell him to pick it up. I'll pay him the delivery charge myself." When she stops, they all pray in the silence that it's over, so they can breathe and rest their jittering hearts and sleep. But then, like thunder rolling in the distance, not really heard but felt, a vibration in a low register, he's saying something, and they brace for more.

Cole jumps at a boom. He has one foot on the floor when their parents' bedroom door latch clacks, and his father goes downstairs. After a minute he hears an exasperated, furious "Criminy!" and she follows him, and now her shouting is muffled, coming up from the kitchen through the floorboards. Then his own latch lifts and Ian steps through.

"What's up?" Cole says. It's nearly midnight.

"Nothing."

"Can't sleep?"

He's looking at the stuff on Cole's bureau—a cigar box holding photos and letters from Liz, a ring made from a penny that she brought him from Mystic, a leather peace sign, an incense burner, Speed Stick. He touches each item like checking peaches for ripeness.

"I can never sleep in this heat," Cole says, and Ian's fingertips hover over a tiny White House encased in Lucite the size of an ice cube, also from Liz; she stole it for him, and the next day was sent home early from the school trip to Washington DC, when she was caught shoplifting in the Supreme Court gift shop.

"Is that why you can't sleep?" Ian says, his voice unusually deep and flat. "Because it's too hot?" Caustic, even. "That's what's keeping you up?"

Ian has always been vulnerable and quiet and hyper-observant. A frightened child, someone might say. This past Christmas, Tilly, Uncle Andrew, and Sandy were over for dinner, and their father was carving and Cole was drinking Scotch in his ginger ale and everyone was in a cheery mood—their mother had just told a story about the year an ice storm knocked out the power on Christmas Eve—when Ian reached for the stuffing and knocked over a candlestick that in turn tipped an empty wineglass onto the table. Nothing was broken. No one much reacted—except for Ian, who burst into tears and raced up the stairs. Their mother went after him, but he didn't come out of his room until the pie was served.

"I'm running away from home," Ian says. He sits on the foot of Cole's bed, holding the miniature White House between his thumb and forefinger, staring into it as if Amy Carter might open the front door and invite him inside. "Not permanently," he says. "Just a couple months."

"Where are you going?"

"South."

"You're gonna hitchhike?"

"Some. But mostly walk. You can take the Metacomet Trail a long way and get food in towns, and it's easy to—" He stops when their mother's shouting cranks up a level; they've both been monitoring it as they talk, waiting for the cry for help. Ian holds the Lucite cube up to the lamp like he's looking at a Kodak slide, and when silence resumes he says, "It's easy to camp anywhere."

"You'll need money."

"I've got money," he snaps.

"Are you going to tell Mom and Dad?"

Ian shoots him a look. "Jesus, Cole, you don't tell your parents when you're running away from home." He's got long, little-boy eye-lashes and soft cheeks, but also the sunken eyes and slanted mouth of a bitter, world-weary man. He shrugs. "I need to borrow your camping stuff. I'll be back by winter."

"When are you leaving?"

"Soon. But my hiking boots are too small. Kelly's gonna drive me to Hartford for new ones."

"She knows, huh?"

"She thinks it's a great idea. She'd do it herself but doesn't want to screw up her chances at the Air Force Academy."

"When's she taking you for boots?"

"I don't know, maybe tomorrow. Anyway, can I borrow your camping gear or not?"

"I need it, actually."

Ian's face turns angry in a flash. "Fuck you!"

"I've got a camping trip planned. But after that—"

"When?"

"Not long, but we haven't picked a weekend yet."

Ian squeezes the cube in his fist much as—years from now—he'll squeeze a tiny toy backhoe, screwing up his face, and then throw it against the wall, hopping on one foot and shouting, "Damnit! I told you to pick this crap up!" And Cole will notice again how the walls feel so flimsy in their cramped Toyohashi house. When Ian's wife appears in the doorway, Ian barks, "Get those kids in here!" and Michiko hurries into the next room and returns with the two boys.

"Look," Cole says, going down on a knee. "Let me—"

"Leave them," Ian commands.

The boys back up against their mother.

"What did I tell you two about picking up these trucks? Do you know what it feels like to step on a sharp hunk of metal? Now get over here."

They remain bolted to Michiko, but she gently pushes them

toward their father, who's sitting on the edge of the couch, and when they're standing before him, Ian grabs the younger one by the arm and spanks him twice.

"Hey," Cole says, jumping to his feet. The boy bursts into tears and runs to his mother.

"Get back here this minute," Ian tells him through clenched teeth, and the sobbing boy returns to the spot his father is pointing to right at his feet.

"Maybe we could all just pitch in," Cole offers.

"You have a lot to learn about this culture," Ian tells him. "And parenting. Talk to me when *you* have a couple hellions." He grabs the older boy's arm and swats him four times.

"Jesus." Cole feels nausea rising. He looks at Michiko, who's staring at him pleadingly, clutching at herself, and cowering in the doorway. The older boy's fighting back tears and the younger one's bawling, both standing at attention before their father.

"Now pick everything up and put it in the *oshiire*." They scramble around gathering up the few toys in view, even sweeping their hands under the furniture, then press them to their bellies and run out past their mother.

She's still searching Cole's face for understanding. A few days later, he'll ask if she needs anything, if they're okay or there's a problem, if there's anything he can do, and she'll evade each of his questions. "Nothing . . . Fine . . . Not at all . . . No, no, no."

But now, hearing the boys whimpering in their room, watching Michiko silently place a tray of bean cakes and tea on the table between him and his brother, he says "Excuse me" and steps into his shoes, then walks down the street gasping for air, trying to get a breath. He's been in Japan for two days and the jet lag has really whacked him. He never sleeps well anyway; but here he feels more awake than ever throughout the night, while during the day it's like he has a low-grade flu. And the strain of contending with Ian certainly doesn't relieve any of these symptoms.

He passes a liquor store with a vending machine out front that sells gallon-sized cans of beer with plastic spouts in the shape of the Kirin dragon. He passes a house getting re-sided—the carpenters three stories up, in black-canvas toe socks instead of boots, shuffle back and forth on bamboo poles lashed together for scaffolding. His stomach is settling down, though his heart's fluttering and he's still gulping down breaths when he cuts through an alley that he thinks will come out at Ian's house. In back gardens, futons are flung over railings in the sunlight. And in Ian's garden he spots a tiny pear tree, its branches weighted down with fruit, and reaches over the wall to wrap his hand around a plump, impossibly beautiful pear. But when he tugs, the stem snaps and his thumb breaks through the skin, the whole pear—completely rotten on the inside—smushing into a soupy, dark-brown goop. He flicks his fingers, but the sickly sweet smell still covers his hand, and he suddenly lurches over and pukes.

Back in the house, one boy's practicing the piano and the other's doing homework in the kitchen while his mother chops vegetables. Ian's in the living room, watching TV and having a whiskey. By the time Michiko calls everyone to the table, Cole is feeling better. Hungry, even. She points to each dish and names it for him and is up and down throughout the meal, running to the stove and back with hot seared vegetables, another piece of fish. She's on the edge of her chair having a few mouthfuls herself when Cole stands up with his rice bowl.

"No, no," Michiko says, lunging between him and the rice cooker.

"That's okay. I got it."

"No, please." She's in front of him, her hands on his bowl, but he doesn't let go.

"Really," Cole says. "It's no problem."

"Please, sit!" she barks, snatching the bowl from his grasp and bumping him toward the table.

He spreads the napkin on his lap as she serves him a fresh bowl of steaming rice, the boys now giggling.

A broad satisfied grin spreads over Ian's face. "You can't try to pull that stuff," he says, nearly laughing. "You'll start a fucking revolution."

IAN OPENS HIS HAND AND RAPS THE WHITE HOUSE ON COLE'S BED-side table as their father comes up the stairs. "Will it be less than a couple weeks? I really want to get going."

"I'll talk to Liz." They're both waiting for their mother to follow him, but she doesn't, which can only mean she's down in the kitchen crying. She might charge up in a few minutes, or maybe she's too exhausted; this might be the end of it for tonight. "Why are you running away?"

Ian shoots him the bewildered look again.

"I mean, what do you hope to get out of it?"

"I just want them to stop. If I run away, maybe it'll distract them for a while, and when I come back they'll be so relieved that they'll quit it for good."

"Or they'll fight about whose fault it is that you left in the first place."

"They'd also have more money if they didn't have to spend any on me, so they wouldn't have that to fight about, either."

"You really think it would make a difference?"

"I thought about killing myself—"

"No, Ian. Don't say that."

"I don't really want to—"

"Good."

"Then I thought about burning our house down."

"*That* would be a distraction," Cole says.

"But I don't want to lose my stuff, and if I stashed it all outside somewhere before I did it, they'd all know it was me."

· · ·

IN THE BAR AT THE AIRPORT SHERATON COLE OPENS HIS LAPTOP
on a table by the window and connects to wi-fi. The waiter lays down
a cocktail napkin and a gimlet, and he takes a long sip. He's come
here to finally finish that email to his sister and brother, but when
he opens his inbox there's a message from Alex right on top. She's in
Budapest. "You'd love it," she says, and she tells him about intricately
carved woodwork in the opera house, massive wood columns and
doors. "And as Antoine had hoped, the smell of thick stews, the faces
of grandmothers in the market, the night sky over the Danube, the
pull of its current—it's all strangely familiar to him." She writes about
their river cruise and the days since spent wandering around and
eating pastry and napping before dinner. "What's wonderful about
traveling is that we can completely let go of control and never have
to meet anyone's schedule or expectations—responsible only to ourselves."

Out the window a jet takes off, and Cole thinks how easy it would
be to grab Daniel and get on the next plane home. To leave his father
and the mess of this house behind. He spins the chestnut ring around
his finger, imagining what all that wood must look like stacked in the
Greenworks shop and imagining the finished timbers in the family
room, wondering if he could get it closed up by winter.

He has no idea what to tell Ian and Kelly about their father. He
can only think of Alex and Antoine on their three-month sabbatical.
He admires their marriage. If he could just figure out exactly why,
then maybe with Nikki . . . maybe there'd be a chance.

He drains the last drops of gin and lime, then slips his computer
in the bag and pays the bill.

THE COMPETENCY PAPERWORK IS SO INVOLVED THAT HE SUSPECTS
completing the forms is itself a competency exam. Since nobody will
give his father a loan, Cole has to submit the paperwork to a judge so
he can apply for one himself and also make other financial decisions

on his father's behalf. Phil doesn't know about any of this, so through a day of working on the bathroom he sneaks in questions that need to be answered.

Setting the toilet—Cole shimming the base while his father tightens the nuts—he says, "So when was your last physical?"

"I'm fine."

"I know you are, but everybody gets them. I go every few years."

"Good for you."

"Do you have a regular doctor?"

"Between the army sawbones and prison hacks who've poked and clawed at me, it's a miracle I'm still alive."

This might be the first time this summer he's heard his father say "prison," which makes him hopeful that he's broken through the armor of denial and convenient forgetting. "Well, who's the last doctor you saw?"

Phil eyes the level stretched across the toilet rim, tightens down the last nut, and slowly stands up, wincing, his hands on his lower back. "He'd press the stick on my tongue with his big rough fingers that stunk real bad of cigars. That scorched smell of smoking them down too far."

"Who was that?"

"I'd look up his nostrils in absolute amazement. Stuffed with steel wool. How could he even *breathe*? But sure enough, when that cold stethoscope moved around all over my back, huge powerful blasts of air rushed out of his nose like a dragon." He rips open the toilet-seat box. "Dr. Engstrom."

Cole takes the seat from him and fits it onto the rim. "Where's his office?"

"At his house, right here in town. Where the Cumberland Farms is now."

He finally catches on. "So this was a while ago?"

"He'd clamp those polio braces too tight on my knees."

They unpack the cabinets. It's been years since Cole bought any—

he has a cabinet shop at Greenworks—but he's got to admit these look pretty good: maple raised-panel doors, quality hinges, laminate shelves, all finished and delivered—too damn easy. "What else do you remember?" he says.

"What a stupid question. I remember everything."

"Like what?"

"Okay," Phil says. "In the summers my father made ice cream with fresh strawberries and peaches?"

"Nice."

"For Christ's sake. Not really. I'm just yanking your chain."

"You don't remember much, do you?"

"Don't start with that crap again."

"Look, if we can transfer authority to me, I can take out a loan and we can finish the house. They're not going to give you one. They don't think you're a reliable risk, and since the crash everything's gotten so tough."

"Let me talk to that little prick again. I'll set him straight."

"What did you have for breakfast?"

He stammers and his face goes red. "Who cares? The reason they ask that is nobody cares. It's unimportant."

"Do you remember Mom?"

"She was an elegant lady. Soft-spoken and very proper, yet she went to work at Ensign-Bickford during the war making munitions. She was there on the day of the famous explosion. Didn't even mention it at supper. She always smelled of gunpowder."

"I'm talking about *my* mother. Your *wife*."

He grins, still yanking his chain, and hefts a cabinet into place.

"Do you remember her?"

"Vaguely."

"Like what?"

"Like a saint. A gift to mankind. A winged goddess."

"Fuck you."

"Don't ask stupid questions if you—" He stumbles, steadies himself on the cabinet, then his head rolls and Cole grabs hold of him as he's about to keel over. They're both slick with sweat.

"I'll get us some water," Cole says, and goes down to the kitchen. When he comes back with two big cups his father sinks a hammer into the sheetrock and tears out a hunk with the claw. "Stop!"

He cocks the hammer for another blow.

"No, Dad. Stop!"

"We'll never finish this if we don't get moving." He turns and points at Cole with the hammer. "I want you to have this whole room ripped out by suppertime."

"Dad"—he grips the hammerhead and gently pulls it away—"this room is done. We drywalled last week. It's taped and primed. Look at it." He puts a cup of water in his father's hand. "Have a drink. We're both so overheated it's hard to think straight." He sits him down on a bucket of mud. "I fell off a roof once from the heat," Cole says. "Reached for a bundle of shingles and the colors started swirling and the last thing I remember was rolling off the edge."

"You fainted?"

"Ninety-five degrees on black shingles in the sun. I make my guys keep an Igloo of Gatorade up on a roof."

"So you hit the ground?"

"The painters had spread a drop cloth over the hedges. I fell into it like a hammock."

"Lucky day."

"You can say that again."

They each take a long drink. Cole's wearing nothing but shorts and boots, but still can't cool off. Phil's clothes are dripping with sweat.

"I knew a guy who took a bad fall," his father says. "It killed him."

"What happened?"

"They call that type of thing an accident."

Cole's heart speeds up a notch. "I've heard *you* pull that line."

His father sucks at the corner of his mouth, as if he's got a cigar stuck in there. "I can't recall the exact circumstances, but it was a few stories onto a concrete floor. They say he landed smack on his head."

"And how about *your* accident."

"I didn't see it. I was in the exercise yard at the time. The kitchen vents blew down on the shady end. Liver and onions. That was Tuesdays."

"I'm talking about Mom."

"Beef was expensive during the war, but she'd bring home rabbit meat from a butcher shop right outside the gates of Ensign-Bickford. We ate rabbit all the time."

"Do you still claim it was an accident?"

"You probably didn't know she also worked at Colt for a time during the war. It takes nimble fingers to insert the firing pins. And she worked tobacco as a girl."

"One day you're going to die," Cole says. "Do you really want to go to your grave in denial?"

"I'd catch her sometimes taking a puff on my father's cigar. It was our little secret. Hers and mine."

"Damnit!" Cole shouts. "Have you thought about the lives you ruined? Not just hers, but the rest of us, too."

Phil reaches for his water and knocks the cup over, then watches it spread across the floor. "Why are you yelling?"

"She worked, she came home, her keys and purse barely hit the kitchen table before she turned on the stove and started cooking dinner. She took care of all of us. She was the reason we were as much of a family as we managed to be. And you can't even admit to my face what you did."

"What did I do?"

"Fuck! I'm talking about Mom!"

"Then ask *her.*"

. . .

THE SUN'S GOING DOWN BUT IT DOESN'T FEEL ANY COOLER. HE made dinner for the three of them, and Daniel's gone to a party with LK. They've both promised to help with the bathroom this weekend. Cole plans to hold off on the back bedrooms until he finds out if he can finagle the loan.

He looks out the kitchen window at the fields of charred tobacco plants. A million-dollar loss, the newspaper said. He loves the look of forests out west after fire, especially in the winter—the straight black trunks slashing the white mountainsides with the spare, delicate beauty of Japanese ink drawings; but there's no beauty here, it's more like cabbage left to rot in the fields. And then he sees someone—oh, no, his goddamn *father*—stomping through the swath of knee-high burnt vegetation. Cole jogs as far as the chicken coop, then turns back, hops in the car and guns it, cutting across the yard to the tractor road. Phil's charging due west toward the orange sun flattening out on the Metacomet ridgeline. Cole comes up fast, dust rising behind him.

"Dad!" he shouts through the open window.

Phil glances over but keeps moving.

"Dad! Come get in the car."

He veers away with his face turned straight ahead, like a misbehaving dog pretending he can't hear he's being called, so Cole follows the road around the back end of the field and parks where he can intercept him. Beyond this point, the field falls away into swamp, shaded by willows and cottonwoods, where he and Ian used to jump from one solid grassy hump to the next until one of them inevitably fell in. As his father approaches, his pace slows; he's apparently resigned to capture. A mosquito buzzes at Cole's ear, and he slaps his neck.

Phil's heading straight for the car, and Cole gets out to corral him, but it's not necessary; he pulls open the passenger door and gets in. Cole throws it in reverse and backs up slowly over the rutted road with one eye on his father, who's still looking straight ahead.

"Where are you taking me?" he says.

"To the house. We've got to get cleaned up for bed." The scorched and rotting smell, as bad as it is, still doesn't mask the reek of his body. He's sweat so much there are patches of dried salt on his clothes, and his hair's matted with oil and construction dust. If Family Services conducted a surprise visit, they'd probably remove his father from his own home. Ha! No such luck.

Cole's still in reverse, craning to peer over his shoulder, when Phil grabs onto the dash. "It's like everything's going backwards."

"We'll get stuck if I try to turn around here."

Phil stares out the windshield and says, "Nice day for a drive."

At the main tractor road, Cole backs around and they roll slowly forward toward the house, and now it's his father looking over his shoulder at where they just came from, then ahead at the house, then behind them again.

When they pull up, Phil says, "It's fine. I just had a shower."

"When?"

Suddenly he's stricken with confusion and fright, like it's a trick question. "It's fine!" But he doesn't fight as fiercely as usual—for whatever reason—and Cole manages to get him in the bathroom. The stink is truly suffocating. Four or five ninety-degree days of hard labor since he's bothered to wash himself at all as far as Cole can tell.

He maneuvers him to the toilet lid. "Okay, first your shirt." But he just sits there, arms hanging at his sides until Cole unbuttons it and peels it off of him. "Pants now," he says, and turns the shower on, but he still doesn't make a move. "Come on, Dad. Work with me."

Finally he comes out of the trance. "Why the hell do you keep calling me that?" Then he stands up and heads toward the door.

Not a chance Cole's giving up now, so he grabs his shoulders and turns him around. "Won't it feel good to get clean?" He unbuckles the belt, releases the button and fly, and yanks the pants down his legs, but now his father tries to escape and trips up and Cole catches him, smearing himself with the slick filth. Before he can run, Cole gets his underwear down to his ankles and holds him steady while he pulls out one foot and then the other. He rips off the socks and shoves him under the water, but as soon as he steps away his father follows him onto the floor.

"Back in."

"I'm clean."

"You need to wash." With a hand flat to his chest he pushes him under the stream. He's not fighting, but not washing either—just standing under the warm water as if it's ice cold.

"Why are you trying to kill me?"

"Dad, I'm—"

"You can't trick me, you know."

And for almost a minute they're in a standoff—Cole holding him under the stream while Phil makes half-hearted dodges to get around him. Finally Cole grabs the soap and scrubs his father's back. There's not a washcloth in the house so he washes with his hands, lathering his shoulders and the ropey curving scar, as big as a banana, along his shoulder blade, pausing there before lifting his elbows to scrub his armpits, then down his thighs and calves—"Steady yourself," he says—lifting one foot at a time. With lots of suds on his hands he washes between his father's legs—first the back, then he turns him around and lathers up the front. He scrubs his chest— thinking, oddly, of Daniel finger painting in his highchair—then his neck and ears, reaching his thumbs deep into the swirls. "Close your eyes," he says, guiding his head under the spray, then lathers up his hair. And then he rinses him off, top to bottom, his hands reaching again into every crevice and cranny, sending the suds and grime down the drain.

After toweling both of them off—his clothes are completely soaked, right through to his underwear—he stands him at the sink with his razor and shaving cream. Phil picks up the Barbasol and rubs the can over his whiskers, knowing that's the general idea but also that it's not exactly right. Cole's never given anybody a shave before but tells him to hold still and slowly, carefully gets the job done; a few missed spots, maybe, but no nicks or cuts.

He's just done a load of laundry and runs to the dryer to get clean pajamas, then helps his father into them. It's still early, but he seizes the opportunity to get him to bed. The sheets smell sour; he can wash them tomorrow. He fiddles with the rabbit ears on the bedside TV until the picture clears up on a cop show. "Good to be clean?" he asks.

"I feel like celery."

"We don't have any celery," Cole says. "How about a peach?"

"Don't try to confuse me. I'm saying I *feel* like a stalk of celery."

"I SCRUBBED HIM CLEAN AS CELERY," COLE SAYS.

"That's extremely clean."

"Cleaner than iceberg lettuce."

"Way cleaner," Nikki says.

In a stretched-out silence, the energy that was building between them wanes.

"I texted Daniel," she says, "but he didn't respond."

"He's at a party."

"Like a normal party with kids making out and sneaking sips of beer?"

"Something like that, I guess."

"What else do they do?"

"I'm not sure. Video games, maybe. But mostly they work. If not in the fields, then on the house. They're both pretty motivated."

"And he's happy?"

"I think so," Cole says. She doesn't respond, and after a beat he realizes she's weeping. "Are you okay?"

"I'm just glad he's not spending all his time conspiring with thirty-year-old freegans. I never thought I'd be so relieved that my son's behaving like an average American."

"That might be an overstatement, but he's definitely got a spark that I haven't seen in a while. He hasn't said 'the world's in the toilet' for weeks."

"Ha! He might as well join the positivity movement."

"He'll be putting aphorisms on the fridge."

" 'Dare to be regular!' "

"Yeah," Cole says, "but I'm not sure you'll get traction with that one. He does seem good, though, and he's really been a help with my father, too."

"*That* I'm less thrilled about."

"It's just that he's another sane person in the house to raise the standard of rationality. My father seems to need reasonable lives to anchor himself to. Otherwise, he spins out. Yesterday we were watching them burn the fields around the house—"

"Who's burning fields?"

"Taybro. One of the big companies. There was a breakout of blue mold."

"In the plants?"

"Yeah, on the leaves."

"Can't they spray something?"

"There's nothing to do but burn it. And they never wait even a second, since it can jump from field to field. It's what the growers fear more than anything. That and smoking bans in New York City."

"Blue mold and Bloomberg."

"Exactly." Cole feels the old ease between them—back to those days they sprawled on his couch watching black-and-white movies. Dialed into each other.

She covers the phone, though he still hears a muffled "Thanks. One more."

"Where are you?"

She hesitates. "The Batignolles." It was always their favorite bar.

"On the patio?"

"Yep."

"Vouvray?"

She doesn't answer, but he listens to her settling into one of those soft chairs in the shade of the bamboo. The clink of a glass.

"Are you alone?"

Again she hesitates, then says, "Yeah." She takes a sip. "Tell me about burning these fields."

The sudden intimacy between them is so profound that he can't remember when he last felt this close to her. "It was wild. The fields run up to the side yard, then wrap around the back, and it was all on fire. It really seemed like we were staring into the apocalypse. Either that or we were acting in a movie about men who fight brush fires."

"*Hell's Firemen*. In theaters this summer."

"So hot your corn will pop by itself."

"But it's dangerous, isn't it?" she says. "Couldn't it catch the house on fire?"

"There's a pretty wide tractor road all the way around. Plus the tobacco's really wet right now so it burns at a low smolder. The smoke smells like a very skanky cigar mixed with rotting cabbage. Burning."

"Nice," she says. "What a place to grow up."

"I only remember this happening once when I was a kid."

"Couldn't they try to just rip out the bad plants?"

"Too much risk of it spreading. There were a few infamous years where the whole valley lost its crop."

"It's all so primitive. With GMOs and Frankenfoods it seems they could just fix this."

"It's a very old-fashioned business. And a dying one. I guess you don't pour money into revamping something that's shrinking year by year. Which is one of the things Daniel likes about it. No one even makes the machines for sewing the leaves together—"

"There's *sewing* involved?"

"They sew the leaves together for hanging, and the machines, they just keep fixing and rebuilding the same ones they've been using for fifty years. The buses, the sheds, the tractors—I swear it's all the same stuff they were using when I was a kid, and even then it was the same stuff from when my father was young."

"If I'd known about the sewing I might've asked you to get me a job too."

He wonders why she says this. A trial balloon? Fishing for an invitation? She'd never come. He knows she's curious about this place, the house, his father. She's never met him, only seen Cole's few photos from back when they were still a family. For her, Phil is frozen in time: a man in 1970s Kodacolor with long sideburns and black-framed glasses, never looking at the camera but caught carrying a sheet of drywall or a sack of chicken feed, carving a turkey, stringing lights on the Christmas tree. A father and husband who will, in a year or three or six, become a murderer. He's as fixed in time for her as Cole's mother is for him.

"So where's Tony tonight? What are you doing off leash?"

She lets that one pass. "How are things holding up for you?"

"Without Ben, Greenworks would be sunk. I'm giving him a raise. He checks in every couple days. I lost a big job, but we'll survive it. And he's keeping everything else on track. He even bid out two small additions."

"That's good," she says, "but I meant you personally. Being there."

"Well, my father needs help, so I'm working on that. And I'm trying to get him to confront what he did, which is probably futile. What I really want to ask him is, even if he didn't mean to kill her, even if he *hadn't* killed her, did he know what living under the threat of violence was doing to his kids? Even if he didn't love his wife, did he love *us*? Was he aware of all the trauma he was inflicting? I actually think the answer's no, he wasn't aware. So does that make it more forgivable? And then I think about how my failure to forgive him has diminished me. *Is* diminishing me. And what you said about my fear of losing control. Basically, I think you're right—I mean, you *are* right."

In the long silence he can hear only his breathing, and hers, the ring of plates and silverware and laughter at the Batignolles.

"To answer your earlier question," she finally says, "Tony's at his house. And I came here, apparently, to call you."

15

HE GOES OUT FOR GRINDERS MOST DAYS AND BRINGS THEM BACK to the house, but it's so damn hot he figures they'd all like half an hour in the AC. Cole's capicola with provolone tastes just like it did back then; he remembers cleaning the slicer at midnight in Simsbury and jonesing for that first Scotch with Tilly, but more he's reminded of sitting right here, at this very table, eating grinders with Liz.

The four of them are quiet—hungry and tired and cooling off—and he can see that Little Kirk's keeping an eye on two men a few tables over—workingmen in oily caps and coveralls. "Who are they?" Cole asks.

"Nobody," he says. "Matt used to be friends with my dad."

"Matt Gosling," Cole says. "Sure enough." No neck and fat hands—he looks the same.

"They had a big blowup," LK says. "I don't even know what about." He steals another glance, then takes a wolfish bite of his grinder and wipes his chin with the back of his hand.

In high school, Matt and Kirk were best friends. Bullies and all-around assholes, cruising town in Kirk's Chevelle looking for trouble. When Kirk was arrested for burning down the sheds, the cops and most everybody else thought Matt was his accomplice, but even when Kirk was offered a deal to rat him out, he wouldn't do it. They kept Kirk in juvie until he was twenty-one.

He's suddenly worried about Daniel. Even back then everyone

knew Kirk got such a harsh sentence because he'd burned a multi-national corporation's property. If they were the barns of local dairy and truck farms, there would've been no FBI and no federal court or federal prosecutors. Daniel, trying to make the world right by taking potshots at Safeway and Bank of America, was picking a fight with some very big dogs.

Cole pats him on the back. "You guys want to take the afternoon off?"

With his mouth full, Daniel says, "I'm good."

"Me too, Mr. Callahan. I want to get that baseboard in."

"How about you?" he says to his father.

"Let's get those water lines connected. Half my life I've been dreaming of taking a dump up there."

The boys laugh and after a moment Phil joins in. He's better today, as he is most days until the afternoon. As the hours click away so does his mind. He resets overnight and by morning he's okay again. But it seems that his reset comes up a little shorter with each passing day—another thin slice of him lost. It's really in the morning that Cole should talk to him about the incompetency declaration, though he never wants to trouble the waters in the hours when his father is doing well. Still, it frustrates him that as soon as Cole brings up anything important, his father's instantly absent.

"Speaking of which," Phil says, "we had two pairs of Chinese geese. Regal birds. Pure white except for their orange beaks and feet. Long graceful necks."

"Ian might remember it differently," Cole tells him. "They were fiercely territorial. If he didn't give them a wide berth, they'd drop their heads down low and run after him, swooping in like fighter jets, and bite his butt or the backs of his thighs and not let go."

"I've seen it happen," LK says, laughing. "They're vicious."

"Once he came in the house crying and smeared with their shit. They'd gotten him so bad he tripped and fell and they attacked. No mercy. And that was the other thing about those regal birds of yours."

He looks at Phil. "In a week they'd covered the entire backyard with shit."

"Nature," Daniel says flatly.

"Were they tasty?" LK asks.

Cole waits for a moment, giving his father a chance to pick up the story, but he's staring down at his plate, so he continues himself. "They were so damn loud that a German shepherd from that house by the creek got curious enough to come check them out. I was upstairs in my room and heard all the honking and barking and went to the window just as the dog split one of them off from the flock. The goose flapped its wings and pecked at the dog's eyes with these quick powerful strikes, and I was about to run downstairs to chase the dog off, but then he got his jaws around the goose's neck, and I still remember watching through the window as the dog made three quick shakes of his head and the goose went limp. He dropped her on the ground and trotted off."

The boys are staring at him, and when he picks up his can of soda he realizes his hands are shaking.

"Are you okay?" Daniel says.

He takes a big swallow of root beer and tries to slough it off. "Yeah, I'm fine. I just remember feeling so helpless watching it all from behind the glass, with no time to get out there."

"Did you eat the others?" LK asks.

"The dead one was a female," Cole says, "and for the next couple days the two males fought for the remaining mate. By the third morning the weaker male was gone. I don't remember what happened with the pair that was left. Do you, Dad?"

"Probably that shepherd got them."

"I was so pissed at that dog." Cole smiles and tips his can toward Daniel. "I guess I still am. Ha! Still mad at a dead dog."

"It's the Baxters you should be mad at," his father says. "They shouldn't've let their dog wander all over like that." He bites into his grinder and keeps talking while he chews. "The dog didn't have any malice. Just doing what comes natural. Just thinking it'd be fun to get that neck in my teeth and shake it around."

THE HUMIDITY IS STILL A SURPRISE, STILL SUFFOCATING. THE CAR, parked in the sun, is like an oven. The boys get in back, Phil up front, and Cole guns it across the parking lot to move some air through. At the far end of the lot they come up on a pickup with a compressor and tangles of greasy hoses and a fuel tank in the bed, with Matt and his friend standing beside it having a smoke. As Cole drives by, Matt flicks his cigarette at his windshield: the ember hits the glass in front of his face and sparks fly. He stomps the brakes. "I wouldn't do that," Phil says quietly, but by now he's slammed the car in reverse, the engine's whining, and he's backing up straight at them. He jerks the car to a stop, flings open the door, and jumps out. "What's your fucking problem?!"

Matt forces a smile.

Cole stares dead at him. "I'll knock your teeth down your throat, asshole."

Matt takes half a step at him.

"Don't even touch me," Cole snaps. "I'll break your fucking arm."

Matt stops, puffs up his chest, broadens his shoulders, and his buddy struts up beside him doing the same. Matt's teeth are bad, the stubble on his chin is gray. "Mouth off like that, you're liable to get hurt."

"Grow up, *Matt*"—he spits out the name with all the derision he can. "You're practically an old man still acting like a delinquent. How long you been flicking cigarettes at people? Since you were like eleven?"

"I didn't even see you there," he says, then grins at his pal. "It was an accident."

"You're a loser."

Matt's face twitches, his jaw clenches, his eyes narrow. Cole has gotten under his skin. "You best get the hell out of here"—Matt's voice drops to a more serious register—"before things turn against you."

In the corner of his eye Cole sees somebody else. It's Phil, coming around the car and stepping between them. "That's right, fellas," he says. "Gotta run. There's some kids and an old man roasting in the car." And he nudges Cole back toward the open door.

For a mile no one says a thing. The air blowing in the window is too hot to cool him down. His heart's racing. The rage is nameless, shapeless. He can hardly see, like the veins in his eyes are bursting with blood. He's ashamed to have done that in front of Daniel. He hears nothing from the backseat and looks in the rearview mirror; his son's gazing blankly out the window, wind whipping his hair. Damn, he was right on the edge. If Matt had come at him, he would've unloaded. What the fuck's gotten into him?

He feels like they're doing ninety and checks the speedometer. Thirty-five. They're almost home when Little Kirk says, "Way to go, Mr. Callahan. My dad's gonna love hearing about that."

"Nothing to be proud of," Cole says. "I lost my temper is all." He squeezes the steering wheel, bites his lower lip. "Nothing to tell stories about."

"Knucklehead like that," Phil says, "he'll hit you with a tire iron without giving it a thought. Next minute you've got a permanent drool."

In the driveway, Cole holds the seat forward and Daniel slides out with his head down. Cole walks out to the apple tree. The chickens run to the wire, crowding and chirping, frantically watching him for a handful of feed. He picks over a few apples before finding one without worms and takes a bite, green and sour. He eats it slowly and stares out at the burnt fields, not plowed under yet. The chickens are making a racket and the blood's still pounding in his ears.

"You wanted to hit *him* with a tire iron, am I right?" It's his father, just behind him.

Cole keeps staring ahead.

"Easy to do. The anger builds and builds, makes you a little crazy, makes it so you don't know what you're thinking or who you are. Mister High and Mighty swooping in here, gonna show me how bad I've been, how bad I am compared to you." He comes up beside him, and when Cole doesn't turn he stands in front of him, facing him down. "You're just like me," he says.

Cole steps away and throws the apple core as hard as he can into the fields. At least his father had the decency to not say it in front of Daniel.

THE RAGE IS PHYSICAL. WEIGHT AND MASS PRESSING ON HIS LUNGS, his skull. Heat and odor. He has a clear, almost mystical vision of himself eventually dying from a heart attack. The rage will get its grip on him someday, too strong for his heart to endure. Rage at the doctors who almost let Nikki die, the cop who gave him a ticket for double-parking to unload twenty sheets of five-eighths drywall in the rain, the woman who flipped him the bird at the intersection of Hawthorne and Forty-First. "You're just not present," Nikki told him once. "You're muttering." And thank God she can't hear what he's saying under his breath—"Go fuck yourself!" directed at the woman who *ten years earlier* gave him the finger at Hawthorne and Forty-First.

Or the time he was washing dishes in the kitchen, rinsing suds off the chef's knife and watching Nikki swing the car door closed with a hip and start across their quiet street with her arms full of groceries, and then a passing car honked and swerved, the man at the wheel yelling, "Watch where you're going, bitch!" and speeding away.

Cole raced out the door with his keys, blurted "Are you hurt?" and dashed by, as she picked up oranges rolling across the pavement.

"No!" she called after him in a panic. "I'm fine. Cole—stop!" But he was already in the car and flooring it after the guy.

He flew down the street, screeching to a stop at every corner, looking both ways for the white Camaro, then gunning ahead. He turned east on Hawthorne and slowed his speed, scanning every parked car, the side streets and parking lots for a mile. But not a trace of the asshole. So he sped back to their neighborhood, up and down every street, searching driveways and alleys, and then heading west on Hawthorne—*where's that bastard?*—with blood rushing in his ears, grinding his teeth, when a woman screamed, "Stop!" He jerked his head and his stomach dropped as he slammed on the brakes, his tires squealing. In the crosswalk, a few feet in front of his growling car, were a woman and a stroller and a little boy and girl hanging on the sides, their faces turned toward him, scrambling, stumbling, the mother's back arched like a cat ready to pounce. Somehow she whisked up both toddlers and was thrusting the stroller ahead, her piercing eyes locked on Cole. She didn't look frightened. She was far beyond that, like she might drop her kids on the sidewalk, stick her head in Cole's window, and rip him to shreds with her teeth.

It was then that Cole saw what she saw: he had a two-fisted grip on the steering wheel, but in his right hand, sticking straight up, was the eight-inch chef's knife, suds dripping down the blade onto his wrist and his forearm.

"What did you plan to do if you found him?" Nikki asked when he got home, and without a word he rinsed off the knife and set it in the drainer.

And it was the same question twenty-five years earlier: winter in Connecticut and they're coming back from Tilly's after dark, the three kids in back, his parents up front, when—*boom, boom, boom*—the car swerves and they all gasp. It's a barrage of snowballs. His father cranes back and muscles a U-turn, spinning out in the snow. There's an apartment complex on the hill above the road, with Christmas lights around the front doors, reindeer and Santas on the stoops, most of the windows glowing with warm light. His father finds a spot close to the top of the hill, puts the car in park, and turns off the headlights, and they sit there: the engine idling, the blower throwing off heat, Christmas lights blinking red and green, and Cole would swear to this day that he could hear the fury surging through his father, the blood roaring in his ears, his gnashing teeth.

Ten minutes later, back out on the main road, snow flurries in the headlights, his mother said, "What did you plan to do if you found them?"

LIZ CLUTCHES HIS HIPS AS THEY RIDE THROUGH THE RAIN, SLA-loming around puddles in the tractor road, half a mile of nets on both sides, until they coast down to three sheds sitting on low land. They bump across the weeds and into the woods nearly to the creek and Liz hops off and lights a joint, the canopy of leaves protecting them from the soft summer rain. It's early evening, but the sky is gray and the mercury lights on the tool-and-die factory have come on, close enough to hit with a BB gun; it's an eerie light, watery and shifting. The cinder-block building is new. Just a year ago you could jump the creek and get lost in those deep woods until finally you'd come up to the chain-link fence topped with barbed wire at the airport's perimeter.

He passes the joint back to Liz and she raises it to her lips. She looks cute as hell in her blue rain slicker, stringy locks of hair wisping out from under the hood. Holding a hit in her lungs she says, "I hate that building."

"I do too."

"I mean, who works there? How do you just plop a factory down in the woods and start making tools and dies? And like, I know what tools are, but what are dies?"

Cole always pictured enormous high-speed lathes cutting foil-thin shavings off of bright flawless cylinders of steel, but he doesn't really know. He takes a hit and shakes his head.

"So they make hammers and crowbars and saws?" she says.

"I don't think it's that kind of tool."

"My brother's a tool. All his friends are tools."

"It's creepy what goes on in that factory." As the weed hits him, the mercury lights get even more wavery, more silvery. "Like Soylent Green in reverse. They suck up a lot of shit from the bottom of the ocean and like every hour they plop out another set of Kirks and his posse."

"And what about the die part?" Her voice flattens, loses its light bantering trill. "I wish *he'd* die." She's staring across at the building, the big lights dappling patterns on her face like rainwater running down glass. Her lips form the shape of a duck's bill, then the tip of her tongue appears and she launches a little bubble of spit. They watch it float off, dodging raindrops, and then she says, as if in a trance, "Let's torch it." A single fat raindrop sparks her cheek, and she comes back to herself. She kisses him and squeezes him between his legs. "*Allons-y.*" This kills him. French is the best class she's ever taken. She feels how turned on he is and rubs him roughly through his jeans—"*Ooh la la*"—and pushes her tongue into his mouth.

They turn. Beside a shed on the hill there's a white car with a light on top, the man behind the wheel watching them. Cole's legs go a little wobbly, but Liz marches ahead. "Grab the bike," she tells him, and as they start walking up the cop gets out of his car and waves them over.

"What's going on?" he says.

Cole answers: "Not much."

"What are you doing here?"

Cole examines the patches on his uniform—not a cop, just a security guard.

"We're exploring nature," Liz says.

The guy smirks. He's young, maybe twenty. "What sort of nature is that?"

"Trees," Liz says. "A babbling brook."

"What are you hiding under your coat?" he says to her.

"Nothing."

"That's not what it looks like to me." In fact, it doesn't look like she's hiding anything at all. The coat's kind of small, tight-fitting.

"Unzip it," he says.

She tugs Cole's arm. "Let's go," she says.

The guard grips the top of his nightstick and moves closer to them, his black belt with a flashlight and cuffs squeaking. "You stop right there, little lady. You two are trespassing on private property. I could take you both in to answer some questions about arson. Not to mention smoking grass."

Grass. Pathetic. "I've been coming here since I was born," Cole says.

"Now you let me see inside that coat."

Liz's face is twisted up. She draws down the zipper to the bottom.

"Open it up. Let's see in there."

She's wearing a gray ribbed tank top, a dark spot over her stomach where she's sweated a little.

"All right," he says. "I'm going to have to take you one at a time into the car to write up a report."

She zips her coat. "Fuck you! You can have our pot, but if you hassle us any more, I'll tell the real cops that I saw you toking up on duty. We both saw you." She takes her Sucrets box out of her pocket and tosses it to him. "C'mon, man," she says to Cole, and they start walking away.

But the asshole lurches toward them. "You first, little missy." He grabs her arm.

"Hey!" Cole shouts.

The guard yanks her toward the car.

"Look," Cole pleads, "we weren't *doing* anything."

Liz struggles against him. She catches Cole's eye, but he doesn't know what to do. You can't attack a cop, for fuck's sake. Not even a rental cop! He pulls her closer to the car, but then she stomps his foot and knees him in the balls, rips her arm free, and doesn't even glance at Cole as she sprints away.

Cole feels paralyzed, his feet stuck to the ground. He looks at the cop, then at Liz racing into the distance, then at his bike down by the creek. The cop's bent over with his hands on his groin—she really nailed him—but then he straightens up, raises his fist, and feints a charge at him. "Get the fuck out of here," he spits, and Cole backs away warily and grabs his bike.

He rides three tobacco roads before he spots Liz up ahead, walking fast and close to the nets. He stops and she gets on, and he rides them to his house, and for a little while they sit on the back porch steps watching the rain tink on a copper weathervane he's never seen before sitting on the lawn. She's silent, distant. Rattled.

"He's not going to file any reports or anything," Cole says. "What can he do?" He pats her knee. "Zilch."

She nods, looking ahead, biting her lip.

"If there's more fires, there'll be more cops."

"He wasn't a cop," she snaps.

"I know that."

She pulls at the frayed ends of her cutoffs. Her legs are wet and shiny, her sneakers muddy.

"How'd you know he'd want the pot?"

"Didn't you see his bloodshot eyes?"

"I was too busy watching his hand on the grip of that billy club. And wondering if he had a gun in the car."

"He didn't want to shoot us."

"If they accuse me of burning down the sheds, I'll have something to tell them about."

"Jesus, Cole!" she shouts so suddenly that it startles him. "He didn't want to fill out any stupid reports." She reaches toward him like she intends to shake some sense into him—"Don't you know anything? Don't you know what the fuck he wanted?"—but instead she grabs both sides of her own head, and the cuffs of her raincoat slide up her arms, where he sees fresh bruises circling her wrists. He pushes the sleeves up farther: purple and brown splotches all the way to her elbows.

"What the hell? Oh my God, Liz." And he wraps his arms around her as if she's been cleaved in two. "Kirk?"

"Forget it!" she says, and pushes him off.

"There you kids are," his mother calls from the kitchen door, and Cole jumps, startled again. Liz tugs down her raincoat sleeves.

"Hey, Mom," he says.

Liz clears her throat.

"Who wants some bread pudding?" she asks, stepping by them with the camera. She snaps a picture of the weathervane, then turns back and says "Cheese!" and takes one of him and Liz.

"That'd be good," he says, blasé, though he loves her bread pudding. But what he's imagining is beating Kirk just short of death—so visceral he can't stop his hands from shaking.

"You two look like what the cat dragged in."

They wander into the kitchen, spaced out, no longer stoned.

"Bread pudding!" his mother shouts through the house. Ian's the only one who appears.

"How's it going?" Liz asks him.

"You guys want to watch *Adam-12*?"

"Sure," she says.

His mother passes around spoons and dishes of warm pudding. "Now, Liz, this is a very typical Early American dessert. The particular recipe comes from *The Williamsburg Cookbook*, but it was common in New England, too. At Christmas of course I make it in the bake oven, but I'm not about to light a fire in this heat."

The pudding is sweet and warm. As good as ever.

His father, still in the pressed shirt and tie he wore to the store today, says, "Smells good," and she hands him a dish. He savors a spoonful, moving it around on his tongue before pronouncing it "authentic."

"*Adam-12*'s about to start," Ian says.

"This," his father says, pointing his spoon at Liz, "is a very typical Early American dessert."

Kelly never comes down from her room, but the rest of them watch TV, his mother ironing, his father in his chair with a catalogue, Liz sitting between Ian and Cole on the couch, still wearing her blue raincoat, looking like a kid on the school bus. The highboy's standing just inside the funeral door, where it was abandoned upon delivery.

"He's lost weight," their mother says about Officer Pete Malloy on *Adam-12*. She hangs another of his father's pressed shirts on the candelabra.

At a commercial Ian turns to Cole. "Do you know when you're going camping yet?"

Cole glares at him. "Paul's not sure if he's free."

Ian nods. Gets it.

When the show comes back on, the cops are called to a domestic disturbance. A swarthy, big-gutted man comes to the screen door of a run-down house.

"A goat," their father says, dog-earing a page of the catalogue. "We need a Toggenburg goat."

They watch the beginning of *Hollywood Squares* and then Liz, who's said almost nothing since they came inside—almost nothing since the guard at the shed—says, "I gotta go."

They put their dishes in the sink and he follows her out onto the porch, and she keeps walking, across the backyard toward the fields.

"I'll give you a ride home," he says.

"I'd rather walk." She takes another long stride, then turns back: "When are you going to get it through your fucking head that you could pound the shit out of your father?"

16

"YOU ARE BANISHED!" UNCLE ANDREW WILL BELLOW A DAY AFTER Cole hits him. The draping arm of his brown velour robe will sway as he points at the front door, his bushy hair backlit by the sun behind him, his face darkened by shadow, all of which will provide a biblical image to match this biblical decree, which is perhaps what Cole wanted all along. To escape and become someone new.

He'll get his own place in the apartments beside the town hall, or call his Puerto Rican friend, who lives with a dozen other tobacco workers in Hartford, or move to Seattle and finish high school there. He will become whoever he chooses to be.

But landlords in Bloomfield won't rent to a seventeen-year-old with a cast on his fist, whose own family just kicked him out; and someone at the apartment in Hartford tells him over the phone they're all in upstate New York picking the last of the apple harvest; and going to Seattle on a thousand bucks and the hope of continuing with his heavy course load and graduating this year seems a recipe for disaster. So he tells Tilly he needs a loan. She orders a sit-down with Andrew, all three of them, business-style, at the Four Chimneys, but Andrew's unwavering: "I won't have him living under my roof. He's my sister's son, but he's *his* son too. We know what he's capable of." There's less slurring already from Andrew's swollen lips. His eye has opened, though the bruise is still pretty bad. He's using the arm in the sling to spread butter on a crescent roll.

Cole reaches for his water, forgetting the cast, and knocks over his glass. He turns to Tilly. "The only option is I go to Seattle immediate—"

"You'll live with me," she pronounces, and a bloody steak sizzling with onions on a hot iron platter is placed on the wet tablecloth in front of him. There's no escape. He is who he's become, simmering, splattering, smoldering. He fists the oversized steak knife—the blade as long and curved as the one they used to slaughter the rabbits. He digs in.

Ian takes it hard. He's slowly prepared himself for Cole's leaving a year early for college, and now it's another six months before that. In the few days it takes him to pack up, Ian barely emerges from his room.

Cole moves into his mother's childhood bedroom. Since the stroke, Tilly doesn't go upstairs. Andrew has put a bed in the room they called the library, and brought down her bureau and her clothes, so he has the second-floor bathroom to himself, a luxury he appreciates. The first night, with Tilly sitting at the head of the kitchen table, he pours her Scotch and she tells him he can use her car until he saves enough money to buy one of his own. He develops an elaborate ritual of making himself a mug of tea, then dumping it out and sipping Scotch from the mug. He still goes to Bloomfield High, driving the ten miles in Tilly's yellow Coupe de Ville. He gets a job making grinders, two nights a week and on weekends. He calculates that it will take over a year to make enough to buy a decent used Toyota. By the third week he's quit faking it with the tea. Each night, when he's done with his homework, he and Tilly sit at the kitchen table and pound Scotch; he tops off her crystal glass and then his Bennington Potters mug, as if they're two old men playing cards into the night to forget their dark troubles.

The home health aide comes Monday, Wednesday, and Friday. She changes Tilly's sheets, cleans up around her bed, refills her pill dispensers, tells her to cut back on the Winston Kings and stop drinking. "Terrible interactions with your medications," she cautions her, holding out the pill bottle so Tilly can see the warning sticker.

"What wonderful eyes you must have to read something so minuscule," Tilly tells her. If it's a Friday, she and Cole are usually drinking before the aide even leaves.

And she does have wonderful eyes. Green and bright, despite being perpetually exhausted. Linda has soft features, a small round nose, pale lips, an oval face so puffy that it's almost as if she lives on pastry, though Cole never sees her eat anything. Tilly doesn't eat either, so he tries to load up on capicola grinders and school lunch. He eats pasta. He eats scrambled eggs, watery and metallic-tasting after the fresh eggs he'd taken for granted.

Linda is divorced with two little children and lives with her own mother, who tends to the kids in the evenings while she works. She wears a silver ankh on a chain around her neck. "Is that a lesbian symbol?" Tilly asks him.

It's late and they've been drinking for a couple hours. Cole eyes her, shakes his head.

"What, then? A hippie thing? Some kind of cult?" Since the stroke her eyes point in different directions and she talks out of the corner of her mouth. Booze exaggerates the effect, like a g-force pulling her face toward her left shoulder.

Cole takes a big swallow. "I believe it's an ancient blood-sucking cult. They slurp down a little each night from an old lady until she dries up into dust."

"Well, then." She pushes her glass toward him for a pour. "At least she's in the right line of work."

He still hasn't made any friends at school, a newbie whose tragedy is known to all, and in a sad realization one night, lying in bed with the spins, too drunk to fall asleep, he realizes that his entire social life is asking people if they want hot peppers on their grinder. Cheese? In the oven? And sometimes bullshitting with regulars; the owner and his son argue in Greek and have no interest in talking with Cole or the customers. And his nights drinking with Tilly. He resolves to drink less, night after night with bed spins or worse, mornings of dragging downstairs and steadying a mug of instant coffee in his hand out to the Cadillac, painful just keeping his eyes open against the headache, driving to school with Paul Harvey's tales of redemption on the radio, resolving over and over to set himself straight.

He starts hanging around the kitchen when Linda's in the house, and the more they talk, the younger she seems. Twenty-four, it turns out, with a three-year-old and a one-year-old and an ex-husband stationed in Manila. Although he hasn't seen Roxanne or Paul since Christmastime, he's made sure they know where he is, and Tilly's phone number, and his plans to leave for college a year early, so Liz can find him. Whenever the phone rings, a bubble rises in his heart.

Linda rinses out glasses and organizes pills; she washes sheets and towels and Tilly's flannel nightgowns, with no-nonsense efficiency. She's staying late tonight because Tilly has a bladder infection and she's waiting until her fever drops. Usually her conversations with Cole are clipped, but he gets her talking about her two years at UConn, her daughters, her saint of a mother, who works in a bakery from seven a.m. till four; Linda works five to eleven. "I barely see her," she says. "I miss her." She twists the dial on the dryer and wet laundry starts to tumble. "Sorry about *your* mother." She looks at him, hands on her hips, already thinking about her next task. "Truly sorry."

"It's a bummer," he says, knowing he's hit a false note after the frank tenderness with which she's described her family. "It's really beat," he adds. Even worse. He never knows what to say about it, how to act. Either he sounds like he feels sorry for himself, or like he's consumed by mourning, or just brushing it all off. He doesn't know how to fold the story of his mother's murder into his own story. In his dreams Liz's face and his mother's sometimes switch.

He passes by Tilly's room—she's snoring over the sound of the TV—and goes upstairs for his chemistry book. When he comes back down Linda isn't in the kitchen and he immediately feels a pang of disappointment that she's gone, of loneliness—and then he smells it through the kitchen window. He startles her out behind the garage, where she's smoking a joint. "Shit," she says. "Keep this between us. Cool?"

"Yeah, yeah, don't worry," and he stands there for a moment before she hands it to him. He takes a deep hit, then another. It's been weeks since he's smoked, and the effervescent rush—a million tiny bubbles scattering through his body, down his arms and legs to his fingers and toes—feels familiar as home.

He tells her it's excellent dope. She says it's good enough for everyday weed, weed she can count pills on. The solicitousness has fallen away from her voice, a frank and world-wise practicality taking its place. She's seven years older than he is, and he recognizes that she was dancing at the fair he missed. A veteran of the sixties. Watching her put the joint to her lips, he thinks Janis or Grace Slick. What does she think, looking at him? Keith Partridge? Greg Brady? God almighty.

After a few minutes they're laughing. She tells him a funny story about finding handfuls of dandelions her older daughter had stuffed down the front of her diaper, and one time three and a half Oreos. He tells her about the cops catching him and Liz drinking Southern Comfort in the cemetery, sitting in the grass and leaning back against the headstone of seventeen-year-old Isaac Owen, who died "with bravery & might" in the Revolutionary War.

She looks at her watch, says "Fuck," and hurries through the breezeway into the house. Cole follows, then stands at the open refrigerator, hanging on the door, and seriously considers drinking a strawberry Ensure, but then spots maraschino cherries in the back. He fishes all six out of the narrow jar, eats three, saving the others to offer Linda when she comes back through, then sucks on his cold sweet fingers. A few minutes pass and he leaves hers in the lid on the counter, then drinks the red syrup from the jar.

Pausing at Tilly's room—she's still snoring, the TV turned lower—he thinks Linda will raise her head and say goodnight, but she's taking Tilly's pulse and notes it on her chart, then reaches in her mouth to pull out the dentures.

Cole goes up to his desk and stares at the textbook pages, watching a swirl of H_2O and CO_2 and Fe and Mg and Nt before realizing his only hope is to go to bed and get up extra-early to study for his test.

In bed he closes his eyes to see elements and compounds zinging around like asteroids, and he thinks of the stars and moon chiseled into Isaac Owen's headstone—"staring at the Face of the Fight"—and he doesn't even know she's there until the sheet lifts away from his body and she crawls on top of him, her bra cool and smooth on his chest, the ankh swinging against his chin. Her hard and purposeful plunges shake the bed, and she licks her fingers, reaches down, and quickly comes in a hot rush; then her rhythm slows and he comes, too. All of her weight collapses on him and she's instantly asleep. He inhales the smell of her scalp, feels the moist skin at the small of her back.

After a time he pulls the sheet over them, his feet sticking out the bottom, and drifts in and out of sleep, and when he opens his eyes, in the yellow-blue swath of moonlight shining in the window, there's Tilly. She hasn't been upstairs in a year, but now she's standing in her nightgown at his door, her cheeks and lips hollowed without dentures, peering into the darkness at his bed. He doesn't move. Linda's breathing is silent, and it's possible the corner is so dark she can't see anything, but through his half-open eyes the moonlight seems to get even brighter, spotlighting Tilly and her bluish hair and nightgown falling straight and empty like it's dangling from a wire hanger with her head on top. She's floating.

She backs into the hallway and he awakens some time later. Tilly's TV is turned up loud. Linda is gone from his bed. The moon must've set. The thrum and whir of being high has left him. Had any of this happened? He squints into the darkness at his door, recalling the triangular beam of light on Tilly.

That Friday, Cole gets home from school and sees a strange car in the driveway and a strange woman pulling a thermometer from Tilly's mouth. She's finally over the bladder infection.

Later that night, when he comes in smelling of ham and spicy Italian salami, Tilly's already at the kitchen table with the bottle. He pulls his mug from the cupboard and joins her. "That kind of thing," she says from the corner of her mouth, and taps the rim of her glass. "It'll drag a bright future right under."

COLE'S GOT THE SHIRT UNBUTTONED, BUT HIS FATHER KEEPS SLIP-ping away as he tries to pull it off of him. "C'mon, it's all down your back and in your hair."

"It's fine," he says. "I just took a shower."

He remembers laughing with Nikki over Daniel's blowout poops that shot up the back of his onesie and out the top, then says, "Do you really want to sleep with mouse shit in your hair?"

"I shook it all out. It's fine."

And it's more than just mouse shit. Cole came down to refill their waters this afternoon—left him alone two minutes!—and while he was gone Phil ripped down a section of ceiling plaster, "for a light fixture," he explained. "There's not gonna be a light fixture!" Chunks of plaster dumped down on him along with mouse shit and a shower of vermiculite insulation—pea-sized, gray and silver-gold with shiny specks of mica and asbestos fibers, poured between the attic joists before Cole was born. Only as long as their work doesn't touch the vermiculite, they can leave it and legally sell the house.

He collars his father and tugs the shirt down his back.

"Get your hands off me! You can't *touch* me!"

"Dad—"

"Stop calling me that! Who are you?"

"I'm your son. I'm here to take care of you."

His eyes narrow and he pokes Cole in the chest. "I know who you are. You're the one who's just like me."

"No, I'm not!" Cole shouts, and yanks the filthy shirt, tearing it below the collar.

That day in Portland when he got back to the house with the chef's knife, he told Nikki, "I was just trying to protect you. It seems like a violent impulse, but it's for the right reasons. I'm not my father, it's the opposite of that." And Nikki said, "I know you're not your father, not at all. But how can I love a man who defines himself by all the horrible things he isn't?"

". . . trying to steal my house. I can see your legal maneuvering, but you can't trick me."

"I'm helping—"

"*Helping* me? What do *you* want out of it?"

"I don't want anything. I'm just here to . . . I just want . . ." He simply wants to do the right thing for his father and for his son.

"Looks like I stumped you. Ha! Your ruse is exposed."

"Dad—" That's why he's here: because it's the right thing to do.

"I'm warning you." He clenches his bent fingers into a fist. "Don't call me that again."

"Listen to me. You're my father."

"Okay, wiseass. If that's true, who's your mother?"

"She was your wife."

"Doesn't ring a bell."

"Remember your wife? The woman you married?"

"Nothing comes to mind."

"The mother of your three children. The woman you played the Brahms with. Piano for four hands."

He's disarmed, looking at a spot on the ceiling, and Cole seizes the moment to rip off his shirt. "She came home from Ensign-Bickford with the smell of gunpowder in—"

"Not *your* mother."

He unbuckles the belt.

"She met Martin Luther King. Of course he wasn't famous back then, just one of the southern teenagers who came up to Simsbury to pick tobacco during the war."

"Your *wife*." Jesus, he's heard this story a hundred times.

"She said he was polite and shy. But after he was famous, someone used to tell her, 'You met one of the greatest men of the century and all you can say is he was polite and shy?'"

He pulls down his father's underwear. "*Who* said that?"

"Somebody. I don't remember who."

"*Mom* said it. Your *wife*."

"In any case, Mother would laugh and say, 'He was just a kid shoveling in food at a church supper.'"

This recollection has softened his father, so Cole tests the water temp and guides him under the spray. Deciding it's futile to try to stay dry, he strips off his own clothes, squeezes into the tight shower stall, and turns the water warmer. "Close your eyes," he says, and moves his father's head under the stream. Shampooing him, he massages his fingertips into his scalp, a deep, slow pressure that eases his fidgety body and soothes his confusion and belligerence. When he rinses out the suds, tiny pellets of mouse shit skim down his father's back. "Arms up," he says, and washes him from his hands to his pits, then the curls of his ears and the loose skin around his neck. "Tell me more about your mother," he says.

Phil burbles his lips in the water streaming down his face. "She loved root-beer floats. I think she loved them more than I did."

Cole scrubs his back, working his thumbs into the tight scapula muscles around the big scar. He lathers up his hands with more soap, and washes the soft folds of flesh at his father's belly, crotch, and thighs, their bodies pressed together. He's never been this close to another naked man. He squats down to wash between his toes.

"I'd fill a little plastic bag with ice cubes," Phil says, "while she poured root beer and scooped in ice cream. We kept the lights off in the kitchen. The two of us sipping through straws at the table, whispering in the dark while she held the ice to her cheek."

Cole's heart misses a beat. Of all the stories he's heard a hundred times, this is a first. As he stands he rubs his father's quads and hips, then rubs his lower back and shoulders.

Yes, he's stayed on at the house because it's the right thing to do. But there's more. All his life he's wondered if forgiveness was possible, if he even knew what it meant. As he kneads the muscles around the scar, their bodies pressed into the shower stall, he comes to realize that forgiveness doesn't happen in an instant—it's not a simple decision, but an accumulation of generous acts, of kindness and taking care. He's stayed on because this summer is what forgiveness looks like.

18

"DO I HAVE TO DO EVERYTHING MYSELF?" SHE SAYS, AND THEN
does it: while Cole and Ian and their father are pulling the old iron
baseboard radiators out of the front room, she calls the antique
dealer in Hartford. The boys keep their heads down. Their father's on
his knees detaching each section, then they carry them out, heavy as
manhole covers, and stack them in the borning room. Hunched over
on the floor, he purses his lips and forces a stuck bolt with a crescent
wrench too puny for the job. The wrench slips and he grunts as blood
seeps from his knuckles.

"Fifty dollars your little adventure cost us," she announces.

He lifts his head from the baseboard, furious and mute.

"The delivery fee all over again, plus you surely didn't think he'd
give you as much back as you paid for it, did you? Oh, he saw you
coming a mile away. Another highboy, when Ian needs braces and
we're still paying last winter's oil bill."

She's won, Cole thinks. The highboy's going back, and she'd like
him to acknowledge that buying it was a mistake. She wants him to
say something. Anything. But they all know he won't.

"Ludicrous!" she yelps. "I have to work myself into a tailspin just
to keep you from bankrupting us. Fifty dollars down the drain. Now
you see it, now you don't!"

That night, Cole is sure it will come. Fan off, light on, no music,
door unlatched. "Why does every decision have to be a fight?" he

hears her plead through the walls. He tiptoes from his closet to the spare bed, piling up his camping gear. They'll just hike up the Metacomet Trail and camp on the ridgeline above Old Newgate Prison. They'll have to keep—"Think about the family . . . Our *marriage*, for Pete's sake . . . I'm up to my ears in chickens and geese and rabbits!"—keep their campfire low and—"Asinine!"

The bruises on Liz's arms were worse than ever. "No damn goat, either!" She promises him she's got it under control, but that can't be true if it's getting worse. He wants to take her away from here. Maybe Ian and Liz have exactly the right idea: instead of camping for a night a mile away—"If you leave me, I'm keeping the money, because I *need* money"—they should just take off. He's heard about cannery boats shipping out from Seattle to Alaska. Factories at sea. You work a few months, then find a cheap place to live until your money runs out. Great dope, and everybody gets high while they're packing salmon into cans. He'd save Liz from Kirk, and get himself out of this fucking house. And maybe save his mother, too. His leaving could shock his parents into changing. "Can't afford a vacation? Don't start lecturing *me* about money."

By midnight it's been quiet for fifteen minutes or more, and he decides he can let himself fall asleep. He leaves the fan off. It's all a desperate game: if he turns it on, he'll be cooler and can sleep more easily, but he'll be listening through the whir, which will keep him awake. And he's gotten worked up. On the edge of sleep he sees Liz's wrists again, ringed with bruises. His eyes shoot open, his heart thumps. He listens to the silence.

Down in the kitchen, he runs the tap until it's cool and drinks a glass of water. He tiptoes back up to his room, sits by the window, and packs the one-hit bowl with his thumb, flicks the lighter, draws slow bubbles through the water, then sucks the smoke up the tube quick as a gasp. Back downstairs he grabs the bottle they keep for Tilly, unscrews the cap, and puts it to his lips for a shot that fires up his face.

He gets back in bed, spinning a little now. He's dulled the sharpness, blurred the hyperalertness, but he's no closer to sleep. He tries to jerk off, but the strings from his brain to his cock won't tighten.

A noise jolts him out of bed. He takes one stride and another, but then halts. It's a goose, startled by a raccoon or possum that's galumphing through the fallen pears.

He rolls a joint and goes back downstairs. He's got to sleep. If only there were a switch he could flick off. He takes his water glass from the sink and pours in a few more swallows of Scotch and sips it on the back porch, looking out at the moonshine, white and bright on the tobacco nets.

From the couch he snags a throw pillow, sticks it under his arm and, with his glass of Scotch in one hand and the fresh joint between his fingers, walks outside wearing nothing but underpants and crosses the yard to the tractor road. The nets are beautiful in the hot night. Though there's no perceptible wind, they shift and billow, tugging on the bailing wire, which tugs on the cedar posts—an old wooden creak to accompany the crickets.

Walking through the deep corridor of nets, each bent a room, a bedchamber, a bed curtained and canopied, dirt between his toes, sweet smoke in his lungs and hot on his tongue, smoothed over by the Scotch—what *gold* would taste like?—he sucks at the roach till it's smaller than a pill, then squeezes it between his fingers and swallows it down with the last golden slug.

He sets the glass on the ground beside a post and keeps moving but after a time realizes he's stumbling and then he's down on his knees in the dirt. He lifts the edge of the net and crawls along the row—the fourth priming, stalks stripped up three feet with a green canopy of leaves overhead. He crawls through to the second bent, and the third, then puts the pillow down and stretches out on the cool, soft ground.

. . .

COLD SHOWER, SUNDAY MORNING, SCRUBBING THE DIRT OFF HIS knees and shins and the palms of his hands. He's dulled, yes, though not exhausted, not hungover. He slept under the nets as soundly as he's slept in years, no idea if the fight turned violent last night.

But now they're late for church. They're *always* late for church. No bruises on his mother's face.

Kirk's an altar boy and gives Cole the evil eye when they clop into the pew during the penitential rite. Father Mally remains aloof at first, but finally *his* glare falls on them, too. "I have sinned through my own fault," Cole mumbles along with everyone else, "in what I have done, and in what I have failed to do." At least half the families come to church fatherless, and he supposes some of them are fishing with pals, talking on ham radios, or . . . what else do men do? He has no clue. *His* father's probably sinking a sledgehammer into the walls of their front room, making a heap of lath and plaster for his sons to contend with after mass. His mother presses a coin into each of their hands for the basket, then drops in two crumpled dollar bills. "Lord, I am not worthy." They take communion, they kneel, they pray. Ridiculous. Stupendously boring. Father Mally's sermonizing, his little insights into human nature, his tips for virtuous living drawn from the Gospel are so fluffy that Cole feels contempt for everyone who wastes an hour of their weekend to be here.

Yet despite the inanity, he lines up and takes communion and holds the wafer solemnly on his tongue, bowing his head, kneeling and clasping his hands. And he prays. He asks God to make them stop. Whatever it takes. It's the only thing he prays for.

And rising from his knees he feels a little refreshed, a little stronger. Like he's done something. "Peace be with you," he says to his mother with a kiss, to Kelly and Ian with a hug, to Mr. Hayes in the pew behind him, shaking his hand, to the Reynolds boys and their grandmother in front, and even to Father Mally, robed and paternal, his knee clicking with each stride down the aisle. He takes Cole's hand between his own. "Peace be with you, Father."

By noon they look like slaves in a gypsum mine, their powdered faces streaked with sweat. Ian's got plaster dust in his eyebrows and hair, straining to lug his side of the garbage can. He looks like an old man.

They've worked quietly and steadily, no groans or complaints. Kelly has been rolling primer on the ceiling and walls of the buttery, setting nails in the trim, spackling and sanding. They're so cooperative because they're waiting for what comes next, which is the van pulling into the driveway with the little Old World man from Hartford, here a week ago, returning to pick up the highboy. Their mother meets him at the funeral door, and the boys follow their father. Kelly doesn't emerge from the buttery, knowing it will only make things worse if she's present to witness his defeat.

"On a Sunday!" their mother exclaims.

"My Sabbath is Saturday," he says, and Cole realizes he's Jewish. Maybe not Italian at all. Cole hadn't noticed the little tassels before, even after going into the shop several times.

"It's just not right," his father says. "Doesn't fit where we'd hoped to place it."

And now they hear another vehicle: Tilly's Cadillac pulling in behind the van. Everyone, even the antique dealer, senses that nothing can proceed until Tilly enters the room, that she is central to any drama that might unfold. So they stand around silently, shifting, staring off, just waiting. And then she steps through the door and they begin again.

"Mother. What a lovely surprise."

"Such a beautiful piece," she says. She introduces herself to the dealer and then says, providing her bona fides, "Marks and Tilly Limited." She shakes his hand. "Some damage on that one foot," she notes, then slides open a drawer and runs her fingers over the dovetails. "It's American?" she says.

"Yes, ma'am."

She moves her fingertips over the molding at the top and then down one side, like a tailor fitting a man with a suit. "The veneer has bubbled out here, you see."

"It's two hundred years old," he says.

In her high heels she walks slowly, appraisingly around it, then says, without looking at their father, "I hope you didn't pay over three hundred for it."

No one says a word. Tilly pivots one foot on the point of a heel, and finally their mother says, "It's going back is what's happening here. Phil decided it wasn't quite right."

Tilly sniffs at the air, knowing there's more to the story, but no one says a thing.

She turns back to the highboy, flicks a fingernail in a gap that's opened up in one of the joints, slides her thumb the length of a scratch. She sighs, pushing a drawer closed tight. "I could probably take it off your hands," she says, then turns to their mother. "We'd all enjoy an iced tea."

The male Callahans troop out at this pause and get back to work. The afternoon is hot and slow going. Now and again their father glances out the window to see whether the Cadillac and the antique dealer's van are still in the driveway, and eventually he turns the radio up—classical music from Hartford—as if he wants to drown them out, even though they're beyond earshot in the far side of the house. He rips out a hunk of lath, mutters, his face twitching. He bashes the wall with the sledgehammer, pinches his finger, groans, bashes the wall again. Other than the outbursts, grunts, and mumbles, he's silent for an hour. Ian and Cole are, too. They know the drill: load the can, hump it out back to the dump pile, break the plaster away from the lath, then heap the lath up separately to pound out the nails another day.

Late in the afternoon, on one of the last trips outside, Cole stops short as he's coming into the kitchen. *"Je vais te rendre plus tendre"*— his mother's stabbing a steak on the counter with a fork; a sprinkle of tenderizer, then stab-stab-stab—*"tendre et bonne et délicieuse"*—

and another sprinkle, her voice singsongy like she's tickling a baby—"*délicieuse pour ma famille*," the dishes in the cupboards rattling with each thrust of the fork.

Sunday dinner. Their father cuts the steak onto their plates, then she spoons on mashed potatoes and wax beans.

"Such timing," she says. "In the Berkshires, just this morning, Tilly was in a shop in Stockbridge that doesn't hold a *candle* to Marks and Tilly, and she sees a highboy displaying tea towels—you know, draped over open drawers, stacked inside. That one was a repro, so as usual Tilly has outdone the competition. And she let your antique dealer know who's who. She went over that highboy inch by inch and in the end he delivered it to her shop for free, gave us back all that you paid, and she bought it herself for fifty dollars less." She takes a folded bill out of her pocket and snaps it open: a fifty-dollar bill. The three kids gawk at it. Cole has never seen one. "That," she says, slipping the money back in her pocket, "is how you do business." She pours gravy on her mashed potatoes. "Now"—she points her fork at her husband—"Tilly had some thoughts about Paris hotels."

ANOTHER WEEK PASSES AND HIS FATHER TAKES A TURN FOR THE worse, forgetting more words than he remembers, wandering most evenings out into the charred and rotting fields so one of them has to run after him; and his increasing, even aggressive incontinence requires Cole to coax him into the shower sometimes twice a day, which thankfully demands less and less arm twisting. He seems to like the rubdown and the closeness of their bodies under the warm water, and it occurs to Cole that his father probably hasn't been touched at all for a long, long time.

He's as sharp as ever at the keyboard and playing even more, though always the same piece. "The soundtrack of the summer," Daniel calls it. It's pretty peaceful, having that soothing, familiar melody swirling in the background. And the wrong notes are now so expected that they sound just right.

Cole has made little or no progress with the VA. They have resent forms that didn't arrive the first time and are suspiciously delayed again. He suspects his father might have intercepted them, and searched his room and the garbage last night but came up with nothing. Likewise, the incompetency paperwork's completely stalled, pending the requisite doctors' exams that won't happen until he's submitted the forms to the VA.

He's been talking to Nikki more frequently, every couple nights. He calls her after he gets in bed, hoping she won't be at Tony's, and he's delighted that more and more she isn't. Daniel is too, although he tries to play it cool. He can hear Cole's muffled voice through the bedroom wall if he's on the phone at night, and in the morning while Cole is making him a crepe or scrambling eggs, he'll casually ask, *"Cómo está mi madre?"*

And tonight he calls her again, and again she answers. "How's Daniel?" she asks.

"Good, I think. He's home more. Getting a little bored with LK, I'm afraid. He still loves the work though, and he won't admit it, but I think he likes banking some money."

"What's he going to do with it?"

"Buy a Corvette."

She laughs. "LK really is an inspiration."

"Nah. The regular-kid thing's run its course."

"He texted me something like that."

"I think we should still encourage him to hang out with LK. He's hardly a great role model, but at least he's a different kind of kid for Daniel to get to know before he's back with his old crowd in Portland."

"Yeah," she says. "I agree."

They're silent for a minute, and he fears the conversation has run dry. He's not sure how much he should say about what he's been thinking while lying awake in the heat at night, when he's troweling mud on the drywall seams and rolling on paint, while he's mashing potatoes for his father and son, when he's squatting down to scrub his father's legs or massaging the muscles around his shoulder blades as hot water courses down his back, how he washes his own body afterwards then directs the shower head to rinse them both, and how he's noticed—their knobby calves, their slightly bowed legs, long thighs, and bony hips—how similar their bodies are.

Instead he says, "Can I ask you a favor?"

"Mmm." Not a yes, nor a no.

The bed is comfortable, his body worn to a frazzle from the day of work, the night cooling off just enough. "Would you sing me a song?"

"You mean like now? On the phone?"

"Yeah."

"That's sort of weird. I mean, I guess so. What song?"

"Any song. It doesn't matter."

"Well, let's see." She hems and haws. "You never asked me to sing before." She's clearly embarrassed, but he can hear that she's smiling so hard she's squinting, her face flushed. She giggles nervously, takes a deep breath, then a second one, then begins.

"Born with the moon in Cancer. Choose her a name she will answer to . . ."

Her voice is wavery, as it never is. She's performing. She never performs, she just sings. "Call her green and the winters cannot fade her . . ."

She eases down into the wellspring of her voice. Cole switches off the lamp on his nightstand and slides down in bed, pressing the phone to his ear.

19

TILLY GOES TO THE BERKSHIRES THE FIRST SUNDAY OF EVERY month. He has always known this about her, and Andrew will continue to drive her even after Cole moves into her house. He'll come over in his own car and they'll head off in the Cadillac for the day. Over the years, "going to the Berkshires" has summoned up images of crab salad at the Turner Inn, followed by drinks in a wicker rocker on their magnificent porch, a sharp-eyed strut through quaint stores, slow drives past rock walls and over covered bridges, an afternoon on the lawn at Tanglewood.

On Sunday Cole's woken by an anvil dropping on his head. "Chop, chop," Tilly calls from the bottom of the stairs. She kept him up drinking late last night; when he quit pouring, she took over topping them off, her hand never steadier than when it's wrapped around a bottle. It turns out that Andrew injured his knee so badly in a race yesterday they kept him overnight in the hospital for surgery.

Cole is behind the wheel by ten, stopping at the Farm Shop for two coffees, adding sugar and cream to Tilly's, then tearing sip holes in the lids with his front teeth. Driving, he takes a swallow, and when it's halfway down he knows it could go either way—to his stomach or back up again. He stows the cup in the holder he bought to hang off the door—plastic and orange and despised by Tilly for its truck-driver cheapness. She sneers at it and lights a cigarette. He powers down her window an inch and she puts it back up. He cracks it again and locks the controls. Knowing what he's done, she doesn't try the button again but simply blows a cloud of smoke at him.

He drives past miles of tobacco fields north of town, the nets removed, everything stored neatly in the sheds, and past the 92 Compound, where Puerto Rican pickers and their families live in the late spring and summer months, paint peeling off the clapboards on bulky buildings that must have once looked grand, like the lakeside family hotel next to the roller rink had looked before Cole's time. Barbecue pits, horseshoes, and tetherball off in the trees. *Family*. At the moment it's just him and Tilly, and he again resolves to regain his brother's trust.

But he realizes within minutes that of course this compound— built for seasonal workers from Puerto Rico and Jamaica—was never anything like a hotel. How easy it is to project an imagined life onto someone else.

He's able to hold down the coffee by taking tiny sips, and his body has achieved a tottery peace with itself. He stops for gas in Southwick and when—with his hand on the nozzle—the tank burps out overpowering fumes, he pukes up the coffee in three insistent heaves into the garbage, blows his nose with a blue paper towel, and goes inside to pay, his headache now blinding.

"I'd better park for a few minutes," he tells Tilly when he teeters back in the car, "just to shut my eyes."

"No," she says, "you'll drive. Grandpapa used to tell your uncle that if you want to play like a man, you can damn well *be* a man."

She directs him from one meandering state highway to another as he repeats to himself "Over the river and through the woods . . ." like a mantra to keep both head and stomach from erupting while they roll and wind through the foothills into the Berkshires, and he keeps thinking they'll come upon one of the gracious historic towns he's visited once or twice. But soon they're passing auto-repair shops, a grungy motel, and an asphalt contractor on the outskirts of a scruffy mill town: crumbling smokestacks, sooty brick factories with bashed-out windows, a McDonald's and a Jack in the Box side by side. The main street's pretty much closed up on a Sunday, though a few blocks later there's a busy laundromat between vacant storefronts. They stop at a red light, where on one corner there's the beautiful old marquee of a long-defunct movie theater, the Egyptian, and on the other a grand art-deco performing-arts theater, shuttered for decades.

"What are we doing here?" he asks.

"Nosy, nosy," she says. "You can drop me at those blinking lights."

"That bar?"

She flips down the visor mirror and dabs powder from a compact on her cheeks. "It's a pub."

"It's called Vic's Bar and Grill and there's a flashing neon Schlitz sign."

"There've been a lot of names through the years."

He pulls up to the curb and stares at the black iron bars over the windows. "Kind of a dive, too."

"You're entitled to your opinion," she says, opening the door. "Three o'clock sharp. Right here."

Watching her walk away—actually rather elegant in white high heels and a rose-colored dress—he thinks that if he weren't so miserable he might try to stop her. The place isn't merely seedy; it looks dangerous. But if he stands, his head so polluted with residue liquor, he'd probably fall over. And if he made it down the sidewalk as far as the front door, one waft from the beer-sticky floor would be the end of him.

Tilly's about to step inside when a blue van rattles up to the curb and its horn toots. She turns. A man about her age hops out and hustles toward her, grinning as broadly as she is. Since the stroke, or his mother's death, he hasn't seen her beam like that. Hell, he's *never* seen Tilly beam like that. They kiss each other on the cheek, not a peck but a long slow kiss, practically nuzzling. He's in a white shirt, his hair combed back with oil, and what Cole finds most extraordinary are the dozen or so keys dangling from a round steel case clipped to his belt. Although she must know Cole's sitting thirty feet away in the car, she doesn't even give him a glance. Together they go through the door, Tilly on his arm. Stenciled on the side of the van is "Bob Dunn Welding."

Cole sits there stunned for five minutes. He grabs fistfuls of his hair, partly for the ripping headache and partly in disbelief. Is this where Andrew's been bringing her every month all these years? It doesn't make any sense. Finally he shifts into drive and inches forward, wondering what he can do to kill two-and-a-half hours, and now he can see there's a patio on the side of the bar where they're sitting at a picnic table. The waitress is setting down what looks like a glass of water for Bob Dunn and surely an iced tea—lemon wedge on the rim, tall black straw—for her. This is Tilly, by God, who orders her first drink before sitting down and her second as the waitress delivers the first. She pinches the lemon and shakes down a sugar packet. Tilly, iced tea, in a bar. Wow.

He hits the gas and loops back through town to the McDonald's, where he orders a Coke. Reaching in his pocket for change, he finds an even better cure: a sizable roach from the night he smoked with Linda. Back in the Coupe de Ville, he torches it up and gets two good hits, immediately soothing, before burning his fingers. The flutter of nausea subsides, the fist in his head unclenches. He drives the mile back to "the pub," parking shy of where she'll see the yellow car from the patio. He reclines the seat.

He dreams of Tilly standing in the moonlight at his bedroom door looking like a ghost—*Cole, Cole*—and when he opens his eyes she's right there in the backseat, the sun lighting up the smoke all around her, the tip of a cigarette glowing orange.

"Cole!"

"Ready," he says. He slept for two hours. "Why are you sitting in back?"

"Drive," she says. "This is how we always do it."

"But why don't you—"

"No talking. Not until we're home."

"Well, I at least need directions if you—"

"Cole, dear. I happen to know you're a very smart young man. I'm sure you can find your way back." Sober as a nun.

So he drives, and at the next traffic light he notices a brown paper bag on the seat next to him. Inside, wrapped in butcher paper, is a sandwich. "Is this for me?" He's looking at her in the mirror, and it's as if she didn't hear him—gazing out the window, her eyes and face pulsing with reverie. So he eats the turkey club while he drives and, she was right—he navigates the route back to her house without a hitch.

When he shuts off the engine, still in the garage, she says, "I'll have a Scotch, please."

In the kitchen he pours her usual and a small one for himself, sitting together at the table. A few sips in he says, "So how's Bob?"

"Mr. Dunn to you, sonny."

"Who *is* Bob?"

She clears her throat and picks up a newspaper.

"Who's Mr. Dunn?" he tries.

"An old friend. He's not your concern."

"I'm kind of curious, Tilly." He smiles playfully. "A secret rendezvous across state lines?"

Her face sparks, the corner of her mouth lifting just enough that he knows she's pleased by his interest, but says nothing.

"And such a seedy locale."

She looks up from the newsprint. "That establishment has been through many incarnations over the years. The Royale had dancing, wonderful bands, limousines lined up out front. You've never seen so elegant a dancer as Mr. Dunn." She looks into her Scotch, takes a sip. "The Royale closed after the war and for quite some time became the Peacock Club."

He's still baffled. This sounds like complete fantasy. "What war?"

"The second, of course. It wasn't until the fifties that the mills started to close, but the town—"

"How long have you been having these rendezvous with Mr. Dunn?"

"Since June seventeenth, nineteen thirty-three. It was a Saturday." Cole throws back a gulp. "Wait! When were you born? When were you *married*?"

She looks back at the paper, pretends to read, turns the page.

"You gotta give me something. Every month since nineteen thirty-three?"

She sets her elbows on the table and gazes at him with a lightness he's never seen in her, genuine equanimity. Even the sagging corner of her mouth seems to rise into balance with the other side. "You never knew my mother, but every story you've heard is true. If Mima were dressed to the nines on a Saturday afternoon, shopping at G. Fox in Hartford, and she passed through the doors onto the sidewalk and met Queen Elizabeth coming the other direction"—she pauses, relishing what's next—"it is Queen Elizabeth who would have graciously stepped aside to let Mima pass." She tips her head, like that explains it all. Then she admires her gold watch.

He scratches the back of his neck. "I'm afraid you lost me there."

She offers him a kind, composed face. "Mima wasn't about to let her only daughter marry a welder. And anyway, he's a Protestant."

"Wait. You're telling me the love of your life—"

"Enough!" She holds up her hand, and he knows she means it. "Same time next month."

THAT NIGHT SHE'LL GO TO BED EARLY, AND THE NEXT NIGHT TOO, but by midweek they'll be back to their usual schedule. She is Cole's best bud and drinking partner, and they both count on the routine. She's reading the paper as he studies chemistry—his most difficult course. He can feel the rhythm of their drinking internally, reaching out to give her a pour just before she tips back the last swallow, pacing himself so he doesn't suddenly have a belly sloshing with booze. Prime the pump, enjoy the period of the alcohol working its clarifying magic and cutting through the blur he's felt all day, and that initial spark that can be extended if done right. He's sharper, chemistry makes sense, as do Shakespeare and cosines and the five root causes of the Cold War. It's something like perspicacious, like a panacea (SAT words). Tilly turns a page, says, "Edith Fallows died," and he gets through the chapter, finishes a worksheet, and pushes the textbook aside, tops up her glass and his mug, and then they get down to serious drinking, not to become merely drunk, not the swirly, dizzy stupidity of drunkenness, but to get plastered. "Damn, that light's bright," he says. "Watch your mouth," she snaps. She looks at the two fluorescent rings on the ceiling, lifting her chin, getting haughty. "Grandpapa insisted on proper lighting. Excellent vision until the day he passed." Cole remembers him with two pairs of glasses on cords, clacking against each other when he carried his warm beer in a shaky hand from the counter to the table, to the very chair where he's sitting now. "You'll have to come home early from school tomorrow," she says, "to take me to the doctor." He swishes, then swallows. "Electroshock?" he says. Her mouth elongates in what might look like a sneer but he knows is a suppressed smile. He laughs. "They gonna zap the crazy out of you?" He's hot, always heats up when he drinks, so he takes off his chamois shirt and tosses it over a chair, leaving him in a *Dark Side of the Moon* tee. From Liz. "It's your father should've got zapped," she says. She gets cold when she drinks, and now wraps his chamois shirt around her neck like a scarf. She points at him. "But you did good," she says conspiratorially. "You did what needed to be done. Now, sit up straight," she tells him. "A man looks weak hunched over. Do you think air-force men carry themselves like that? What do you think your sister would make of your posture?" He recently got a letter from Kelly recounting impressive morning runs through mud, all rigor and discipline, signing off with "*Aim

High!" She seems as permanently gone as his mother and father, and although he'd like to see her he feels guilty that he doesn't miss her more. He stares into the booze in his mug, thinking that all of this is temporary, the stage before living resumes, and suddenly it's his mother's voice he's hearing. "When we've completed the restoration" began any of a hundred lines she repeated over and over: "Phil and I are going to do Europe right," "we'll actually take a *family* vacation," "I'll start reading," "I'll start yoga," "I'll start cooking more gourmet," "I'll start enjoying the weekends," "we'll actually start *living* in this house." But she never got that far, and he feels a rush of sadness, which Tilly calls self-pity, so he never lets her see it. Like his mother did, he's living in the in-between, but soon this will be over and he'll be in college on the other side of the country, all rigor and discipline and Aim High! But Tilly rings the rim of her glass with a fingernail, and Cole does the only thing that makes sense: a stiff pour for her and a stiffer one for himself, and he throws it back in two hard swallows and bellows, "Tell me again, Tilly, about the time you and Grandpapa took the goddamn train to Atlantic City!"

20

CROSSING HATCHET HILL TO THE NEXT TOWN, IT'S NOT JUST A FEW turns he knows but every curve and rise in the road, every stretch that narrows along a hillside or flattens out by the river. Today is the anniversary of his mother's death, always a day when he feels a shiver of finality—she was his mother and then she was gone. But this time he's restless, as if that night continues on, much like his father and the unfinished business of this unfinished house.

The cemetery and their old church aren't far from the restaurant in the converted mill where he had lunch with Liz, almost two months ago now—months in which he feels like he's lived outside of time. Coming around the corner, he sees that the church has been sided in vinyl. Still, it's an attractive, broad-shouldered little building with a stout bell tower, perched on a hilltop with the cemetery spilling down the gentle slope behind it.

He parks in the lot and climbs the steps to the front doors, but they're locked. Across the lawn, there's no activity in the rectory, blinds drawn, and he stands in the shade for a moment. When he was last here, he was helping carry the casket down to a hearse that drove it the few hundred yards to the grave site. Since his right hand was in a cast, he was positioned so he could grasp the casket rail with his left. He was surprised by how light it was, what little effort was required to bear the body of his murdered mother.

He walks back along the street and into the cemetery, stopping at a statue of the Virgin Mary just inside the gate and gazing down the slope to the left where she's buried next to Grandpapa. Tilly's grave must be right beside them.

White peastone crunches underfoot as he steps along the narrow drive, and he's passing under a shade tree when a car pulls into a side entrance. His legs and then his whole body slosh like vertigo, so wavery that he grabs on to the tree trunk. The car's a canary-yellow Cadillac, identical to Tilly's. It stops by the grave and the driver's door swings open. Even from this distance, even after these years, he recognizes Uncle Andrew from his lanky and streamlined runner's body, his pitched-forward neck, his long narrow head. He opens the back door and extends his arm; a hand takes it, and an old woman rises out of the car. Cole squints, watching her navigate the uneven ground over to the headstone. He's seen her before. He *knows* her. But it can't be Sandy, because then the passenger door opens and a tiny woman with a long silver ponytail and a Guatemalan dress gets out.

How easily the old emotions rekindle. He has focused so much on rage, but now shame burns him like a branding iron. Andrew and Sandy took in all three kids—happily!—and Cole completely cut them out of his life. He's tempted to wait under the tree, just allow them to pay their respects and leave so he doesn't have to face them. But he regains his legs, takes a big breath, and walks across the grass through the headstones, not knowing if he'll be met with cold shoulders or even hostility.

Sandy's the first to recognize him, her somber face overcome by something like elation. She throws open her arms and he rushes to her, and once he's in her embrace he's sobbing like a baby. She holds him until he composes himself, then he wipes his eyes and turns to Andrew, his face leaner, a Band-Aid on his cheekbone, but really looking just the same. "It's wonderful to see you," he says, taking Cole, his back heaving again, into his arms.

The pitch of emotion in the air is exhausting and exhilarating.

After a time they introduce him to Sandy's mother, Faye, and he says, "I think we met thirty years ago."

"Yes, I remember it well," Faye says.

Sandy squeezes Cole's arm and discreetly shakes her head. "Actually, Mom, that's when you lived in France. You never met Cole."

"I lived in France?" she asks.

"Yes, Mom. You and Daddy lived in Lyon for eighteen years."

She pulls a face, sly and girlish. "How fabulous."

They leave it there, but Cole still feels a familiarity about her. He wonders how old she is and almost asks. His mother would've turned sixty-nine this year, and Faye must be a lot older than that. It's always been impossible for him to imagine years onto his mother; even seeing how Andrew and Sandy have aged, he can't conjure an image of her being any older than she was that night. But maybe—Faye has a round, gentle face and soft eyes—maybe she would've looked something like that.

They ask him if he's still in Seattle, and he says, "No, Portland." When they ask about Kelly and Ian, he's ashamed that he doesn't know any more about them than Andrew's question suggests *he* does. He tells them at length about his brilliant and compassionate son, realizing that not mentioning his wife is explanation enough.

The conversation turns to why Cole is in Connecticut, and he provides the broad outlines, speaking mostly about Alex and Antoine and the beauty and functionality of chestnut.

They talk about everything except the reason they're all at the cemetery today. Instead, in a lull, they subtly shift their footing to face the grave. After a long silence, Andrew clears his throat. "Why don't you come back to the homestead with us for tea? Stay for supper."

He'd like to, and says so, but leaving his father alone much longer could be disastrous. "I'm actually trying to fix the old house up a little and put it on the market," is what he tells him. "Hey, want a screaming deal on an old colonial? Needs some work, but it's a gem." They all chuckle, even Faye. "I really do need to get back to finish something, but I'd love for you to meet my son. Could we come by another time?" He doesn't mention Phil, and they don't ask. Maybe they assume he's dead.

"That would be wonderful," Sandy says, tearing up again.

"Where do you live?" he asks, wiping his eyes.

"The homestead," Andrew says.

Cole shakes his head. *Homestead? He's not getting it.*

"Tilly's old house."

In one beat he's sitting at that kitchen table, craving a few big swallows of Scotch.

As he's saying goodbye, he gives Faye a hug and makes the connection: she's who was painting in the side yard of Tilly's house. And it was Sandy who brought her the tea. Strange that he didn't recognize her then.

They offer Cole a lift to the church lot, but he declines, and Andrew makes a slow loop through the cemetery, the polished yellow car sparkling in the sun. The chrome shines like mirrors, the tires oil-black, the whitewalls gleaming. It's obviously his prize possession, a cherry '70s Coupe de Ville with white leather seats, acquired from the original owner.

WHEN HE GETS HOME HE WALKS FROM ROOM TO ROOM, DISCOURaged by all that remains to be done just to get the place presentable enough to invite realtors in. And Ben called as he was driving back: all their jobs have hit snags, manageable snags, but issues that Cole could best handle on-site. On top of that, they lost a remodel for the fall because the city made demands about the design, something about the angle of the driveway and a retaining wall, and the customer got tweaked that Cole couldn't meet with them immediately to fix it.

He squats down and pulls at a dried-up bead of caulk where the shower stall butts up to the plaster: wet and spongy right down to the floorboard. Since arriving in East Granby he's been living across time, through time. It would solve a lot of problems if he could figure out how to live across *space*, to be here and in Portland at once.

He makes pasta and a big salad for dinner, then drives Daniel to a party at LK's, and coming back he can hear the piano from the driveway. As he walks behind his father, he stops and lays his hands on his shoulders through the end of the movement. And as the next lighter, trillier movement begins, he opens a second beer and listens while he washes the dishes.

For a couple hours he sits in the wing chair in the parlor with his laptop, trying to solve another issue that Ben mentioned on the phone. They're adding a second story to a bungalow, and in his original design the stairs rise up directly opposite the front door; but now the client says he doesn't want to walk inside and look at nothing but staircase.

"But it's going to be the most beautiful goddamn staircase they've ever seen," he told Ben this afternoon. "I was thinking I'd even use the chestnut. There's four times what I need for my family room."

"Well, he says he wants a sightline straight through the kitchen and out the back windows."

So Cole nudges the stairs over by four feet, then tries to fix the size of the new bedrooms and deal with a load-bearing wall in a living room that's four feet narrower. In building and design two rules typically hold up: there's always a solution to a problem, and you can get used to anything. But as he looks away from the screen and notices it's gotten dark outside, he fears he might not find the solution to this one. Ben's right, it would really help if he were there and could see it for himself.

He closes the laptop and shuts his eyes to study the image that's stayed with him all day: the old mint-condition Cadillac, rolling at a walking pace past headstones and hedges and mounded earth, Sandy and Andrew and Faye waving in slow motion behind the glass until they passed through the gate and were gone.

He calls Nikki and tells her about the graveside meeting.

"Wow," she says. "I'll bet that stirred up a lot."

"It's kind of incredible that Andrew welcomed me with open arms after I broke his nose over my own misunderstanding. I've got to stop denying my fucked-up role in all of this or I'll never forgive myself, ever. This isn't just about forgiving my father."

"You were a kid," she says. "In hindsight, yes, it's a bummer you beat up your uncle, but your mother had just been strangled and you thought he was hitting Sandy, and anyway he was screwing his high-school students. If one of those girls' fathers had found out, it would've been even worse. And with your parents, how could you have stopped it? You did much more than any kid should be expected to. Imagine Daniel blaming himself for our problems."

"I know. But Daniel doesn't go into a rage and lose control—"

"Cole, you did what you had to do to protect your mother and it still wasn't enough, but that isn't *your* fault."

So Nikki, like him, has come to believe the story she tells. "Remember what you said that night when I was stranded out there at the prison? You're totally right. I can't tell the difference between letting go of control and losing control, and the reason is that I've never faced what I did, so how can I forgive—" His phone beeps. "Sorry," he says, "I'm getting another call." He checks in case it's Daniel, but it's Liz.

"I should go anyway," Nikki says.

"No, that's all right. I don't need to answer it."

"No worries. I gotta get back. Tell Daniel goodnight, and we can talk more tomorrow."

And then she's gone. In the dark window he stares at a reflection of himself in the wing chair, holding the phone until the beeping stops. Get back *where*? he thinks. What's Nikki getting back to?

A minute later, Liz calls again. "Liz, hi," he says. He hears music throbbing in the background.

"C'mon over to Kirk's," she shouts. And when he doesn't reply, "Cole, are you there?"

"Yeah, I'm here."

"We're having a party," she says, her voice loose and loud.

"I thought it was a kids' party."

"They're in the basement, but Kirk and I are upstairs and it's sort of boring since he doesn't drink."

"Bite me!" he hears Kirk shout in the background.

"And he's being sort of inappropriate." She laughs.

"I really need to keep an eye on my father," he says.

"You said he has no sense of time. Just tell him you're coming to pick up Daniel. So you're gone for an hour instead of fifteen minutes. It's all the same to him, right?"

He's grateful for the lightheartedness and says he'll come over, but when he finds his father in the kitchen, all the burners are flaming and he's pulling everything out of the fridge and heaping it on the floor. "If we don't get going on those currants, there won't be any jelly. I can't find the . . ." He scrunches up his face, confused but not angry. "The sweet salt."

Cole turns off the stove, but doesn't dare tell him that he dumped the currants in the trash long ago. After scooping out the mold, it would've made an excellent batch of prison wine.

"I need to go get Daniel. Maybe you should come with me." Cole covers his father's hand with his own—he's holding a jar of relish—and guides it back into the fridge. "Let's put this stuff away and we'll take a drive."

Recognition sparks his face. Maybe he wants to say *Nice day for a drive,* but he can't find the phrase. "We need to make hay while the day, ah . . . while the day's not old."

"It's already old. Look out the window. It's dark."

He doesn't look, suspecting a trick. "I want to get the countertop in today and tile the backsplash and wire in the exhaust fan."

These are the tasks they finished this morning before Cole went to the cemetery. "Why don't you just come along, Dad?"

"It's fine," he says, and sits down in his chair at the head of the table. Once there, he looks at the salt and pepper shakers, the stack of paper napkins, and says, "What are we having?"

"How about if you play piano while I pick up Daniel?" Cole rubs his shoulders for a minute, then lifts him gently by the arm—he doesn't resist—and leads him to the piano. As soon as he sees the keys, he gets his bearings and launches in from the top.

"I won't be long," Cole says. He tiptoes out and quietly closes the door, praying his father doesn't burn down the house.

AT THE SCREEN DOOR LIZ PLANTS A WET KISS AND THE TASTE OF A Manhattan on his lips. "Thanks for coming," she whispers, and in the bright kitchen Kirk shakes his hand heartily. He's shaved and trimmed his mustache and is wearing a Hawaiian shirt, so when his teeth aren't showing he looks almost decent. Liz looks good too— all in white except for a violet scarf, gauzy as tobacco netting, that's draped over her shoulders, her hair pulled back, her face flushed. Music thumps up through the floor.

"How's it going down there?" Cole asks.

"Haven't checked it out." Kirk puts a Manhattan in Cole's hand. "What happens in the basement stays in the basement."

"We were just remembering," Liz says, "when kids used to skate on the pond."

"Yeah, I noticed there's a strip mall there now."

"That's new," Kirk says, then sucks air through his teeth. "But years ago, long before that strip got built, a kid fell through the ice and his parents sued the town. The board of selectmen, in their infinite wisdom, closed it off to skating."

"And years later they filled it in," Liz adds, "on the absurd notion that it would cut down on mosquitoes."

"Idiots," Kirk says, shaking his head in disgust, and then muttering, "Total fucking idiots."

"We sort of met at the skating pond," Cole says, smirking at Liz, but her eyes are on Kirk and the agitation that's suddenly got his face twitching.

Drunken screeches and hollers boom through the floor with the pulse of the music. He hopes Daniel isn't drinking too much.

Kirk cracks open another can of Dr Pepper. "Speaking of the old days," he says, "I never thanked you for narking on me. Reform school really turned my life around."

Liz stiffens. She puts her glass to her lips.

Cole sits forward in his chair. Cautiously, he says, "Really?"

"Fuck no!" he shouts. "I was gonna be a cop, our own town cop, and that was the end of that. But hell . . ." He smiles. "A lifetime ago, right? Water under the bridge."

Liz is staring into her drink. She crosses her legs.

"What I figure," Kirk says, "is look at your life. Would you want it to be different? Because if you like yourself, if you think everything turned out okay, you can't wish something in the past was different. I'm not talking time-machine bullshit. I'm talking about being good with what you got and knowing that everything that came before brought you right up to it."

Though the sentiments are simpleminded, Cole's pretty impressed that Kirk could've even come up with them. He doesn't seem like the bitter person who torpedoed a chestnut timber at him on his first day back in town. "Lots of people need a decade of therapy to reach that understanding," he says.

"Why would I do that? I got my health, a nice home, a sister I recently reunited with, and the greatest young man in the world as a son."

"He really is remarkable," Cole says. "You can't believe all the help he's given me on the house. He's so solid, shows up ten minutes early, ready to work. I've never heard one complaint out of him. I got pretty good guys on my crew in Portland, but the truth is most of them aren't as solid as LK. It's been good for Daniel too, to have that friendship."

"He learned that from me. Loyalty. The value of your word, of hard work, of doing your best. As I said, all the life experiences—good and bad—bring you to who you are. There's been some rough patches, but we come out stronger. No harm, no foul. When something's not right, then make it right. I can't stand people whining about all the injustices done to them. Everybody survived, right? Nobody died."

Cole sits back in his chair, silent. He hadn't realized the dishwasher was running, but it comes to the end of a cycle and the motor's quiet for a moment before the pump kicks on, blasting dirty water into the drain.

"So *sometimes* people do die," Kirk says. "But *you're* not dragging around feeling sorry for yourself, right? You understand that shit happens and it's made you stronger and you wouldn't be who you are today if she hadn't died. I mean, obviously that's how you feel. A big architect—all the way out in who the hell knows where, but never mind that—so successful you can blow into town after all these years and buy up thirty thousand board feet of our heritage and for old times' sake fuck my sister."

"Shut up," she says. "Jesus."

"More power to you. I mean it. You're a real hotshot." He raises his can of Dr Pepper. "Cheers."

Cole stares dead at him.

"Look, you gotta feel that even the bad shit makes people stronger to sit here in my house drinking my liquor knowing that because you're a narc I spent four years in juvie."

"Enough, Kirk," Liz says.

"My whole point's no hard feelings. Getting arrested and doing time made me who I am, and being the narc who put me there made *him* who *he* is." He opens his hands. "We're a greatest hits of every-thing we've ever been. And we're good with that."

Cole's phone chimes and he pulls it out of his pocket, keeping one eye on Kirk. It's a text from Daniel: "Come get me now!" "I guess my boy's ready to head out," he says, and takes the last swallow of his drink.

"Let him party awhile," Kirk says. "It's barely ten, and summer'll be over in no time."

A house-rattling boom and a shout through the floor speeds up Cole's heart. It doesn't sound like rowdy fun, but confrontation.

"I'm leaving too," Liz says, glaring at her brother.

After another more muffled shout that might be Daniel, Cole rushes across the kitchen, yanks open the door, and pounds down the stairs into dim light and smoky air, the stereo speakers buzzing with bass. A couple's slouching on stools at the bar over shot glasses and bottles, kids are splayed out on the couches, and beyond them—when he turns the corner—his son's getting flung backward.

Cole jolts toward him, tripping over a kid on the floor and stumbling as he sees Daniel cock his fist and punch Little Kirk on the side of his head. "Hey! Both of you!" he shouts. "Stop that!"

But LK swings and catches Daniel right in the mouth. Cole shoves by one kid but a second jumps in front of him, grabs his shirt, and throws him aside. "Mind your own business!" Not a kid at all—bigger than he is, with a blond mustache and hands the size of mitts.

"Out of my way!" Cole shouts, ramming with his shoulder and knocking him down. By now Little Kirk's got Daniel's shirt in one fist and he's pummeling his stomach with the other. "Stop it!" he yells, just as Daniel head-butts LK on the bridge of his nose and he falls back, blood spurting across his face. Cole stands between them, pushing his son away. "Enough, for fuck's sake!" But LK licks at the blood on his lips and charges them, so he grabs him by the shoul-ders. "Cut this shit out!"

Just then he's blindsided, his whole head on fire, his ear stinging. It's Kirk, standing between him and his own son with his fist raised for another shot. "What the fuck?" He points at Cole, as if to tell him to stay put, and roughly grabs LK's chin to examine his bloody face. "Did that asshole do this to you?"

"*I* did it," Daniel says.

"Is that true?" Kirk says, and his boy nods. "You let that skinny faggot do this?"

"What the hell's going on here?" Liz plants herself between the four of them, but they're all growling and grunting like dogs until Daniel says "Look" and nods at the corner behind the couch. Though Cole's vision is swirling, he sees a girl lying on the floor. Unconscious, naked from the waist down. And LK cinching up his belt.

"He was raping her," Daniel says.

"She wanted it, you fucking dumb-ass." LK wipes at the blood running from his nose.

"She's passed out! She's been passed out for an hour."

"She doesn't care."

"Oh, my God," Cole says.

"Who is that?" Kirk asks his son. "Rita Gruber?"

He nods.

Kirk smiles, shakes his head. "Gimme a goddamn break. That tiny skirt she strutted in here with? We all know why she came over and drank herself unconscious. *Everybody* knows about Rita Gruber."

Quick as a gunshot, Liz smacks Kirk's face so hard he shouts out, then she rushes to the girl's side. "Get me something to cover her up with!" She touches the girl's forehead, feels the pulse at her neck. Cole tosses her a sweatshirt flung on the back of a recliner, and Liz gently slaps her cheeks. "Rita. Wake up, Rita."

Retching comes from the far end of the room, where the girl slouched on the stool is puking on the bar as her boyfriend jumps aside. Kids are scurrying out from dark corners and bounding up the stairs. Then there's a police siren in the distance.

"I called the cops," Daniel says.

LK lunges at him, but Cole stops him with a stiff arm, then Kirk grabs his son by the collar and throws him to the floor. "Find her clothes," Kirk tells him.

"You said you were my *friend!*" LK screams at Daniel, then bursts into tears, blood still running from his nose and into his mouth. "How could you do this to a friend?" He slaps his hands around his own face, sobbing on the floor.

Kirk kicks him. "Find that little whore's skirt and clean yourself up. Now!" The siren's getting closer, and he turns to Cole. "You two next. Get the fuck out of my house."

Cole takes Daniel by the elbow, but he doesn't budge. "I'm the one who called them," he says. "I shouldn't leave."

Cole eyes Kirk, his hands, gauging the level of his violence. The big blond guy he knocked over has taken off. Liz has rested Rita's head on a throw pillow, her blouse straightened, buttoned, the sweatshirt covering her from knees to waist. She hasn't come to. The sirens are now out front, and Cole's aware that he should be having flashbacks, reliving trauma. Expecting this, he's already reminding himself that now is not then, though he's still pulsing with heat and sorrow and grief. He wants to help the girl, to protect her, but she's safe in Liz's care, and he also feels that as a man he should keep some distance from her trauma. He used to believe that all boys grew into men who beat their wives, and tonight he can't help feeling that all males, even witnesses after the fact, are implicated. Except—he looks at his son—for Daniel, so his protective impulse shifts to him. Again he's the reasonable, sane one, who understands fairness, right and wrong. Of course they can't run.

"You'd better go let them in," he tells Kirk.

"Get her out of here," Kirk tells Liz. "Drag her into the laundry."

"Don't be stupid," Cole says. "The best thing you can do right now is meet the cops at the front door." His calm is all thanks to Daniel, as if his son's speaking through him.

A few minutes later Kirk leads a cop down the stairs. "Some of the older kids might've snuck in some booze. Careful there." They step around a puddle of vomit by the bar.

The cop is young, not far from Daniel's age. He kneels beside the girl, feels her pulse, opens an eyelid with his thumb and shines a small flashlight on her eyeball. "How long has she been out?" he asks Liz.

"She was like this when I came down, maybe ten minutes ago."

"Over an hour," Daniel says.

The cop looks up at him and then he radios for EMTs. "Drugs?" he asks Liz.

"I don't know."

He stands and steps toward Daniel. "Do you know if she's taken any drugs?"

"I just saw a few shots of tequila," he says.

"Are you"—he looks at his notepad—"Daniel Callahan?"

He nods.

"I'm Cole Callahan. I'm his—"

"I'll get to you. What happened here, Daniel?"

"She was passed out in this recliner when I went in that other room over there"—he nods at it—"to watch a movie, and when I came out Little Kirk had her in the corner and he was raping—"

"*Raping her*," Kirk mocks. "Did you see her resist? Hear her say no?"

"Oh, Jesus," Liz says, still kneeling beside Rita, and drops her head.

"He wasn't even in the room," Kirk says. "It's a *he-said-she-said*."

"If you don't stop interrupting, I'll have you wait in the back of the cruiser."

"When I realized what was going on I tried to pull LK off of her, but this blond guy and another one held me back."

"This is *bullshit!*" Kirk says.

"Last chance to shut up," the cop tells him.

"You don't have to believe me," Daniel says. "Just look at their phones. They were taking pictures."

"So where are they all?" the cop says.

Daniel looks around. "Gone."

"Where's your son?" he asks Kirk.

From the foot of the stairs he shouts, "Get your ass down here!" But for as long as the cop takes statements and photos, finally ordering Kirk out of the basement, Rita still unconscious, Little Kirk doesn't show.

TOGETHER, COLE AND DANIEL COAX AND TRICK PHIL UP THE STAIRS and into pajamas. "You smell like bourbon," he says to his son, "and you both look shell-shocked."

"Yeah, well," Cole says. "Long night."

"What time is it?"

"After midnight."

"You used to stay up past midnight doing pull-ups and . . ." He mimes it.

"Isometrics." That was Kelly.

"In prison, when I couldn't sleep, I'd remember my own kid having the gumption to keep his body fit, and I'd roll off my bunk and do push-ups on the cold floor."

Cole settles him into bed and pulls the white sheet up to his chest. "Do you want to watch TV before you go to sleep?"

"What I'm saying is that my kids inspired me long after I went away. I'd punch up my pillow, my muscles warm, half awake, half dreaming that I'm in the keeping room and the house has been finished for years, *not* snaking wires or sweating pipes but just reading by a fire, and thinking how relieved I am that I'm sitting here looking at bed warmers hanging next to the fireplace, brass candlesticks on the mantel, instead of lying on a bunk in prison." He smooths the sheet over his bony legs and bloated stomach, looking like a corpse that's woken up in the morgue. "I'm saying I appreciate you two and the Schaler boy for pretending we're ever going to finish the house."

"We'll get it just where we want it." Cole squeezes his leg through the sheet.

"Not a chance," Daniel says. "Only us working? Now *you're* dreaming. That would take years. We have to get back to our lives."

Cole gives him a pleading stare.

"Just tell the truth," Daniel says. "Give it a shot. He's already paranoid and now you're telling him something he knows is a lie. That confuses him more. No wonder you and Mom can't communicate well enough to keep from torturing each other. You're both so pissed off and defensive and proud you don't even know what you're saying. I've heard you on the phone and you're all like 'Everything's great here . . . Daniel has a friend his own age . . . Working my father toward a retirement home.' Truly batshit, Dad."

WHEN COLE'S GETTING INTO BED, THERE'S A BEATING ON THE door so violent that his first reaction is to grab the gun from the nightstand. But there is no gun, so all he can do is slip into his clothes, sneak stealthily downstairs, and peer out a window at Kirk's truck in the driveway, engine rumbling, high beams glaring. He kicks the door and shouts, "Open up, Callahan!"

The dome light in the pickup comes on. "Stop that, Kirk! Stop that right now!" It's Liz and she's hurrying up the driveway.

Cole goes to the door and listens to them on the other side. "If you can't calm down, we're leaving," Liz says. "I swear to God, Kirk, I'll call the police if you don't control yourself." He doesn't respond, but Cole's so close—just the thickness of the door away—he can hear his heavy labored breaths.

Liz softly raps her knuckles and says, "Can you open up, Cole? We're just trying to find LK."

Wishing he'd taken the time to put his shoes on, he slides the deadbolt and pulls the door back toward him a crack, and with the moist night air comes the feverish smell of trouble. Kirk pushes inside, and when Cole gives him a hard shove, his head snaps back against the wall. Before he can recoil, Liz jumps between them. "Stop it, for fuck's sake!" she shouts. "Both of you. You're middle-aged men. You look ridiculous."

Kirk's arms slowly drop to his sides, and then Cole realizes his own fist is raised, so he lets it fall.

"Nobody can find him," Liz says. "He texted Kirk and said he was coming over here to set things straight with Daniel."

Daniel! He's got to make sure he's safe. He spins around—and there he is, standing on the keeping-room hearth.

Cole says, "I haven't seen him," then notices his father sitting on the piano bench, watching.

"He didn't text you?" Liz asks. They all scrape into the keeping room, everyone still tense. Phil switches on the small lamp on the piano. Cole keeps an eye on Kirk.

Daniel looks at his phone. "Nothing."

"He took off on his motorbike," Liz says. "The police want to talk to him." She shakes her head. "He needs to turn himself in."

Kirk stares angrily at Daniel. "He didn't come here?"

"If he did," Daniel says, "I'd call the police."

"Listen, you little fuck!" Kirk snaps, pushing past Liz, knocking her to the floor, and charging across the room.

From her knees she pleads, "Stop it, Kirk!"

Cole blocks his path, the two of them chest to chest grabbing fistfuls of each other's shirts. "Get out," he shouts, "or I'll—" and he cuts himself off, but the truth is that seeing Kirk go after Daniel makes him want to unleash on him, to pummel him until his own fists are bloody and broken. Old fantasies of beating the hell out of his father and all the men who've stood in for him and his long-buried desire to do the same to Kirk merge in a vicious, immediate urge.

Liz seizes her brother's shoulders from behind and he swipes her hands off and she's on the floor again. "This is my *son!*" he says, nose to nose with Cole, his face oily with sweat and smelling of scorched cigars. "One little mistake that we don't even know if he made—all on the word of this little shit. You said yourself what a good kid my boy is. You don't destroy his life over something so measly."

"Out, right now!" Cole growls. They're pushing at each other so hard that his bare feet start to slip.

"Not till I find my son."

"He's not here. So go look somewhere else."

Liz is pulling Kirk off again and he's relenting, still clutching Cole's shirt, but his body going limp, his arms flaccid. They both take a step back, and Liz guides her brother toward the door.

"But why won't he answer his goddamn phone when he knows it's me?" His eyes are red, a tear runs down his cheek. He wipes it away, as surprised as everyone else. And embarrassed, so he snarls again. "I can't believe I thought you might be good for him," he says to Daniel, bitterly. "That's not friendship, what you did. I draw the line at calling the cops."

Daniel puts his hands in his pockets, looks down at his feet, then back at Kirk. "I draw the line at rape."

Kirk lunges so fast that he knocks Cole over and grabs at Daniel, who slips away sideways, but then Kirk catches hold of his T-shirt and cocks his fist, and as Cole's still scrambling to his knees, a hammer suddenly pounds into Kirk's shoulder blade. Screaming, he crumples to the floor, writhing, then gasping when Phil steps on his neck, waving the hammer over him.

"You're a delinquent," Phil says calmly. "The whole town knows about you."

Cole gets to his feet, rubbing the back of his head where it hit the fireplace brick, and covers the hammerhead with his hand. "It's all right now, Dad," he says, and just like that he steps off of Kirk's throat and the hammer disappears behind his back where he'd been hiding it all this time.

Kirk gets awkwardly to his feet, moaning and holding his right arm tight to his side. Phil sits back down on the piano bench. Daniel stands by the bathroom door. He seems unhurt. Strangely, in fact, unrattled.

"Get him out of here," Cole tells Liz.

"I'm so sorry," she says, taking Kirk by his good arm and leading him out. On the steps she turns. "I just thought I could keep him from going ballistic. I thought I could handle it. But it had already gone too far."

Kirk's tires spin out on the driveway and screech when they hit the road, the pickup bucking, his greasy tools crashing into the tailgate, the hose on his fuel tank popping loose and flinging out over the side of the truck. He speeds down Old Newgate Road, the nozzle dragging on the pavement and shooting off a trail of sparks.

"Did he hurt you?" he asks Daniel, moving his hands over his son's shoulders and arms, touching his face.

"I'm fine. Good move there, Kung Fu Grandpa."

"How hard did you hit him?" Cole asks his father.

"Oh, he'll be fine in a day or so. I got hit there myself once or twice. Clumsy as hell eating soup left-handed."

"I'm sorry about this," Cole says to Daniel.

"I'm thinking it's about time for me to be getting home. This has been cool and all, but if you really think it's better than the occasional can of spray paint in the name of social justice, then we have some serious talking to do."

YET AGAIN, COLE GETS INTO BED. HIS PHONE IS TURNED ON NEXT to him, and he told Daniel to do the same. The fan's blowing. He lies with the sheet pulled up to his waist, his chest bare. Just one cool night would be—as Nikki loves to say ironically—"a blessing." It's only ten o'clock in Portland and he considers giving her a call, but he really doesn't want to explain how he's taking care of their son. *Get-*

ting to know his family history has really been a blessing. He imagines her smiling at that. He longs for the time he could make her smile. And he feels himself relaxing, relieved that for now the hell of this night is over. But only for now. Daniel will have to give a deposition. He might have to be a witness at a trial. He's tangled his son up in his own past. Brought him across the country to save him from trouble and instead plunged him headlong into something much worse. And the girl. Rita. Tonight will follow her through the rest of her life.

He gives up on sleep. In the kitchen he runs water into a glass and takes it into the keeping room, where he stands beside the piano gazing out at the stars. Phil will put up a fight, but Cole will get him living in a facility where he's cared for. The house can sell as is. In the moonlight he looks at the sizable dump pile they've amassed from the summer's work, on the same spot as when he was a kid. Daniel's right: it's time for them to go home.

This decision is a relief. He sets the glass in the sink, and coming back through the keeping room stops at the fireplace, stripped of its iron crane and hanging pots and brass-knobbed andirons. They'd had a reflector oven on the hearth that his mother cooked the Christmas turkey in before a roaring fire. There'd been trivets and the brass bedwarmer. All that remains is an oversized iron nail in the paneling that the poker used to hang from. It was a hearth as impressive as any in Sturbridge Village.

Back in bed he remembers the day his mother spoke French with the Quebecois on the stagecoach at Sturbridge, the day his parents held hands for those few steps across the common. The evening was beginning to cool when they got in the car with a paper bag of salt-water taffy. As his father drove, they passed the taffy around, all five of them chewing and sucking on the colorful sweets. The sun went down not long after they were on the highway, and in the darkening car he and Kelly and Ian stayed silent: they were listening to their parents have an easy, intimate conversation in the front seat about pewter salt cellars. For a minute neither of them spoke, then his father remembered a cellar they'd bid on at an auction in Deerfield, which reminded his mother of a hutch table from a house there that she'd seen in a Skinner auction catalogue, and how it looked very similar to their own. Nightfall and the soothing hum of the road cast a spell over the car. Ian rested his head on Kelly's shoulder, but his eyes remained open. They let the candy slowly melt in their mouths so they wouldn't make a sound chewing, sprawled together across the backseat witnessing the effortless drift of amiable conversation between their parents.

HIS DREAM IS THE OLD ONE OF MAKING LOVE TO LIZ HIGH UP ON A platform in the burning shed, then grabbing their clothes and scrambling to escape, but this time it's all twisted up with those soothing, seductive early years in the Hawthorne apartment with Nikki—until it's interrupted like a needle dragged across a record and, as if he was never asleep, he's racing from his bed, racing toward his son, who's calling "Dad!" over and over. Smelling the smoke, he yanks open Phil's door and sees Daniel ransacking the bedding. "He's not here!" he shouts, and Cole checks quickly under the bed and inside the closet. "Let's go!" he says, and pushes Daniel ahead of him as they thunder down the stairs, hotter as they drop, and now he smells gasoline. There are pockets of fire in every room.

"Dad!" Cole shouts when they find him sitting at his place at the kitchen table. "C'mon, let's move!" He and Daniel grab him and they stumble out the door into the yard, turning back to see the house ringed in low-burning flames. "Did you call 911?" he asks. Daniel shakes his head and Phil just stares at the house. Senselessly Cole pats his hips for his phone—he's wearing nothing but underwear. "Phone?" he asks Daniel, who shakes his head again and, already lurching forward, says, "I'll run up for mine."

"No, stay here with Phil," Cole orders him, then runs inside and up to his room, grabs some clothes and the phone, and bounds back down.

Daniel and his father have backed away from the house, and Cole's dialing as he joins them. In a minute they hear the long wail of the firehouse siren, but since it's a volunteer department it'll take some time. Phones are ringing automatically all over town, summoning them to the station to suit up and roll out.

"Is there a hose, Dad?" Cole says, but his father has slipped away and is peering into the chicken coop. "Shit!" He turns to Daniel. "See if you can find a hose out back."

Then he dashes to a hose bibb and forces the rusty handle, but when it breaks free, nothing happens. Around the front of the house he tries another with the same result. If they could just find a hose he could tape it to the kitchen faucet, and when he gets around back Daniel's hauling junk off a pile—old lumber and corrugated fiberglass, an ancient lawnmower and a shattered TV—but looks up and shakes his head.

Fuck! Curtains flame through the windows and Cole sprints into the kitchen and runs water into a pan, and while a second fills he splashes the keeping-room curtains; one spot snuffs out and smokes briefly before the flames spring back. With the empty pan he runs into the kitchen. Standing there in the smoke is Daniel, who reaches for him saying, "Forget it!"

"I want you out of here!" he shouts, pushing his son toward the door.

Daniel takes him by the arm. "We can't do anything, Dad. It's too late." He coughs, and Cole does too. "Too late," he repeats.

The rush of resignation is so physical that Cole lets the pan drop to the floor. It's calming, almost a relief. He gently closes the tap, and they abandon the house to the fire.

The siren from town is still sounding—a low moan slowly rising to a fevered wail, then dropping silent until the moan builds again.

No sign of the firefighters yet. His father, watering the chickens from the cistern, might think it's morning. In fact, the keeping-room windows are so lurid with flames that Cole can see the mantel and the tin wall sconce holding a candle stub. And now blue lights come flashing down Old Newgate Road and a speeding cruiser stops just short of the house but then guns it up the driveway and onto the grass, and the same cop he met a few hours ago at Kirk's jumps from the car and calls, "Is everybody out of the house?"

"Yes," Cole shouts.

"How many?"

"Three." He points. "My father and son."

The cop turns toward the fire, flames curling out an open window, and shakes his head. "That motherfucker," he says, mostly to himself.

"I smelled gasoline," Cole tells him, then hears a siren drawing close.

"Do you have keys to this car?" the cop asks, waving at Phil's old wreck.

Cole touches his pocket and nods.

"Then pull it forward. Clear this area."

As he's starting it up, red lights streak over his windshield—fire trucks now turning up the road off School Street. He rolls the car straight ahead, past the pear trees and where the rabbit hutches once stood, past the cistern and the butchering post, and stops where the grass ends.

He gets out of the car, and Daniel comes across the yard to join him as a fire engine and tanker rumble into the driveway and the volunteers get to work with astounding efficiency, dragging out hoses across the yard, pulling open valves, smashing a window with a long pole. Very quickly water is surging into the house. He feels a breeze, and a minute later a stronger gust, which despite all the water stokes the fire.

All summer he's been hearing the melody, either from the piano or inside his own head, and now he thinks nothing of the occasional note that emerges over the gushing water, rumbling trucks, and crackling fire—a phantom playing from the flames.

But Daniel's face is contorted by panic. "He's in there!"

Cole bolts for the back porch and bursts into the kitchen, squinting against the thick smoke and lifting his shirt up over his nose. Flames lap up the walls. Water cascades from the ceiling light and splashes onto the table, and he sloshes through the flood into the keeping room. In the glow of red and blue and white lights flickering in the windows he sees his father, faint and gray through the smoke, playing the piece as routinely as ever.

He coughs and squeezes his eyes closed, then calls "Dad!" over the racket of shattering glass and the mean snap and roar of the fire that's combusting everything. He horse-collars him, but Phil spins and pushes him away. He gasps and coughs while his father, coughing too, turns back to the keyboard. Cole reaches both arms around his chest and lifts him off the bench, but then he squirms and elbows Cole in the ribs and, when his hold loosens, pops him under his chin. "God damn you!" Cole shouts, blood and thick saliva seeping over his tongue.

"Get away from me!" His father's face is paranoid and afraid.

Once Cole locks his arms around his torso again, the bench tips over and they both hit the floor hard. On his knees he tries to drag him out, but he's clutching the piano leg and the whole thing rolls when Cole jerks. He kicks the bench aside and tries to peel back his father's death grip. "Let it fucking go!" The piano skids another few inches across the floor, and looking over his shoulder Cole sees that Daniel's got hold of Phil's ankles and is yanking on him. "Get out!" he shouts at his son.

"Pull!" Daniel shouts back. Even through the smoke Cole can see how red his son's eyes are, that he's pressed his shoulder to his nose, doubled over coughing as tears stream down his cheeks.

"Okay," Cole shouts. "Pull!" They tug together and the piano doesn't budge, the wheels caught between floorboards. How the hell can his father's grip be so powerful? Next there's the crash of a wall collapsing in the bathroom. They've got to get the hell out of here. "Dad," Cole says, and when his father turns toward him he punches him square in the face. He goes limp long enough that Cole can pry his hands free and Daniel can drag him away, until Phil grabs the *other* piano leg.

"Jesus Christ, you're gonna kill us all!" Cole cocks his fist to hit him again.

"*That's* the Cole I remember!" he shouts.

And Cole holds back. This is the first time all summer his father has spoken his name.

"Put another beating on the old man. Do it! I know you want to, but don't stop short this time. Take it all the way."

Daniel releases his ankles and looks at Cole as if he's suddenly weighing all the different versions of the story he's heard. And even through the smoke Cole can tell his son understands that Phil's telling the truth.

Cole lowers his fist, then stands up and steps on Phil's wrist with more and more weight until he finally lets go. Daniel drags him away from the piano, and they carry him out.

On the porch Phil kicks himself free and scrambles to go back inside, but the young cop and a fireman run up to them. "You dipshits!" the fireman shouts.

"We went in to haul him out," Daniel says.

"You trying to murder your whole family?" the cop barks at Phil. Blood runs from his lip. "I'll do as I please on my own property."

The cop twists Phil's arm behind his back and marches him to the patrol car, shoves him in the door, and slams it shut.

Daniel and Cole straggle across the backyard coughing up phlegm. Cole's about to tell his son he should never have come back inside the house, but instead he says, "Thanks for the help." Nearly to the chicken coop, they turn around. It's clear now there's no hope of saving the house, flames creeping up hidden spaces around the chimney right up to the attic and the cedar roof. He rubs the back of his hand, still smarting from the punch, as they sit by the old swing set. In the firelight he watches his father through the black metal mesh between the cruiser's front and rear seats. Daniel leans back on his elbow in the grass.

"It's true," Cole tells him. "What your grandfather said."

"I know. I've heard Mom tell the story before. But you were just trying to protect your mother." He sticks a blade of grass between his teeth. "It's hard to imagine Phil being so violent. With LK the truth is I wasn't really surprised. But Phil seems so gentle."

"I never protected her. Not like you did with that girl tonight."

"You tried, though."

"Not like you think I did. I went after him in anger, to hurt him. Not to protect your grandmother. She was already dead."

Daniel sits up. "That's definitely *not* how I heard it."

"But it's the truth," Cole says. "Those other stories started when your grandfather was still lying there on the floor with his face . . ." He stops there: a fifteen-year-old boy needs to hear only so much. Fifteen, the same age as he was that night.

They're silent for a time until Cole slaps his son's thigh, squeezes his knee. "What a fucking mess," he says. "What are we doing here?"

"Dude, it's like you went down the rabbit hole. This isn't our life."

Our life. He likes the sound of that. "When we get back, can you try to quit committing class-A misdemeanors?"

"I can sure be smarter about it."

"Can't you just stop—"

"Doing the right thing?"

"Yeah, I guess."

"You thought you were doing the right thing staying here, and look at this disaster. If you'd just left with that wood and gone home, he'd be living right now in a nonburning *old colonial.*" He employs the DAR emphasis of the grandmother he never met.

"And you'd be in jail in Portland."

Daniel sweeps his arm toward the flaming house, the fire trucks, and the tremendous arcs of gushing water. "So you did this all for *me?*"

"That's not what I mean. Look, there's got to be some way to honor your principles without breaking the law all the time."

"Don't get me started on laws."

In the back of the police car his father reaches to one door, then the other, trying without success to get out.

Daniel's watching the fire—*everyone's* watching the fire except for Phil, who tries the doors again, confusion and a growing panic on his face behind the metal grille.

"Just a sec," he says, and heads to ask the cop, who's talking with a fireman in the driveway, if he'll let his father loose, but suddenly the window beside the piano blows out, and as the splintering pieces start flying, something inside him blows too and tears come streaming down his face, so he detours under the pear trees and squats down against a trunk while his breath catches in his throat and he erupts into sobs. He cries for the girl waking up in the hospital right now and being told what's been done to her. He cries for the house itself. "Antiques," his mother said. "This candlestick"— or "blanket chest" or "sampler"—"has passed from life to life, hand to hand, for two hundred years, and it's your responsibility to usher it through the short time it's in your possession." Isn't it the same with our children—we usher them safely through the few years they're with us? And isn't it one of the many things a husband owes his wife? He cries for his broken marriage, for the family he's lost, for the isolated sufferings and joys of his sister and brother. A floor inside the house collapses, the thunderous boom shaking the ground, and he cries for his mother. The last thing she saw before an excruciating death was *her* husband's face disfigured by rage. Thirty years ago to the day.

Did he look into her eyes as he choked her? One hand clapped over her mouth and the other squeezing her throat while she struggled to breathe, pounding at his shoulders?

When he can finally let that image go, when Cole himself can breathe again, he walks over to the police car and peers through the glass. Phil, sitting calmly in the middle of the seat, turns to look at him, his face blank and passionless, his eyes milky. The blood on his lip and in his whiskers has dried, his hair matted to the side of his head. His shirt is filthy. He needs a shower.

Now the cop is nowhere in sight, but Cole approaches three firemen gathered in the driveway around the tailgate of a pickup laid out with sandwiches. "Help yourself," says one of them, who Cole realizes is the fire chief, before adding, "This was arson."

Cole nods. "That seems right."

"Did the old guy set it?" another one ventures to ask.

"He *loved* this house."

And at that point the cop walks over and joins them, saying, "Thanks, Captain," into his cell phone before slipping it into his pocket.

How's he supposed to move on, Cole would ask Liz if she were here, when once again his father's in police custody and he's about to accuse Kirk? After Tilly's stroke, after the prosecutors and social workers and the certainty that they'd be leaving both the house and the town, Cole was seized with panic that he couldn't protect Liz from her brother; worse, he'd *never* protected her. He told a cop then the same thing he tells this one now: "Kirk Schaler likes to set fires."

The cop smiles. "You got it partly right," he says. "Kirk's sister called the station worried out of her mind. That's when I came rushing over, but I was just a little too late. According to the sister this here's a father-son deal."

The chief sighs. "Kirk's always been an asshole."

"Well, he'll be out of our hair for a few years. They got him at the station already."

"How about the son?" Cole asks.

"He's a slippery little shit. Jumped out a bedroom window and shot off on his motorbike. He can't be far, though. I doubt that kid can even think beyond the town line. Same as his dad."

The firemen get back to work, and Cole stands beside the cop watching them, the truck at their backs, its surging pumps as loud as a factory. Flames are shooting through the roof despite the drenching. The tanker truck comes screaming back from town and stops beside a folding pool they've set up on the road, and when the valve opens, water gushes out to be sucked up by the pumper. A dozen men are shouting over the racket.

"My father, he's not all with it," Cole says. "Dementia. But he's settled down now. Do you think you could let him out?"

The cop looks dumbfounded. "Isn't he the Old Newgate Strangler?"

Cole nods. "He was."

"So this is the house?"

"Yeah."

"And you're one of the kids?" he asks.

Cole nods again. He flexes his sore hand. "Could you let him out if I keep close tabs on him?"

Cole follows him to the cruiser, where he opens the door. "Step outside, Mr. Callahan." His father looks suspicious and tired. "Turn around and face the car." Phil knows the routine, reaching his left hand behind his back even before the cop asks. He clicks a handcuff around his wrist, and another when Phil reaches the other hand back, and then walks him over to the swing set. "You put other people's lives in jeopardy with a stunt like that." Phil doesn't respond. "Sit here on the grass." The cop helps him to the ground, uncuffs one wrist, and locks him to a rusty crossbar.

Daniel comes strolling across the grass, eating a sandwich. "Want one?"

"What kind?" Phil asks.

"I don't really know," Daniel says. "Meat, I guess."

"But you don't eat meat," Cole says.

Daniel chews. "I know."

"What kind?" his grandfather asks again.

Daniel opens up the sandwich and tears off a piece of boloney, wiggles it in front of them.

"Boloney," Phil says.

Daniel slurps up the scrap of meat and says, "I never heard of it."

Phil asks for one, and when Daniel comes back from the truck he's carrying food on a stack of blankets and pillows. He kneels down and unloads the sandwiches, cans of soda, and Fig Newtons. They all chow down, Phil using his free hand. Eventually, one by one, they lie back on the blankets, looking up at the stars, and when the wind shifts, gray smoke moves in front of the twinkling light.

"That was a good thing you did tonight at Kirk's," Cole says. "Not an easy thing."

"It was very easy," Daniel counters. "You see rape, you stop it and call the police. Pretty basic."

"I mean, it took guts to stand up to him like that."

"I didn't give it a second thought."

"Jesus. Will you just let me be proud of you?"

"You would've done the same thing," Daniel insists, and hearing this from his son makes Cole tear up again, and he closes his eyes, at peace with the knowledge that his son believes in him.

When a section of roof caves in, Cole lifts his head: explosions of sparks whirl skyward but then are sucked back down into the house, as if to keep the fire blazing. And drifting into sleep he hears a low ping, and another, and another. It sounds like laser guns from a space movie—*ping! pang! zong!* But it's the piano, burning now, the high-tension strings snapping free with one last note.

. . .

THE NEEDLE CLAWS AROUND AND AROUND THE DEAD ZONE AT the end of the record, until he finally lifts it. Yes, he knows why their bedroom door's ajar. He knows with certainty what's happening. Knows he's failed to stop it. Down in the kitchen, reaching deep into the ice bin, he hears a familiar sniveling animal noise, so he reaches for the poker as he steps across the keeping-room hearth, looking for the glow of possum eyes in the dark.

And then he jumps. Off in the corner his father's sitting on the floor, his arms crossed over his knees, his head on his arms.

And there—a smear of moonlight glinting off a bare white leg. He bends low to see under the table: her bunched-up nightgown, the inside of her wrist. He rushes to her and drops to his knees where she's slumped against the end of the upright piano, and he shakes her. She's warm, but her head drops forward. "Wake up!" he pleads. He puts his face to her mouth—no breath—and his ear to her chest— still nothing—and then jumps back to his feet, looming over his father whimpering pathetically there on the floor. Nothing in any of their lives will ever be the same. He squeezes the poker in both fists as if he could crush the iron with his hands. "Jesus Christ," he yells, raising it over his head. A shadow of his body, twisted and ready to strike, hurtles across the ceiling in this frozen light.

But then a gurgle rises from his mother's throat. The poker thuds onto the floorboards. He grabs her under the arms and drags her beneath the windows and lays her out flat, pinches her nose and holds her chin in his fingertips, then fills his lungs and presses his mouth on hers and blows, his breath vanishing into a void, so he blows harder, blood rushing to his face, and he rests his hand on her chest, feeling it rise, then lifts his mouth from hers and pushes down on her lungs, his breath, mixed with the smell of his mother, rises through her teeth and lips. He spreads her mouth open wider, and then his own, and blows a surge of hot air from deep in his belly, and what comes back when he pushes is the sour air that seeps beneath the iron door of a dungeon, the smell of fear. Again he blows and now it comes back warmer and smelling more like her, his mother, the scent of her scalp when he hugs her, the smell of her tears and knotted-up anguish when he puts an ice bag on her cheek, the smell of their kitchen and her body powder and lotions. He tastes her blood on his lips, and at that moment she chokes, two quick spasms in her chest, and he holds an ear to her breast and feels his father's hand desperately clutching his shoulder, his voice telling him, "Keep doing the mouth-to-mouth." Cole rears back until the tips of their noses touch, his father's face red and slick, and then he uncoils: he lunges from his knees, thrusting out his arms to shove him off, meaning to scream "Get away!" but it emerges only as a long, crazed grunt as his father, lifted off his feet, flies into a pedestal table, the candlestick clattering to the floor, and stumbles over a Windsor chair before crashing through the door into the parlor and falling on his back, a final thunk when his head hits the floor.

Cole lowers his face to his mother's mouth—*still* no breath—so he presses his lips to hers again and blows.

"What's happening?" Hysterical, already in tears, Ian comes weaving into the room as if he's balanced on a scrap of debris barely afloat in a roiling ocean.

Cole doesn't throw him a line. He offers nothing at all. Just turns back to his mother and exhales deeply into her, feeling neither desperation nor hope. They knew this night would come, they all knew it. What he feels is resentment, disgust. Toward Kelly, stubbornly awake up in her room; toward Ian for his weakness; toward his mother for never divorcing, for ever marrying him at all; and for his father, whose simmering anger and flashes of rage have defined each of them and defined their family. But his most profound disgust is reserved for himself. For retreating into ecstasy with Liz instead of trying to put their family right; for not coaxing Kelly back into the fold; for not working harder on the house to help bring them harmony. For not standing up to his father. For not saving her. Kneeling over his mother's already cooling body, he puts his lips to hers and sucks in the dead air.

Kelly screams, rushing up and palming their mother's cheeks. "No!" she cries. "No, no, no!" She puts her ear to her mother's chest, frozen there for a moment before collapsing against the wall. Cole continues breathing into her body, his fingers pinching her nose. Those deep breaths are meditative, the only thing he can hear, all that any of them hears. And he goes on like this for some time because there's nothing else he can try to put everything back the way it should be. He's suddenly disgusted with himself for thinking that if he doesn't bring her back to life, their family's secret will be out.

But finally Kelly touches his cheek, and when Cole looks up at her she's shaking her head, so he stops. And when he does he can hear the rocker squeaking. His father got off the floor and is sitting in it, and now he turns to see what it means that all the loud breathing has stopped, and once he figures this out his animal moans resume. When Cole snaps "Shut up!" he falls quiet. And never has Cole known such silence, with his hand on his mother's chest, resting on her stillness. Her face is contorted, her jaw out of line. But her lips, wet from his own mouth, are glistening pink.

Kelly rises up from the floor, standing tall and straight. He thinks she's going to comfort Ian, but she walks to the phone in the kitchen and dials. "Yes," she says. "We'll need the police." Her voice is measured, dignified. "We'll also need an ambulance. Ninety-three Old Newgate Road. There's a post lamp in front. The big white old colonial." She sounds like Tilly.

Ian hasn't moved from the spot where he stopped, although he's now crumpled on the floor, sitting on one ankle, his arms pulling a leg to his chest, tapping his forehead on his knee. He looks as if someone has broken his body into pieces and then arranged them in a neat pile.

"If she just would've . . . *just stopped!*" His father is mumbling, jabbering.

Cole touches her face. Cool as porcelain.

"If she would've just shut up."

"I told *you* to shut up!" Cole bellows, and he can't even be sure he actually shouted this except that his face heats up from the explosive effort and he feels the scrape in his throat.

"She goes after me and after me. All night long."

Cole's heart starts pounding and somehow he's thinking about going camping with Liz. About waking up with her in the tent as the sun slips up over the horizon, cooking breakfast on a fire. He thinks of the food and mess kit and hatchet piled on the spare bed—

"Won't just *drop it!*"

—and that if not for all the gear his father would be in that bed right now beside him, his mother alive, everyone asleep.

When he stands up her fingers pull at his ankle, hooked around his foot, so he lifts her wrist and rests her arm by her side. Then he backs away. *A corpse*, he thinks. *Laid out.* So he squats by her head and gets a grip under her arms and—in an impulse he'll never fully understand, as if to put everything back as it was, as if he'll be blamed—he drags her over to where she was, heavier now, and sets her upright, leaning into the angle where the side of the piano meets the wall. Then he goes to his brother, his forehead banging on his knee with the rhythm of a beating heart, and touches him lightly on the nape, and Ian snarls so fiercely he snaps his hand away.

"Never," their father growls. "She never lets *anything* go."

Cole charges across the room. "I told you to shut up!" He's never spoken to him like this, but everything has changed.

"Oh, she really knows how to push my buttons. Bitching and bitching—"

Cole slaps both hands on his father's chest, the rocker tipping back, and grabs his pajama top in his fists, pulls him up and throws him against the wall. The sampler hanging there, a poem about mortality stitched by a little girl now dead for a hundred years, shoots off the wall, frame and glass shattering on the floor. They both stare down at it, then Cole looks across the room at Ian, who at last has lifted his face. He's turned toward Cole, gently nodding. In the kitchen doorway, Kelly's nodding too. He glances at his father leaning against the wall, and even he seems to be slowly, pleadingly nodding. Cole takes a big step forward and swings, expecting a crisp thwack like in the movies, but his father's nose crunches, his head slams into the plaster, and he gives a deep, quiet grunt. Before he falls, Cole swings again and catches him on the jaw and then—once he's on the floor—drops on top of him, swinging blindly, his father's glasses long gone, some of the punches on hard skull, others on the softer cheek and the side of his neck. And he isn't fighting back at all, so what stops Cole's furious assault are Kelly and Ian pulling on his bare shoulders, trying to get him off their father, but he keeps swinging until finally Kelly grabs him by the hair and yanks him away. Cole turns and sees their horrified faces, both running with tears. "What are you, fucking *crazy*?" Kelly screams. "You're gonna kill him!" She's been screaming for a time, and she still is. Ian's cowering, and his father has rolled onto his side, moaning, his hands covering his head. Kelly hauls Cole to his feet by his hair. He steps on the fireplace poker, and when his sister lets go, seizes it with both hands, raises it above his head, and thumps it like a sledgehammer into his father's back. He tries to pull the poker loose, but the hooked end is lodged under the shoulder blade. He jerks, and his father cries out. The blood puddles warm around his bare feet.

THE SMELL OF SMOKE THAT COMES IN WITH THE COPS IS A RELIEF, a new sensation; they've been to the burning shed tonight. One of them lifts their mother's eyelids and looks at her pupils with a flashlight. The other stares at the folded bath towel that Kelly has pressed to their father's back, now soaked with blood, then he says, "Your name, sir?" and, when there's no reply, "Can you hear me, sir?"

Once the ambulance arrives, they don't take their mother, just their father. Cole has a swollen spot the size of a cherry on his right hand, but he keeps it tucked under his arm, sitting there on the floor beside Ian, who hasn't moved from this spot for an hour, still twisted up like a heap of limbs. Kelly kneels on the other side of their brother, her arm over his back, his head tapping on his knee more slowly now, a metronome for a dirge losing time.

"My brother tried to fight him off," Kelly says. "He tried to protect her. To protect *all* of us." As the cop examines the black eye Cole got from the corner of the bureau, Cole confirms everything his sister says and adds details of his own, telling the story of the fight he'd always wanted: his father coming at him with fists raised and Cole striking back hard and decisively. He'll go through years of his life wanting *that* fight, a *real* fight instead of this one-sided beating, resenting his father for not delivering on his end.

There will be more questions later at the hospital after they put him in a cast from the elbow down. "Boxer's break," the nurse will say. The fifth metacarpal in his right hand. They'll pick the broken glass from his feet. There will be interviews and counseling and through it all Cole will stick to Kelly's version of events, which included nothing of what actually happened, and their father—two weeks in the hospital—will never contradict it. And over the decades Nikki will innocently help him shape it into the only story he could possibly live with.

COOL, DAMP AIR BRUSHES HIS FACE AND HE WAKES FROM THE sleep that carried him deep into the night. He pulls the blanket up over his shoulders. Daniel's next to him, and just beyond, his father's uncuffed and curled in a tight ball. The sun shows through the treetops to the east.

Stiff and sore, Cole slowly gets to his feet and crosses the yard, an overwhelming smell of wet, charred wood, of a doused campfire.

The chimney's still standing. And so is the far front corner: the parlor below and his bedroom above. The fire went wild once the roof collapsed and it became more a matter of waiting for it to burn out than extinguishing the flames, and that's when Cole fell asleep. But at some point in the night he was awoken by a truck, the headlights casting their beam fifty yards out into the field . . . and he gasped: caught in the sudden wash of watery light he saw the ghostly figure of Little Kirk, as if he were floating there before turning away and running through the burnt, rotting tobacco and disappearing into the weeds edging the swamp. Then the truck backed onto the road and the lights swept away like a black curtain dropping.

The cop's gone. Only three firefighters remain, rolling up wet hoses, their truck idling. There's coffee and a box of Hostess powdered-sugar donuts on its chrome sideboard. He steps around the currant bushes to the pear trees, stretches out the front of his shirt, and fills it like a sack with a dozen pears snapped from the branches, then brings them to the truck and lines them up one by one on the chrome. Over the clucking diesel engine he tells the men, "They're still a little crisp but plenty sweet," and he crunches into one.

Where the first floor caved in he can see into the cellar, the beehive chimney base, the ancient asbestos-wrapped furnace. When the house was built in 1780, there was no Connecticut Shade growing in the fields, no pavement on Old Newgate Road, no Hostess donuts or Styrofoam coffee cups. But surely there was brutality. Along with brass candlesticks and ladder-back chairs, angry men passed their violence to their children. And surely sons rose up against their fathers, the same blood surging in their veins.

Across the yard, Daniel's sitting there straightening the blanket covering his grandfather. He stands up and gazes toward the house. When he sees Cole, he tilts his cheek to his hands pressed flat together: *He's sleeping.* Then he ducks under the apple trees and takes a leak in the weeds. All summer Daniel's been saying they should go home. Why the hell didn't Cole listen? Last night they witnessed violence handed down through generations—an old story Cole knows by heart—but where are the accounts of legacy handed backward, of the father learning from his son?

Daniel crawls back under his blanket and pulls it up over his face against the light. Cole slides his hands down in his pockets and leans on the rumbling truck. It occurs to him that his wallet got burned in the fire—credit cards, a little cash, all of his ID. But at the bottom of his pocket he feels the chestnut rings. In the sunlight he admires Alex's stellar lathe work, Antoine's precise carving; they, like their gift, make an inspiring pair. He slips one on his ring finger and the other on his pinkie.

He needs to tell Nikki, once and for all, exactly what happened that night. From the start he told her a story closer to Kelly's than the truth, and his attempts to correct the record through the years have been half-hearted. Anyway, they both preferred the story she's come to tell, continually revised to affirm his heroism. The more times she told it, the truer it seemed.

Tires screech, and then the yellow Cadillac lurches onto the tractor road and skids to a stop in the dirt. The driver's door flies open and Andrew sprints toward Cole, shouting, "Is everybody okay? What happened?"

"Everyone's fine."

Andrew is panting, still in a fright, rubbing his knee. "So you all got out?"

"Yes, we did," Cole says. "Is that Sandy and Faye in the car?"

He nods. "We're meeting Sandy's brother in Suffield for breakfast and came this way to see the house."

"You just missed it!" Cole jokes, but he can't get the look of devastation off Andrew's face.

Beyond the weeping willow, Sandy's helping her mother from the car and then leading her over the yard. Andrew's staring into the ruins, entranced. He's thinking, Cole suspects, that the house has been smoldering for thirty years, a funeral pyre that's nearly, finally, extinguished.

And his own thoughts are much the same, starting with the resignation he felt when Daniel convinced him it was too late to put out the fire. He could feel himself letting go of this house and its traumas, letting go of the simmering rage that's haunted him. He watched as the cycle of violence was reduced to ash.

He didn't realize his father was awake but sees him now examining the yellow car, then hurrying after the women. Cole meets them on the grass and says, "Hello, Faye," then hugs Sandy as Phil, out of breath, catches up and scrutinizes all three of them. When Andrew turns from the embers to stare dead at his brother-in-law, Cole fears the worst.

But Faye inadvertently breaks the tension, addressing Phil with an air of boasting. "For quite some time I lived with my late husband in France."

"My wife lived there," he says. "Rosemary."

Everyone stiffens, except for Faye, who touches her forehead as if to remember: "She died."

"I'm sorry," Phil says, his face turning white.

THE SUN HAS RISEN HALFWAY TO NOON AND COLE SITS DOWN NEXT to Daniel, who's thrown off the blanket but is still asleep, with his arm flung over his eyes. Phil's holding Faye by the elbow and leading her to the chicken coop. The chickens seem to delight her. The more they cluck, the more she laughs.

Cole presses his nose to his sleeping son's scalp, and he's fifteen years back in time, at dawn, in front of the woodstove he's just stoked to warm the dampness out of the house; baby Daniel has fallen asleep at Nikki's breast, and she lays him down on the bed between them, swaddled and hot as a coal, his lips still creamy and puckered; he and Nikki roll to their sides and cocoon him, their foreheads and knees touching. Contained in that small, sweet space is everything that matters.

His phone rings and by the time he gets it out of his pocket, Daniel stirs. Cole looks at the screen: Nikki.

21

THE RICH SCENT OF CHESTNUT AND TOBACCO COMPLETELY ENVEL-
ops him when he walks into the shop, like he's entering a cloud of
leaves curing in a loaded shed. He flips on the overhead lights and
can hardly believe all the wood—a stack as neat and massive as a
wooden ship, an arc—that has divinely appeared under the roof. He
walks the length of it, from the roll-up doors all the way to the back
wall. Seventy feet. A few boards that Ben has run through the planer
are laid out on the table saw. He smooths his palm along the grain,
figured like smoke.

He raises his forearm to his nose. For days afterward the smell
of smoke stayed on his skin, and even now he thinks he sometimes
catches a whiff on Daniel. As he was leaving for the airport the day
after the fire, Daniel reached into a jumble of half-burnt lumber and
wiggled loose an iron nail—not a little one for lath but a 16-penny
framing nail, forged and shaped by hand, that he now keeps on his
dresser.

He'll always smell that burning house when he remembers saying
goodbye to his father at the VA in Hartford, where he's getting the
tests he needs. In a matter of weeks he'll be living at the Charter Oak,
on their top floor, in Memory Care.

At home he spreads out the plans for the family room on the
kitchen table. Some of their September work fell through, so he's putting a couple of his guys on the framing as soon as the foundation

is done. Daniel wants to work on the addition, too. Since learning he doesn't have to go back to Connecticut for a trial—LK took two guilty pleas, sharing the second with his father—his spirits have been high. He started his junior year yesterday—all forgiven at the high school. A clean slate.

Cole hears the shower turn off in the upstairs bathroom. Nikki is drying her shoulders, her arms, her thighs. The bathroom window is open to a sunny Oregon September afternoon. Her skin is moist from the steam. When she steps lightly with bare feet down the hall to their bedroom, he closes his eyes and listens, because she's singing.

ACKNOWLEDGMENTS

FOR FRIENDSHIP, SUPPORT, AND INSPIRATION I'M GRATEFUL TO Gary Fisketjon, Genevieve Nierman, Abby Endler, Kim Witherspoon, Maria Whelan, Alexis Hurley, Claire Friedman, Nathaniel Jacks, Patrick Dillon, Tanya Katz, W. Wilson Keithline, Jason Brown, Sara Jameson, Peter Betjemann, Joy Jensen, Tim Jensen, David Vann, Peter Wogan, Aria Minu-Sepehr, Sean Crouch, David Robinson, Christopher McKnight Nichols, OSU Center for the Humanities, and my colleagues in the School of Writing, Literature, and Film. To John Daniel for *Looking After: A Son's Memoir,* the Corvallis Fire Department for their generosity, Bob Grigg and Gregg Mangan for their research on Old Newgate Prison, and Nick Van-Olden and Brandon Seettje for a day in the sheds and under the nets picking Connecticut Shade. And I'm grateful to my family—Jen, Luke, and Chloe—for their constant and boundless love.

ALSO BY

KEITH SCRIBNER

THE OREGON EXPERIMENT

Naomi and Scanlon Pratt are at the threshold of a new life.
East Coast transplants to small-town Oregon, Scanlon has a
position at the local university—teaching mass movements
and domestic radicalism—and Naomi is pregnant with
their first child. But everything changes when they meet
Clay, a troubled young anarchist who despises Scanlon's
self-serving attempts at friendship but adores Naomi. As
the Pratts welcome their newborn son, their lives become so
deeply entwined with Clay's that they must decide exactly
where their loyalties lie, before the increasingly volatile
activism that they've been dabbling in engulfs them all. A
love song to the Pacific Northwest, *The Oregon Experiment*
explores the contemporary civil war between desire and
betrayal, the political and the personal.

Fiction

VINTAGE CONTEMPORARIES
Available wherever books are sold.
www.vintagebooks.com

Printed in the United States
by Baker & Taylor Publisher Services